ALSO BY J.L. HUGHES

BROKEN JADE

Dark Justice

Dark Divide

R.A.Y. A Step Too Far

PRAISE FOR DARK JUSTICE

Think homicide detectives don't take their work home–think again. Unravelling this criminal entanglement will leave you breathless.

To paraphrase Brad Pitt's character in the hit movie *Seven*, Ladies and Gentleman we have a Serial Killer!

In DARK JUSTICE, a prolific serial killer's methods echo the murder of homicide detective Jade Carmichael's mother, launching her into a relentless pursuit. This story will keep you on edge, up late, and haunt you long after the final dark twist.

DARK INTENT

DARK INTENT

DARK INTENT

BROKEN JADE
BOOK 3

J.L. HUGHES

**ROUGH
EDGES
PRESS**

Dark Intent
Paperback Edition
Copyright © 2025 by J.L. Hughes

Rough Edges Press
An Imprint of Wolfpack Publishing
1707 E. Diana Street
Tampa, FL 33610

www.roughedgespress.com

Editing by My Brother's Editor

Paperback ISBN 978-1-68549-371-4
eBook ISBN 978-1-68549-370-7
LCCN 2025946512

DARK INTENT

PROLOGUE

Machias knew evil well enough to see through its most elegant disguise she only wished others she trusted had eyes to see it too. They didn't and hadn't for almost sixteen years. She knew better than to fear the killer who left the driver's seat to wander the outskirts of the truck stop. Anyone catching sight of his scarred face read the villainous origins of his story. The most dangerous predators went unrecognized as evil. Hiding in plain sight they painted their young victims as difficult, unruly, rebellious, unworthy, troublesome and wild. Those that went so far as to label them as damaged she had no use for. They never bothered to investigate who caused the damage. Even her name, Machias, translated to "bad little falls" and that's how they'd been explained away when she was young enough for people to question the bruises and battered state of her tiny limbs.

Her eyes, burning, absorbed the details of the van's dirty interior searching for something, anything she could use to defend herself. Jack told her to fight until she found peace. He always said that, but it meant more this time because it'd be the last. He repeated it as the man with the facial scar dragged him yelling and flailing from the vehicle alongside an abandoned county road. Chained to the floor she couldn't raise up high enough to see out the upper back window as the echo of his protests receded in the distance then silenced.

Sliding her hands on the gritty floor she searched its surface until catching something soft, coiled, and smooth. Jack's necklace, he ripped it off in the battle out the door and flung it, accepting his fate, to leave it behind for her. His grandfather's dog tags from the war still hung on the broken chain reminding her of Jack's legacy fought for by generations preceding him and ended by his vow to keep her safe. Three years of hideaways, rescues in the night, and camp and couch surfing landed her days away from moving into his new apartment where no one could auction her off, and then this. That dream fading, vanishing into the night like Jack, she was back inside the nightmare, alone.

The sickly sweet smell of chloroform, reminiscent of acetone nail polish remover, coated her face. The rag left its taste dry in her mouth as the offensive odor of circling diesel fuel, potent from the long-haul truckers filling up, forced her to draw breaths through her nose. Trapped in the haze of it she fought the urge to gag. No way to gauge how long they'd traveled while she'd slept on the soiled metal floor. All she knew for certain was it was night, Jack was miles behind them discarded somewhere along the route the scarred man was taking her, and his destination was a hell she had no intention of ever reaching. If not for herself, then for Jack. He made her promise.

Mac didn't want to live. She decidedly didn't want to live without Jack. He said it was the only peace she could give him, promise to survive and get away before the murderous driver arrived at his next checkpoint. They heard him talking to someone waiting for "the shipment" to change hands. Machias was a shipment. Well aware she wasn't alone in her plight, she also knew the how and why of her circumstances few shared. She prayed this was the case unsure she wanted to remain in a world where the generation before, tormented and jaded, were in competition to wound their offspring into submission and stand on their broken souls to embolden themselves to higher ground.

Mac's worst enemy wasn't the killer who claimed the driver's seat of the van transporting her across country to be sold before she reached the age of seventeen. What Machias feared most was the goal of the twisted and tortured soul of the man who staged the kidnapping, who scattered breadcrumbs over social media feigning desperation in dealing with his troubled teen runaway for months, maybe years, to claim his role of victim. The one wildly evil in his version of Munchausen syndrome by proxy who planned all along for his child's destruction to pay back the world, her mother, his mother, and every other for his own undoing.

"You evil bastard," Machias whispered into the quiet of the night, her head pounding with the pain of grief. "I'll live to see you pay for whatever happened to Jack. I will keep my promise just to end you, Dad, you heartless, vile monster."

There was so much more she had to say but she fell mute again hearing the jangle of keys accessing the driver's door. Her transporter returned from the truck stop they'd pulled onto the edge of. Far removed from patron congestion, swallowed by overbearing echoes of Cummins X15 engines, and too far for any protest she may launch to risk being heard. A cutout fashioned with a sliding tray box had been created between the front and back cargo hold so he could pass water and food without opening the back door of the vehicle. This was her moving prison cell.

Scanning the heavy bolted down loops on its floor and walls Mac's eyes stalled on something odd she couldn't make sense of in the limited light filtering in from overhead of the break wall to the front cab. Despite her father's efforts to destroy everything inherently good about her, Mac had impeccable vision. Blinking to clear the resin of tears she concentrated on the metal loop and coiled chain midway up the wall left of where she was bolted down. Stifling the instinct to scream in horror her vision captured the details of the skin left entangled in a metal hook affixed to its end as unmistakably female, a woman's delicate flesh. Her head whipped to the opposite side, perceiving the equal placement of hooks at mid-torso level on the walls and ankle length on the floorboards. She understood why Jack gave his life fighting to free her of this cage. He had been chained to that side, blocking her view. This was not her fate. She was destined for a different torturous end. With thick sound insulation, the bars on the small windows at the back, and the absence of anything useful to her it was clear it had been customized for this hedonistic purpose.

Which meant one thing. Machias wasn't its first passenger and if she didn't survive to expose the truth, she wouldn't be its last.

ONE

NYPD homicide detective Jade Carmichael approached the new office of Dr. Abraham Maxwell fully prepared to lie through her teeth about the spider crawling inside her head. She didn't lie easily or frequently, when occasion called for it against the worst criminals she confronted but never to family, never to friends until now. Lately it became a necessity in response to one singular topic—her murderous half brother that disappeared into treatment leaving her and the team without legal access to track his movements in the world. And the world was not safe if his incarceration was not guaranteed. Having been the catalyst and focus of his twisted criminality, she believed the duty to ensure the wall between him and the rest of society remained impenetrable fell to her. Those closest to her didn't agree, including Captain Grey. His concern for her sanity landed her back in the capable hands of Max, the unit's trusted shrink. The team, Kane Kolton her partner on and off the force, Jackson Swan their best buddy and fellow detective, and Amy Logan the junior serving a formal timeout, shared history.

The kind that forced trust and tested it.

Jade included them all in every piece of evidence she unearthed.

She just wasn't willing to allow them inside her mind. There, spiders roamed and some were deadly.

Arriving before Max she was comfortable being in his newly designed space but brimmed with annoyance that the visit was compulsory. She wanted to see Max since during her last case there was no opportunity to; she'd been out in the field and missed their face-to-face talks. But today, being forced to go felt too much like old times she'd rather forget. Jade did a lap of the room breathing in the scent of reclaimed wood and aged texts, her hands smoothing over the cutwork in the pillars framing his space and the heavy linen of the new sofas before claiming a seat. Old memories flooded back, nonetheless.

Reading it all on her face, Max smiled, walking in to take his position opposite her behind his desk and sat leaning into the protesting leather wingback.

"A little too familiar, I'm guessing?" he said, settling in.

"I'm glad it's a new office and you switched up the décor. Anything less and I'd be out the door," Jade admitted. "I don't think even you want to relive those dark days."

Max sat forward, folding his hands on his desk. "True. I don't any more than the rest of you. Honestly, you're the one client on the force who I don't know what to say to."

"And Amy? You know what to say to her?" Jade brought up fellow detective, Amy Logan to gauge Max's reaction. Being the junior in their unit and on forced leave, Jade wondered how she'd fair under the scrutiny of one as wise and crafty as Max. Amy hadn't done anything wrong. She'd done everything wrong. Loopholes existed to navigate her away from suspension and possible prosecution but that didn't mean everyone was onboard.

"I have a treasure trove to say to her," Max said, his eyes rolling skyward. "Not that she'll listen to any of it. That one requires oversight."

"She's not the only one. She's still having nightmares about Nickolas, even after the attempted murder case closed, after Errie came home safe," Jade said, knowing Max would eventually steer the conversation back to the real reason she sat across from him.

"Having a killer almost take out your whole team, literally wounding all three senior detectives, and live to talk about it grates on the nerves. Amy wasn't stable, hell no one was after Nickolas attacked you, shot Kane and Jackson, and almost killed his mother and grandfather." Max shook his head, losing his doctor's decorum. "I really prayed for them both to live. I wonder if I would've if I'd known they'd jump to his defense and shield him from the law? I don't think any of us anticipated that one-eighty.

"Anyhow, after her actions processing the outcome of the Redeemer case and the abduction last summer of her fiancée, she's struggling. I'm hoping together we can find solid ground."

"The team is hoping that too but if you see her sliding—"

Max's lips pulled tight and he studied his hands. "There's only so much I can say."

Jade smiled and drew a deep breath. "I understand. We just don't want to lose her. Feels like we all abandoned her when the Redeemer's case was at its worst."

"You didn't have a choice," Max said. "And Jade, that's the job she signed up for."

"Yeah. The one you and Grey just barred her from doing." Jade made her point and left it just as quickly. It wasn't Max's fault, the position Amy was in, temporarily suspended with pay, under a very uncomfortable microscope, and walking on eggshells. She put herself there. And though none of them spoke it out loud, she did it angling to rid the world of Nickolas Leigh, well known as the Redeemer; few knew he shared a biological father with Jade.

In a flash of clarity she realized her half brother was always why she sat across from Max.

"So...from what I've been told by Captain Grey no one knows where Nickolas has been shipped off to. The judge, his grandfather, made dispensations to manipulate the judicial system handing down an insanity plea and linking his care and incarceration to a five-star rehabilitation facility." Max spoke while studying her reactions.

"Which essentially means the man drenched in guilt for who he became controls Nickolas's freedom. If the doctors in place to work with him deem him well, no longer posing a threat to society, they could set him free and we don't have a clue where he is. Am I seeing this right?" Jade asked, more than a little on edge.

Max exhaled, staring at his notebook before facing her. "Yes, that about covers it. Jade, I can't explain how any of this could result in his freedom, and Leigh Senior is well aware of the carnage that resulted at the hands of Nickolas Leigh. Let's face it, he's suffering permanent damage from it and so is his daughter. He has also been explicitly informed of the personal blowback his family will face if a single criminal act resulted from such a decision. Personally I don't believe there's a scenario where he's out of custody but it's you who has to go on with your life without knowing his whereabouts. Can you do that?"

Jade didn't answer. She knew the response he wanted and needed but couldn't give it. At least not without taking a moment to process what he and the department were asking of her. Forget that a half brother you never knew existed murdered a string of people and then came after you, the man you love, your friends who were your family on the force and, wait for it, got away with it scot-free if you exclude the bullet Kane planted in Nickolas's neck that all but paralyzed him. Well...until recently. His other side of the family was pouring their endless funds into mass rehabilitation and damn if it wasn't working. Talk about insult to injury.

"I have to be," she said. "He took all he is getting from us."

"I wish that were true but Jade he has an intense attachment to you and he's using it." Max locked eyes with her, a fatherly concern behind his stare.

"The letters? Yeah. They're still coming one every couple weeks." She shifted her position, becoming more rigid.

"You could redirect them," he said.

"If I did that, I would lose any chance of gaining a lead on his location." Jade avoided eye contact surfing the room's interior.

"And he knows that desire keeps you at the mercy of his correspondence." Max didn't sound happy. His tone revealed frustration he rarely exuded.

She turned her attention back to him, facing it head-on. "I know it. I am well aware this whole situation from word go is completely and utterly fucked up, but I can't change my blood, Max. He is connected. I have Kane and Jackson analyzing the letters with me, and I'm not laboring over this night and day. I actually think I'll be happy when we get the next call to actively work a case and refocus." Jade slumped in her seat. "Working with neighboring towns on their drug deals gone wrong and domestics is growing old. I don't wish anyone to become a victim of homicide. You know that. I just want to be useful and get back to what we were designed to do."

"So you're asking for me to tell Grey you're good to go should the next call arise?" he said, pleased with her candor and perhaps at a rare loss for advice.

"I am," she said, flashing a grin, glad to shed some of the emotional weight she walked in with. She pushed the spider into the dark corner of her mind where he belonged.

"I'll let him know you have my blessing. I guess it'd be pointless to warn you to be careful what you wish for?" he asked it with the knowledge of her past ever present.

Jade stood, scanning the space a final time, then glanced back on her way to the door. "It would, but you already knew that. You know me so well. I approve of the whitewashed ancient Rome-inspired décor, arches, woods, and pillars. It's very you."

"Do I?" he said, ignoring her nod to his design choice a shadow fell on his bright eyes. "I'm not always so sure I know you so well."

"No one really knows another completely," she said, pausing at the threshold. "Life clings to its mysteries, Max, and I guess we do too."

TWO

"Few days on this earth are perfect or painless," Axel's grandfather warned him repeatedly. "So, if you find one don't be distracted, stay present, burn it into memory." The breeze catching Rocklyn's golden hair whipping through the cab of his new truck, her seat dancing to the song blaring out of its speakers, and her pirate's grin when she glanced his way, scorched forever on his soul. Zane and Hailey, best buddy and girlfriend, were all smiles in the rearview and for good reason, they won against all odds, decimating their worst rival and did it with scouts in the stands. The perfect start to the football season with a foothold on future options he once deemed impossible. Axel admired his grandfather, his success in business and life. So he wasn't distracted, he was present when taking Hook's corner after the bend on Blacktop Road. And the image of the slumped figure he came within inches of running over was burned into memory right over top of his perfect day.

Death had a way of reaping the focus of the living and tainting every experience close enough to grasp. Axel knew this truth as his family survived its ruthless devouring before, when he was nine. And once you brush shoulders with death you recognize the shift when it surfaces, even if this time it's not coming for you.

Axel's hands jagged right then left, course correcting while the treads of his new tires left rubber etching the near miss across pavement. Rocklyn was tossed with the violent jarring motion, her seat belt slamming her into the leather as she clutched his arm, screaming. The truck careened dissecting the corner and skirted the road's narrow edge before he regained control. Inches further and it would've caught the transition into farmland throwing them into utter chaos and ending everything good forever. The screeching and screams died at the tracker access point to a field. Sliding off the main road and out of the way of possible oncoming traffic Axel pried the death grip of his hands from the hot leather steering wheel, checked on Rocklyn and his passengers, then searched the rearview for the body at the road's edge in the distance.

"Fuck man, what the hell?" Zane asked breathless from the back seat, his eyes on Hailey who took a bump to the head against the side window.

"Did you see him?" Axel said, turning to Zane then back to Rocklyn. "Are you okay? Are you hurt?"

"No I'm good. You guys? Hailey?" Rockie asked, swiveling to face her friend.

Hailey rubbed the side of her head. "I may have a headache but I'm okay. What the hell happened?"

"Him who?" Zane asked, patting Hailey's hand and springing from his seat out the door. "What the hell? Stupid ass will get killed passing out on this stretch."

"What?" Rockie removed the seat belt, crushing her into the leather, and slid out the door to stretch and absorb the near accident. "Someone passed out on the side of the road?"

"Assholes," Hailey echoed, still in her seat, staving off the dizzying spell from meeting the window. "Next time, give us a warning."

"No time," Axel said. "Sorry." Snapping on the hazard lights, he stepped out as Zane took off striding toward the prone figure thirty yards behind them. "Wait up," he yelled, jogging the space between to approach in the lead. With the girls left by the truck he shouted back. "Stay there until we check it out, okay?"

Rockie waved in agreement turning back to where Hailey sat in the second row of the truck.

"What you worried about, bro?" Zane said. "They've seen a guy trashed a time or two before." Zane made to laugh then, catching the seriousness in Axel's stare, stopped. "You don't think he's lit. You think it's something bad?"

Axel met his eyes. "Yeah, I think it's bad. I swerved hot pavement inches from him and...he didn't flinch. When we get up to him stay behind me okay."

"Shit." Zane's typical excited aura dipped. "Yeah. Okay."

Checking for oncoming vehicles, they crossed to the side where the body laid, both pushing hair back for a clear view. Several feet away Axel threw out a tanned arm blocking Zane's approach. "Hold back. I don't want us tainting evidence. See that tire tread mark?" He pointed to a partial tread print running from the body at an angle back onto the blacktop.

"You sound more like your dad every day, bro," Zane said, keeping his distance. "No question where you're heading after grad, scholarship or not. It's in the blood."

"Yeah, yeah. Just wait here." Mindful to walk parallel to the tire tracks and avoid disturbing possible footprints, Axel made his way near enough to confirm the figure was male and determine if there was any chance he was still breathing. Coming in from the far left opposite the road, Axel inspected the body from the side hidden from his earlier view. He didn't make it more than a few steps before halting abruptly. "Oh damn."

"What?" Zane asked, shuffling his feet back near the roadside where Axel left him.

He stepped closer and Axel held a cautionary hand up. "Don't move. Go back with the girls. Get them inside the truck and lock it until I come back. I'm going to snap a few photos just in case and get a hold of my dad. This is bad."

"Bad like what? The guy's beaten or—"

"The guy's dead." The tone of Axel's voice echoed the seriousness of the situation and Zane retreated a couple steps. "Keep the girls calm and safe. I don't think he's been here long." Axel's eyes dropped to the discarded man at his feet and then panned the distance surrounding them.

"How do you figure?" Zane asked but made no move to come closer.

"Fuck, I can see tear stains on his face," Axel said, glancing at his friend, he shook free as remorse weighed on him. "This is real bad and whoever caused his death could still be around. Move, fast."

Zane sprang into motion with the determination of his typical quarterback tackle for the truck and their girlfriends. One glance back said, as much as he was having trouble believing the deadly detour of their plans, he trusted Axel's judgment enough to shift into full protection mode. With the girls safe under Zane's care, Axel pulled out his phone and snapped photos of everything around the scene, ending with multiple angles of the body dump. And that was exactly what it was. Steadying his breathing he hit his dad's private line in his recent list and waited.

Callum Macleod answered on the second ring, a few hours shy of his usual departure from the cop shop on a Friday he was in work mode, short and direct. "Hey, Axe. I thought you were all heading out to the lake," he said, the sound of shuffling papers reverberated down the line.

"I was, we were. I'm on the side of Blacktop Road, mile marker seventeen just after Hook," Axel said, his eyes tracing the sad figure left to rot at its edge.

"Don't tell me you blew a tire. We just—"

"I'm standing over a body. It looks like he died here recently and it's…" Axel drew in a deep breath of hot summer air and swallowed. "He wasn't hit, Dad, and it wasn't a loner wandering back to town high, it's a body dump."

"Are you okay? Are the kids?" Axel recognized the tone of fear filtering into his father's voice.

"We're all good. Zane's with the girls. Hailey bumped her head when I swerved. Dad, I think Mom had her hands on the steering wheel. An inch difference and this would be a very different scene."

There was a pause, the one you come to expect surviving the loss of a parent and partner as a team. The space where nothing needed to be said but so much existed. Then, "I have no doubt she was, son." Furious typing clicked in Axel's ear. "Mile marker seventeen? Just after Hook's corner? What side of the road?" Callum asked.

"Westbound," Axel said, waiting.

"What time did you come across it?" he asked, still typing.

"Maybe ten minutes ago. Haven't seen a vehicle through here yet, but the second the party breaks up they'll be all over this roadway and—"

"Hold on, son." Axel listened as his father barked orders for the nearest patrol unit to rush the area and set up blockades. "They should be to you in a few minutes. Mitchell is on county east of you. Are you in any danger?"

"I don't think so but this guy expired a short time ago by the looks of it and he left a message...someone murdered him and reading this, his killer isn't done yet."

"Son, get back in your truck. Pull in ahead of the site, off the road a safe distance with full lights flashing to warn traffic until Mitchell arrives to take over the scene. You did great, Axe. Did you happen to take any—"

"Yeah, I'm forwarding them now." Axel heard the ding through the phone confirming his father received his photos of the scene in all their gory detail. Only a second or two passed in silence before his voice boomed over the line as he yelled across the police station. "Get homicide on the line and patch me through." Back into the phone he said, "Axe, get in the truck and text me when you're locked inside it."

THREE

The officer Mackenzie Daughtry spoke with on the phone never gave an exact time for when they'd be dropping by to discuss his missing daughter and he wanted to be prepared. He'd written down pertinent details, the time he discovered her missing, the last place she'd been seen prior to, a listing of her friends, teachers, classmates and their numbers. He gleaned a great deal from her social media pages and those of her closest friends. The public plea he issued had a flood of hits and he'd agreed to link real-time police access so they too could see any new leads it may generate. He turned his life into an open book but before they reached his door there were a few details requiring his attention.

Chiefly, the attic over the barn.

It certainly wouldn't be the first place they would go, if they gave it more than a passing glance, but there were things there he'd rather not have inspected. A shame really, he thought, to dismantle the space when recent modifications elevated it to match perfectly with its intended purpose. And prying the heavy bolts free from the wall hooks sunk deep into its thick roof studs would take no small measure of effort. Carrying a leather craftsman's satchel to save the iron in for a later date, he went to work removing the foundation of the restraints used to contain Machias before he handed her over. Inspecting the room, its temperature rising early in the mid-August heat, pangs of regret surfaced. He could've, should've had a second daughter if Mac's mother hadn't become so rebellious. One younger to take Mac's place. He imagined ways to get around that failure, to fill the space. So many were easily available and searching to replace a bad home experience with a worse one.

A grin slithered out lifting the left side of his lips. He couldn't allow such things in the presence of the law and he'd studied micro expressions, body language, and actions to avoid as much as he'd researched the failings of those who came before him with similar propensities. The result of such created a disappointment he hadn't anticipated. And a knowing, he was so much better than them. Perhaps it came down to a question of intelligence or a lack, on their part, of imagination. In his mind their shortcomings might have more to do with timing. He'd been a student of the art of deception his entire life, well at least since the age of eleven, and that was a long time to master a class.

And master it he did.

Hooks and plates removed he installed a regular upturned hook in place of the restraint ones, hanging aged tools in their stead. He spread a new shift of hay over the floorboards masking previous stains beneath and collected all the blankets in a basket for laundering. The mattress he pulled up on its side, slid it against the wall, covered it with a tarp, and piled old furniture before it. Disassembled, it appeared as any other barn attic. For good measure he opened the previously nailed shut window and left it ajar. If birds came to roost, so be it. The air, though warm, would serve to mask or confuse any telling scent.

Surveying the transformation he left confident no one would ever suspect what occurred there. They hadn't yet and he'd give them no reason to moving forward.

Striding across the yard to the farmhouse he adopted the disposition of a grieving father. Passing a hall mirror prior to entering the kitchen, his reflection confirmed his mastery. Pleased with his work, he headed up the refinished wooden stairs, admiring the perfection of the stained corbels and banister. Left of the top landing sat an ideal teenager's bedroom designed with the typical placeholders signifying youth, independence, and nurturing, none of which Machias experienced after her mother left.

She never truly left. She was driven away in a similar fashion to how Machias was removed. By a man they called the Ferryman and possessed a gift in ridding the world of certain troublesome individuals by means that ensured they never resurfaced.

Mackenzie entered the bedroom. He pulled out the desk chair and left it askew, checked that the diary he forced her to write in was haphazardly stowed under a bed pillow, left the log of songs teenagers gravitated too embedded in her computer for school, and threw a few choice items of clothing lying on the bed or crumpled on the floor as if tossed off in a rush.

Content with the staging he opened the window, the appearance of freedom being subtly ushered into the subconscious of anyone who entered. This he did with gloves on. He had her open it times before when she was permitted to be inside the house. She never knew why. She never saw this day coming until it was too late. The entire kidnapping played out exactly as he orchestrated until her friend Jack decided to become a hero. Her wide receiver boyfriend was out of commission with an early season injury. Their relationship hadn't developed into one where Machias felt comfortable sharing any of the harsh details of her home life as of yet but he suspected if their time at school allowed them to draw much closer secrets would be shared. This was why her move date had to be pushed up.

Jack, a lifelong friend from the community and one she could never become romantically involved with because as cool and attractive as the kid was, he played for the other team, knew too much. Be it their budding maturity or his personal strength of character breaking down her barriers, the truth had been spilled. More than evident in the young man's eyes the last time he'd picked her up from school. Jack failed badly to conceal his contempt and that slip cost him his life.

The Ferryman called from a truck stop using a burner phone the night before to confirm Jack was no longer an obstacle to Machias meeting her delivery date. Mackenzie wasn't privy to where the killer held his cargo, those destined to be shipped elsewhere, and he damn sure wasn't fool enough to pry. Honestly it didn't matter as long as delivery was made as scheduled and he was paid.

Ten days and she was off his hands for good and worth the years he spent enduring her presence. Tortured by the fact that she resembled her mother so accurately, the saving grace in the hell of it all was that both had been such pretty girls. That fact alone became his bartering chip, and in the end, it'd pay him back. Maybe not for all of it, but at least a fair portion of the past humiliation. If Machias hadn't been the spitting image of her mother, maybe everyone would've forgotten her, but they couldn't with a walking replica reminding them. Now with them both gone, and him left heartbroken, the tide was set to turn.

Angling for the door, he glanced out the window, a direct shot from the two-story house to the barn and the driveway in that split them. Flashing lights marked his queue and with a spin toward the staircase his stride grew labored, his head hung lower, his eyes burned from lack of sleep, and his hands so steady moments earlier gain a tremor of weakness.

Ten days.

Riparian never used his name except with club contacts. To everyone else in the business he was simply the Ferryman, a take on the Grim Reaper. Those unlucky enough to be transported by him met a version of hell after seeing him. A few survived for a time after he handed them off, others did not. The name fit and served to mask his real name, though he didn't fear it being used. No one had ever encroached on his dwelling. No one would ever find him or track him effectively. He didn't fear discovery, as far as the law or any government was concerned, he didn't exist. Born into the club, with no birth record or traceable history, he was a figment of imagination, the worst kind. He didn't fear being identified. He didn't fear at all. The evilest man in the room no matter the room he was in since he turned nineteen, Riparian couldn't recall the sensation of panic, dread, or terror though he witnessed it in some form from every piece of cargo.

No one traveled with him without displaying fear. The young girl in the back, interestingly, hadn't shown it yet. Anger, grief, rage, she mastered but not fear, not yet. It made him question her past. Her skin appeared flawless from what he'd seen of it. Her hair long, thick, and bright. She didn't wear the signs of malnutrition or physical abuse like so many of the others. No cigarette burns, scars up her arms, or rope burns shadowing her wrists and legs. It didn't mean she hadn't suffered. It just meant whoever hurt her was careful.

Riparian wasn't necessarily careful. He didn't have to be.

Pulling out of the truck stop and back on the road, having sent through water and food to the cargo hold, he expected a quiet ride through the night. If there were more than one passenger, whispers would echo through the cab, futile plans for possible escape at the next gas station or his washroom break. Those traveling alone seldom uttered anything but tears, eventually succumbing to exhaustion and collapsing into restless sleep.

This one, now alone and aware her friend had departed this earth, was different.

"Can I know your name?" she asked, the question reverberating through the food tray as if she was using it for a rudimentary game of telephone. "If you are to be the last person near me before my life as I know it ends, I'd like to know your name please."

She said please? He'd dragged the boy kicking and fighting from the van while she cried and pleaded for his life while chained to the back wall, unable to assist him. Their expressions revealed the intense bond they shared, more than typical of the teens he dealt with. A "my life for yours" bond. Of all the years he witnessed such circumstances it occurred less than a handful of times. Rare, it ensured her instant hatred of him, but she said please.

"It's not like I'll be telling anyone," she continued. "We both know I'll never have that chance."

The girl waited, and he contemplated. Thinking back over the years, he couldn't remember being asked or answering.

"My name is Riparian," he said, picking up speed on the open road to make time in the hours least traveled and monitored by highway patrol in these parts.

"Riparian," she repeated it slowly. "It's unique like my name. I'm Machias. I'm guessing we'll be driving for a long time, far away from anyone who might recognize or help me. I've read when teens are trafficked, they're normally taken across country, across the world even. The further away the less chance of escape or detection."

The girl was speaking to be heard and that was not new. The tone of her voice, level and calm, didn't match anyone he moved in recent memory. And she read, like him, researching and expecting likely outcomes of her future.

"Could you tell me if that is accurate, please?" she asked and waited not filling the uncomfortable empty silence as most did.

He drew a breath, let it slide out, and spoke. "It would be in most cases. Unfortunately it isn't the case for you."

Silence hung in the air between the cab and the cargo hold barrier for the better part of ten minutes then he heard her again. "Yeah, my life has never been typical. Like our names, unique but not in a good way. In another life I might say I like your name, nothing else except that you were willing to speak to me. You're a killer; I would've known if I'd glimpsed you across a room. I know the type. So Rip, what kind of hell is in store for me and where are we headed?"

Odd at first, he suddenly identified the interesting quality in the girl, the part that encouraged him to respond when he hadn't so many other times. Familiarity, the girl in the back, the sixteen-year-old promised to a destination possibly worse than one he would choose, with a whole lifetime ahead of her reduced to days, she wasn't afraid either.

"You have six hours to sleep before life is unrecognizable," he warned. "Use them."

FOUR

The call came into homicide, patched through from central, and with Max's approval, Grey sent it Jade's way. Kane, out of the office on an assist, was due back shortly. She used the time to glance through the initial report expecting the body discovery to link to an unfortunate OD. The back road, commonly frequented by teens escaping the town for the lake, had seen its fair share of accidents related to the pitfalls of youth. The first officer on scene confirmed the victim was no more than eighteen to early twenties but there was more. The son of Callum MacLeod, a respected cop on the town desk, made the discovery nearly running over the corpse.

Jade didn't just know of Callum, she knew his story and could attest his skills belonged in homicide. After the illness and passing of his wife, he scaled back to put his son, Axel, first, a decade or more ago.

She kept reading, jotting down the exact location Axel reported and was entering it into the GPS on her phone when the note written below shot her up from her chair. He confirmed the death was the result of homicide because the young man, dead beside the blacktop, wrote as much and more in a message in the dirt where he met his end.

From a standing position, Jade scanned through the details logged into the computer but the full message wasn't to be seen. Snatching her keys off the corner of the desk, she bolted for the door, texting Kane the coordinates to meet her. She wasn't waiting for a rookie patrol cop, weather, or any other stupid threat to disturb the first and perhaps most crucial clue of her new case.

Not yet noon, the intense sun of summer beat down cooking the paint of her Denali. Mindful she opened the door using a cuff of her sleeve as a shield and slid inside. She sat behind the sun guard covering the windshield until the air conditioner pumped cool air, then twisted it back into the small circle it reduced to, shoving it beside her seat pulling out of the shop parking lot. The heat would not bode well in terms of preserving the body or evidence shed onto it. Throwing on her lights, she sped the quickest route of back roads arriving through strategically placed patrol cars impeding motorists from clear view of the body. For this she was grateful, knowing the victim hadn't been ID'd and anyone driving by may be related. Small towns almost guaranteed close connections. This time that fact wouldn't be beneficial.

Pulling off the road a fair distance from the site, she struggled to be grateful officers had erected a tarp, worried it came at the expense of surrounding evidence. Recognizing Callum as she closed the distance, her fears abated.

"Well this is not what we should be doing on a day like today," she said, flashing an easy smile.

"That's for damn sure," Callum agreed, walking to meet her. "Axel and the kids were heading to the lake after a morning game. It's lucky he drives like his dad or this would've been far worse."

"Well, he has a lot of you in him by the looks of the report. Mile markers, time stamp, everything except—"

"The dirt note before the dirt nap," Callum said, pausing Jade before walking the grid to the body. "We can't formally identify this boy, but Axel is fairly certain he's a kid from school. A year his senior, so eighteen, nineteen and you'll have to consider the death may involve a hate crime."

"Hate crime?" Jade peered over Callum's shoulder catching sight of the body. "How so?"

"He was super well-liked and developed a popular podcast that was…going viral?" Callum explained.

"Doesn't sound like a whole lot of hate there unless you think someone jumped on a jealousy bandwagon." Anxious to take over Jade motioned for him to step aside.

"He was gay. Apparently super cool, unfairly handsome, intelligent as hell, and gay. Axel was concerned maybe someone from out of town came after him."

"Thanks for letting me know. If he's right, and this is who he suspects it is, what am I to call him?" Jade brushed by Callum seeing the path of least destruction he'd cut to the body.

"Jack," Callum said solemnly, waving the patrol guys standing guard to lift the tarp's side and allow Jade proximity to the deceased that they were denied. "Jack Wells."

Jade spun on her combat heels to face Callum. "The *Getting Wells* podcaster? Oh shit. I love that kid. I really hope your boy is wrong."

"He's not," Callum broke off, heading back to the road to be the barrier between passersby and tragedy.

Entering the tented site, Jade came in from the roadside. From that vantage point only a curved figure was recognizable. It's back facing her. What Axel would've steered free of smearing across the blacktop. Shifting positions, the case expanded to not only investigating who stole Jack's life but a hunt for his best friend, to save her before she met the same fate.

Jack spoke to Jade through letters he'd carved into the dirt beside him, commanding her to do what he no longer could…*save Machias*.

You have 10 days
Save Machias

Merc Cargo Van Blk –> W
His fault
M M /=

Questions erupted as Jade studied the young man's corpse. He was long departed but left her with all he could in his dying moments discarded by the roadside. Her heart broke a little wider knowing the potential of the person at her feet. Beautiful in so many ways, she could only think of him as a true gift to this world. One needed, wanted, paving new paths for so many, and now stolen, obliterated. Jade chose, hovering over the vessel turned evidence, to make certain at the closure of this case his efforts were not forgotten. But today was about extracting every possible clue he left to follow and there were many. None as glaring as the link to his killer and the urgency to stop him from taking another life.

"Okay, Jack," she whispered inside the tent. "I will do everything I know to save Machias. And I thank you for putting me on the right track. I'll let you know when your friend is safe."

Jade's eyes memorized the slant of each letter, opening her mind to the intention of every word, cementing them to memory. Ten days. Jack had strong reason to believe a deadline hung over Machias's life or it wouldn't have been the first thing he etched into the dirt. Her life was doomed to share his fate or worse. Worse because Jack had obviously gotten in the way, was quickly killed and dumped in the path of a destination awaiting her. Jack, being Hollywood handsome, would fetch huge money in any trafficking ring but perhaps his fame made him unsellable. It appeared she was the target and Jade knew too well all that meant for young women these days. A hell and brutality society had become all too complacent against. Jade imagined Jack's last sight in this life was the back end of a black Mercedes-Benz Cargo Van fading into the distance heading west. With a mandatory two-plate requirement displaying license plates on both front and rear, the vehicle could've gone either way leaving its plate and the make identifiable. If he hadn't mentioned the direction, they could've easily assumed the vehicle responsible for disposing of him headed east. His body placement suggested this. Jade assumed he'd crawled through the grass and collapsed here fighting for unreachable help. Jack told her as much. Who Jack blamed for his death and Machias's cursed fate Jade wasn't certain but the perpetrator Jack fingered was male. It was 'His Fault.' The trail extending after what appeared at first glance to be the letters MM followed by the number one and an indiscernible scribble said he had more to say but ill fate silenced him.

She kneeled carefully close to the dirt note analyzing the angle of Jack's hand, certain he was mid-word when his life drained out. Photographing every detail she didn't register the footfall drawing near.

Callum lifted the tent behind her but didn't enter. "You've incoming," he said, nodding to indicate Kane's approach behind him.

"Callum, I assume you put out an APB for the vehicle heading west with plates starting with MM, can you have me notified of anything on that? And do you know who Jack is talking about?" Jade asked.

"I did and will. Who Jack is? Oh, Machias. Yes. She's local, a grade eleven student at the school. Her father put in a missing person's report. We have officers scheduled to meet with him in a few hours but didn't know it was anything more than—"

"Cancel them," Jade demanded, the authority flooding her voice had him pulling out his phone. "I want us to be the first and only ones speaking to him and I don't want him tipped or prepared." Callum dialed and was on the phone issuing her orders before Kane slid by into the tent to join her. "And no one calls him, notifies him of homicide's involvement, speaks to him at all, understood?" Callum nodded and dipped out speaking into the phone.

"Damn. Well this is definitely not the summer he deserved," Kane said, inspecting the scene from the outskirts. "And we have a second victim."

Still kneeling, Jade tipped her head to the side to face him. "Yes, and a tight schedule."

"And a partial?" Kane asked, motioning to the last two letters trailing the message.

"Callum put out an All Points, nothing yet but I'm not sure he was writing a plate." Jade focused again on the scene. "The Machias girl was reported missing by her father. We're heading there next."

"Oh shit," Kane said, his tone shifting to reserved anger. "This is Jack Wells, the *Getting Wells* podcaster we watch! Well now I'm properly pissed."

Jade glanced up. "Yep, I was getting to that. Me too."

"He's a great kid. Fuck. We need more of him, not less." Kane restrained himself from stomping the scene but his body went rigid fighting against it.

"Exactly. And it makes me wonder, with such an obviously bright future, who would he risk his life and lose it for? Whoever this Machias is, I'm betting she is not your average girl."

Callum peeked his head back in. "Okay, officers are standing down and were two miles within the farm so it was close. I sent the MPR to you so you have everything we have on Machias. They hadn't interviewed at the school yet, so her class schedule is attached. There has only been one potential hit on a Mercedes van west of here. License plate is unreadable, go figure, from the CCTV capture. It could be unrelated."

"Send everything you have to Detective Swan," Kane said. "I'll jump on with him and get him on it. How far away was the capture?"

"Highway 87 and there's a hundred destinations it could've gone from there," Callum said. "I'm having everything reviewed from anticipated time of body drop. I placed it between midnight and early hours the previous night. Any sooner and the kids would be all over this back road, any later those coming into town for the early game would've spotted something. We've had no reports except my boy's."

"I need a map." Kane stepped by Jade their eyes meeting on his way out. She read his relief dropping together into the comfort of a case that wasn't related to them. She felt it too.

"Come with me. I've got one in the truck," Callum offered and disappeared behind the dropped canvas with Kane.

Alone again, the clock to rescue Machias started ticking in Jade's mind. Nothing else mattered. Until she was recovered, they would focus on nothing else, do nothing but build the case. A voice deep in her psyche wouldn't be fully extinguished, the one questioning the whereabouts of Nickolas Leigh. Jade shook it free placing a hand on the still body of Jack Wells. "I'll find her, Jack."

With so much evidence to filter she was anxious to get back to the shop and build the case out in a way that made sense following the collection.

Jade inspected the condition of Jack's boots. The clothes he wore, so distinguished by a splash of unique and daring cool for the recorded podcasts, didn't disappoint even here, down to the custom laces on his Balenciaga ankle boots that had to cost over a thousand. "You're breaking my heart, Jack. Only you and me can truly appreciate these."

They remained undamaged, soiled in such a way visions of him fighting his assailant standing in a half-drag position to meet his fate filled Jade's mind. He wasn't thrown around postmortem, he crawled back to meet the roadside fighting to avenge until his last breath.

She gazed at his face. His eyes were closed, and being abandoned to die roadside in the dark, he was the one who bravely chose to close them. His face was beautiful. She recalled him laughing on the screen doing a satire piece about what parents worried about opposed to what they should. He had a smile that lit from within and a laugh to match, one that had you roaring with him before you took notice of doing it. And his delivery was always fair, balanced, even wise. Every homicide they investigated struck a nail in the coffin of an elevated humanity but some hurt more. This hurt more.

That thought cushioned Jade's approach to their interviews at the high school. Knowing how devastating this news would be delivered. She chose to delay their arrival until counselor support could be established. On hand and prepared for an outpouring of pain.

Speaking to the kids, those closest to Jack and Machias, would be crucial to rebuilding the state of their lives prior to their abduction. Interviewing Machias's father, the one who reported her missing so quickly on the heels of her disappearance, became her priority.

Jade expected the glimpse behind the walls of that home to tell her even more than Jack had.

The coroner, a woman assigned the position between Jade's last need of one and today, introduced herself as Meg with a gentle entrance into the tent that Jade respected. She came alongside Jade as invited and placed a hand on Jack's arm, an area undamaged.

"Can I check him?" she asked.

"Please," Jade said. "We have initial photos and collection done surrounding this space."

Meg carefully lifted the body, rolling it slightly to view the portion of his side and back in contact with the soil. "Ah...here we go," she said, waving Jade to lean nearer his torso. "Stabbed, I'd guess, and with a precise direct hit to the liver. If he'd fallen the other direction, it would've been obvious but with this angle he bled out into the soil and he's wearing black so harder to see."

"How precise?" Jade asked, inspecting the area.

"Perfect placement. It may have only damaged a singular lobe but I won't know until I get back to the lab with him." Meg looked at the victim's face for the first time. "Oh no. This is—"

"Yeah, Jack Wells. This one is particularly awful," Jade agreed. "If it damaged a singular lobe how long?"

"Would it take for him to bleed out? If it hit a major artery as little as ten minutes, less vital places a couple hours. If the weapon hadn't been dislodged, he could've made it until being discovered. I'll narrow the range when he's on my table. Either way it's a damn shame." Meg glanced up from her inspection of the wound and met Jade's eyes. "I'd say whoever inflicted this had practice."

"That's what I figured you'd say. This isn't some lucky hit." Jade scanned Jack's body. "No other fatal injuries."

"No." Meg confirmed, her voice dropping in volume. "One and done I'm afraid...and I'm wondering how afraid we should all be."

Jade met Meg's stare, a knowing passed between them. "I don't think his killer stuck around," Jade said, elevating from her crouched position. "But he chose the right time on the right road not to be seen so—"

"Very afraid," Meg answered for Jade and, skirting Jack's corpse to exit the tent, she didn't correct her.

FIVE

Raven peered down from the brick warehouse apartment
he shared with Jack, his silver balayage hair catching the
light in his reflection off the floor-to-ceiling tinted
window. They loved the space. Gutting what once was a floor of
leased random businesses to create their dream home and studio,
every detail painstakingly arrived at recreated it to its current splen-
dor. And Raven couldn't see any of it. His eyes burned from lack of
sleep. His stomach churned and crushed in against the fear escalating all night after Jack missed their preplanned check-in.

In this case no news meant bad news and Raven felt it in every
cell of his being.

Jack pre-taped the next two podcast releases for *Getting Wells* and
Raven set one for the coming Friday and one for the following as
instructed. There was always work to be done but he couldn't stop
his mind from its downward spiral enough to focus on breakfast,
forget anything requiring mental substance.

The day was hot and bright but he stared at the outside world
waiting for dark foreboding clouds to roll in matching the storm he
sensed brewing in the distance, wherever Jack was.

He'd asked, well, more demanded, Jack confide what exactly his plan was regarding Machias. Knowing she was moving into the room at the opposite end of their home, one reserved for guests, wasn't enough. Raven was excited to expand their family to include her. They were close and Mac was the only one who made Raven laugh harder than Jack. Still, dark secrets existed between Mac and his partner. Jack would never betray a confidence. And though Machias came close to revealing whatever caused the shadow lurking behind her bright eyes, Raven remained outside the knowing between them. He didn't envy the burden Jack carried. It weighed heavy and he'd come to realize being left out was by design to protect him.

But who was protecting Jack or Machias now?

Jack left their apartment late the previous night. Urgency drove him out the door without pause to say goodbye. He packed a bag, with what Raven wasn't sure. A flashlight. He'd retrieved it from their pantry earlier that day for Jack. The rest of the contents were gathered before he came home from a run to the market. Jack explained the need to be prepared to pick up Machias at a moment's notice. That wasn't unusual. He'd spent the better part of high school coming to her rescue and for good reason.

Raven helped once. That one time stopped any previous questioning he pressured Jack to answer. Battered and terrified at thirteen, two years younger than Raven at the time, she refused to speak to the counselors at school or identify who harmed her. Raven didn't need an explanation, so saddened by the damage inflicted he wasn't willing to contribute to more. Jack kept her safe and allowed her to heal before returning home so her father didn't see any physical evidence. Raven suspected someone much older had taken advantage of her. Her shame said as much.

She trusted no one completely except Jack. And Machias was Jack's champion too in every way she could be. The podcast was her idea. As it exploded with success much of the content was hers yet she refused to acknowledge her contribution. Jack set up a bank account for her, deposited a salary into it, and vowed to maintain it until she graduated. Mac didn't know.

Raven wondered if she ever would.

He fought fear in waves; it hit and receded then hit again from a new angle. He couldn't escape it.

Jack and he met because Raven dialed a wrong number. Jack's response made him laugh so hard he called back and never quit calling. Now Jack's cell phone kept connecting to voicemail.

No one was answering anymore.

Tempted to call Machias, he fought the urge knowing Jack warned him not to under any circumstances once he left to bring her to her new home. Raven knew her father would never permit her to move in with them. They lived outside his limited, archaic spectrum of acceptable partnering. Mac explained that her only way forward would be to make a clean break. This didn't feel clean.

It was more than an adolescent response to a friend in trouble, one who dipped into a deep end and couldn't swim ashore safely alone. A dread drifted in as soon as Jack left and Raven couldn't shake it. Unwilling to stay glued to the windowpane, he grabbed his wallet and keys and headed to the Daughtry's farm. With no intention of confronting her father or entering the property, he would go to observe it from a distance hoping to catch sight of anything that might steer him to Jack.

Axel dropped Zane and the girls off at his house and continued on to the police station to give a full statement. The others were questioned at the scene but it was Axel who first recognized the body and approached it viewing the scene in detail. Leaving the station he grabbed an iced coffee and headed back to meet his father where Jack died. He hadn't told the others he identified the victim as fellow graduate of Shadow Hook High and near famous podcaster Jack Wells. He didn't want it to be true. Jack's face was all over the internet, dancing with the coolest moves to the latest songs, visiting the most obscure locations and making them popular overnight, and bravely confronting the hottest topics of conversation their generation faced with grace to walk both sides and join everyone in the middle.

He was their version of Jagger, Indiana Jones, and Dalai Lama all rolled into one.

As Axel recounted all the ways Jack made life better his anger rose to meet them. Damn whoever was responsible for extinguishing his short but brilliant life. This moment for Axel, without doubt, cemented his future in law enforcement and he couldn't get there soon enough.

In fact, formal training or not, he considered this his first case and intended to see it through.

Pulling his new truck alongside his father's off the side of the road at the crime scene had a different feel. Arriving at such a place to meet his dad was not a first for him. Their lives veered far left of normal after his mother's death. Accommodations had to be made in an only-parent household and he grew with far greater independence, responsibility, trust, and awareness than his friends. It set him apart at times but also drove him ahead beyond his years. His father didn't micromanage his life, gave him more respect, and included him in decisions most kids were completely barred from. He read Axel's purpose for returning in his eyes without a word and instead of minimizing his part he did as he always had since their loss, he acknowledged and welcomed it.

Axel closed the distance between them with one arm casually behind his back, his dad crossing the empty roadway to meet him. "Where's mine?" Callum asked.

Axel brought out the hidden cup and grinned. "Right of passage," he said handing the iced coffee over. "So what do we know?"

"The body was transported to the coroner minutes ago. We won't know much on it for a while. No doubt it's a homicide and Detectives Carmichael and Kolton assessed the scene and dug in with both feet. Wheels are in motion. Unfortunately the bastard responsible left town and there's a hundred routes he could've left on. They'll dig into Jack's life, time leading up to his disappearance for leads." Callum swallowed down half the cold brew having been in the hot sun too long.

"Dad, his circle won't talk to the cops like they would me. Has anyone notified Raven?" Axel asked, his eyes watching evidence collection on the opposite side of the pavement.

"Who?" Callum asked, waiting for Axel's full attention.

"Raven is Jack's partner. They've been together for a few years now, live in a sick warehouse convert on the edge of East Block Street." Axel tried his coffee while his dad processed.

"Okay, so Jack is a moneymaker. Nothing down that street that's not worth a small fortune."

"He was loaded, Dad. His followers were nearing thirteen million last I checked but his bank account may have nothing to do with it. I know his success because we were buddies and shared mutual friends but they were pretty quiet in the world outside their posts. And the thing that makes me wonder the most about who killed him is Machias. She was still attending school, younger than him by a couple years, and it was common knowledge they were tight but you never saw them outside of campus together." Axel inched to cross the road as the team finished up and prepared to leave the scene.

Callum crossed first, paving the way for him to follow without being stopped by the new guy who didn't know who he was. "Why do you think that was?" he asked, still walking.

"Her upbringing was pretty strict. We all figured it was because of her mother's disappearance when she was a kid. Everyone knew the story, she walked home against her father's judgment from a church auction and was never seen again." Axel spoke while stepping carefully into his father's footprints nearing the site where the evidence tent was being dismantled, the body gone and collection complete.

"Yeah. Whispers Lily left him and her daughter, ran off with someone else, circled town. Can't blame the knitting bees for that one." Callum parked his feet at the back edge of where Jack had taken his last breath and motioned for Axel to join him. "Daughtry isn't exactly a prize."

"That's for damn certain," Axel said enthusiastically. "Had the misfortune to run into him after a game. He was picking Machias up. She was chatting with Rockie. The guy's an ass. Honestly, I didn't want him anywhere near my girl. Couldn't read if he was critical of what she was wearing or what but…bad vibes."

"Well, he'll be put under a microscope…actually could be under it as we speak. The detectives wanted to catch him dry so he'll be blindsided by Jack's confirmed homicide. They'll see his first response. But creepy doesn't equal killer."

Axel knew the guidance his dad issued wasn't to berate. He said it to teach him to safeguard his approach coming into a crime so he didn't miss any angles of possibility. He raised his eyebrows and his dad chuckled. "Heard that one before?" he said.

Axel kneeled, scouring the surface where Jack laid. "Just a few times." He traced the letters still etched into the dirt with his finger in the air without touching or contaminating evidence by habit though there was no longer a need to protect it. "Wonder who he is?"

"The killer? Yeah, we all are," his dad said, his shadow blocking out the sun.

"No. The Main Motherfucker," Axel said it, pointing to the last entry of Jack's note where two M's were followed by what appeared to him to be a half scribbled F.

"I thought that was a partial plate," Callum said, grabbing his phone.

"Not if you're our generation. And why wouldn't he write a plate directly under the van information? Why wait until after the accusation? And if this killer is as good as he appears to be, plates wouldn't matter. He'd switch them out." Axel glanced up to see his dad grinning while his fingers sent messages, presumably to the detectives working the case. "If it's okay with you, I'll take a look around and then head to check in on the gang. I'll start asking questions. Maybe one of us saw or heard something."

"Carefully, son," Callum warned. "We don't know who did this, where Machias is, or who is involved and I do not want you or one of your friends being next. You stay together, don't go anywhere alone, and tell the girls to stay indoors at night or in a group until this is solved."

Axel stood to meet his father's stern expression. "I will and I will tell you the second I hear anything, if I do. I just…he was one of us…I can't do nothing."

"I know." Callum crushed the empty plastic cup in his hand tossing it perfectly overhand into a garbage bin not yet removed from the site. "So I guess I will be signing the recruitment papers? You're staying local? It's law enforcement?"

Axel smiled, a weight lifting from him as a new determination settled in. "Yeah, sign away and quit grinning like that. It wasn't that hard of a shot."

"Hardest one I've had to make in years," Callum said.

Axel knew they weren't talking about the cup. His dad desperately wanted him to stay close but refused to say it or put pressure on Axel's academic future. Little did he know it was a desire Axel shared and Rockie supported. His crew was staying together and he planned on leaning on them harder than ever.

He had a case to solve and intended to do it from the inside out, for Jack.

SIX

Machias woke to the rattle of chains, a crushing realization that the location Jack was yanked from the van and dragged away became his final destination over the course of the night, and a brutal awareness that no one could rescue her now. Not because they wouldn't try or want to but her stark surroundings brought unmistakable clarity that they'd never stand a chance..

An abandoned bomb shelter somewhere within a night's driving distance, large enough to park several long-haul trucks inside and constructed of impenetrable cement.

A soundproof, unyielding, bombproof cage made all the more devastating by the fact she wasn't inside its walls alone.

Riparian was feeding a five-inch thick chain through iron loops sunk into the concrete walls flanking the solid steel gate he closed behind them after driving inside the shelter. Machias woke to the sound but hadn't managed a glimpse of what lay outside the huge echoing arched space. When her driver was done securing an entrance that clearly didn't require additional measures, he pulled a lever by the door and overhead lights flashed on in succession down the tunnel ahead. It was then she noticed, though still locked inside, the van's back doors were ajar allowing her full view of the shelter's interior. Seeing that it proceeded into the distance for what appeared to be miles she wished she'd been spared the secondary illumination.

The light announced in glaring clarity this wasn't a cubbyhole hideout, it was a world Riparian had years to convert and make his own for perhaps this very purpose or worse. As if sensing her thoughts, he entered a code into a keypad and, staring at her, crossed back to where he'd left her.

"Time to get you out of there," he said, his eyes never leaving hers as if reading and assessing all her private thoughts. "I will allow you a measure of freedom within this space if you do not cause issues. You cannot get beyond the doors, so don't try, wasted energy."

"Rip, how many people have seen the inside of this place and lived to speak about it?" she asked, not expecting an answer.

He studied her for a moment; leaned in and unlocked the restraints holding her but kept her hands cuffed and helped her to step out, aware her legs would be weak. "One," he answered.

She read his eyes passing beneath them. He was the one.

Seizing the cuff at its center behind him he guided her to the left and then stopped midway across the vast open space. He swiveled his head to her briefly making eye contact again, then deciding against that direction, veered right. Walking her around a corner, to a smaller room than the first but still large by any house standard, she witnessed the first glimpse of how the transporter lived. A bank of surveillance monitors embedded into the wall above a large concrete desk with a keyboard on its surface kept tabs on activity outside the bunker. Here she stole her first glance at what existed immediately beyond its sturdy broad walls. Not what she expected. Similar to sitting on the edge of a forested property, she thought at the deepest point a scattering of matching buildings existed. Was it a government site? Private property in close proximity to a power plant or mass construction base? Unlike the scenery back home this had a manicured appearance. A corporate location cared for on a regular basis. Without time to make a judgment, she turned her attention straight ahead so he didn't witness her curiosity.

Her bare feet were freezing though it was summer, telling her the temperature within was controlled. She stared up as he walked ahead clutching to her cuffs with one hand trailing his back. High above the ceiling had no gaps, sealed with pipes running the length on the inside. Fans turned in a soft rhythm every twenty feet sending a shiver ricocheting from her core down her limbs. He noticed when it hit her hands. Pausing he opened by keypad a large storage locker down the next hall, grabbed a heavy gray blanket from within, tossed it over her shoulders yanking the edges to meet her pinned hands, locked the storage unit and continued on.

"Thank you," she said. Clutching tight to its border, she stayed in stride with him.

His eyes ventured down, not lingering on her but to the floor they walked over. He searched it then her, opening the blanket, inspecting her for damage. He scooped her off the ground in a single swoop and onto a metal hall table where she caught sight of what had him so distraught. She'd left a blood trail in footprints.

"He uses tiny razors," she said, his eyes searching hers for explanation. "It's not bad this time; you kept me off my feet. Jack brought ointment with him, he always does…did. That's why my shoes were off. He meant to put them back on but…"

"Who did this?" he asked, inspecting the abrasions on her soles.

"You know who. It doesn't hurt too badly. My feet are cold." She sat still while he lifted and checked each foot.

"Don't move." He disappeared for a few seconds down the hall. She thought of running but to where? Possibilities circled once and he was back with gauze and medical supplies. "This will sting," he warned before spraying both feet with an antiseptic and wiping them clean with a soft cloth. She didn't flinch. He paused at her feet glancing up at her. She said nothing. Repeating the procedure he applied ointment and began wrapping them in the gauze. Once complete, he taped the top edge so they wouldn't come apart.

"Leave them wrapped. I'll check them tomorrow," he said, helping her off the table.

"Thank you," she said, waiting for him to pile the supplies and garbage the bloodied cloth. He opened what appeared to be a small bag he brought with him and placed the cloth inside. Etched on it she read the words 'Burn bag' as he led her forward.

The hall ahead paralleled what she could only describe as a cafeteria. Storage on one side held can goods, dry goods, and all manner of food supplies behind bars. The opposite side, also a mass of shelves, contained packaged items, of what she couldn't tell. Metal tables were stacked and locked down at the far corner as were chairs, but in its very center perfectly placed opposite a large television screen, sat a long, heavy wooden trestle-like table. Machias studied the habits of Vikings, and the table before her mimicked any depicted in a Long House banquet. A lone chair sat before it.

He caught her staring.

"I studied Viking history. The table is amazing," she said, keeping her eyes on it and not his facial scar.

"I thought you were hungry," he said.

"I am, but I've never seen a table like that one. Did you make it?" she asked.

He stopped to keep the room in view, glanced at her and then the table. "Yes."

"In another life, if things were different and you hadn't killed my best and only true friend, I would've said you missed your calling. It's beautiful." Machias never lifted her eyes from the wooden work of art but started moving in step as he did. Feeling his eyes on her she dropped hers to the ground when the hallway wall blocked her view.

"Wait," he said, stopping in front of a closed door. Again, a keypad left of it required a code to gain entry. When he entered it, she memorized the numbers. He didn't shelter the keypad from view, and she assumed he didn't fear her ever having use for the code. She repeated it, storing it to memory anyway. Opening the door he nodded his intention for her to enter inside the room she did so without delay or complaint. Just inside the door, he instructed her to stop and removed the cuffs on her wrists. "You'll eat soon."

Without another word, he locked her in. She listened to a suction seal engage. No way out but at least she was alone. She wished Jack was with her.

Facing the room, she absorbed each detail from the built-in bunk, reflective of those in movies that soldiers sought shelter under during incoming bomb strikes, to the folded supplies on a shelf protruding from the sidewall. Striding from back to front and side-to-side, she estimated the space to be close to twenty square feet. The roof dropped lower here, maybe eight feet and over the toilet, a sink was cut out of the wall. Beside it a first aid kit took the place of a medicine chest. Checking inside it she found nothing useful in terms of protection but knowing her assailant, if she located a steel bat under her bed holding it would only equate to offering him another weapon.

Jack worked out six days a week, had trained in Muay Thai, and didn't get so much as a viable swing in against her seasoned trans-porter. Machias didn't stand a chance at least not in hand-to-hand combat.

The lighting, not as bright as the hall, cast down from deep-set holes overhead and away from the sleeping area. The contents on the shelf included a large sweater, another blanket, a pillow, and slippers. Slippers in her exact size.

He prepared for her arrival, and looking around at the space she wished her departure was much further out. Having dealt with survival in circumstances far more atrocious, this was a hell she could endure. The existence Jack tore her from, what happened before they landed in Rip's van, what happened over the course of her life escalating in its violence was worse. And Riparian wasn't interested or paid to ravage her. She knew the predatory eyes of such men. He didn't have them.

The only pain inflicted in this journey was Jack's and he made her swear she would not grieve, mourn, wallow in guilt or any self-destructive emotion until she was home with Raven and safe. "Then," he told her. "You can have at 'er, but not until."

With nothing else to give him, she promised this, and to continue the podcast.

Here, sliding her bandaged feet into new slippers and collapsing beneath her two weighted blankets, she recounted all the ideas they discussed while chained in the back of the cargo van. She organized them into categories in her mind, making up a riddle to lock their titles into her psyche should she live to produce them with Raven.

Tears welled in her eyes and her body curled into a ball at the thought of him. Raven would be devastated without Jack. She couldn't help wondering if he'd blame her and harbor resentment. Jack's face clouded her thoughts.

"I know," she whispered into the empty room, kicking free of the slippers and drawing her feet under the blankets. "I won't, Jack. I'll fight to survive until I reach peace, but did you ever consider death might be the only way for me to do that?"

Drying her eyes on the blanket, her nerves settled some revisiting the first podcast they discussed. Planning, even if futile, calmed. She hadn't made it very far when the sound of the door disengaging spun her to face it. Sitting up, she waited.

"Come," Rip instructed. "You can eat in the mess hall if you behave."

Sliding back into her slippers, she met him at the door and, keeping her head down, asked. "At your Viking table?"

He paused before leading the way out. Again she sensed his stare but didn't turn her face up to meet it. "Yeah. The Viking table." His voice consistently low, raspy, and hard didn't sound quite as threatening.

Machias followed, wondering with every step behind Jack's killer if they overheard the timeline wrong, and if it would be her last meal. When she rounded the corner, two chairs sat at the table. Forest scenery played on the screen opposite her seat, steam rose from stew set before her, and Rip had relocated his chair to a far end to watch her but not converse. A wooden spoon was provided along with a cloth napkin and a wooden cup of water.

She waited until he motioned for her to take her seat. "Thank you," she said, inching up to her bowl. Having not eaten in almost two full days prior to the night she was taken her stomach grumbled despite the nausea Jack's death incited. *He would want me to eat for strength to make it back to Raven.* She repeated the mantra in her mind with every bite.

It wasn't unreasonable to consider the food was poisoned, but a freedom existed in the darkness of loss and hardship. If she died by treachery, like Vikings of old, she'd be on her way to Jack, a far better fate than the one her sick father surely had in store for her.

SEVEN

The Daughtry farm was a short drive beyond the outskirts of Shadow Hook down a less traveled county road and though its buildings failed to impress, the beautiful land surrounding it surprised Jade. "How many acres did they say?" she asked as Kane approached the turnoff onto the winding entry road.

"Near fifty," he said, raising an eyebrow as shocked as she was. "I guess it was a camp home at one point for wayward teens, the county version of a halfway house but not for many years now. Mackenzie Daughtry is blind. Who would let all this beauty go to waste?" Kane studied the first building. "And would it kill the guy to pick up a paintbrush?"

"I was thinking the same thing. Shame. From what I read, he hasn't worked since the inheritance. I'd get it if he was father of the year but according to most, he is anything but. Why is it the most breathtaking places are owned by idiots?" she said, drinking in the view of lush rolling hills and treed backdrops in contrast to the dilapidation of the barns and structures leading them in. "Wonder what it's worth."

"I'll get on it. I think it was originally owned by the wife's family," Kane said, starting down the interior road for the unkept farmhouse.

"The one that went missing?" Jade ignored the view to meet Kane's stare. They were both thinking it. One case, at least in their history, tended to expand to encompass a broader investigation. This one barely began and they sensed it turning that direction.

"So how do you want to play this?" Kane asked, finding a parking area on the edge of the core grouping of buildings so they could deliberately take more in walking to and from the truck.

"We'll see how he reacts and gauge it but you take lead." Jade sprang from her seat before Kane killed the engine.

"Right," he said, undoing his seat belt. "I can see how well that'll work."

She smiled, shut her door, and waited for him to walk ahead of her. He chuckled. "You couldn't take second before you made detective, no way you can now."

"I'm great with it, enjoying the view," she said, teasing but losing the smile as Daughtry appeared on the porch to wave them in. "Here we go," she whispered under her breath. It wasn't the disheveled state of the place responsible for turning their opinions. In truth, it was everything amassed in the file they were handed. By all accounts he was a suspect in the wife's disappearance over a decade earlier but a lack of evidence eventually exonerated him in the eyes of the law and he collected on her will and life insurance. Jade planned to dig deeper into his history after questioning him. Local police hadn't the budget or resources to pour over her case ten years ago the way their unit could with all the latest tools afforded them. They'd throw the kitchen sink at it and see if any new leads washed in.

"Mr. Daughtry?" Kane asked climbing the five steps to porch level.

"Yes…officer—" Daughtry's expression said the plain clothes weren't expected.

"Detective Kane Kolton, and this is my partner, Detective Carmichael. We're from the homicide unit." Kane extended a hand as Jade analyzed Daughtry's response. He hesitated.

"Homicide? Oh my, are you saying Machias has…" Daughtry's voice lacked an authenticity Jade had the misfortune of being exposed to far too many times.

"No, sir. We're here to discuss your daughter's disappearance and connection with a possible related homicide," Jade said, noticing he forgot to invite them into his home. "Shall we go inside?"

"Yes. Sorry. My manners. You startled me. I expected the officer I filed the missing person's report with to visit, not homicide. And I'm really hoping the death is not connected to Machias. She ran away before you know, teens, but she's never been involved in anything dangerous that I'm aware of." He held open a screen door and waved them into a front sitting room. Conveniently, it allowed little view of the greater home. The furniture, matching and of sturdy quality hadn't been dusted…well ever and no family photos adorned the space. Jade remained standing and looped the room while Kane distracted the man before taking a seat on a chair opposite a small sofa he claimed. A sideboard one would expect to hold antique dinnerware or crystal instead displayed strange camera-equipped drones, miniature robot devices, magazines face down, and cords to what she didn't know.

Kane pulled out his notes and pen and leaned imposingly forward closing the distance between him and Daughtry. Daughtry shifted back on the sofa preserving it.

"When was the last time you saw your daughter?" Kane asked, waiting and refusing to fill the air for the man.

"As I explained to the officer when I called in, the last time Machias was with me was before school Thursday morning. I dropped her off as always. She planned to stay late and have a friend bring her home after history club. I ran errands in town and arrived here by seven that night. I waited up. When she wasn't home at nine, I started calling around for her." Daughtry's eyes scanned the tables on either side of him locating his water glass. Gulping as Kane wrote, he smiled casually at Jade but didn't release the glass.

"You said she ran away before?" Kane asked, not raising his eyes from his notepad. "Why and when did she do this?"

"A few months back, the school would have exact dates, she missed an exam. I think nerves over the test set her off. She had been irritable and difficult, if I'm honest, for days before. She stayed with a friend who I didn't approve of. Came back home Sunday after church." Daughtry ran his hand through his hair and repositioned his feet angling them diagonally to the screen door. "I won't lie, being the only parent of a teenage girl whose mother vanished when she needed her most has not been easy."

Seeing the opportune opening, Jade intervened. "I can only imagine," she said, taking a seat closer to him. "I don't have children but raising a girl on your own? That would have a particular set of challenges."

"It does, but I wouldn't trade it for a small fortune." Daughtry refocused all his attention on Jade. "You said her disappearance might be related to a homicide? How so?"

"We can't discuss an open investigation," Kane said, catching a quick glance from Daughtry before he turned back to Jade.

"Who did your daughter stay with?" Jade asked. "When she ran away?"

"Actually, I'm not certain. She has two male friends who live together. She wouldn't admit which one of them invited her to stay. I only know one is named Jack and the other has a strange name. I can't remember it now. At the time I was so glad to have her back I didn't push." He explained, saying the right things but the words failed to match the vibe Jade read below the surface. "I wondered if she was back with one of them," he added.

"Did your daughter take any belongings with her that you noticed missing?" Kane asked, his stare demanding a direct response.

"No. That's the strange thing. Her cell phone and wallet were in her locker when I went to the school Friday morning. That's where she keeps them usually when she's there. I toured the school with head of school's permission. Thinking it might have been a one-night event. No one had seen her." His eyes darted first outside in the direction of where Kane parked the truck, then toward a staircase Jade glimpsed walking in. "She has a fair amount of clothing so I'm not certain I would notice if a few items were taken."

"Can we have a look at her room?" Jade asked, feigning a pleasant report.

"Of course." Daughtry sprang off the sofa and was at the door before either stood to follow. "This way."

Jade preferred staircases that didn't lead to the front door of a home, too direct like all the nurturing within intended to escape before being absorbed by its occupants. This one was not only in perfect alignment of the front door but also so narrow and steep as to appear threatening. The banister was Douglas Fir, she appreciated wood and could identify most, but the newel posts didn't fit the railing, ominous in their design from a different time period they had to be deliberate additions. She watched him ascend and wait at the landing blocking the right side of the upper hall leaving her and Kane access only to the left where a bedroom awaited them.

Daughtry hovered in the hall content to monitor their every move, smiling awkwardly when they glanced his direction. Initially the room held all the markings of a typical teen's space, but the more Jade analyzed the dwelling the more it failed. She jotted down notes making mental reminders to discuss with Kane in private. Pausing at the open window Jade swiveled to see Daughtry keenly observing her. "Lovely view," she said, turning her back to him and blocking the space before her. "The land is amazing." While he issued words of agreement, she ran her finger over the sill noting holes along its smooth surface where the wood was compromised by nails. The nails removed left ragged edges. Interesting.

"So has this always been your daughter's bedroom?" Kane asked moving to the doorway to fill it while Jade inspected behind him.

"When she was too little to safely navigate the stairs she stayed in mine," he said, a defensive tone underlying his compliance.

"Didn't you install a baby gate? Something to protect her from falling? One tumble down those steep stairs could kill a child." Kane used his accusatory tone to deter Daughtry from interfering with Jade's review and she was well aware. Seizing the moment Jade ran hands under the mattress, peeked below the bed, noticed a diary half tucked beneath a pillow, and addressed the laptop left in clear view.

"Do you mind if we take her computer with us? It may hold clues as to who she was in touch with," Jade asked from around Kane's shoulder. "And I see she kept a diary."

"Oh. Okay, I wasn't sure she still did. Where did you find it? You're welcome to both if you think it will help find her." He used the question to push by Kane and enter the room.

Jade waved the diary, retrieving it from its hiding place. "We'll return them once we've reviewed the contents and we'll likely have other questions for you. Thank you for providing the list of friends, class schedule, etcetera."

"Of course," he said, shifting his position to funnel them back down the uncomfortable staircase.

"You don't work, right?" Kane asked before descending. Daughtry's face crumpled almost into a sneer until he smoothed the lines of tension. He didn't answer. "I'm asking so we know where we can reach you should there be developments in your daughter's case."

Daughtry relaxed back into his mode of helpful father. "I will be here, at the church, and I volunteer at the Shadow Shelter at least once a week, more now until Machias returns."

To this Kane stared Daughtry down. Jade read the look in his eyes and so did the father who was off in countless ways. Either a visual order to pray for her safe return or a declaration Kane intended to ensure Machias lived to explain the truth of the man standing before him, it threatened. Daughtry stepped to the side placing a measure of empty space between him and Kane.

Kane started down, Jade glanced to Daughtry and said, "Please lead the way. I know how difficult the not knowing must be. We'll give you updates when we have any solid leads."

Daughtry hesitated and then followed Kane, glancing back twice during the short trip to check if Jade followed. The day was heating up but Jade bet the beads of sweat formed across the back of his scrawny neck wasn't from the temperature in the house. He hustled to open the front porch screen door for Kane to leave and closed it promptly after Jade walked through. On the porch, Jade stopped. Kane waited at the base of the porch steps on the dirt. "Where do you think your daughter is?" she asked.

"Well...I don't know. If she stayed local then perhaps with the same friends, she—"

"She isn't with Jack." Jade spoke quickly not allowing him time to reframe his words. "Jack was found murdered this morning."

Leaning on the framing post at the top edge of the steps to ground level, Daughtry didn't falter, flinch, or fall to pieces at the prospect of a close friend of Machias, one she ran to, having been killed or the risk to her sharing his fate. He didn't budge. Jade read everything he wouldn't say in the flash of a second before he spoke.

It took time to orchestrate a lie. And whatever fell from his lips next would be just that. He knew Jack was dead and it placed him in the crosshairs of their target.

"I...I had no idea. I don't know him. I..." Daughtry struggled and squirmed under their scrutiny.

"We'll be in touch soon," Jade said, taking the steps without turning back.

Kane stood, a barrier between them, his eyes memorizing Daughtry's stance for no other reason than to cause discomfort. "Don't leave town," he warned, his tone said such action was expected and would be met with an unforgiving force.

"I wouldn't...I have no reason to except to find Machias."

Jade glanced to Kane as they crossed back to their truck, the corner of her lip curled and his eyebrows raised ever so slight in response. Neither spoke until inside the vehicle, concealed behind its reflective windshield and closed doors.

"That bastard had everything to do with his wife's disappearance and Machias going missing and I'll be damned if he's getting away with it twice," Jade said.

"What I want to know is how he slipped through the cracks for so long." Kane spoke, guiding the truck off the cursed property.

"Evidently Daughtry isn't the only one who's blind. The rest of this town has been since…when did she go missing?"

"Ten years ago," Jade said, anxious to be back on the county road.

"At least that long," Kane predicted. "Maybe longer."

EIGHT

Barracutta watched the tracking device embedded in the Mercedes cargo van go dark three hours after the scheduled retrieval point and it hadn't resurfaced some twelve hours later. Whoever the Ferryman was he appeared to be as smart as he was dangerous. It didn't matter a damn as long as he showed up with the cargo intact as predicted and on time. Using someone new always posed risks but on short notice he was the only one the gang vouched for delivering without incident or attention.

The attention part was believable because despite proven methods the fifty-thousand-dollar custom modified van had vanished.

The transporter's next check-in was twenty-three minutes out and Barracutta gave the henchmen at the door strict orders, no disturbances would be tolerated. Though countless such calls were fielded on a regular basis this particular one held more weight. This cargo, promised to the highest paying buyer, would fetch more than a dozen others. A payday rare and not to be messed with. A shipping container left the docks three days earlier without complications and would land at its destination in eight days unless weather factored in. The next wouldn't leave for a couple weeks. The window allowed the sole focus of the day to be on this call and ensuring the product's safety while in transport.

Tapping fingers over the desktop keyboard, Barracutta's eyes searched manifests on the computer screen ahead looking for opportunity. Preplanning and amassing options kept their system of delivery going when so many others folded and failed. Cargo was cargo in this business and having learned industry challenges running a leading corporate export company taught lessons others in this particular avenue couldn't forecast. It made Barracutta the best, a force no one could stop, one cushioned from all sides and well aware of the pitfalls to avoid.

It did nothing to remove the nerves when money was on the line but there were outlets, ones Barracutta slated to indulge in after-hours. Reviewing the contract request from the buyer, though most of it read as typical, the clause at the bottom caused concern. The seller guaranteed the product met the requirement, but they all did that. Whether true or a bald-faced lie. This time if the new client was stretching the truth the consequence was deadly. Any deception would result in death and not necessarily for the seller alone. Barracutta's reputation and continued survival could be jeopardized right along with the client's. Not a standard allowed with others, the buyer had endless money and needs. A constant stream from him, even over the course of a couple years, equated to a clean escape from the life, the country, the criminal history always a step behind and threatening to gain the lead.

Age altered one's perspective, Barracutta knew the days of evading were numbered and felt more in the rearview than existed ahead. This buyer dangled a golden carrot one relatively easily delivered. One success would set the train in motion but only if it was carried out flawlessly.

Ensuring every detail was managed expertly. All that was left was to wait. Waiting had never been Barracutta's strong point and resentment built so when the phone didn't ring at the precise time anticipated a fever started. It spread quickly and forced a dip in the air conditioner setting for the offices. By seven minutes after the hour Barracutta didn't care if the rest of the crew froze to death. An icy breeze was the only factor contributing to a measure of calm.

The phone alerted to an incoming blocked call nine minutes late. Barracutta drew two cleansing breaths before answering.

"You're late. Not a great show of trust. I expect an explanation." Intended as a demand, Barracutta's opening didn't insight the targeted response most delivered.

"I'm not on your clock," the Ferryman said, his voice an octave lower than one would assume possible and completely unapologetic.

"Remember who you're—"

"Talking to? Are you for real? You don't want to hear my description of you. I have a cargo to protect and hand off and that is where this ends."

Barracutta wanted to jump through the line, slit his throat, and retrieve the cargo early. Lacking that option, the next words were chosen carefully. "You're new to our operation. Minutes can mean disaster on this end. Protocols are enacted on almost immediately in protection of the greater business and clients. I'm asking that you respect the timelines because of this."

"How much do you trust your seller?" Ferryman asked but didn't wait for a response. "He damaged your product, looks like he enjoyed it too."

Barracutta heard an instant acceleration in the rhythm of heartbeat echoing up from a now tight chest cavity. "What exactly is damaged?"

"The girl can barely walk—"

"Are you fucking serious? Our client planned a complete medical confirming she's still a virgin prior to payment if—"

"Her feet have been cut," the Ferryman said it in disgust, evident by his tone. "A thousand tiny gashes. I'm guessing a micro-razor. He ran the length of natural lines and it wasn't the first time." The Ferryman sounded irritated.

Barracutta considered he might share the frustration caused when cargo was messed with. "Are they noticeable, will they be at time of transport? And, have you found any other damage? You should strip her down and inspect so we know what we're up against."

"The feet have been treated and will be until delivery. There's no other damage that I have witnessed. I'll check back with you in two days. And, I don't give a damn what you're up against. I don't answer to you."

Before Barracutta could protest, the line went dead. Punching in their tracer did nothing to produce a location or even partial digits from the phone the Ferryman called in on. Whoever he was he was bold and possessed tech that trumped theirs. Not reassuring. Making a mental note to reach out to the gang member who connected them for more on his background Barracutta's hands wrung, now cold from the drop in temperature. Readjusting the thermostat until heat poured in, options spun for dealing with this new problem.

The seller.

Barracutta had obtained the address, routine, and contacts associated with the man having had him followed for days during the finalization of the deal. The idiot really believed he would see a fortune on his end once delivery was made. Now more than ever he posed a risk that couldn't be gambled with and required possible elimination. He did what everyone in the business, even the seediest of characters, knew not to.

He compromised valuable product, one already sold to the highest bidder.

Unbolting the bulletproof fire door, Barracutta glanced at its guard, the one quick look enough to prompt him to relock it and signal the worker at the hall's far end of their pending approach. The process set months earlier had at least one man ahead for protection when entering the open warehouse structure central to the outer buildings. Though signs surrounding the location and surveillance cameras deterred and alerted to unwanted visitors on site, if an enemy or law enforcement entered crossing this space posed the greatest risk and opportunity for apprehension or attack.

Once inside any of the secured outbuildings Barracutta had tunnels and hidden access doors for quick evasion. Still, the roof height and its catwalk and the array of equipment one could hide behind weren't ideal. The construction site for the highway expansion nearing the docks was, however, the perfect disguise for their base of operations. Accommodating and concealing a large inventory of product in close proximity to the shipyard with built-in restrictions on who was authorized on the property. The actual construction crews picked up supplies from an outer building at the front of the greater yard. Their work went on as any other would and the highway expansion progressed with a timeline set by the needs of the more profitable business it masked. It would be completed when Barracutta decided to relocate. The couple of occasions when outsiders ventured in for safety checks Barracutta welcomed them and toured the facility proudly. They had no reason or interest in visiting the gravel holding tank, who would?

No one.

Soundproof, with a custom manufactured interior shielding a hidden space any worker familiar would be blind to, it all but eliminated the fear of discovery. Barracutta added a feature designed to flood the area with tons of stone should threat warrant it. The product would parish under a volume of rock burying the evidence. Genius really. The only flaw was the dust. Shifts in the level of loose gravel created suffocating dust. Filtering it away from the product was not as seamless as hoped. Engineering a successful method of disbursement without compromising the lungs of the women in holding was tricky so, for now, Barracutta was content to time the replenishment of stone on offload product days. Planning was everything.

The back of the tank had a horizontal window twelve feet up with bars on its interior. With slick walls consisting of solid steel there was no way to reach it. The bars were set apart every couple feet and couldn't be seen from the exterior. It too was protected from sight by close alignment to the back wall of the warehouse. Barracutta motioned for the pit guard to open it further for the exchange of fresh air.

"Leave it open tonight, it's rank in there, but post someone capable of staying awake," Barracutta instructed. "I don't want visitors because one of them decides to try screaming their way out."

The guard nodded walking ahead to open a side door at the back of the tank a few feet from where the upper window began. Barracutta had the window left ajar for hours before scheduled product checks to mitigate the stench. Ran like a solitary confinement but en masse, portable toilets were provided and cleaned regularly by the guards, the smell lingered and grew pungent as the days in holding extended. Day three for this small group with additions incoming until the next shipment, it wasn't unbearable.

Nor was it pleasant.

Barracutta entered the space examining the product cowering at the back of the holding cell, shielded by dim lights lining the walkway. "How can I guarantee quality product if I can't see it?" Barracutta glanced at an interior guard. "Do you have the sanitation soap handy?" He nodded and shuffled to a metal cabinet on wheels set at the end of the makeshift hall. Retrieving an industrial-size container with a squirt tip end he hustled back awaiting further instruction.

"Where's the fire hose?"

To this, a guard standing close to the exit furrowed his brow then fought to smooth it. "Around the corner, boss. Right of the door outside here."

"Bring it in," Barracutta said, tempting the confused man to disobey. He didn't. Returning seconds later with the business end of the hose he met Barracutta in the hall at the center of the cell. "Well, hand it over and call when you reach the valve."

The guard left quickly yelling confirmation he was at the site of the hose's on-switch seconds later.

"When I say, you lather and I'll rinse. They don't comply exactly as they're told we do it again, understood," Barracutta said to the interior guard.

He nodded, his brows dipping before speaking, "That hose can slice through metal if it's too close…you may damage…the product." His warning was work related so Barracutta let it slide choosing to nod acknowledgment.

"Don't open the valve all the way!" The deep throaty command was met with compliance from the guard waiting outside the tank. "I don't want to cut them in half just clean them up a little."

Shifting attention back to the guard with the soap, Barracutta said, "I wish I had that car wash song playing." His expression said he didn't know the song or understand the reference. Securing both hands tightly on either side of the nozzle, Barracutta aimed at the young women across the cell. "Okay, if you take your shower quietly you can get on with your night. If not, we may be here a while."

The astonished faces vanished behind a flood of torrential freezing water and soap but as the screams and chaos ensued Barracutta felt infinitely better about the Ferryman's disrespect and the seller's meddling. No question who was in charge now. That fact resonated on every face in the complex as they scurried like worker ants containing and cleaning up the aftermath of the visit. There'd be no sleep for any of them tonight, which predicted Barracutta was assured to sleep like a baby.

NINE

Axel drove the long back road home windows down, allowing the fresh hibiscus-scented air to clear his mind. He called Rockie and checked on the gang telling her to expect him in the next hour and not to leave. He wasn't wasting time digging into Jack's last days on earth and what lead up to his murder. Machias was still out there in the hands of a killer. Axel's talent on the football field and prowess on the debate team made him an accepted central member at large with a tight core group of friends. Despite this he sympathized with those on the outside helping, on occasion, to break down barriers setting them apart. The distinction grated on him. He reasoned it had much to do with the loss of his mother and the isolation belonging to that category caused.

There were many days when he played a part, feigning tolerance, when inside he fought the urge to blow into pieces or crumble.

He respected Jack and Raven. Instead of quietly drifting on socially accepted fringes they ran screaming into hot zones so often the general public, definitely the student body of Hook High, missed them and felt off-kilter without their opinion blazing trails of conversation.

How Raven would do that alone? This was a question, among Axel's friends, only he was qualified to answer. Difficultly. Half-hearted for a time. Then, brutally honest and fearlessly.

And Axel would help.

The fork branching back to his side of town, continuing on to meet the main highway, or right on the secondary road was in view. The secondary road linked to another route into town and also skirted by the Daughtry farm. His hands guided by a force greater than his own, veered the truck right, its tires spitting up dust and forcing him to close the windows to keep the cab clear. Five minutes later, at the last intersection branching off for town, the dust plume of an Alfa Romero sports car approaching from the opposite side and signaling to turn Daughtry's direction blurred his path. Its emerald-green exterior confirming its owner and Axel's need to head it off long before it pulled onto the property. Speeding up he closed the distance between the two vehicles cutting off Raven's approach. Slowing, Axel guided them both to a gravel turnout near a bank of trees, forcing Raven's pretty car onto a rough edge of the road where they could safely park.

Waving from the cab into the rearview mirror, Axel waited until Raven confirmed he recognized him. Parking alongside Axel, Raven remained in the car expecting to chat window down from the driver's seat. Rolling down his passenger window Axel yelled over, "Too low, can't hear you, turn it off and jump in."

Sounding casual, in truth Axel's nerves churned at his core knowing what he was about to do. From this second forward he would be grateful for grace in every step. He knew, having experienced a similar devastation, none would ever be forgotten as long as Raven lived.

Seconds later Axel heard Raven extinguish the Romero's engine, open and shut the driver's door, jingling keys on the way over. Recognizing these would be Raven's last normal moments on earth Axel was glad the day was so beautiful. It poured rain when his mother died and he found nothing good about the rain since. Bright and beautiful on the day of her memorial, he felt a sense of her then. He hoped this picturesque day offered the same for Raven.

There was life prior to tragedy and life after. Death shifted you to another dimension, one where you could never see or experience living as everyone else did ever again.

For Raven, Axel would usher in that shift, heartbroken but willing to carry its weight.

When the door closed behind Raven, Axel watched his hands and which one held his keys. Left-handed, the keys were within reach. "Let me guess, Axe, you hate the color green and thought you'd give me a free coat of dust?" Raven asked, happily distracted by the surprise of running into a friend.

Axel smiled then asked, "What kind of fob is that? I've never driven a Romero but Jack gave me a lift in your last one."

Raven handed over the keys, unaware of why Axel had a desire to hold them. "The blue one? Yeah, it was great but when the opportunity came to switch it out for green, he raced to the dealership. He hasn't driven this one yet so you'll have to get in line."

With this, Axel quietly dropped the keys in his driver's door pocket, unbuckled his seat belt, and swiveled to face Raven. Head on he read mounting worry in his eyes and knew why. Loss and death more than known were sensed. "Why are you on the road to the Daughtry farm?" Axel asked and waited.

"Why are you? I was...Jack left last night to pick up Machias. Now that our renovations are finished and address unknown to her father, she's moving in with us. We planned to pick her up on Sunday when her dad was volunteering but she called...Jack said he had to get her last night."

"What time did he leave to get her?" Axel asked, knowing any information he could pull from the conversation had to be garnered before Raven knew about Jack.

"I think it was around eleven. They were waiting until dark to sneak her off the farm without her dad knowing." Raven had been staring out the window. As a dreadful clarity started to land, he locked eyes with Axel. "Why are you asking me?"

"I don't think approaching the Daughtry farm is wise. He filed a missing person's report and a case was opened," Axel said, inching toward the whole truth.

"That fast? Jesus, she hasn't been missing all of a day." Raven's processing bought Axel more time to gain insights desperately needed to help find Jack's killer.

"According to her father, she never came home Thursday night after study group," Axel offered.

"The man is lying. Mac talked to Jack on the way home Thursday night. They made plans to move up her extraction in case—"

"In case of what?" Axel prompted.

"Mac didn't trust weekends. Too much time alone with that creep. I don't know what she said to Jack but he started packing a go-bag after he hung up. That might explain where he is, why I haven't heard from him." Raven's eyes lit with a glimmer of hope. Axel swallowed hard to fight the swelling pain. "Jack was meant to call, to check in at certain times if anything went wrong and I haven't heard from him. Maybe Mac ran and never went back home after they talked. Maybe they had another rendezvous point, somewhere without cellular service. She could've bolted."

"What did Jack take with him?" Axel asked, redirecting the conversation, the time for questions fading fast. "You said he packed a bag? Could you describe it, its contents?"

"It's a black canvas coach pack. I know which one because I bought it for him last Christmas. I gave him the flashlight I use to venture down to the utility room. I think he packed an XPLR hoodie. I was looking for it after and couldn't find it. Black with an 'X' covered in roses on the back. Why would that matter? Are you thinking he's gone missing with her?" Raven couldn't find rest for his hands. "I can't stay here wondering where they are I—"

"They aren't together," Axel said. He reached for Raven's shaking hands and place one of his over them. He didn't speak. He waited until Raven raised his eyes from staring at their hands to meet his own.

"No." Raven's eyes filled with tears that spilled over his dark lashes before Axel confirmed a thing. "No. Why are you here? You came to find me? You know…what happened. Where is Jack?"

Axel breathed in deeply, his eyes locked in for the downward spiral visible in Raven's begging him to keep breathing. His mind imprinting the moment, he realized he'd never truly seen Raven, not the way Jack did. His eyes were mesmerizing. So dark and etched even without the black eyeliner he wore. And inside that stunning outline sat crystal clear ice-blue eyes, possibly the prettiest eyes Axel had ever seen close up, though he'd never admit it to Rockie. He saw in that moment what Jack must have and never would again. Witnessing the purity and depth of his love for Jack, his heart ripped at the truth of this loss. Axel shook his head, tears of his own blurring the pain before him. "Jack is gone, Rave. And I wanted to be the one to tell you so I could say you will not deal with this pain and loss alone."

"Gone?" Raven's body sobbed, reading a truth his mind hadn't accepted. "Axe, what the fuck are you telling me? Gone where, how?"

Axel gripped Raven's hands tight. "Jack is dead. He was found murdered this morning."

The sound erupted from the depths of Raven's soul. Though indescribable, it was familiar to Axel. He heard it before from his own father. Axel grabbed Raven and held him tight as waves of pain rocked his body. Until, bursting upright, he pushed back, caught his breath, and fought to speak clearly.

"They could be wrong. What if they're wrong and it's not him they found? I haven't identified him. They would need to confirm it's him." Raven fought futilely to cling to a few more seconds of a world where Jack's death wasn't a certainty.

Axel searched his eyes until he captured Raven looking back. The black eyeliner perfectly placed earlier now bled in streaks down his face. "Rave, it was me who found him."

Raven fought for his keys, hitting Axel till the rage turned to anguish. He tried to jump out of the truck too but Axel had engaged the child locks aware he might. When the shock set in sapping Raven's energy Axel sent Zane a text to bring the girls and drive Raven's car back to the apartment for him. They arrived and Axel slipped the keys to Zane out the window and drove away with Raven to get him inside and settled.

At the apartment Raven designed, built, and shared with Jack he located natural sleep relaxant pills in their medicine cabinet. He made Raven take two on autopilot and helped him to bed. Sitting on the edge, unsure anything he said would be received, Axel promised to stay until he fell asleep and would return the next day to check on him.

Raven never said a word, he'd snatched two sweaters of Jack's from the back of the kitchen chair and a hook outside the washroom, buried his face in one while curling his body and broken soul around the other and was out before Axel met Zane at the door.

"You get the car in his parking space?" Axel asked.

"Yes. He okay to be left here alone tonight?" Zane asked, handing over Raven's set of keys.

"No, but I can't stay. I'm going into the station to see what I can find out. He'll want answers when he comes around."

"If he comes around," Zane warned. "I'll stay, at least until morning. I'll make sure he is okay before I go and let him know when you'll be back."

"Okay. I'm running down to the hardware store two streets over and I'll be right back," Axel said, switching places with Zane to head out.

"What for?"

"I'm having a copy of his keys made. I don't trust him alone. We need access even if he doesn't want us here, especially if he doesn't."

"Smart." Zane scanned the living room and then turned back to Axel, his eyes searching the ceiling. "Do you know the alarm code? 'Cause I'm not all that comfortable staying here knowing whoever killed Jack is still out there."

"I do. Raven said it's Jack's graduation year but don't arm it until I hand off the keys." Axel said, crossing the doorway. "You don't need to worry. I have a strong suspicion whoever did this wasn't after Jack. He walked into the path of something much bigger than he knew. I just wish to hell he told me, someone, hell, anyone. Why is it the most dangerous shit is the stuff no one talks about?"

"It's not that, buddy," Zane said, reaching to shut the door. "People try, no one wants to listen."

TEN

Jade's eyes followed Grey as he walked the evidence board absorbing the initial mapping of the case. Being back at the shop with the team, seeing all the changes with new tech and security measures blend with familiar patterns, gave comfort in the intensity. And it charged the air. Hours drifted by too quickly. The timeline Jack set hung above his picture central to the case. A recent photo of Machias, given to them by Callum's son, Axel, from a school event sat directly under Jack's. Even here he watched over her. Grey read the details of Daughtry's missing person's report, put his back to the board to face her and Kane, and nodded.

"Okay," he said, finding a table to lean on bringing his height down to match hers. "Give me your thoughts. What's your sense of it?"

Kane glanced to Jade, then spoke. "Daughtry, the father, is guilty as hell. Of what or how much, we don't know but the vibes coming from him were undeniable. And you don't become what he is without history."

"How so?" Grey asked, eyeing Jade for an answer.

Jade drew in a deep breath. "Fifty acres of pristine land was

67

motive enough for the wife's murder ten years ago, the inheritance he received gave him permanent unemployment for life and he let the place fall to ruin even with means to maintain or expand it. Local cops investigating then had limited resources. We want to interview them if possible and dig into her disappearance. Her leaving on her own was unlikely ten years ago. It's all but complete bullshit now."

"I think at least one of the officers involved in that case is still active," Grey said. "If he retired chances are he's still local. It's worth checking into but stay focused on the missing girl."

"We are," Kane assured. "We suspect it may be connected. I mean think about it Cap. If he got away with it once and Machias discovered something or became a threat, what stops him from reoffending?"

Grey nodded waiting for Jade to break in.

"The farm has a main house built in 1896, stately inside but the exterior is rough, and six outbuildings. We want in all of them but especially the largest barn, closest to the house. Every time a window put it in view Daughtry was eyeing it. He's concealing a lot but that barn definitely holds secrets he didn't want us finding. Without reason, if we pushed it, he would've known we're suspicious. I don't want him aware of a thing yet," she said.

"Agreed," Grey said. "Keep him in the dark for now. We don't want him tipping off whoever has his daughter before we can get to her. You don't think he has her somewhere on the property, do you?"

"It's big enough to hide the football team," Kane said, walking from the desk he was resting on to the aerial map on the board of Daughtry's farm. "We'd need reinforcements to do a proper search. And it's one of the oldest farms in the county. We can see what's on it. Who knows what's under it. Some properties from that long ago had cold storage cellars and full-height basements. An operation that size could have many."

"What else?" Grey asked, settled in and following Kane's focus on the landmass.

"He expected a visit from law enforcement but when he saw us, he forgot to invite us inside. His reaction to homicide showing up was telling, and that was just the start." Walking to the center of the board Jade followed the evidence with a hand while elaborating. "He isolated us into a confined sitting room, his mouth went dry almost immediately, and his body language said he was ready to bolt for the exit."

"He did," Kane added. "When Jade suggested seeing the daughter's bedroom, he was halfway up the stairs before we stood up."

"Exactly," Jade agreed. "He blocked further access at the landing of the stairs and did everything possible without being overtly obvious to steer our investigation. No family photos, a collection of drone camera equipment, magazines out but flipped face down to obscure their subject matter or target audiences all said he staged the house. If she was out of the picture Thursday night, he had plenty of time."

The corner of Grey's lips curled, driven by fatherly pride. "So if I asked what you think his game is at this point?" he asked.

"The window in Machias's so-called bedroom, which we question the validity of, was nailed shut at one time. The nails removed, holes still visible. Outside of the staging and suspect behavior three things stood out for me, none of which point in any positive direction."

Kane caught Jade's attention, his grin and raised brows encouraging her to lay out their conclusions despite consequence.

"The newel posts and spindles weren't original to the house," Jade said, indicating images of posts almost exact replicas of those at the Daughtry home. "They were acquired and installed after the wife's death." The photo next to the image was one taken at a fundraiser run from inside Daughtry's home to organize a search for his missing wife from a decade earlier. The posts clearly in keeping with the rest of the then well-kept home. "Notice the difference?" she asked while Kane smiled, in on the joke.

"What am I looking for?" Grey said, striding over to inspect the images closely.

Kane met him at the board and pointed to the spindles. "Originally they were set in upside down."

"So he had them fixed?" Grey asked, still examining the photos.

"No," Jade said. "These were deliberately installed upside down in keeping with a Victorian tradition. Placing them this way"—she tapped the original photo—"was said to keep the devil from climbing the stairs while those in the house slept. It was done for protection."

"You do realize Daughtry may not be that bright. He may have just seen it as a flaw."

Jade shook her head arguing his logic. "Do you know how much it cost to replace these? A lot. They are carved out of cherrywood probably farmed right off the surrounding land. Why spend the money to correct a flaw no one is going to see? Why correct it at all if it's a protection, especially after your wife goes missing never to be seen or heard from again? He was welcoming the devil upstairs."

Jade paused and Grey stepped back awaiting further explanation, his expression demanding one.

"Okay so we dug around and found someone to interpret the markings on the new newel posts he installed," Kane said. "Jade snapped a photo coming down the stairs behind Daughtry. They're pagan symbols saying exactly that."

"They welcome the devil," Jade explained. "Even if he corrected the spindle direction because they simply were set the wrong way, incorporating custom carved toppers of this nature shatters the likelihood of it being done by chance. Then there's the evidence of him being at odds with the kids. Callum's son, Axel, the one who discovered and initially identified Jack's body, said no one had ever been invited onto the property. Anyone dropping Machias off following school or church events did so at the gate—"

"And it's a hike in from there," Kane added.

"There's more?" Grey asked, locking eyes with Jade and reading her as he had since he rescued her from the scene of her mother's murder at age eleven.

The lure wasn't obvious, but if the tide turned and the reason Machias was targeted revealed itself in the manner Jade expected, she'd remember the underlying clues guiding her to that truth as subtle, a quiet disconcerting that screamed from afar something was terribly off. And, she needed Grey to hear it.

"He never acknowledged her as his daughter once. He called her by her name the entire time. No find 'my child,' 'my baby,' or 'my daughter.' His detachment was evident. And there's the history." Jade glanced for Kane to jump back in.

"The property served as a group home for wayward teens when Daughtry arrived on the scene, which ended with the disappearance of Machias's mother. He claimed to be too distraught to keep things going. We haven't traced where the kids living there went yet but we will. He volunteers at the church, apparently working with vulnerable youth." Kane paused as Grey read both their faces.

"Christ," he said, having processed the path their evidence was leading him down. Grey backed away from the board and into the front of the table nearest it. He barely acknowledged contact, glued to the evidence, his focus shifting from it to them and back again. "You think this is about the kids."

"We do," said Jade. "Given what we have between our initial inquiries, the previous case on the mother, and what Jack left us, it's pointing that way. Oh and get this…" Jade repositioned to the side of the evidence board where the analysis of the message Jack carved into the dirt hung. "At first glance the end of his message appeared to be partial plates but it didn't feel right. Then Callum calls and says his son—he went back to the scene to meet his dad after the body was removed—had a drastically different take on it. Youth today has its own language and he read it as Jack scrawling the letters M, M, F at the bottom of the note."

Grey cut in, not able to stop himself. "What the hell does that mean to him?"

"Main Motherfucker," Kane said, smiling.

"He wants us to find the person central to why he was killed and there were a million ways for Jack to deliver his last words. I think he was telling us whoever killed him may only be a player in a much larger game." Jade watched the color drain from Grey's face, living up to his name.

"Great." He collapsed into a chair. "This is the worst scenario realized if you two are right?"

Kane walked over, patted a hand on Grey's shoulder and said, "Yep but it may lead to the most important takedown Shadow has ever seen."

ELEVEN

R aven's eyes studied the loft apartment ceiling high above the bed some fifteen feet. The first night he and Jack slept there they fell asleep watching moonlight dance across its metal beams from the upper set of windows, the light pouring in over the nine-foot wall separating their room from the main open spaces. Now that the world had slid off its axis, his eyes saw but he couldn't register the sight the same way. Everything was static, nothing solid, nothing reliable. Like freefalling off a mountainside blind expecting to die, he waited for his heart to hit bottom and kill him in a final burst of pain.

That would be the kind thing to do.

If he lived to see his twenty-first birthday, he would've already suffered the most crippling agony of his lifetime. And no one would understand. They'd say he was young and there'd be other loves, his whole life was ahead of him. All wrong. Every aspect of his life was tied to Jack. From the home they only kicked the final construction workers out of weeks earlier, to their business, the podcast channel, all the future commitments professionally, their families and every friend they loved.

There was no Raven without Jack, no Jack without Raven.

A face mixed within the clouded thoughts swirling in Rave's mind, Axe. Axe found Jack. He couldn't remember if he explained how and he blocked it out or if he never got to that part. Everything after the word 'murdered' became like smoke in his head, he couldn't hold on to it, couldn't find clarity and he didn't care. Did the how matter? The why? A grounded reason could not exist. Anything he learned wouldn't alter the outcome.

Static.

His eyes grew heavy under the sedation of the sleep aids he'd swallowed. Before closing they scanned surfaces searching for the bottle. If he downed them all quickly, he could skip enduring a single night without Jack and wake wherever he was. No luck, no bottle, no energy to reach for it if it had been left there. Axel was crafty, he'd taken it with him. As sleep took over Raven expected no peace but hoped the drugs killed his ability to dream as they ushered him out of consciousness.

Before Jack left out their door for the last time Raven sensed a shift. A quiet disconcerting whisper warning him of certain trouble heading their way. Why hadn't he stopped Jack? Why didn't he demand to go with him? At least then they'd share the same fate and he wouldn't have to face the world alone. Exhaustion prevented resentment. That emotion called for energy and he possessed none. Not enough to acknowledge the rage brewing beneath the surface as his brain succumbed to silence. His last discernible thought was oddly not of Jack. It landed like a grenade, exploding and knocking him out. A vision of Machias, appearing as she did on that night long ago, beaten and damaged. Jack was gone. Jack wasn't coming back and Machias was out there alone with no one to save her.

Axel offered to identify Jack formally at the morgue for good reason. Aside from sparing Raven tainted memories of how he envisioned the person he loved and would mourn, it provided the best opportunity for further insight on how Jack was killed. Those details may hold clues he could track down but they'd be demanded by Raven when he regained his fight.

And regain it he would.

As much as Jack was the front man behind the screen for the podcast and held that position in public, Axel wondered when the roles would switch. Raven, stoic and reserved, was instantly brilliant when called on, the voice of reason and wisdom when the shit hit the fan, and uniquely compelling almost so much so it gave weight to shielding him from attention sure to spread like a wildfire.

He feared the limelight while Jack stood proudly in it. And Axel knew, especially now, if Raven survived this tragedy, it was sure to find him. Axe expected, having endured great loss, Raven being forced to embrace his greatness may be its purpose in the end. Ensuring Raven outlived the pain to meet it was the obligation of them all now. Thinking back, it was Raven's advice Axe clung to when his grief overwhelmed in the days and weeks following the diagnosis and later death of his mother. When no one saw it. Raven did. Few realized how close a friendship they all shared. Axe sensed, walking into the waiting space at the far end of the hall outside the coroner's lab, it would be undeniable soon.

The day had drawn out, containing such importance and devastation when others drifted by simple and routine. Axe saw the sun as out of place, having forgotten to allow the moon its rightful position soon enough. Now darkness reigned and he'd heard from Zane that Raven woke restless and inconsolable but was back out, the available minutes wouldn't adequately fit all he meant to accomplish.

Machias was out there, alone with a killer for soon-to-be a second night and he didn't have a lead. As the coroner waved him inside, he hoped that'd change.

Detective Carmichael stood near the body but back a few steps, waiting to confirm the inevitable. From there they'd contact his parents on the West Coast and news would spread quickly in school and throughout the town. Like a freight train barreling down, no way to stop it or lessen the impact. With his first glimpse of the outline of Jack's body under the sheet the atmosphere in the room altered. He could almost feel Jack's presence there, an intense sadness mixed with regret and urgency. When he caught the eyes of the detective, he knew she felt it too.

"Are you sure you're up for this?" she asked, stepping forward. The coroner waited for her approval holding the top edge of the sheet covering Jack's face.

Axel wanted to scream "no" but giving in to emotion wouldn't help Jack and it certainly wouldn't allow him to be trusted with any insights to find Mac.

"I know you found him," she said. "But this part is…different. The finality of it hits hard."

"I'm okay," Axel said, motioning for the coroner to drop the sheet lower. Glancing to the detective, who nodded her approval, she pulled it down evenly to expose Jack's face. "It's him. This is the body of Jack Wells and if you need further certainty, he has a tattoo on his left ankle, Aramaic symbols, it means 'Boldly go forward.' He had it done for graduation. It was in his speech."

With this the detective shifted positions lifting the corner of the sheet over Jack's ankle viewing the etched symbols that appeared as a strange stream of upside down and backward letters. She pulled out her phone, snapping photos from different angles and then typed for a few seconds and waited. Axel assumed she was confirming the translation. She nodded at the coroner and dropped the sheet back over Jack's feet. "Would you like a few minutes alone with your friend?" she asked.

"Yes," Axel said as Carmichael waved to clear the room. When he heard the door slide quietly shut behind him, fighting back the tears became a losing battle. "Damn, man, you could've told me. You should've. Why didn't you reach out?" Axel stared at the face below him aware Jack was so much more than the body on the cold table. He hadn't reached out then but he was now and Axe felt it at his core. He thought of Jack's speech, they'd all attended graduating or not to hear him. "Okay, buddy. I'm boldly going forward. Gonna need your input. And you better help Raven survive this because we can't lose you both. I expect you to lead me or that detective to Mac before she ends up here, you hear me?" Axel's eyes searched out the window where Jack was. The body couldn't hold him anymore and that was exactly how he planned to explain the experience to Raven.

Detective Carmichael entered the room, waiting near the door.

"Please," Axel said, waving her back in. "I'm okay. I'll be better when we find who did this. How did he die? It may help his partner carry this to know or be something I shield him from but I need to know which."

Carmichael paused, locking eyes for a beat, then said, "Meg isn't done with her examination but he died from one wound. A direct hit to the liver by what we're anticipating to be a hunting knife."

"Did he suffer for long?" Axe asked, holding his ground to gain her trust. "I believe he crawled to the roadside, wanting to find help or be seen. Did you locate the place he was stabbed?"

"I'm going back at first light and we have patrol guarding the area overnight. We think he survived for ten to fifteen minutes before expiring. He fought until his last breath to give us what he thought we'd need to pursue his killer. Damn brave. With the injury he sustained it was a herculean feat."

"That's Jack, master of the impossible." Axe glanced down one last time, placed a hand on Jack's cold forehead, and pulled up the drape. "We'll all be crushed by guilt. Whatever was happening with Machias was always on the periphery, you know? A constant shadow that no one faced except Jack. He shouldn't have had to deal with it alone."

"No he shouldn't have but that's for my unit to figure out and we don't want another person compromised by getting involved." The detective's warning fell on deaf ears.

"There are people who won't talk to you that will talk to me," Axel said, locking eyes. "Anything I hear I'll bring to you but I won't sit idly by." Axel stared at the body of his friend inches from him, with all the knowledge of how to find Mac and catch his killer, and unable to speak a word.

"I won't be silenced or barred from helping him find justice and finding Mac before I end up here again viewing her. I'm months out of joining the academy but I've lived law enforcement my whole life. I've never been on the sidelines and I won't stand there now.

"He wouldn't be cool with it, so it's not happening."

Detective Carmichael allowed the hint of a smile to escape; she scanned Jack's still form, then lifted her head. "You listen to me. Do nothing that even comes close to taking a risk. And anything you hear that feels relevant you bring to me immediately. Okay?"

"Yeah. I got it." Axel realized why his dad was a fan of Carmichael. She was real and he wanted to know more about her. "Jack took a go-bag. He was prepared to rescue Mac and planned to move her into his home where her father wouldn't have any access to her. I wrote it all down, the timeline, what he brought, and everything I pulled out of Rave before I told him Jack was murdered." He handed the prepared notes over. "I'm going back to check on Raven in the morning and can let you know if he remembers anything else."

Carmichael accepted the notes. "Thank you. We'll be coming into the school, anyone you think may have information you text me their name." She motioned for him to hand over his phone and typed in her direct line and the numbers for her partners working the case. "If anything comes up." She locked eyes. "You reach one of us immediately and remember you're a civilian. If I don't have your ass your father surely will have both ours. You want in my unit?"

Axel nodded and listened, his pain becoming fuel for determination.

"You stay safe and alive so I can request you out of the academy."

TWELVE

Riparian locked the girl in the shower room with soap, towels, and a change of clothes he piled on a side table at the door. After showing her how the faucet worked, he hung a watch over a safety bar, secured it by its strap, and told her he would not return to open the door for forty-five minutes giving her a window of privacy. Then, before returning her to her holding room, he would treat and bandage her feet. The bastard who cut her did a fine job of all but hobbling her. No way would she be capable of fleeing to escape. Any significant impact and the wounds would reopen.

The thought angered Rip, as she called him, and it wasn't the only thing.

Every aspect of this job was pissing him off deep at his core and that never resulted in good things for anyone involved. When he agreed to the gang's request, he had no idea the product would be a young girl. His forte existed in transports of adults, predominantly males, and all indebted to the gang or its affiliates in such a way that amends were not possible. The risk posed was too great and an exchange into the hands of those most interested or the meeting of finality was necessary and desired.

Rip didn't know a girl was at stake because the gang didn't know. They simply couldn't. The current situation limited Riparian's response time and availability. They'd never cut access to his services off willingly. Thus, he had calls to make. Well aware of the criminality Barracutta represented, the expectation framed by past dealings said he'd be moving a woman, one inside the life and deemed a risk detrimental to the greater operation. After speaking to Barracutta Rip knew the narrow margin presented of this buyer's game revealed all but a card in a deck of dealings they'd want no part of.

They'd been lied to, deceived, and put at risk.

Mistake number one.

The seller wounded this girl prior to transport and not to ensure she didn't run, but for entertainment. The injuries were new but similar scars told a lengthy tale of abuse. And she was different. He killed her best friend, a young guy who clearly knew the odds were stacked against him and gambled anyway, believing any chance of rescuing her was worth his life. Not a typical friendship. The bond spoke to the girl's worth and plight. Whoever negotiated a path to usher her into the vile underbelly of society did so with no regard for her existence or future potential.

Mistake number two.

And then there was the boy. Riparian learned his name was Jack by listening to their conversation echoing forward into the cab of the Mercedes while driving them. He knew Jack planned to identify him if freedom presented the opportunity and he also realized no one held knowledge about the crime save these two. One eliminated, only the girl could tie him to the kidnapping and what was to follow. Understanding more of how her current circumstances may have evolved, he decided he wasn't cool with them and his choices reflected and were always in keeping with the gang's. To back out of this contract meant blood and complications he didn't welcome but had accepted before making his way down the tunnel to allow her shower time.

He told her forty-five minutes but gave her extra knowing the process of redressing would be emotionally difficult. When he opened the door met by her fully clothed wearing her late friend's hoodie with her face freshly awash in tears, he expected the questions to come.

"Why?" she asked, her voice cracked and more broken than he'd heard it previously.

"He gave his life to save you. That depth of friendship deserves honoring." He himself had only experienced one other in his life who possessed that level of dedication, his brother on the inside of the gang. The reason he sunk into the life to begin with. And the reason he could never leave it.

"Then…why? Why did you kill him?" she asked, locking eyes with her friend's murderer and showing no fear only remorse.

"I'm a killer. I didn't know who you were. I've learned my reaction time sometimes exceeds understanding. Necessary for survival but in this case, not favorable."

The girl breathed slower, her voice steadying. "You sound smart."

"I am smart," he said, standing in front of her motioning for her to hop up on the table so he could administer to her feet.

She slowly climbed up and settled with her feet dangling over its edge, the tension of her movements revealing details to him.

"Then why do what you do?" she asked.

"Some people have to die to keep a greater number of others safe. I became the one called in to even that playing field in a time of war and never quit. The passion your friend had…Jack, I recognized it. I had the same for someone once and it landed me here. The difference between him and me is that I was far better prepared to meet the challenge." He set the first aid kit beside her and lined up the necessary items to clean and wrap her feet. "Climbing onto the table was painful for you. What else did he do?"

Reading his eyes hers registered shock. He noticed pain she expertly mastered concealing from most everyone. "He has ways of inflicting damage that doesn't leave visible marks," she said, staring past him to the floor. "He's mastered the art. It's his only passion."

"You know this for certain?" he asked, watching her body language and reading only truth in it.

"I do. That's why he sold me to whomever you work for. I needed to go away before I got away...and I was close." She said this last part with a defiance underlying her tone.

"You were not sold to us, and I work for no one. Those I work *with* would never have taken the job of transporting you if we were told the truth." He cleaned her soles noticing her extreme tolerance for pain. Her eyes caught his, a flash of confusion mixed with a hint of hope shone through. Her resilience was astounding. "Truth after the fact tends to complicate things considerably."

She studied his face, mere feet from him, and her eyes didn't rest on his scar. Instead they appeared to drift over it in tandem with the other characteristics, not halted even for a second. He tried but couldn't recall experiencing such an altruistic reaction.

"So you don't agree? With whatever he has planned for me. Where I'm destined for?" she asked, still dialed in.

"No." Her feet rewrapped, he was ready to walk her back to her holding room, but holding for what? He couldn't return her to where she'd left, nor be sent into the hands waiting for her. Complicated.

"Okay," she said, inching forward to the edge of the table to slide off it for her slippers. "Thank you for helping my feet."

Before closing the kit, he tapped two mild pain relievers from a container into his hand. Offering them and a fresh water bottle he said, "They'll ease the other injuries and help you sleep."

She stepped down gingerly, accepted both, and swallowed back the pills ready to make the trek to where she'd be alone again. "I'm sorry," she said, avoiding eye contact.

"For what?" he asked, curious.

"For whoever you were forced to kill for. If Jack were trained to kill, like you were, you would've ended up dead like the person you fought. I'm sorry both of you made that choice. I tried to stop him, he wouldn't listen." Sadness clouded the clarity of her words.

"I didn't either."

Fatal mistake number three.

82

The walk back was met with silence and not an uncomfortable one. Riparian sensed the girl knew, as he did, there was nothing more to share and what had been earned a time of processing. Twenty minutes later, alone again in his lair, his mind, as expected, set the problem on a turnstile in his head and spun. Viewing it from every possible angle.

He didn't particularly like what he saw.

He knew when he entered the life, at the place he came into it from, there'd be no exit save death. He expected one day a contract would arrive to place him on an impossible path leading to a grave. He just hadn't predicted it would come in the form of a sixteen-year-old farm girl.

Strutting to an office he set up across from his sleeping quarters used solely for his personal business and protected as such, he pulled open a desk drawer, reached far into the back for a cell phone he used least, and found a comfortable position in a nearby leather chair. His eyes swept the space strangely aware of how cold it appeared. Abandoning the chair, he ducked into the hall, aimed for a cabinet, entered a code, and brought a blanket into the room. Settled back in the chair, blanket draped loosely over him, he pressed a speed dial button and waited for the connection knowing what came next would change everything and quite certainly end in the death of him. Despite the truth of consequence, he hadn't felt more at ease in years.

A shelf above the desk inset into the stark white cement wall cataloged a gruesome legacy. Each zip stored there laid out his deeds, those orchestrated by him but ordered by the gang. The details of which followed every person involved, names, locations, times, and history. Only one made him proud. The rest added weight to the purse paying his entry into hell.

There were a few times he walked into trouble expecting the probability of death but knowing, with every part of his being, the outcome was worth the odds. Most contracts didn't merit the time or effort forget risk. He didn't anticipate facing a meaningful challenge after leaving the service and saving his brother, his position diving always into deeper darkness. Today he glimpsed a worthwhile path to one potential good deed. One to go out on. And, as the voice on the other end sounded, a grin escaped his scarred lips and this time they weren't turned up by the rival of evil.

"Hey," he said, acknowledging the baritone matching the depth of his own echoing over the line. "We've got a problem."

THIRTEEN

S itting quietly across from the desk in his office, Jade watched Max examining the case file analyzing Daughtry and the events the team mapped leading up to the disappearance of Machias. Given ample time overnight to absorb pertinent information, he was reviewing points of interest before issuing his thoughts on the man Jade believed stood at the heart of the matter. Setting his glasses on the desktop, he closed the file holding it in his hand to meet her patient gaze, ready to deliver.

"So?" she asked. "What do we have?"

"Trouble padded and packaged in the socially accepted behavioral wrappings of a typical struggling single father. Under the starched and ironed exterior a monster operates with impunity afforded by paying taxes, living on the outskirts of town with a perimeter fence, and volunteering at a church outreach too trusting to see the devil in their midst," Max said, slapping the substantial file down. "What part he has or how big I can't help with but the signs exist. You were correct in questioning his true intention. In my opinion, he's deviant, criminal, and likely murderous if it serves him. The clinical label has no impact on the urgency of uncovering this man's past."

"I couldn't agree more, Max. I want to reopen the missing wife's investigation. We're obligated to have evidence justifying doing so and we'll work on it. The girl and the death of Jack is priority one. Is there anything in what you read that might shed light on how or why Daughtry would be involved in his daughter's abduction and Jack's death? I sense Jack is key to the puzzle."

"Well young Jack found pointing you in the right direction worth considerable pain and the sacrifice of his life. What he said is key, but it's the matter of deciphering it accurately that poses the challenge. He knew more than time allowed him to write but the facts surrounding his goal of retrieving Machias from the farm to relocate her to his home speaks volumes. And I read that Jack's warehouse apartment is new, armed with an alarm monitoring system and safety protocols due to his vast following on social media. I wonder if the protection was established more in anticipation of Machias's arrival and need of a deterrent against Daughtry's threat to her?"

"Agreed. Jack didn't trust her to stay on that property another night but she lived there for years so why the sudden urgency? I think he learned Machias was in immediate danger. He couldn't get her out fast enough and it cost him his life." Jade ran a hand over her arm feeling a chill in the air. Her skin, warm to the touch, didn't hold the cold but allowed it instead to pass through to her heart. Instinct said if Jack and Machias activated their plan days earlier they might be safe with Daughtry behind bars. "We're picking up Jack's computer and diving into phone records to check for viable links but what I want to know is, if Daughtry set his daughter up to be taken, why?"

"The cursory view says whatever triggered it served him and him alone so I'd start there," Max suggested, flipping again through the file. "Yeah here, his actions after the mother went missing reveal a concern for public opinion, maintaining a staged image, and manipulating access to information to avoid interference with the processing of the life insurance. Self-serving. So how does the girl's disappearance work to his benefit now?"

"We're looking at that from every angle," Jade said. "And

Jackson is searching highways out of town in every direction for a hundred miles to catch a break on the transport vehicle. I want back on the property. While Kane and I were interviewing him his eyes kept drifting to the barn closest to the home whenever it was visible. My gut says there's evidence in there. He's had time to clean it but…I want inside.

"If he catches wind that we're on to him?" Jade dropped her head and exhaled, realizing the panic underlying the knowledge Daughtry held the cards and Machias's life in his grimy hands threw her breathing rhythm out. "Max, I don't know if the girl is still alive but if she is, the last thing I want is to jeopardize her survival by tipping him off."

"So don't," Max said, leaning forward on the desktop. "Create a diversion, have Kane bring him into the station while you search the barn. If your instincts are drawing you there, follow them. If you find anything worthwhile, activate a search warrant and tie him up so he can't send word. That, I'm guessing, is the other complication."

"Yes. If we decide Daughtry is involved, he isn't alone. Who he is working with, using, or was hired by him is a mystery." Jade shook her head. "The thing is…this guy doesn't strike me as a mastermind."

"And that may be imperative to solving Machias's case and her mother's, if it was in fact due to criminal involvement. What if whoever helped him in the past has done it again? If that holds true, the implications are…have you told Grey your suspicions yet?" Max asked, his expression exposing deeper thoughts. "Did anyone else go missing around the time the mother vanished?"

"Not from Shadow," Jade said, having checked missing person's from the period and recent days. "I'll expand to nearby towns. I suspect Grey landed there before us."

"What has me thinking this could be a part of a much larger whole are Daughtry's actions. He isn't running."

"I was considering that too," Jade leaned her elbows on the opposite edge of his desk, hand in fist she rested her chin on them, the bad energy resonating off her conclusion weighing on her physically. "What if he can't? What if he is following the protocol of someone bigger and far more dangerous than him?"

Max studied her eyes when they drifted back up to meet his. "If that's true, than Machias and Jack may not be the only members of our community this ends with and you all better track the perpetrators down before anyone else goes missing. This happens too often, especially on the edges of small towns. No one talks about it much around here but we are so close to the ports."

"Jesus, Max." Jade's brow knitted into a knot at the mention of their seaboard proximity. "If this bastard put that girl on an ocean liner he sure as hell had better of armed the boat because I'll chase them from shore to shore to bring her home and sink the motherfucker on my way back."

Jackson's eyes burned like they'd been dipped in Grizzly hot sauce after twenty hours of viewing CCTV footage. He feared staring away from it the world would reflect back in grainy images, his eyes no longer capable of seeing clarity but when Kane walked in holding fresh coffee, he was gratefully recognizable.

"You get maced, Tex? The cool kid stand you up at prom?" Kane joked but delivered the coffee and followed it up with a breakfast burrito he hid behind his back. "You'd think after all the advances in technology they'd give us clear pictures, right?"

"Yeah, well they haven't." Jackson accepted the breakfast and pushed back from the desk to consume it. "I have three possible partials. Whoever was driving knows evasive tactics. No direct captures. I think he mapped the route."

Jackson consumed while Kane reviewed the pictures he froze on the computer screen from over his shoulder. After a few moments of intense analysis Kane turned his attention back to face him. "He knew the camera placement," he said.

"Oh I'll do you one better," Jackson said, shifting the cursor over to bring up new photo captures. "These five cameras along the route with the easiest accessibility and options are all disabled. Two within days of the abduction."

"He tampered with the cameras?" Kane asked, leaning in to scrutinize the information Jackson referred to.

"Yep, I'm betting this was not a run-of-the-mill opportunistic snatch-and-grab. It was carefully planned and executed."

"That kind of planning—"

"Takes practice," Jackson finished the thought for him.

"Where is the last exit or destination?" Kane asked, grabbing the mouse and clicking back to the previous screen grabs.

"There." Jackson pointed to a fork in the highway branching off out of state or to a secondary route toward the largest nearby college and access to government-protected forest leading to a communication center.

"Well that's terrific. The options are every other state heading west or a campus with thousands of students for her to blend into. Can you say needle in a haystack?" Kane's frustration deepened his tone.

"Yeah, that's where I left off right before I went blind," Jackson admitted. Not all searches in the stream of evidence proved worthwhile, at least not at first glance. "She was on this road though. It is the Merc responsible for transporting the girl." Jackson leaned back into his chair and closed his eyes while Kane, rolling his chair over, stole center stage to examine every detail Jackson had memorized. "The reflection from the light. Can you see the bars in the back window? That's not standard." Jackson opened his sore eyes again to see Kane staring between the expanded image and him.

"Damn, you're good, Tex," Kane said with a smile.

"Yes, my friend, I am. Unfortunately, so is our suspect."

FOURTEEN

Axel entered Raven's place with the key he had cut after patiently waiting through several bouts of knocking and almost breaking the damn doorbell. Zane, with obligations that would impact his scholarship if he pulled a no-show, left sending word Raven was quiet in the bedroom. The wreckage at Axel's feet said he didn't stay quiet. Stepping through broken glass, glad he traded Converse for work boots, he questioned how far down the rabbit hole Raven sank and elected to call out just in case his rage turned outward again.

"Rave? I'm inside, man. I came to tell you everything I found out at the cop shop, figured you'd want to know." His voice echoed up to the high exposed rafters and spiraled back at him but was met by silence. The extent of Raven's pain was splashed across every surface and evident wherever the eye landed from his six-foot height to the baseboards, nothing had been spared. Their home, new and meticulously appointed was unrecognizable. Crystal glasses, dishware, expensive art from the wall to tabletops, pillows torn and shredded only accounted for the obvious first layer of destruction. Mixed in were components unidentifiable at first glance.

"Looks like you brought my grandfather's combine in and drove crop circles," Axel said under his breath, mildly concerned about what lurked around the next corner.

A sudden panic shot him across the open hall to the office and studio knowing if Raven did to it what he'd done to the living space he may well have compromised valuable evidence. Sticking his head through the threshold relief washed over him until a chill traveled the length of the spine he'd exposed by placing it to the bedroom where a very manic Raven was likely waiting. Spinning on the heels of his boots, he saw Rave sitting on the edge of the unmade but undamaged bed. The defeat he wore couldn't be reliably put into words.

"Guess I can't give you shit for not removing your shoes," Raven said, lifting his face enough for Axe to read the streaks of pain painted on it. "I stopped breaking shit when I came in here but only because I had no energy left."

"Thank God for that," Axel said, coming over to sit next to him, close enough for Raven to lean in if he crumbled. "I'll call the girls in tomorrow. They're better at cleaning then we are but I'll stay and do the heavy lifting. You trust them to take your credit card for replacements? I'm pretty sure you don't own a single solid plate."

"Oh definitely, I'll give Rock the company card and expense it as renovation cleanup." Rave said, his voice refreshingly familiar.

"Cleanup? At the very least." Axe smiled and they locked eyes for the first time. Seriousness in Raven's burned oddly green, like that inexplicable sundown flash across the horizon striking in a second and easily missed if you blinked. Axel wasn't blinking.

"I want him dead, Axe. And, I want to be there for it. You understand? If anyone tries to stop me, they'll be next." Raven's voice birthed a new unsettling deep tone. "If there is any chance of apprehending the bastard that stole Jack from me, I want you to make sure I'm there when it goes down, and I don't give a damn how."

"I figured you'd say something like this. I can't guarantee anything but I can vow to stay close to the case until it's resolved, not matter how long," Axel said, standing and peering around the doorway. "There's no safe place to sit out there and I want to go over the case with you, office?"

"Yeah, there's an attached deck, it's covered from the sun and quiet, looks over the backside of the building," Raven suggested.

"Okay, destroyer, after you," Axe said, ushering Raven out ahead of him and toward the office away from the aftermath of his breakdown.

A few minutes later they were comfortably seated beside each other watching a breeze rustle the leaves at the treetops across the park from them. Axel envied the space for a beat and then, realizing the death of every dream built into it by Jack's murder, thought better of it. "It's a beautiful life, the one you two built together," he started. "I know Jack wouldn't want you to waste it or destroy it." Axe glanced inside. "There's more for you to do here and now you have to live for you both."

Raven's hands braced the sides of his head, resting there, then brushed through his cool locks. "I hadn't thought of it like that," he admitted.

"It's a burden but one you have to carry if you love him." Axel spoke the next sentence facing the park. "Love constructs a cross and it weighs heavy but it's a reminder too of the truth of its existence. Now you have to fulfill both his dreams and yours. I would know."

Raven studied Axel's profile until Axel was ready to face him head-on. "Does the pain ever heal?" Raven asked, obviously hoping it was at least possible.

"No. It becomes easier to live with and then one day it becomes inspiration to live better but only if you allow that." Axel couldn't lie. The loss of his mother cut like a knife, more the second and third year following her death. The first year was a blur of grief. He navigated his life ever since with her in mind just as his father did. Now one of his best friends would have to come to grips with doing the same. It was a league he didn't want anyone he loved joining but here they were.

Raven sat with the truth. Axel was grateful he saw him

accepting it. Perhaps the hellfire that toppled the apartment's interior burned hot and burned out. Wiser mindfulness prevailing.

"Who killed him?" Raven asked, sitting up and staring straight on.

"They don't know but whoever did it wasn't an amateur." Axel braced for the follow-up.

"How did he die? Was he made to suffer?" Raven asked, pain resurfacing in his voice. Axel was glad he phrased the question as he had. He couldn't and wouldn't lie to him but there were aspects to Jack's death he didn't want haunting his broken buddy.

"He was stabbed once. A direct and fatal hit to his liver. He was not made to suffer. No other wounds existed. And it all happened quickly." Axel offered no more.

"I love Machias, you know I do," Raven said, his face creasing, fighting swelling emotion.

"Of course I do," Axel reassured.

"I hate myself for it but I wish Jack never got involved." Raven inhaled deeply turning to search the leaves of the furthest tree his eyes could lock onto.

"We all wish he never put himself in a position where this could happen but Rave, Jack is a hero. He scribbled information in the dirt beside him. I can't discuss what it said but it is being used to track down his murderer and find Mac. And I have a strong sense where he leads may have a greater impact than we expect."

"What? How so?" Raven only half heard, his mind expectantly tortured and caught in a loop assessing the way Jack left this world and him behind.

"The expertise with which this crime was executed says it's not a first time and unlikely to be a last. Something bigger is at play," Axel said, not wanting to expand further.

"He was killed by a professional." Raven said it for him and then shifted the conversation. His hands were shaking. He slid them under the sides of his thighs. "So you're heading to the academy? Don't even try telling me there's another path for you."

Axel let a smile escape and caught Rave almost smile with him.

It was everything he needed to focus every human effort in him on finding Machias and Jack's killer. "I am, and now I have a sole reason driving me."

Raven's posture slumped; his eyes, swollen, left all but slits to see out of and Axel knew he hadn't the strength for much more. "Rave, you guys put in a substantial security system. Is it because of the fan base growing so fast or—"

"It was to protect us and Machias from her father. That man is a monster and as much as I thought the abuse I witnessed came from outside her family, now I think I was wrong. Jack was fighting to take her out of her father's influence. Of that, I am sure."

"They picked up Jack's computer from Zane while you were sleeping to see if anything on it can help but would there be any other—"

"Mine," Raven offered. "We share access so anything on his is on mine. I know his password to get in. I never had reason to use it." Rave spoke while getting to his feet and leading the way back inside the office. "I'm not posting anything until Friday and I can do it off our mainframe. Take my laptop," he said, handing over an orderly computer bag. He jotted codes and passwords on a note pad placing it into the side pouch of the bag.

"Thanks. I'll give you an update when I know more," Axel promised. "Tell me you'll go to bed and ignore the rest of the house?"

"I will," he said. "Not much I want to be present for in this world currently except finding whoever did this."

Axel swung the bag over his shoulder and left for the exit, hoping Raven didn't follow, choosing instead to cross the hall back to bed. Not hearing footsteps behind him, he called out. "Rave, I'm locking you in and setting the alarm system. Can you share the app with my phone so I can see if you need me?"

"Okay," he said, his voice receding as he disappeared back into the bedroom, emotionally and physically spent.

Axel didn't worry about new waves of destructive behavior. Sadness, overwhelming grief, sure but he sensed Raven would store any rage or building violence for Jack's killer and him alone.

Unfortunately, the more he examined and sat with the details surrounding Jack's murder, the more he suspected whoever *he* was, he wasn't working alone.

FIFTEEN

Daughtry considered postponing the youth outreach fundraiser at the church given the circumstances with Machias, the police investigation, and the swarm of public opinion sure to explode as word of her disappearance spread throughout town. A flash flood in the small county, bad news flowed to and consumed everyone who had ears to hear it. As far as he knew the detectives hadn't hit her high school yet but they had no obligation to inform him when they did. If they wanted to question her classmates they'd have to wait until Monday. Certain that was on their agenda he figured the Sunday prior to may be his best and only opportunity to host a productive event without all eyes on him.

And, Barracutta made it clear, any deviation from the plan he consented to carry out and consequences would be dire.

Daughtry hated being under the thumb of anyone but given Barracutta's considerable power and long reach, he wasn't willing to gamble against it. The current state of things didn't offer much in the way of reassurance. He'd been told Machias remained tucked away safely in their possession, awaiting the proper time for handoff to the buyer. And if he expected the agreed upon amount to hit his offshore account the terms of their agreement must be realized exactly as instructed.

On that front he'd procured a possible acquisition that met the parameters requested and devised a plan to deliver not only the intended product but also a bonus. With this goal in mind he set about isolating the girl when the event wrapped up. Recognizing her desperation and vulnerabilities he tested his line, dangled the bait, and began reeling in the catch to satisfy his quota.

Having done it for almost two decades, he'd become scary brilliant at it. Sometimes, on days like today, surprising even him. He could only hope Barracutta would be pleased and not stand in the way of his payday. He had so much riding on it.

"Melody, was it?" he asked the girl, drifting off to the back corner of the room where she was quietly sitting and reading their outreach pamphlet. "Did I get that right? I work with so many young people every week I'm not always great with names." He lied.

"Yeah. You remembered right," the young girl said, a shred of hope in her eyes.

"I volunteered for cleanup when the event ends. If you and your little brother would like to stick around, maybe roll up the streamers for me, you can help finish off the leftovers in the kitchen." Daughtry's eyes focused on everything but the girl deliberately nonchalant. "Usually my daughter helps with that but she's away."

"Oh, you have a daughter?" she asked. Bait dangling easily in sight.

"Yes. She's a little older than you, I think. I find it harder to tell age every year. She's sixteen." He gathered information pamphlets on the nearby table, restacking them into piles and collecting them into a box for storage. Lifting his head, he scanned the room checking the number of workers and visitors that remained, gauging timing. "Looks as if we had a fairly good turnout. I wish we could do more but the church only has so many available spots. I ran a teen house on my property, to expand available beds, until my wife...." Pause for affect. "Life without her has been more challenging than I anticipated and my daughter needs to be my priority."

"I'm sorry," she said, melancholy sinking her tone as his bait sank into the tender part of the flesh. "Bobbie and I lost our mom too. I turn fifteen in November, too young to be employable and our aunt isn't parenting material. That's why we ended up here. I thought the church might have a program that could help."

"Well," he said, amping up his attitude and putting on the shine. "You came to the right place, at the right time. And, I dare say, found the right guy to talk to. Help me with the tablecloths and when I'm done, I can go over our program specifics and see what we can make work for you and Bobbie. How does that sound? Fair trade?" he asked, noticing the church coordinator heading their direction.

"And who do we have here?" she asked, looking at his new prospect too closely.

"This young lady offered to help me with cleanup so we're heading over to put the tablecloths away." Daughtry led the girl quickly into the adjacent room squashing any chance of shared details.

"Thank you," the coordinator yelled as they left her behind.

Twenty minutes later with linens stowed, tables and chairs stacked, and everyone gone but the half-deaf minister who retreated to his second-floor apartment an hour earlier, Daughtry watched the coordinator's Toyota pull out and disappear down the long drive onto the main road leading back to the center of town. He'd had Melody organizing member requests information alphabetically, a very important task. Her need to please in the hopes of placement was exactly the distraction he required.

He discreetly relocated her into the back room nearest the employee parking lot stressing the sensitivity of the applications. A smaller lot facing the forest, it was out of the line of sight of the road in and passersby. A single door accessed the lot and he carried the key. The staircase leading to the upper floor was across the main auditorium and he'd locked its double doors on his way back to Melody.

She focused so intently on the job he gave her she hadn't noticed or asked about the absence of her younger brother. The kid was maybe eleven and slight. Attacking him from behind, he'd been blind to the chloroform and slid into the confessional pew in the storage room with ease. An older version of the one currently used in the main church, it was meant for restoration but doubled nicely as a holding cell for the unconscious child. Once he dealt with Melody, he'd fetch the boy and dump him in the back of the van with her for delivery. Knowing the law had new interest in him because of Machias and the discovery of Jack, Barracutta arranged a quick exchange point under a bridge a ten-minute drive from the church.

The van, owned by the church and used regularly for such events to transport supplies, would attract little attention and couldn't be directly traced to Daughtry. Painted with a string of doves in flight, it didn't scream, "Hey, this is carrying kidnapped kids inside." One short trip and Barracutta's henchmen could take over the cargo leaving him free of further involvement and on his way to financial freedom.

The townspeople assumed his inheritance and ownership of the farm equated to a free ride in life. They were wrong. The inheritance came with stipulations and a monthly payment structure dependent on Machias's coming of age. If he left the land the payments ended and were rerouted to its caregivers or the next in line. The land also could not be sold to anyone outside the family until Machias reached adulthood and was presented the option to take it over. If she decided to remain on the property everything, absolutely everything would transfer to her. Her place in his life benefited him until she reached sixteen. Then, the money allocated for him decreased over the course of the next two years until her eighteenth birthday. Resuming to original levels only if she rejected the opportunity of ownership. Her late mother altered the will without his knowledge. Not as unaware of his intentions as he assumed she was, she punished him from beyond the grave and used her daughter to do it. He made certain Machias paid for her mother's sins resolving a modicum of revenge but doing nothing to free him from financial constraints.

Daughtry was a year and a bit out from losing it all and the one standing in his way was also the only possession he had to bargain with. Selling her off to Barracutta was a win-win for him. Freeing him of her, and the restrictions preventing him from leaving it all behind.

Images of the new life waiting for him swam in his mind. Justification for what came next.

Melody's head was down sorting the last of the paperwork. On a shelf across the back wall of the room, a collection of vases filled with roses and used as centerpieces during the event had been carefully arranged by the girl. The air was heavily laden with their sweet aroma. Fitting. His footsteps audible in the small room, she addressed him without glancing up. "I've almost finished," she announced, pride evident in her tone. "There are three files here where the writing is too difficult to read. The rest is in order."

Saying nothing, standing as a barrier to the only exit, he stared at her assessing her build and how much effort would be required to subdue her if she decided to fight him. The fast-acting sedative dispersed into the cloth he held at his side would render her unconscious until the transfer was completed. The boy, turning his head at an angle, may have lessened the drug's potency. He made a mental note to re-administer it before carrying him to the van as a precaution.

"You would make a fine assistant if that was your path," he said, watching her eyes rise to meet his. Seeing the anticipation of good things fade away, replaced by the animal instinct alarming her to a predator's presence, he reveled in it. He hadn't witnessed it in Machias for years. Surprise perhaps when he devised something unexpected but not this. This was pure shock. The second the prey realized they were caught. He didn't rush it. He drank it in. "But we both know it's not meant to be." His tone dropped the volunteer façade revealing its sinister nature as her expression registered panic.

Melody's eyes banked left and right taking measure of the tight quarters and lack of options. Only a single table and three feet stood between them. Nowhere to run. Not a big man, he was still twice her size and several times her strength. He blocked the doorway, filling the frame issuing no space for escape save plowing directly through him. And though she didn't know it, he was armed. This process worked well. He used it countless times. With no alternative, she'd eventually rush him hoping to spin clear on the outside of the room and race to freedom. She'd collapse in his arms, terror aiding the delivery of the chloroform, and he'd deposit her into the van and be on his way. The boy was an easy afterthought, already sedated.

Tracking her eyes and her grip on the table's edge, he leaned in and swiped the only pen and viable weapon onto the floor, eliminating it. Jerking up from the chair, she swayed calculating odds. Calm, he waited knowing he possessed the upper hand. Staring beyond him, she screamed for help that wouldn't come.

"We are the only ones around for miles and the minister has retired to his rectory. It's several cement walls away and he's deaf, so scream all you want."

For fun he jogged right then left, enjoying her quick attempt to counter his movements. It wouldn't be long now. He cushioned an allowance of extra time to ensure no hiccups in the delivery but he didn't have all night.

Her focus was locked on him, and he read her thoughts as she fought to arrive at a beneficial course of action. When the realization none existed hit, defeat shadowed her bright eyes. Ready to advance and force the end of the standoff, he braced to lunge at her. In a rarely unexpected flash, she moved, not left or right around the table, but over it in one fluid leap. Unprepared for this maneuver, he ducked, leaving too much available space at his left. Swinging around to seize her and chloroform her into submission, he caught the business end of a shovel wielded by her little brother.

Impact landing on the right side of his head, stars circled and blackness closed in as he heard the boy's voice.

"I'm young but not stupid and I mastered playing dead a long time ago, you asshole."

SIXTEEN

Jack broke free of Riparian's grasp and ran like a track star. Unable to see, too far for highway lights to be of use, Rip's feet slipped on the uneven surface of the field leading to the forest, racing to close in on the boy. If he managed to disappear inside the cover of foliage his chance of escaping increased exponentially and Rip, with cargo waiting inside an unprotected van, didn't have the luxury of time to hunt him down. He considered without these factors at play, maybe the kill wouldn't have happened. But he was trained to do nothing else, instinct took over, and before he could stop the momentum of the moment his hunting knife penetrated the young man's liver.

This was Riparian's newest nightmare, creating a torrent waterfall in an endless stream of meaningless deaths.

Not all jobs resulted in restless nights of regret. Killing a dealer responsible for decades of depravity didn't keep him awake. If anything, those contracts eased his conscience. Enemies he'd hunted and terminated on foreign soil, known for using kids and wives too young to be wives as human shields and destine to slaughter innocent civilians to make a political point also failed to resurface in his mind. In the years he served the gang following his professional service, there existed two jobs he declined. He remembered them both clearly. The files of contracts locked away and cataloged in his private bomb shelter didn't hold a single person worth weeping over.

His brother said he did the work of a hero. He allowed that because it wasn't implying the actual label fit. Careful to deliver the compliment in a manner he could stomach, he knew that was how his brother saw him. He didn't agree.

What he was, what he became, didn't allow for delusions.

Riparian was no hero.

What he did for his brother, offering to become a weapon in trade for his life, left a terrible scar but wasn't the act of a hero. A hero would've devised a way to free them both of the life and every darkness associated with it. In essence, all he did was buy them time. Or freeze them in it, still owned, controlled, and imprisoned.

Lying in the quiet of night, visions of the boy called Jack, fallen to the ground mere steps from the forest's edge and possible freedom, he was haunted. And the only path to any sliver of redemption, he realized, slept in the room down the hall.

The girl Jack died trying to defend.

Knowing rest wouldn't come and time couldn't be bought, he threw on pants and sauntered to his office, dropping into the chair at the desk. Rebooting the computer and running a security sweep, he confirmed the backdoor into the nearby university's mainframe remained free of detection and typed in two words.

Machias Daughtry.

His interest wasn't in the state of her missing person's case or current suspicions on how she vanished sometime between Thursday night and Friday from the farm. Instead, he sought background on the girl and everyone associated with her. A decision to make, he wanted it to come from a place of as much knowledge as he could expedite with the window to transfer quickly approaching.

The first information to surface was a well-written piece on the vanishing of her mother when she was still very young. Sliding a leather journal across the desk to open in front of him, he began as he always did. Breaking down elements associated with her to build a likely puzzle of her history. Typing in the mother's name, he was uncomfortable with the images surfacing. The girl down the hall as a baby and child—protected, laughing, and nurtured by a beautiful woman who couldn't have been much older in the photos than Machias was currently. Her biological mother had no clue about her family legacy or inheritance until arriving in Shadow Hook, vulnerable and within Daughtry's reach. Giving him a hint at when her current path was truly born.

The journal page filled, he flipped to the next blank one and continued writing.

After four pages, he knew more about the girl's mother, Lily Lincoln-Daughtry, than she ever would. This part he was exceptional at. Absorbing the tendrils of interactions, connections, choices, and repercussions, he could trace them back and rebuild not just the life lived but the core of the person who lived it. In the service it allowed him to excel at hunting and acquiring targets no one else could track. With his present proclivity it made him inescapable and lethal.

As baby pictures painted a backdrop on his screen, he wished the girl hadn't witnessed this truth firsthand. She was not yet six at her mother's funeral service, a memorial without a body. A date jumped out at him from the newspaper articles. Pushing back from the desk he walked to the locked cabinet, entered a code, threw back the door and slid out a leather-bound book containing all the damaging details he archived. Flipping the pages close to the start of his union with the gang, he located the reference he sought. The timing too close to be coincidence, he was all but certain the girl's mother was the first job, and one of only two he refused. Crossing back to the desk, he stared at the photos before him. Seeing the progression of Machias aging before him and the obvious light in her blue eyes dimming to a single point of illumination threatening to extinguish, he knew exactly where he desired to aim his talents.

It wasn't at her.

The man's name was Mackenzie Daughtry. Riparian back-checked basic personal information after acquiring the girl. The contract file never mentioned it, a fact he saw as confirming Barracutta's talent for compartmentalizing each leg of nasty business and everyone associated. This fracturing made it difficult to trace and or pin responsibility on the head of the organization, if you weren't Riparian.

In less than two hours, Rip uncovered three outreach youth programs the so-called father of the girl was associated with, two ran out of his church and one with Shadow Shelter. Within the span of a year he linked seven missing girls who were at a time connected to one or more of them. He wondered how many more he'd identify if he pushed out the timeline. All were under the age of eighteen. None resurfaced after being listed as runaways.

Rip believed they were all indeed runaways but not in the context given. He suspected not one was successful at running or getting away. No more so than Jack.

Jack's voice echoed down a long hallway in his head, back to a place existing before he was ever deployed. "Don't let him hurt her." He'd said it clutching his side staring up from the earth where he was left to bleed out. "Hurt him for me. You owe me now."

Riparian hadn't spoken a word in response. He didn't feel it necessary. The young man read his regret with clarity only allowed by one so close to death. He nodded and walked away, his footsteps heavier than when he chased Jack across the field. With darkness surrounding them, he still recognized a peace in the boy's dying eyes. His mission handed over to one more capable of seeing it fulfilled.

And he would.

Watching as the pieces fell into place constructing a hedonistic picture of Daughtry's true identity, he walked down the hall to where he disposed of the cleaning cloth used on the girl's feet, glad he hadn't burned it yet. Retrieving the cloth with gloved hands, wielding sterilized scissors he cut a small section free. He placed the sample in a test tube, then it in an envelope, and discarded the rest and his gloves. Back at the computer, the envelope sat left of his notebook and a dozen pages of recorded ammunition necessary to make things right. Or, as right as his capabilities permitted.

With clarity on much of the situation, he decided to retire and catch enough hours to be sharp the following day. Convincing his brother where intuition was leading hadn't been difficult. Handing down his response may not go as smoothly. For the action he intended to take would not only put them both at risk, it was likely to cost them their lives. Not seeing freedom from a life neither wished to continue living, it posed the best scenario. At least this way they left on their terms, not the gang's, not the law, and certainly not Barracutta's.

The challenge was timing. Success required keeping all players in the dark until the last move and resolving issues of finality in an order that allowed none to warn the next in line and all to meet their end.

The one thing Riparian didn't deal well with was loose ends. And this game, having taken on a new and powerful meaning, had no room for failure. In his eyes, he failed himself years earlier, his brother almost as many, Jack mere days ago. Only one other remained that mattered, the girl sleeping down the hall unaware.

She didn't know it, maybe never would, but in the course of a day he'd become her greatest champion. Falling under a blanket of exhaustion, hearing Jack's voice beckon his loyalty, he vowed Jack would be the last to fail Machias.

Machias slept with dreams of Jack watching over her. He was now, wasn't he? In life he adopted the role of her protector and savior without hesitation, recognizing her plight when no one else could. After death he reassured her in dreams, she was not alone and he "had influence" from the other side, she'd be okay. He said to apologize to Raven for him and then asked the impossible of her.

Before she could answer, he faded away and she woke in the dark questioning the exchange and remembering where she was. What were the odds she'd ever set eyes on Raven again? If she did, how could he ever forgive her? She cursed her mind for playing tricks on her dangling false hope but fought to remember the words Jack spoke, somehow unable to dismiss their importance. Like catching raindrops in her hand, they landed, skimmed the surface, but couldn't be contained, losing structure and slipping away.

Frustrated, she allowed the quiet of the space to calm, and closed her eyes, focusing her senses. Tormented for years in countless ways she'd learned to connect to peaceful aspects of life while ignoring pain. Her mother taught her this meditation tactic at a very young age. She bestowed tricks of survival to prevent Machias's true nature from destruction despite her father's efforts to turn her. A vile and calculating manipulator, he had many tells that her mother pointed out so Mac knew how to gauge his moods and end punishments swiftly. Thinking on this her eyes sprung open, identifying the source of the underlying peace she sensed.

Since her arrival at the bomb shelter, she hadn't felt threatened. Not once.

Rip didn't torment, challenge, or intimidate. Imposing and menacing in his appearance from the speed and finality of his actions to his impossibly low voice and obvious facial scar announcing him as a warrior, she didn't fear him directly. Her circumstances? Yes, the not knowing what Daughtry had planned for her. But Rip didn't seem a willing partner in keeping her surrounded by darkness waiting to violate her yet again. In fact, he'd done the opposite. He explained Jack's death and his regret, he showed reproach when he discovered her injuries, and he cared for her needs down to distracting her with entertainment when her pain and fear were at their peak.

Something was off with her courier.

She knew evil. Lived in its house her whole life. This wasn't it.

Maybe this explained Jack's visit? Or, perhaps between the loss of her best friend, the torture endured before waking in Rip's van, and sheer exhaustion, delirium found a strong hold.

She struggled to get comfortable but the torn muscles in her back made her usual positions of self-soothing impossible. She stared at the high industrial cement ceiling and without warning envisioned the rafters in the barn. She swore the scent of sawdust, hay, and blood waft in the air. As if he knew it presented the final opportunity to inflict pain before offloading her to the fate he served on her mother, Daughtry laid out a smorgasbord of his favorite weapons and administered abuse wearing the grin of a kid unleashed near the desert end of the table. Until Jack appeared.

She'd been so ashamed and embarrassed for Jack to see her in that condition, strung up and virtually naked at the mercy of a beast. For Daughtry it was not sexual, it was strategic. To ensure no marks, no evidence, and no apparent damage to her as a product. He mastered inflicting internal injury shy of demanding hospitalization for recovery.

Machias heard him on the phone too many times. She feared for others for whom he doled out worse. Those she could never save. And the level of his fury said he'd uncovered her efforts to try. She knew too much to ignore and not enough to be useful but she told Jack all of it nights before they were taken.

Too young to recall many details of the days preceding her mother's disappearance, she assumed they shared the same disquiet knowing signaling their time to break free was anticipated by him and thwarted. Daughtry, a superior player with a lifetime of experience, rigged the game cursing them fated to lose.

For a few moments Mac thought she'd won, beat him. Jack had cracked Daughtry in the back with a blast from a broken ladder. It sent him flying off his feet and across the floor. He'd landed unconscious and stayed out while Jack pried her free of restraints and restored her dignity, gathering her clothes and standing as a barrier until she was ready to run. They made it to the ground floor and outside the barn, across the farm and to the edge of the property, and even to the truck. When they jumped inside and locked the doors, she thought they were home free. They didn't know a predator was locked in with them. She recalled the smoke emanating from the floorboard, white like the cement encasing her now.

She wondered if Daughtry was smart enough to tamper with the vehicle. Aware he took direction from a loftier enemy, she assumed planting an airborne drug to knock them out wasn't his idea. Eyes were everywhere but nowhere. And it hit her, as hers began to weigh heavy, another aspect to the calm that made Jack's ghostly promise somehow believable.

No one could see beyond the bombproof walls securing Rip's place. Falling asleep, she didn't fear the door to her room opening, only the one to the world beyond.

SEVENTEEN

J ade hovered on the edge of a desk, Kane within reach in a chair, Jackson pushed his chair away from his desk to stretch his Texas legs and boots out, and all eyes were on Grey as he reread the mapping of the case and their projected plan.

"There's too much real estate and too few of us to cover the docks at the coast, every highway Tex caught the van on, and possible sites capable of holding victims," Jade said, drifting off the desk and up to the map of the town and surrounding area pinned in front of Grey. "We know Daughtry has a connection. If we focus efforts on everything touching him, he'll slip."

"You're hoping," Grey said, still studying the details of the team's potential approach. "Whoever he's in with they'll know he's a target. His daughter's missing and his wife years ago. You really think they'll risk contact with heat all over him?"

"Yes," Kane said, his legs rocking his chair from side to side in debate. "This guy…no way does he make an exchange knowing the attention it'd bring without a payday. And we don't see evidence of him celebrating. I see a holding pattern."

"You don't think the deal is done? If there is one," Grey asked, checking the faces for disagreement as he always did.

"There is one," Jade said, returning to lean on the desk near Kane. His space was hers and it felt good to be back in it at work. "Cap, it's a damn shame and a miracle Daughtry wasn't arrested a decade ago. He made mistakes with us. He cannot be orchestrating this on his own. Revisiting the wife's disappearance, he had a solid alibi, a dozen witnesses-many of whom didn't like him a bit. Someone else disappeared her."

Jackson saw his opening. "She's right and whoever they are they're damn good. I mean professional. I tracked the model of van down every road outta here and for every hit there was a different plate. Same horse, Cap." Jackson spun his chair over to his desk and pulled up a feed while Grey walked over to view it. "See these three captures?" He expanded the photos to make the plates easily readable. "Three different plates. But if you focus here." He shifted the images one after the other to reveal custom bars in the back windows and a scratch across the van's exterior paint near the seam of the door.

"Same horse," Grey repeated, examining the pictures.

"I calculated it and the driver would've had to map out three safe zones, without CCTV or building camera range, within a one hour period to pull this off. Three plate changes, in the dark, with victim cargo and without drawing suspicion. Tactics more military than civilian."

"Well shit, Tex, you're just a ray of sunshine tonight," Grey said, running a hand through his silver hair and backing away to take in the board as a whole. "So you couldn't narrow exactly where this van ended up but you're running it down. You haven't put a finger on the puppet master but you know we have one. And the girl's still missing and we're on a very uncomfortable timeline. So what else did you drag me in here to see because you're all looking nervous as hell and that's never good news for me?"

Jade cast a glance at the boys bracing them to back her up before speaking. "The Daughtry farm once served as a youth safe house, were you aware of that?"

"I think I recall it being shut down," Grey said, searching the room for the most comfortable open chair and dragging it center stage of them.

"While Kane was tracking current activity and Tex was chasing cars, I searched the background on every youth organization Daughtry has ever been affiliated with." Jade stood again, marching to an easel displaying a poster board pad off to one side. The thick pad, new, remained closed. Flipping it open Jade revealed correlating unsolved missing person's cases and those deemed runaways all under the age of eighteen, some as young as ten, with organizations Daughtry was associated with at the time they vanished. Grey's expression turned deadly serious. The shock he wore was shared by all of them but her team had more time to absorb her findings. They were devastating.

"Over the last ten years, since Machias lost her mother to an unsolved disappearance, forty-seven teens have vanished and not one has resurfaced. At least, not that we can find so far." Jade waited as Grey drank in the harsh reality before him.

"Holy fuck," he said it under his breath to the air, not making eye contact with anyone, still glued to the brutal stats. "Worst-case scenario, like I feared."

"And I back traced the girl's mother. Her name then was listed as Lily Lincoln and she was a runaway seeking safety first at Shadow Shelter and then at the Daughtry farm." Jade turned from the board where all the detailed connections were outlined to face Grey. "She was sixteen when he met her. The same age as Machias. He must've married her out of state, forged the papers, or claimed to but never did. No record of it officially in our courthouse."

"So this girl's mother was just another victimized teen but he decided to keep her?" Grey suggested.

"For a while, anyway," Kane said, the inference hard to swallow.

"Okay, next steps?" Grey asked, sold on their perspective.

"The farm," Jade said. "We want inside the main barn. Well, all of it, but until we can conduct a proper warranted search without putting the girl or case at risk, I want to take a cursory glimpse and we've devised a plan for that."

"Anything you find is inadmissible," Grey warned.

"I won't disturb a thing only confirm my suspicions. Then we focus on the school and the kids. We think Jack was killed interrupting whatever Daughtry had in store for Machias."

"If Jack knew or suspected, maybe other kids have information we use against Daughtry," Kane said, standing and closing the distance to the area of the board where details from the original crime scene were displayed. "And Callum's boy, Axel. He poses an opportunity to get the kids to open up."

"I don't want him or any other youth put at risk in any way." Grey's tone hit the familiar depth signaling a line dangerous to cross.

"Of course," Jade reassured. "But he may smooth things over with classmates or Jack's partner, Raven, enough for us to be trusted with the truth."

"Speaking of, when are you interviewing him?" Grey asked, his stare still fixated on the list of forty-seven missing kids.

"Later tonight," Kane said. "Axel will be there like Jade said to provide a buffer for us. Jack's partner gave us access to everything without hesitation. I'm not sure what we'll get from him on the heels of Jack's murder but we're planning on using the timeframe to encourage cooperation."

Grey walked to the poster board, turning to Jade. "Send the list to my phone." He had access to all their information via the shop's system but, requesting a direct copy, she knew the case had taken a sharp turn becoming personal to them all.

Tex, recognizing the inspiration for the move, spoke up. "Cap, I'm running them all for connections in town. So far most are from out of area. I'll let you know what I find."

"Thanks, Jackson. Keep me in the loop. Every step you take from here forward is a minefield." With this, Grey made his way out the double doors, his stride altered by the weight of each name on the list. When the doors closed and the room was theirs alone again Jackson answered Jade's inquisitive stare.

"Seven years ago, a guy Grey came up with committed suicide. They were like us, close, brothers. The word was he couldn't recover from the loss of his daughter. She was fourteen and vanished in a storm three blocks from home. Grey carried the blame. No closure. The case is still open and…" Jackson walked up and tapped the list. "She's number three."

"Oh shit," Jade said, dropping into the large chair Grey had warmed.

"Yeah," Tex said. "If we're right and they'd stopped this then?"

"Grey was right, Tex," Kane said, softening the blow as he did with humor. "You really are a ray of sunshine tonight."

EIGHTEEN

After swabbing and testing the last five letters Nickolas Leigh sent to her home address opening one without gloves became less intimidating for Jade, reading its contents, the fear never diminished. Filled with hints and clues yet undecipherable but mounting in annoyance, they hadn't pointed to anything useful in locating him. They did serve to remind her of his ever-watchful eyes. He knew when Kane completed his recovery and when he and Tex were fully reinstated. Amy being reprimanded and placed on suspension, even her mandatory psych evaluation, came with not only acknowledgment, but also his opinion on its pointlessness. Jade hated to agree but did.

Her violent, murderous half brother, who came close to ending her life and the lives of all she loved, knew too much and her far too little. And the inclination to feign something useful to that end compelled her to run the letter opener across its edge, break his customary wax seal, and submit herself again to his dark influence.

Dear Sister,

You have a predator in your midst. Life has called me to serve you in your desire to hunt him down. I am still healing. My progress in this regard is inspiring. This endeavor you are not on alone but fear, blood of my blood, the reach of the threads of this nasty web. They stretch as far back as they could forward and must be severed severely to kill the spider at the center. So I'll ask you this, what is true about the maker of the web?

Your Loving Brother, Nickolas

So much for a good night of sleep. Jade knew without doubt his words would cycle on repeat all night long while she studied them from every angle to no avail. Precise details of the workings at the shop said he had eyes inside their department. It wasn't the first time. The last time cost them dearly and was thanks to the computer upgrade he funded under an alias. Though experts broke down and retraced the data breach, she didn't see it as out of the realm of possibility they missed some backdoor he hid behind waiting to access at a time such as this.

Grey had an internal investigation underway to expose any potential person he may be in contact with. Chances were, if a person existed, delivering the information was paying out a pretty penny and they'd have no idea who they were handing over the confidential facts to. The details weren't particularly scandalous and were common knowledge in due course so they wouldn't be detected as damaging to anyone who wasn't aware of the team's private history with Nickolas Leigh, known previously as the Redeemer, a serial killer few targeted survived. Amazing the power of an aptly timed name change, family judicial power, and a near-death event.

Jade and the team suspected there were tendrils snaking in more than one direction from the incident of Jack's murder and the abduction of Machias. Nickolas all but confirmed it was so. Starting at the furthest point and following each back to the center required time. Time Machias was short on. With every cell in her being screaming to crumple the letter, disregard the words within, and wipe any subsequent thoughts from her mind, Jade wasn't willing to gamble with the girl's life.

Setting her alarm back an hour, with the prospect of actually grabbing a modicum of shut-eye when her and Kane returned from interviewing Raven, she planned to drop by the shop before everyone else Monday morning. All the information Nickolas was privy to was accessible outside of the case data on the personnel mainframe. Jade intended to sprinkle breadcrumbs for Nickolas to follow but only so far as to open the door for a widened explanation of the claims within the letter. How far back in time exactly did the web travel and where was it aspiring to go? And just as importantly, how the hell did he know about it?

If he wanted to "help" her this was his chance.

Kane and her scheduled a visit to the school first thing Monday. They'd drop an invite for Axel's help at Raven's, if their discussion went favorably. Jade liked the young man and was curious how the interview would go with his coaxing.

Standing at their bedroom window overlooking the yard, their bushy spread of Foamflower and forest beyond, she didn't register Kane's approach until he stood next to her. "You ready?" he asked, his eyes dropping to see what she held. "Not another one? How many is that?"

"Six, I think," she said, not directly offering to hand it over. "He knows what we're working on."

"It seems he always does. You think he's back inside the department?" Kane asked while staring at the paper with intensity sure to have it burst into flame. "Did he say—"

"He's not referencing enough to be inside but maybe the first layer of the mainframe, what's accessible to all on-duty personnel. And by all, I mean the cleaning staff and the lot guy." She relinquished the page and stood silent while he read it. "It might give us an opportunity—"

"No." Kane's tone lost its melodic calm as his eyes shot up from the page. "There's no chance we risk him knowing another damn thing. We give this to Grey and have him shut it all down."

"Again? You know what that would do? Other than hitting the six o'clock news and headlines? No. We use it. We isolate potential access and use it against Leigh, draw him out while we unearth what he knows. You read it. If he knows something that could help this case, help us get to Machias in time, I'm not ignoring that." Jade's voice rang back with a harsher edge than expected.

"We can fight about it later," he said, dropping the letter on the foot of their bed and marching out the door. "We're expected at the Raven kid's apartment in a half hour and it's a ways. I'll meet you in the truck."

A killer, a monster, a murderer, a menace, a demon even, Nickolas Leigh wore many atrocious labels but invalid was never among them and he rejected it now though the therapy pool, staff, and exertion said otherwise. Refusing to accept limitations from meeting the bullet from Kane's weapon or the following attempt on his life while in hospital, he regained full upper body movement to the amazement of his carefully selected and highly compensated doctors. Not content to be reliant on a wheelchair, he demanded continued physiotherapy through his grandfather's influence and support financially. The past months had been grueling, his stomach turned at the scent of the detoxifying minerals most found calming, and on days when embracing a handicap appeared preferable to continuing to push beyond current capabilities only his end ambition fueled his resolve.

Jade was reading his letters and with the delivery of each one he constructed a new link in the bridge between them. Up until recently they'd consisted of mere check-ins while he waited for a chance to do more, be more to her even from afar. No one knew his location and that fact protected and isolated him. A necessary sacrifice toward a greater goal. But latest developments offered a path to connection and proof for Jade to solidify who she suspected he truly was all along.

Sharing the same father meant sharing the same brilliant decisive analysis of criminal behavior. Though standing on opposing sides of the fence, he knew how to lead her to the evildoing underlying the case she stumbled on. A cursory search of the missing girl's name and family history awakened him to truths long buried but requiring exorcism, nonetheless. And who better to initiate it than the devil himself?

Gripping Hydrotherapy float boards on either side of him with strong hands, he thought of how best to serve the situation while ignoring the pain shooting through to his spine with every advancing step. He contemplated serving a visit on the man he knew specialized in defiling youth through drugs and abuse, hooking them on a variety of addictions before handing them over to be used for other purposes. He was but a link in a long chain. Known as the Candy Store owner, he'd never voiced his name but the memory of him hadn't dissipated with time. As fresh today as it was when he was disposed of at the Candy Store to be toyed with as punishment one afternoon, serving justice on the criminal now served multiple purposes.

Fury had taken hold and without awareness he crossed the pool. Reaching the far side, he was met by the glowing face of his primary physical therapist. "I can't believe it," he said, with unbridled emotion. "You're walking."

Realization sinking in, Nickolas devised the next letter in his mind, deciding the timing of couriering though, staring into the waves at the muscles in his legs, he considered going home to deliver it in person.

NINETEEN

A xel surfed through Jack's personal computer files until over-the-counter drops failed to dispel the sandpaper coating his eyes. He jotted timestamps and facts he suspected as relevant reorganizing them searching for some clue to leap off the page. Hours, and he'd lost track of how many, spent pouring over every detail in a futile effort until Raven called to remind him when to show up for the interview with the homicide detectives on Jack's case. They'd requested the Sunday evening timeframe to "exchange information before interviewing at the school." A light went on in Axel's mind and he reached for the phone.

His father and him were particularly close with the head of school. They'd remained so after she'd helped them both with an outpouring of support and a hedge of protection following his mother's death. She was literally on speed dial, though none of his fellow classmates were privy to the depth of their relationship to avoid criticism or talk of favoritism. She was fair but in Callum and Axel's view, part of their new extended family.

Being it was a Sunday and just after the dinner hour he

expected her to be home and was relieved when her calm voice answered on the third ring.

"Axel? What a pleasant surprise. How are you, son?" she asked, her tone taking a solemn dip signaling the impact of Jack's death.

"Hi Evelyn. I hope I didn't interrupt your supper. Do you have a minute?" Axel said, avoiding the depressing emotional discussion.

"For you? Of course. And I ate an hour ago all you're doing is providing a welcome distraction from dirty dishes."

"I hate to narrow the focus of a situation that deserves a much broader conversation but I'm about to sit with Raven for his interview with detectives working Jack's case and I'm helping him clarify a few important details you may be able to help with," Axel said, his pen at the ready.

"Okay. If there's a way I can help you know—"

"That's why I didn't hesitate," he assured. "My father informed me that Daughtry came to you on Friday searching school grounds for any sign of Machias."

"He did come but I don't know if I'd characterize what he did as a search, maybe a targeted one at best. He looped the halls, then asked for her locker number. He rejected my offer to escort him to it. I came around to check to see if he had trouble with the combination and he was gone," she explained. "I know better than to ask how this relates to Jack's murder, Axe, but should I be worried for the safety of our students?"

Axel hovered on the line silent. Telling her not to worry seemed a lie. "I don't know yet," he said honestly. "As soon as I do you are my first call. For now I'd caution the students, particularly the girls, to use the buddy system and avoid vulnerable places and circumstances."

"But it was Jack who died?" Evelyn's confusion was certain to be shared.

"I believe he was killed fighting to protect Machias from whatever fate she's dealing with." He clarified and didn't allow time for speculation. "Do you have access to the camera footage in the hall during Daughtry's visit?"

"Yes. I can log in and view it from home for security reasons," she said, her voice no longer as calm as it was on answering his call.

"Can you trust me with the login code? I will only be accessing it once on my own then I will hand it over to the detectives. Anything we can rule out or gain clarity on quickly may make the difference on locating Machias and Jack's killer."

"Do you have a pen?" she asked, then proceeded to walk through the three-step process of tapping into the footage.

An hour later, Axe was sitting on Raven and Jack's sofa waiting for the detectives to request access to the elevator and the top-floor apartment. He figured they had a half hour alone and not much more. Raven was nervous and fighting emotions. Axel used his questions as a template for what was to come and a distraction from the dark avenue of thoughts plaguing his friend.

"You remember telling me Jack had a go-bag?" Axel asked, sliding one of the glasses of water he brought to the coffee table earlier in front of Rave and motioning to suggest he take it.

Raven accepted the drink, clutched the glass with a sweaty palm, and gulped before answering. "Yep. He packed it saying he couldn't risk the time it'd take if she called and needed out of there earlier than planned."

"Did Machias have one too? I mean do you know if Jack would've put things in motion for her to take essentials? The intention being for her never to go back."

"Yes. I know they ordered a second copy of her birth certificate to be delivered here because her father kept it locked in his safe and wouldn't allow her to see it. And Jack advised her to keep her student ID and health card in her wallet and it and her phone never out of reach," Raven said, his hands releasing the glass as he settled into investigative mode. "There was a hit list of priorities we reviewed."

"So would she have left her phone and wallet locked in her locker at school?" Axel asked.

"No way." Rave shifted positions, angling to face him. "Jack suggested keeping possessions at school thinking they'd be easy to grab and out of her father's reach but she said he had her combination and made it a habit of dropping by to inspect it randomly. She knew it wasn't a safe option. She created a hiding spot on the property. One she could get to quickly."

Before Axel could answer Rave's inquisitive stare the buzzer rang and the doorman requested permission for their guests to ascend the elevator. Axel placed a level hand on Rave's shoulder and offered to answer the door. He called down using the intercom and waited to inspect familiar faces from the security window. "Send them up, Tae. Thanks." He thought it weird staring at detectives that didn't know he could see them. He registered the seriousness of their expressions and sensed their urgency before unlocking the door.

Detective Carmichael appeared pleased to see him and whispered out of Raven's earshot as she entered. "You good to help us at the school tomorrow?" she asked.

Axel nodded and showed them the way in, making kind but unnecessary introductions. "Rave, this is Detective Carmichael and Detective Kolton from the special homicide unit working Jack's case."

"Please have a seat," Raven said, stiffening physically less comfortable than he had mere moments before. "I can't say I'm glad to meet you, but I will do all I can to help you find my partner's killer."

"We understand. You can call me Kane. Is it okay if we call you Raven?" Detective Kolton asked, taking a seat directly across from Rave.

"If you called me anything else, I wouldn't answer, haven't used a last name since I could talk," Rave said. "I understand you have questions for me, but I have a list of them for you. I want to know who you think did this and why?"

"You can call me Jade, Raven. And we will do everything to answer your questions though no answer we could give will justify the loss you've endured. Right now, there is a clock ticking down on our chance to bring Machias home alive. We believe Jack gave his life in an attempt to save her. So for him and her, we'll focus on what we know and need your confirmation on. We will make time for further discussions on anything you need closure on after she is home safe."

Recognizing the directive of the officers, Raven opened up to their inquiries, limiting interruptions, respecting the active case. Axel did what he could to trigger Raven's memory and aid his cooperation. After fifteen minutes, the stream of questions shifted to appear more varied and arbitrary. Axel listened intently catching the underlying focus of their asks. Then, when the subject of the school came up, he intervened.

"You're aware, Detectives, that Jack grabbed a pre-packed go-bag before he left?" Jade and Kane acknowledged, then waited. "There's reason to assume Machias did as well. She and Jack decided on essential items she'd need, which she stored in a hiding place on the Daughtry farm. What's interesting is that two of those items Daughtry claimed to have located at the school Friday morning when he pretended to search for Mac." This last line was met with expected inquiry. "I say pretended because of this…" Rising and leaving to collect his booted up and waiting computer from the kitchen counter, Axe set it in clear view of the group. "This is Friday at 8:47 a.m., time stamped here in the left corner. The screen was paused. You're watching the school camera feed Evelyn, head of school, was kind enough to patch over for you to see. Watch carefully who appears from the right hall to access Machias's locker."

Axel hit play and the trio was glued to the screen as Daughtry entered the hallway, walked directly to the locker, opened in without hesitation, and after a few moments scanned around him once and ducked back out. When the video frame ended all eyes turned back to Axe.

"Now watch it again and focus on his left hand," Axel instructed and then hit play. There in cheap monochrome color Daughtry opened the locker, pretended to rifle around in it, and then, as he was closing it, pulled a wallet and phone from an inside pocket. "He had her belongings when he walked in. Showing up there was staged, and I'd like to know what else he's hiding."

"That motherfucker," Raven said unapologetically. "I should've stormed that farm long ago. I'm betting Jack would still be alive and Mac would be sleeping down the hall if I had! If I get my hands on that prick before you two do, God help him." Raven didn't pause or excuse his behavior. He didn't guard his thoughts or his words. Instead he flew off the sofa, marched down the hall smashing objects within his path, and slammed his bedroom door.

Axel attempted to smooth his reaction over. "I'm sorry…he isn't—"

"Himself? We understand," Jade said. "You calm him down, explain the only way to help Mac and prevent the criminal responsible for Jack's death from winning is to refrain from reacting just like that." Jade scanned the room, her eyes landing on the remnants of the wreckage from Rave's first outburst. "It isn't the first time his anger ended a night, is it? It should be the last, to protect him, the case, and the Julie Mehretu original." She tilted her head to admire the wall art mirroring an architectural blueprint. One of few framed pieces left unscathed. "We all need calmer heads to prevail. But you did great spotting this clip of Daughtry. I take it you're sending it over to us?"

"I did before you arrived through Dad, he was at the shop. The last thing I want is footage of the school I just graduated from." Axel smiled, and they smiled back. "I never knew Rave could get mad, never seen him like this but Jack was his whole world and they were…amazing together. Like…better than the rest of us could ever hope to be. To say he's devastated is like calling nuclear holocaust a crop dusting. He'll be okay but not for a long time. I would know."

The detective's expression gave merit to his words. "What made you focus on Daughtry's trip to the school?" Kane asked.

"The timing, so soon after and the fact that he hadn't done it the last time she ran. I was at school that day. And I figured if Jack planned in advance, he would've made sure she wasn't left without money, essentials, her phone. Jack would've made sure she was safe."

On their way out they gave him their ETA for the next morning and instructions on where to meet up with them. He hadn't any formal training but as they closed the door, officially or unofficially, he damn sure felt like he was working the case and nothing mattered more. Except perhaps his damaged and enraged buddy in the next room.

TWENTY

Riparian lived alone in seclusion for so many years he'd forgotten how he might be viewed by another sharing his space. Not taking stock of talents falling outside the demands of his employ, the girl was reminding him of qualities he possessed that had gone unappreciated since the service and before the scar. The marked flesh wasn't so bad that it made him undesirable; in fact, some women were drawn by it. The symbolization he assigned to it, how and why he earned it; this encircled him with a wide berth of negativity capable of dispelling anyone who slinked in too close.

The girl thus far was impervious.

"Why didn't you become a chef?" she asked, gobbling the breakfast burrito he made her like she'd come off a coffin ship during the Irish potato famine. "You totally could have."

"I was destined for another path," he said, realizing he enjoyed watching her eat like he had his brother when they were young.

"There's an expectation to be wicked with knives for both but I think you'd be happier in a kitchen." She chewed and swallowed, sighed, inhaled and continued. "You should consider it."

He chuckled halfheartedly but the sound rang back with the

force of a belly laugh to his ears for he couldn't recall the last time he'd done it.

"I have to leave you here later today for a few hours." The words left his lips and she stopped eating, chewing, breathing. "No one will come in. I will lock you inside and be monitoring the whole time. You will be completely safe until I return. My venture outside can't be avoided."

As if the mention of a shift in current circumstances sprang to life a reality she'd buried, she withdrew. "Should I go to the room now?" she asked, pushing her plate away.

"No. We have hours before, and you can stay out as long as you promise you won't tamper with any of the locked cabinets or doors. I'll treat your feet again before I run my errand and can set up a feed for the screen if you want to watch something."

"Are you being kind because you feel guilty for Jack's death or for the fate you're handing me into?" she asked.

Bold, he thought. *No, damn courageous. Deserving of honesty.*

"Jack."

She stared at him for a couple seconds, and not the scar part, then tucked into her plate again and resumed eating. In truth, knowing his days were numbered in single digits he desired to hold on to a few interactions worth keeping for the dark road ahead.

"Where were you before you ended up in the back of the van?" Not sure how she'd respond, he started slow and waited.

"You know where," she said, her expression crinkling with confusion.

"I don't. I acquired you when I was given the van, cargo included. They didn't offer up details on what happened prior to when they opened the back. I could've left, but..."

"You didn't know what, who you were transporting until they handed you the van?" she asked, eyes ablaze.

"Exactly. And I don't trust the information I was given. Jack wouldn't have died if I'd...taken the time to ask more, so where?" he asked, maintaining a level tone so as not to scare her or open the door to a battery of questions.

"My farm, where he...where Jack saved me," she said, her voice beginning to crack. "We got away. Jack knocked him out cold and we ran. Made it off the property and into the truck but someone was inside. I remember smoke rising off the floorboards, getting dizzy, and a blurry figure, a man, appearing from the back seat."

"Okay. That helps. One more question and I'll show you the best energy smoothie in the world." He nodded at the double steel doors of the refrigerator. "You can help."

She sat still, staring at the kitchen, then back at him and waited.

"Who is Daughtry to you?" This was the kicker amid the distraction he would use to gauge the truth by.

"That monster is my father." The girl locked eyes with him and every ounce of her disgust registered inside them. And there it was, the confirmation he needed. The girl didn't know the truth, had no clue of it. Rip voiced nothing, but internally he pledged before he departed the world, he would make certain she knew it all. And to do that, his next move would be gaining access to the farm Machias was taken from.

Although they didn't anticipate an epiphany through interviewing classmates at Mac's school, Jade also didn't expect it to be a complete bust. She left disenchanted and finding it hard to swallow that Machias was surrounded by so many every day all day Monday to Friday and virtually no one suspected Daughtry of any serious wrongdoing. Or, if they did, they weren't inclined to act on it leaving the girl doomed to a fate that was painting a horrific abstract on the backdrop of Jade's mind.

She and Kane met Jackson back at the shop to regroup before she embarked on the Daughtry property. Kane would provide a distraction for Daughtry after Jackson picked him up to come in for a second formal interview at the police station. Dangling the hint that information gathered at the school had taken the investigation down a new road of inquiry, Kane lured him into cooperation if only to accommodate his fishing expedition on what they knew and how close the case was coming to his front door. Intent on keeping him engaged of an hour or more by stretching out questions and sprinkling in details of interest they'd give Jade a solid hour to investigate.

Her focus was narrowed on the barn nearest the farmhouse and the house itself. She wouldn't have time for much more while conducting a thorough search. Kane reminded her to check for a full-height basement and the three mapped out her approach and time allowances at each main site. Being that Daughtry couldn't return freely without Tex driving him back home, they were left with a modicum of control.

"You sure we want to deliver him back?" Tex said, walking from where they were hovering over a field map to the coffee maker. "I could just give 'em the Texas boot out along the highway and save a whole lot of time and money for judicial prosecution."

"As much as I'd love that," Jade said, rising up from her focus on the plan to motion for him to grab her a coffee too. "If we decide to go down that road, you know it wouldn't be right unless Kane and I were traveling behind to use him as a speed bump."

"I'm with Tex," Kane said, sauntering over to grab Jade's poured coffee and return it to her desk. "But since we have no idea who is pulling his strings or how far they reach I think we have to let him live a bit longer."

"Who are you three conspiring to oft now?" Max said, taking up the doorway to the unit.

"Just the asshole you're watching us interrogate tonight," Tex said, grinning and gulping his hot brew. "That's why we're keeping you hidden behind the glass, Doc. Plausible deniability."

"'Cause that's worked so well in the past," Kane said, waving Max in. "This one is definitely a head case we need you to weigh in on."

"And you and Tex are conducting the interview so where will you be?" Max asked, focusing on Jade. Before she answered Kane closed the distance, patting Max on the shoulder.

"Don't ask, Doc," he said. "She doesn't have time to explain and really shouldn't."

"Great," Max said, eyeing the group.

Jade finished gathering the map, her phone, a walkie, and her jacket. Passing the three men for the exit she flashed a pirate's grin and disappeared outside the door. They set up her comms to be monitored by Callum while the interview was live in the event she ran into any trouble or required a delay in Daughtry's release. In the hall, she ran into Grey heading into the unit to be briefed prior to Daughtry's pickup time.

"Heard the warrant came through; you leaving to gear up?" he asked, stopping her alone midway to the exit for the parking lot.

"Yeah, meeting the tech guy to pick up the bugs. Max is enduring his directive from the boys. Should be an interesting night. I'm hoping he can provide useful insights seeing Daughtry in action," she said while tucking her phone away and snapping the walkie on the black belt matching the rest of her attire, camouflaged in stealth mode.

"Check comms before you leave your vehicle and expect to be monitored by someone more lethal than the victim's father," Grey warned. "Not sure how much intel the sound monitoring will yield but it's a first step. As tempting as it will be, don't even consider interfering with any evidence you stumble on. We go back for it when we have cause and authority to rip the Daughtry farm apart."

"About that," Jade said, anxious to leave, checking her watch. "The Daughtry farm. He had the name formally changed on land titles. Previously, and for three prior generations, it was known as the Lincoln farm. I couldn't find Machias's mother's approval or signature on any of the paperwork. So I'm guessing he never had it. It speaks to motive for the mother's death. The worst part is, if our suspicions are correct, chances of ever finding a body or real closure on her case is—"

"Nonexistent," Grey said in agreement.

"Yeah." Jade motioned for the door and heard him whisper under his breath as he headed to the lion's den.

"What a fucking mess."

TWENTY-ONE

S linking onto the property without detection wasn't as difficult as it'd be for someone lacking Riparian's training and a night vision tactical monocular. Identifying two types of cameras monitoring the place, the standard property and home alarm system rigs and a second, more powerful, set of equipment complete with repeater and remote site monitoring capability. Skirting the common cameras, he moved in close enough to disable viewing on the high-tech feed from the angle of his approach and future exit by dropping a tree branch over its face.

A questionable intrusion perhaps, but undetectable as deliberate for his purposes.

Waiting until nightfall provided cover, he entered at the forested edge dipping into each building to assess its use and potential opportunity for evidence. Too many structures to cover effectively, he moved in closer to the main farmhouse after cursory glances at abandoned lodge-like sleeping quarters, one holding what appeared to be transport weigh scales and long thin lead plates, and farm equipment storage barns. Most of which were confirmed as long uninhabited by the cover of cobwebs, dust buildup, and absence of footprints accessing them.

Through the monocular he viewed a trampled-down pathway cut into the ground cover leading from the house to the largest of the barns in close proximity. Advancing using the blind side, he snuck along its outer wall until spotting a first-floor window. Tipping a discarded log piece onto its side, he gained enough height to push it open and hoist himself up and over its sill. Dropping with an erupting dust plume and thud onto a canvas-covered uncomfortable pile, he later confirmed as stacked leather saddles, some of which were worth thousands, he swept the area to identify interior cameras or alarm measures. Locating none, he began investigating the space.

Trained to see beyond the surface, the barn began whispering an expected and unpleasant story. The items cast aside, covered and stored, were those carrying the most value, but not to one unfamiliar with agriculture. The structure and collection of tools within said the original owners were serious and dedicated to the land and the life. The one who assumed control knew nothing of it. Scanning the space for access to the second, loft-style, upper level he found the first in a sequence of telling clues.

The ladder used to access the second floor was removable from below and stored away from the hole it fit within on a wall with hooks that didn't match those holding original apparatus. A hatch had been constructed of material much newer than the rest of the barn and locked from the lower floor. A shorter, five-step, A-frame ladder sat collapsed against the wall complete with drag marks revealing consistent use. Someone locked the hatch regularly and Rip assumed someone else was confined to the upper space.

He knew who and the realization made his temperature spike despite the cooling of nightfall.

Moving it all to go up posed a risk though he witnessed no movement near the house for the hour prior to his advance. With a singular purpose driving him he used the system in the dark, shifting the ladders back and forth with relative silence. Peering up cautiously when his head inched level with the second floor, his eyes met a shift of hay, its scent heavy and new overlaying another, all too common to him.

Blood.

If the barn had been used to slaughter animals the scent of blood would be most potent when he first entered. And being it wasn't and he'd seen no animals grazing, that option was unlikely. The fact that it assaulted only when his head breached this isolated area said the upper level was reserved for acts more sinister than storage.

Pulling up and standing in the loft he spun around using moonlight to examine the surroundings at first then employed night vision to inspect areas of interest more closely. Sliding the hay aside with his boot he cut a path to the opposite wall where he caught the reflection of metal hooks spaced on either side. An expanse of discoloration a few feet out marked the area of torture, that and a single broken fragment of razor stuck in the aged floorboard. Rip was standing where the girl had been violated prior to racing away with Jack. So, he thought, where Daughtry was knocked out had to exist here, within feet. Snapping out his hunting knife he kneeled, and with gloved hands, cut a sample from the area most saturated in Machias's blood. Tapping it into a collection tube he brought, he sealed it with its cap before returning it to one of his many pockets. He searched until locating a second area with a much smaller stain and repeated the procedure, careful not to cross-contaminate the samples.

Stowing his night vision, he shone a penlight close to the hooks anchored and flanking the blood pool. The hooks held items out of sync with those stacked and stored, adding another clue in the harsh tale rebuilding before him. Spotting a mattress haphazardly hidden by a poorly draped tarp he was about to move in to examine further when a single light traced across the field approaching from the roadside of the farm.

He wasn't the only one interested in Daughtry or he'd been made. Either way, it was time to pull back into stealth mode and monitor who he was up against. Preferring to stay a few steps ahead he'd remain in the shadows until fully armed and guaranteed the target wasn't pointed his direction. Machias was waiting and if he didn't make it back, she'd never learn the truth he owed her and so wanted to deliver.

TWENTY-TWO

J ade abandoned her truck behind a chaparral of trees to conceal it from occasional drivers traveling the side road nearing the Daughtry farm. Before leaving it, she checked comms, her phone battery, weapon, and the package of sound monitoring equipment she planned to activate on the property. She reviewed the optimal placement and installation method with the tech team at dusk while Jackson left the shop and retrieved Daughtry so they wouldn't pass each other on his infrequently used stretch of back road. Still she was cautious about being seen or identified by any other motorist.

Enemies were everywhere and you couldn't always see them coming.

Having walked this side of the property in the light of day she knew where the three cameras covering this angle were and mapped an advance intending to avoid them. Crawling forward in the shadow of night and light of the moon, she almost stepped directly into a tracker blade concealed in tall grass and rusted from too many seasons without shelter. Cursing at the stupidity and waste of it she altered her trajectory switching on her flashlight to avoid injury.

Common sense said to enter the house first. Where they lived and operated from appeared the logical choice. Following her gut she swung left and made for the barn. It called to her from the first second she crossed onto the land to interview Daughtry. Currently she could hear it screaming. Switching off her light before exiting the field, she made for the side of the barn closest to the forested edge and away from where the cameras pointed. Knowing the possibility of a monitor being hidden and missed, she'd worn full tactical camo from head to toe, exposing only a thin strip framing her eyes.

Tracing the back wall of the barn she hadn't made it halfway when she came upon a log beneath an open ground-level window. Laying on its side a few feet away it may have been coincidental or a stroke of luck. With the proper door on the opposite side and in full view of the first camera measure this presented a far better option to remain undetected.

With nothing but moonlight to rely on and the sill inches above her reach even with the aid of the log, Jade jumped to it scrambling for balance. Hovering on its edge she pulled her light out tipping it to her drop zone confirming safety. The pile rising off the floor inside the barn appeared harmless enough but also disturbed. A huge canvas tarp overlaying whatever sat underneath was creased and its dusty coating wore smears as if something large had recently been dragged across it. Unlike the other buildings on the grounds this one remained in use.

Drawing in a last deep breath of fresh air she pitched forward, the landing was hard and loud. Rising off the pile mildly bruised and coughing her lungs free of dust she glanced at the walkie on her belt grateful for the tiny green light reminding her backup waited on the other end. Just because they'd eliminated Daughtry as a risk didn't guarantee someone else wasn't there watching, waiting, or in this case listening for an intruder. She stood in the darkness quiet for a time before retrieving a small penlight and switching it on low to the ground and away from reflection that could be caught outside. Taking in the interior, she clipped her light into her belt, pointed just beyond her feet and grabbed the walkie.

"Callum, I'm inside building B," she whispered into the mic knowing he wouldn't speak back risking exposing her if an enemy existed. Two clicks rang back and she holstered the walkie and forged ahead. The interior smelled as any barn would only older, more aged and musky. She prowled a few steps to where it opened up to a two-story space, looked down on by an upper loft. Crossing to its midpoint she flashed her light overhead, a shadow catching her attention. Hanging dead center a large chain dangled, its reach descending down stopped short of hers ascending up. Contrasting the metal in the barn surrounding, though she couldn't inspect it closely it appeared new, shiny, refracting light.

"What the hell would this be used for?" she whispered, staring up analyzing its heavy links and large roof brackets.

Her eyes followed the narrow flashlight beam searching walls, shelves, tables, and benches until coming to rest on a worktable and items cluttering its top. The closer she drew the clearer the image became until she stood peering down at wrist restraints made of thick leather, padded with a Sherpa lining, and locking with metal cuffs attached to a large iron ring.

"You fucking monster." She breathed the words, suppressing the urge to bag the restraints and have them tested against Machias's DNA. Bringing out her phone, she snapped several pictures without touching or disturbing their placement. She knew what the chain was for.

Shifting her focus deeper into the room, she caught the ladder to the second floor in the light beam and snapped a few close photos before heading up.

"Ascending to the second floor," she said into the walkie before trading it for the rungs.

She paused within inches of the opening to take a couple zoomed-in shots of the hatch. As she breached the new level, she panned the loft with her light ensuring no one lurked in a distant corner waiting to rush her. Standing at full height a chill snaked its way down her back. A window facing the forest at the back and close above the one she'd entered through was left open.

"The hayloft windows were left wide open up here," she said

into the walkie, putting Callum on alert to note it. "Pretty sure they were closed when we were here."

Scouring the floor she chose a path to the window avoiding two areas where the hay cover was swept free. The panes opened like doors, matched her in height but far wider, and folded inward and then out to either side. Passing the one closest her light reflected off something small along its edge. Leaning down she ran a finger to inspect it and stopped short of cutting it on a twisted nail. The panes had been nailed shut and torn open with force by the appearance of the edges. This time, unlike the window in Machias's so-called bedroom, the nails hadn't been removed. Again, recording the condition of it via photos, she put her back to the opening for a fraction of a second before spinning to face it.

A tendril of fear reached out and tickled the length of her spine. Dropping to the floorboards, she employed a soldier's crawl to the far left edge of its lip to peer into the darkness without remaining an easy target. Seconds passed with her heartbeat echoing in her ears as her eyes trained on the trees and bushes. Deep within, and flanking the property's backside, the isolated shifting of leaves flushed adrenaline into her veins. Jade waited, frozen, for movement elsewhere, hoping she wasn't suddenly being surrounded by a team infiltrating the farm. The thought rang back as paranoid until an explosion of disturbed branches erupted at the furthest reaches of her sightline. An owl took flight, swooping over treetops and across her field of view. She hugged the hay-coated floor until the forest fell silent, then retreated before rising off its planks.

The night was still but her hackles said the owl wasn't the source of the movement she spotted. He, like her, reacted to an intruder.

Checking her watch, she realized how much time had passed and what little she had left to investigate with. Fluffing and spreading out the hay with a boot she ensured no sign of her crawl was left obvious. Furniture was stacked in the back right corner. She closed the distance keenly aware of the night beyond the open window. A canvas drop cloth poorly thrown covered a mattress leaning on its side against wooden pieces. Lifting its edge with a gloved hand she swept her light over its surface identifying areas soiled and stained. The mattress was otherwise clean and new in its condition. Out of place among antiques it stood out as though the intent of whoever placed it there did so to conceal it.

Backing away, a hook caught her just below the shoulder. On close inspection, she identified an imprint scored into the wallboard. What once occupied the space held an outline slightly larger and more rectangular than the existing hook's square base. Surveying the area, she found it was one of an existing pair. Standing between them her eyes traced out dead center landing at the site of the offset hay. Stepping forward to a proximity close enough to view the space without intruding on it, her flashlight lit a clearly defined stain. Kneeling she pulled out a swab kit, one Grey strictly warned her against bringing, wiping a sample from its center. Seconds later she confirmed it as human blood. Seconds after that she stored it in a sealed tube safely stowed inside her inner pocket.

To the untrained eye the barn was like any other, full of aged tools, hay, and items outgrown but still taking up space. To hers it rejected its misuse, revealing the culprit who violated it and those held within, begging to be cleansed and rid of him.

Daughtry.

Jade swept a boot under the pile of hay allowing it to fall over the stained area, smears caught by moonlight said it wasn't the first time the method was employed. And why had the stain been left exposed? A lucky twist of fate or deliberate? Hoping if Daughtry was slipping up he'd continue until they could hang him from the rafters she concealed possible traces of her presence.

Intent on denying him any forewarning.

Jade extracted the sound recording device, located a space near the area of violence, activated the device and made her way back outside. Leaving the wooden structure almost as she'd found it but better served.

Gaining ground toward the farmhouse she considered the exposed area where the blood pool sat. Rubbing the edge of her gloved finger where the twisted nail threatened to gouge, she paused at an exterior basement hatch on the back left of the farmhouse. Why would Daughtry go to such lengths to stage the girl's room and areas of the home her and Kane were given access to and leave damning evidence in plain sight in the nearby barn?

Daughtry didn't strike Jade as particularly bright but to avoid suspicion or, at the least, accountability for any crime for decades he couldn't be unintelligent. Was he so arrogant he believed he controlled the situation and had nothing to fear? Or was it that he'd escaped justice for too much and too long to fear a thing?

Entering the unlocked and undefended cellar Jade guess it was the latter.

Sweeping the exterior walls of the open cellar, Jade found nothing of interest except the space itself. Covering a considerably smaller footprint than the house above she panned it again for a door leading to an adjoining room but saw none.

Scouring over shelves holding nonperishables that perched there long enough to not only parish but decompose and be reborn, all appeared untouched, dust and cobweb coated. An old door laid over two short wooden stepladders became a table holding leather-bound trade logs. Jade had seen similar ones in the local museum from the Great Depression when farmers traded goods instead of money to help townspeople survive famine. A trip down historic pathways though fascinating wouldn't help Machias.

Jade continued searching until identifying the staircase leading into the upper realms of the house. Concealed by a cloth drape, first mistaken for another tarp over stored items, she pushed it aside revealing steps up to an interior hatch. Before climbing them, a cold draft pushed her to inspected a second tarp right of the stairs.

Her flashlight beam drifted over rows of shelves containing glass, pickling jars holding a variety of contents from basic pickles to beets, carrots, mixtures of peppers, and onions in a variety of colors behind a brace bar to secure the bottles. There had to be close to fifty in total some with dates aging them beyond a decade. Jade snapped a picture of this adding to her collection though not quite certain why she bothered. Grabbing the last shelf in a final quick shot the flash from the picture illuminated a drag mark cut into the dirt floor. The shelf moved.

Backing up, she checked the time on her watch noting she had

fifteen minutes before hitting the hour marker on Daughtry's interrogation. Snapping her walkie from her belt she notified Callum.

"Callum, I'm in structure H, full-height cellar, and I've located a
hidden room. I need more time to finish here and vacate without
bumping into Tex returning Daughtry to the property. Can you ask
them to stall?" she whispered and then clicked the PTT button
twice indicating he could respond without his voice placing her in
danger.

"You have thirteen minutes by the clock but I'll interrupt with a
coffee drop off and buy you at least ten more. Check in on your way
out and don't get locked in down there." Callum warned.

Jade said nothing but felt instantly lighter with his reassurance.
Heaving the shelving unit forward the pinned jars barely shifted as it
opened to a full back room equipped with camera security feed
monitors, a desktop computer, a catalog of disks, and a logbook
similar to what a long-haul trucker would use to report on cargo
trips.

Opening the log Jade snapped photos of page after scribbled
page until she reached the last entry. At a glance it meant nothing
but presented potential tracking information, viable evidence to use
against Daughtry showing a history of his criminal behavior. She
wanted to collect everything and take it with her and radio the team
to arrest Daughtry but cases were never that simple.

Realizing she was working on borrowed time she rushed to
replay the camera feed and erase any sign of her infiltration. She
caught one three-second clip where she crossed from field to barn
and tailored it to leave Daughtry blind. Then, switching to the side
camera, with a partial view of the forested edge meeting the barn,
she pushed the tape back to a time before the owl flew over. Nothing. Rewinding, then fast forwarding she sped through footage until
a branch dropped over the camera possessing the best view from
that angle.

Convenient.

Her walkie clicked and she responded back signaling Callum.
"Your suspect is becoming difficult and insisting on leaving. Jade, get
out now," he warned.

"I need seven minutes to get free of the property and then have to cross back to my truck," she said, planting the listening device beneath the desk and ensuring everything she discovered was left exactly as she found it before backing out of the hideaway and across the cellar. Secrets the upper floors held would remain mystery.

"You don't have time to drive out without crossing paths. If it cuts too close, I'll get Axel to create a diversion but you've got to move now."

"Don't risk Axel, I'm heading out," she said, exiting the stairs leading outside. "I'll check in when I'm inside the truck."

Careful to avoid the camera range, clear on its capabilities, Jade ran retracing steps in the darkness that dropped heavier onto the land. Clear of the buildings and nearing the truck a flash caught her eye. Lowering she stared at the origin but having her head down, focusing on navigating the uneven ground in the dark, she missed a clear grasp of the illumination. Sure it came from opposite her off the understory of the forest floor she watched and waited. Without confirmation she couldn't be sure but her hackles said there might be more than one intrusive party scouring the property tonight. One hand clutched the walkie the other rested over the pocket her phone and the evidence occupied. Instinct said after she left and Daughtry arrived everything she witnessed could vanish and along with it the chance of finding young Machias alive.

TWENTY-THREE

K ane imagined nothing more infuriating than interrogating a creature as vile as evidence thus far revealed Daughtry to be while the woman he loved risked discovery stealing onto a property that held too many horrific memories to exorcise. As minutes ticked by and tension grew his treatment of the man shifted from cold indifference to palatable disgust. The glances Tex shot him from behind the man's back as he paced the room said he'd lost the directive and crossed into open hostility.

"I've repeated what happened so many times I'm about to start confusing myself," Daughtry complained.

"The truth is not confusing," Kane shot back. "You said you suspected Machias ran away because she'd done it in the past yet you reported her missing within hours."

"I was worried. I thought it was the proper course of action. Aren't you supposed to be out there looking for her? Why are you interrogating me?" The man had a point and one that was becoming increasingly difficult to hide.

"This isn't an interrogation," Tex said, pacing the floor behind him with the exaggerated heavy steps of his cowboy boots adding to the drift of his voice looping the man to unnerve. Kane, familiar with his technique, was about to applaud when Tex froze behind the suspect. "If it was, we'd be asking a whole battery of intrusive questions, like who hit you?"

Kane watched the intensity in Jackson's stare lock onto target.

"That looks painful and fresh," he continued. "I'd say a horse got the better of you during shoeing but you aren't much for working the farm, are you? Kane, come have a look at this shiner." Tex leaned over the man's head to inspect the wound closer, raising his eyebrows with interest.

Welcoming the invitation, Kane pushed back from the table and skirted it never lifting his eyes off Daughtry. The man's face confessed everything he refused to voice. Standing shoulder to large shoulder with Tex, they inspected a serious gash on Daughtry's head. Kane invaded close enough to feel the heat rising off the snake as he shifted uncomfortably. He hadn't expected them to notice the wound.

"I live on a farm," Daughtry blurted out, swinging around in his chair to face them and deter further inspection of his head. "I've been so distracted worrying about the Machias situation I wasn't paying attention and walked into equipment in the barn."

"What kind of equipment does that?" Tex asked. "I'll definitely avoid it."

"It doesn't matter," Daughtry barked, readying to stand.

"Slow down there," Kane warned, placing a heavy hand on the man's shoulder nailing him to the chair. "You may have a concussion. How long ago did this happen? Today? It appears to still be bleeding. Did you have a doctor check you out? I'll call ours in to be sure you're safe to go home on your own. If it's serious, and I don't know, Tex, doesn't that look serious to you?"

"It looks pretty bad," Jackson agreed, hovering over Daughtry, his shadow all but swallowing the man.

"If it is and you fall asleep, well," Kane said, reaching for a handset on his side of the table while waving Daughtry to stay in his seat. He pressed a button and spoke into the speaker. "Can you have Doctor Maxwell swing by here if he's still kicking around? Our abduction victim's father suffered a head injury and I'm concerned for his safety returning home alone."

"Of course. I believe he is still in the building. I'll send him over," a male voice answered back. Kane knew it was Callum but didn't identify him.

Smiling, he fell back into the chair across from Daughtry, the satisfaction emanating. Daughtry, on the other hand, appeared ready to come out of his skin. Trapped, he could do nothing without lathering himself in further guilt. Tex grinned from ear to ear, holding open the door for Max to enter the room moments later.

With all they'd endured as a team Kane came to appreciate how brilliant Max was and how useful his involvement could be when employed effectively.

"Max," Kane bellowed. "I'm glad you hadn't left. This is Mackenzie Daughtry. His daughter Machias is the girl who went missing with our latest homicide victim. He suffered a head injury and I thought it best you weighed in given the risk of concussion. We need his mind clear. He was likely the last person to see her."

"I see," Max said, appearing nonchalant. "Concussions are nothing to ignore. Nice to meet you, Mr. Daughtry, I'm so sorry about your daughter's abduction. I mean what kind of human garbage takes a straight-A student from her hometown? Does it hurt?" Max joined Tex behind Daughtry and, laying a hand on Daughtry's head, guided its position so the wound was in clear sight of the overhead light. Daughtry squirmed against the intrusion but without reason couldn't divert the attention.

Max raised his phone camera mode ready and snapped a close-up of the wound and his hand, graduate ring visible for evidence confirmation. Daughtry flinched realizing what had happened and twisted, shooting daggers at Max.

Max, releasing Daughtry's head, pulled out his glasses, appearing oblivious to the man's cold stare. "Sorry, comes to us all, can't see much clearly without expanding it and throwing on the old spectacles."

Nope, Kane thought, *nothing dumb about Max*. In one fluid second, he cataloged vital evidence, justified its collection, and could substantiate it in court.

"See, it appears serious," Kane insisted, watching Daughtry's face flush to a deeper red.

"This is worth heading into the hospital for cleaning, stitches, and a cold compress," Max offered, examining the photo. "Looks to be from a substantial blow to the head. Who did you make mad? Or…did you get hit trying to defend your child?" Leaving no space for answers, Max turned his attention to Kane and Jackson. "Sorry, I know you can't discuss the details of an ongoing investigation."

"Thanks, Max. The injury was sustained after the abduction," Kane clarified. They were all enjoying inflicting pressure on Daughtry.

"Oh, I see. So not part of the case?" Max asked, almost believable with his false ignorance.

"We didn't say that," Tex chimed in. "Exactly."

"Doctor of what?" Daughtry piped up, sick of the game swarming around him.

Max casually made for the door seizing the moment. "Oh I have three doctorates, most substantially in criminal psychology and forensic psychology. I recommend having your head checked."

Daughtry's expression melding into bafflement and fierce tension while Kane studied him. "Basically, Max is a decorated expert in reading monsters." As the words dropped from Kane's lips, Daughtry pushed out of his chair and past Max.

He almost hit the hall when Kane called after him, "You're forgetting your ride. And when you reach home, you may want to stay there. I recommend you don't leave town."

———

Before Daughtry's interview began, Max requested a comfortable chair and Grey rolled one from his office into a separate "Sexton's office" housing the CCTV monitor, long past the days of one-way windows this was how he observed the suspected criminal in detail. Jackson and Kane, expert in their approach, caused Daughtry discomfort on multiple levels making it all but impossible for him to shroud his true nature.

Kane gave Max the broad strokes of where the case led them, showing him Jade's map of potential victims over the last decade before coding in the monitor for the interview room housing Daughtry. Forty-seven girls vanished from the surrounding towns and area within a fifty-mile radius stretching from the seaboard to Shadow Hook. All were reported missing or were never heard from again after involvement with one or more of the outreach organizations Daughtry was tied to.

Twenty minutes in the room with the detectives, and Max believed him capable of not only having involvement in some of the disappearances but all of them. The man was born of resentment twisted into hatred and solidified by rage. What seeded his creation Max didn't know, not yet, but he wanted to. This creature required study to dismantle.

Years earlier, Max wouldn't have taunted the suspect with his play on words on the way out the door, but this wasn't then and he'd lived through too much to waste decency on one so undeserving.

Officer Callum gave Max a heads-up on Jade's timeline exiting the Daughtry farm prior to him entering the interrogation under the guise of possessing a medical opinion on the man's recent head wound. Anxious to be up-close and personal Max was thrilled to assume the role buying Jade more time. But as the suspect departed with Jackson back to his home, Max was sure of three things. The man's capability and need of violence, his complete detachment to the girl who shared his name, and a certainty he was not acting alone. Besides the evidence confirming this through facts demanding he be required in two places at once to carry out associated acts, he didn't have the restraint or connections to orchestrate the moving parts necessary. Not to mention the finesse to do it repeatedly spanning many years without detection.

The man was simply put a hothead and not particularly bright.

Curious to see what insights Jade returned from the property with, Max decided to hold off on offering his opinion until he revisited the interview. After Max traded the photo he snapped of the man's head wound to be analyzed by experts, Kane packaged and sent the recorded file over for Max to study overnight with plans to reconvene early the next day. Reminded the clock was ticking on the girl according to the message the young, murdered man scrawled before dying.

In the peace of his new BMW 5 Series cutting through the winding road to his estate home, Max's gut said there was no question who the Main Motherfucker Jack referred to was. The question instead remained, could they unearth enough to tie him to the crimes, and not just those associated with Jack's murder or Machias's disappearance? And if they did, what else would surface?

The dangerous truth Max sensed rolling forward, shadowing the case and those who worked it, said whoever sat behind Daughtry possessed a volume and breadth worthy of a criminal enterprise existing off a horror affecting too many for too long not to be viciously defended.

What he would lay out for Jade and the team would be nothing short of a warning, they were about to engage not one man, a cog in a wheel, but the whole damn machine.

One he suspected was well insulated, armed, and lethal.

This wasn't solely a crime initiated by Daughtry to serve his selfish purposes. Machias was a piece in a jigsaw puzzle with razor-sharp teeth. As dangerous as Daughtry was, he was but a pawn.

The team stumbled on a game played for years by masters with every move being costly. Jade and the unit wouldn't quit until their opponent was defeated. Unfortunately, he feared this time their opponents were many and they had the upper hand.

Pulling into his garage he wished he could read the case another way and intended to examine the tape all night for better options. But the facts were, if one organization was behind the vanishing of this magnitude of victims and managed to escape justice for this long, they should be feared.

Even by police.

TWENTY-FOUR

A xel, never capable of inaction, became all but compelled seeing the impact of Jack's murder on Raven, his friends, and the town. The detectives bared witness to a version of Raven damaged so deeply he'd become consumed by the dark and demanded vengeance more than justice for Jack's death. Axe feared if resolve didn't come swiftly Raven may not resurface and he refused to lose any more friends.

Keeping tabs on the case through his father, he knew the one lead in clear sight had yet to produce useful connections to the abductor or the reason behind the crime. In his mind's eye he stared at Jack's message etched into the dirt, focusing on the details related to the vehicle that drove away with Machias inside. Detective Swan, who they all called Tex though his name was Jackson, was tracking down leads on the Mercedes van, scouring every available piece of footage he could find aimed at any road leaving Shadow Hook. Considering this, Axel brought up a road map on his computer screen, searching routes and possible destinations for something, anything, to stand out.

Until something did.

The game of football did much for Axel's social standing and one of his best teammates, two years his senior, ended his athletic career with an ankle injury. Instead of mourning the loss of a possible professional future, Dylan Barclay recovered while building a career online in cybersecurity. There was no back door safe from the former left tackle. And being that his family business tied to the docks, his uncle was still employed as security for import arrivals, he had access others didn't without breaking down firewalls.

Axe swiped his computer bag off his bedroom floor, left a scribbled note for his father, and headed over to speak to Dylan in person. Ensuring no trace of what he had to discuss. Swinging by the local coffee shop he picked up a box of Onyx coffee, leverage for negotiation. Twenty minutes later he stood outside Dylan's walk-up, waiting as intrusive cameras captured his image to allow him access into the foyer.

"Hey, man. What's with the cryptic message? Sorry to hear about Jack," Dylan said, dressed casual but stylish, his wild blond hair grown out into a surfer wave, he leaned on the open door owning his space to welcome Axe inside.

"Thanks. I think you might be the perfect person to help me with something, didn't want to broadcast it," Axel said, walking into the computer haven that could've doubled for a pretty cool family room if owned by another man. "Do you have access to CCTV footage of roadways around the closest harbor?"

Dylan laughed, motioning for Axel to follow him into the kitchen, heading for a heavy wood table sitting dead center of a floor-to-ceiling bank of windows framing a garden beyond. "You mean currently?"

Axe smiled and grabbed a chair, then pulled a box out of his bag setting the coffee on the table.

"Yes," Dylan said. "I can get you access. It's not like it's protected interior workings of the docks. You're looking for traffic flow?" Dylan sat a chair away where a laptop waited.

"A particular customized vehicle," Axel said, handing over a sheet of paper with the suspected van in a screen grab, model, make, and distinguishing window bars highlighted. "And you never saw this."

"When and where?" Dylan asked as his fingers clicked on the keyboard. "Any direction? And what date range?"

Axel handed him a second paper with the date range in August from a week prior to when Machias was confirmed missing up to current date. If someone was sent into the area to pick her up, they may have entered on one of the highways adjacent to the shipyards. The detectives were tracking from the day she was taken forward, Axe wanted to go the other direction in time hoping to catch the vehicle prior to Machias and Jack's abduction. A long shot but better than sitting on his hands.

"Okay. I have three directions covering the three major roadways. I'll set a search moving back in time from now. Ten days," he said, typing away. "I'll enter the screen grab and have it search for an identity match." In seconds Dylan fed the screen grab into a scanner in the outer room and returned to modify a program. Staring over his laptop at Axe his forehead crinkled in thought.

"What?" Axel asked quietly, not wanting to interfere with Dylan's mastery.

Dylan didn't answer but dropped his head down, refocused on the screen, and typed in additional parameters. After a few minutes he pushed back from the monitor and regained his casual stance. "So are you okay? Is Raven...how is he?"

"As good as you'd expect so shit," Axel said. "How's life in the cyber tech world?"

"I'm still a solid left tackle but this time they really can't see me coming," Dylan said, a grin escaping.

"I wondered you know...if it was fate, your injury or—"

"Well this is my life now, so fate," Dylan said. "Let's brew some Onyx! The aroma helps me think. Hey, how is Falcon doing? I mean with Mac missing, Jack's murder, and the leg injury. Unlike me he knows his future is in football. He's the next big thing. Humble as hell but the talent in those hands is crazy, right?"

Falcon was quietly dating Machias. Axe witnessed their chemistry more than once and hoped they stayed together and outlasted her situation. He hadn't thought of him or what he must be suffering through and made a metal note to pay him a visit.

"He said the doc thinks he'll be better than before. Falcon's lucky his dad found him. I guess the guy was all over his recovery to the point the coaches have him on speed dial for the rest of the team. I'll check in on him." Axel promised.

Dylan drifted behind the island to a coffee bar space with the box in hand. Axe stood and neared the window surveying the yard beyond it. His head twisted as he traced the outer edges of its pane. Dylan, coming in close silently, startled him when he lifted his eyes off the floor.

"What are you looking for?" Dylan asked, the sound of coffee brewing echoed behind his question.

"Well your front door is like entering a level four clearance room but I see no cameras on this huge window, which, by the way, gives full view of most of your main floor," Axel said, glad for the company and Dylan's infectious easy nature.

"The cameras at the front are for delivery dudes. I still work out five days a week." Dylan laughed. "Who would want to try me on? I'm not working for Interpol. I help companies who require protection. They love me don't fear me. Besides, the nonstop construction out back keeps messing with my feed. I'll activate surveillance there when it won't pick up workers twenty times a day. They're annoying and, building rock gardens and retaining walls, noisy as shit."

Axel laughed and followed Dylan back to the coffee bar waiting for the fresh brew. The scent of perfect beans waft through the house, inspiration no doubt. He made a mental note to go back to the coffee house before checking in with Raven. Dylan handed him a glass and wood container filled with thick cookies. "They're addictive but actually pretty healthy, try one."

Carrying his coffee and dessert back to the table Axe couldn't remember when he last ate or slept through the night. Chances were sometime before the last game he played...before discovering Jack dead. He hadn't finished chewing the first bite of cookie when Dylan's program alerted. He waved Axe back into his seat, speaking while crumbs escaped his lips. "Relax it's telling me the program is set. It'll take a few minutes to run through the data unless—"

A ding rang out and Axe abandoned the chair to shadow Dylan

as he checked the computer. The screen filled with a mess of pictures, grabs time stamped and reorganizing automatically into a chronological order from first sighting. The strange thing was none of them appeared to be on a highway. "Where is—"

"Yeah, yeah, it's not from the road. I thought of imports, you know, like what if the vehicle came off a ship so as not to be traced? You said it had been customized, what better way to keep it off book? This is from the lot." Dylan froze one particularly clear image of the van driving out from beneath a camera. The bars in its back windows were unmistakable. "Shit. This is from inside the dock security at the import deck. Where imported vehicles arrive and are normally offloaded onto transport trucks."

Axel slid his chair over close to Dylan. "Can you run the program further back and focus it at entrance points to confirm it didn't enter and then leave? Backtrack it and send me this data?" Axe knew what this would mean for Dylan, how it could put his career at risk. "D, this is the vehicle that abducted Jack and Machias and whoever that is." Axe pointed to the best screen grab of the front windshield. "It's likely the bastard that killed our friend and you may have the only photo of him."

The coffee aroma fell dead in the room as they studied the dark image of the driver in the van. The weight of what Dylan obtained hit Axel and the undercurrent left a bitter taste in his mouth that wasn't from dark roast. "Have you ever done this before? Anything as intrusive as this?"

"You having second thoughts? Little late, bud. Yeah, but not without being paid in more than coffee beans. You tell the cops I found it by accident after we were talking and you didn't share the specifics with me," Dylan said, turning to lock eyes. "Make and model only, okay?"

"Got it," Axel said, astonished and unable to suppress nervous excitement. "You might have just found a way to save Mac, buddy. I owe you."

"Yes, you do," Dylan said, fingers tapping over the keyboard. "And if my uncle ever hears what I just did you may be putting in a word for me with the cop shop for a new job and a lifetime supply of the best coffee on earth."

"That's an easy trade," Axel said. "You lead them to the driver and you won't need me. They'll be hiring you on the spot. I'd like that, working together."

"Ah, so you are heading to the academy. Knew it," he said, still tapping out instructions with the keys.

"One better," Axel said, pride releasing for the first time. "Heading there with a recommendation for homicide unit."

"Good to know. If you were there sooner, this could've played out different," Dylan said, pushing back from the keyboard.

"I wouldn't bet on it." Axe tapped a photo of a corner of the van's rear left side. "That is about as much of this case as the detective are seeing right now. A distorted partial picture. And they're the best at what they do."

Dylan transferred the data into a file, typed in Axel's name bringing up his email address, and sent it over with a heading that read "Fourth and Ten." Then without warning he deleted everything 'Axel' off his drive.

"Well…I just risked my well-paid ass to bring it into focus and if I'm taking one for the team, I expect you to carry it across the end zone."

TWENTY-FIVE

Riparian entered the bomb shelter with caution to refrain from startling the girl. The outer entrance was as it always appeared, cold, drafty, hollow, and empty. He all but tiptoed down the hall to his locked office. Once inside he stored his gear, the vital evidence collected, and changed out of black on black. Resealing the space he ventured down to the area where he left her with food and the large screen monitor streaming an endless supply of Sam and Colby YouTube videos as requested. With the whole bunker to explore at will without his watchful eyes on her, she was here, asleep in front of an episode on a potentially haunted asylum somewhere in Ohio. Rip never liked Ohio but loved the show and its creators. He ended the feed studying her sleeping form knowing a truth that could set her free from a past no one her age could possibly deserve.

Center screen she'd constructed a makeshift bed by pushing chairs together and padding them with pillows and the extra blanket he gave her. He encircled it noticing how she butted the ends against the wall on one side and made wedges bracing the other to prevent it from separating. It required time and thought to make, revealing she possessed what so few did these days, patience. Not wanting to alarm her by moving her down the hall, he removed the sweater he wore, draping it over her feet and left, turning the lights to low but not fully off.

In his bedroom he chose a burner, dropped onto the bed pushing back against the pillows, and dialed. His brother answered on the second ring.

"Titan," he said, offering nothing more knowing their time constraints.

"You find anything connecting the guy?" Rip asked.

"Dates back to him working to lure girls in when he was underage. It's at the drop. This is what you thought, isn't it?" he asked.

"Yes."

"Any way we get out of it?" It was a fair question.

"Can't see one yet but I'm not done looking," Rip said, wishing he had better news.

"How's the kid?"

"Okay," Rip said, thinking of her ingenuity with the chairs. She found a way to do with them what Rip longed to do with their situation. Pull together something to sustain and protect them from pieces that didn't fit together cleanly.

"Don't quit looking," Titan said. "I've got a feeling. We aren't the only ones interested from this side. Gotta go, bro." The line went dead. Rip pulled the card, crushed it, and tossed the phone and it in a half-full water glass on the nightstand. He didn't need to protect inside the shelter but old habits died hard. He could only hope to say the same for him and Titan. His brother was worth saving a thousand times over. He lacked clarity on where he stood but Titan reminded him whenever possible. They'd gone undercover together and he was out first and dove back in when he knew they made Titan. Life inside or death out. It hadn't been much of a choice. A problem? Definitely. One so far that proved unsolvable but he wasn't done, not yet.

Creeping down the hall he peeked in on the girl, sleeping soundly, hoping to make it to their revolving drop point and back before she woke. Tonight it was east; if a pickup occurred tomorrow, it'd be in the west. The established cycle kept them safe. Now, it worked to do the same for Machias Lincoln.

Titan said there was another interested party asking questions about the history of Mackenzie Daughtry. Whoever they were they weren't doing it officially but outside legal channels, so not the detective who crept onto the farm. Rip considered who his competition was and how far behind him they were as he locked up the bunker and drove to the drop concealed behind a helmet on his Harley Fat Boy. The bike and attire said, "made gang member" and kept civilians from getting in his way. It also made him unrecognizable to any capture from footage monitoring the area. He altered his appearance and plates regularly as a precaution though he had no record. According to any official dossier he never came back from abroad and, though not declared dead, failed to resurface.

The night was crisp in the aftermath of a rainstorm that hit between his outings. He drew in deep breaths recalling what it was like to feel free on his bike before him and Titan were owned. Rounding a tight corner banking the woods, visions of the young man he abandoned to die at the forest's edge a few short nights ago clouded his mind. There was no salvation for what he'd done. At first, he had trouble piecing the memory together. Like flashes of clips out of sequence in a movie, nothing made complete sense. Used to the process since suffering with PTSD after returning from war, he learned to abandon focusing on traumatic events. Allowing them to return on their own he'd eventually retain the whole of the experience. He hadn't suffered a memory distortion for quite some time. The people he killed never left him with regret or remorse until…

The death of Jack hadn't returned fully yet but horrible fragments plagued him with an incoherent buzzing of angry voices, visions of the hunting blade impaling the young man's liver, his boots slipping in the mud retreating to the van, and slamming its door against the night defeated. Enough to send bile into his throat.

Arriving at the marked area, he wasted all of three minutes collecting the package before circling back along a different route than the one which brought him in. The leather bike satchel strapped on as always but this time he wished he could secure it with armor. He flipped through it briefly before driving. A name he caught within hinted that Titan may have truly been onto something.

An inroad he could use.

Anxious to examine the new data he flew through the winding stretch of road but two switchbacks before his final turn he noticed he wasn't alone on his midnight quest. He picked up the attachment at the highway exit that paralleled the road leading to the docks. Focused on Daughtry, his connections, the girl, and a way to rid his family of the gang he'd made a dangerous mistake. Dismissing the power and scope of Barracutta's network and why he had the girl in the first place. He was a placeholder until it was deemed safe for the dock drop to occur.

In the saying "trust then verify" he was a proponent of the verify part not so much the trust. So, when he was handed the contract, he put the docks under surveillance monitoring inspection rotations and the routines of staff. The girl's drop was mere days away, after a final inspection of the construction site and when a skeleton crew made distraction easy. That didn't mean Barracutta forgot about the payday, the girl, or the transporter holding her.

Eyes were everywhere and if he intended to keep her safe and avoid suspicion, he couldn't allow the hired henchmen now tailing him to confirm who he was or where he was going. He loved his bike, like all true riders do, but wished it transformed into a crotch rocket. His mind mapped the back roads surrounding his current location and he when to work weaving, speeding up, disappearing in the shadow of transport trailers, and driving under bridges killing the engine until clear of them.

By the time he secured the bike inside the bunker and sealed the world out his mind was running at pace with the ride to get there.

Not as careful as he usually was, he opened the documents his brother obtained, spreading them across his desktop. He grabbed his journal and pen and began the process of tracking Daughtry back to the start and within a few hyper-focused hours he located the trifecta he searched for. A place when Daughtry's history put him within range of Lily Lincoln and Barracutta's organization simultaneously but it wasn't what he expected.

A prostitution ring, a drug mule scenario, even a black market baby adoption scheme wouldn't have surprised him. Running drugs out of a care facility for the elderly, using the corpses to transport, and shopping the Candy Stripers for viable product, back then? The operation highlighted the criminal mastermind at work long before the law would've suspected a multifaceted illegal approach such as this. Barracutta acquired Daughtry when he was a nurse's aide there. The informant Titan pushed said Daughtry's record, though expunged, confirmed he was caught stealing meds. Barracutta struck a deal recognizing the potential. Lily Lincoln was a volunteer Candy Striper whose vulnerability became all too convenient when the grandmother, and last family member who cared for her, died suddenly inside the facility.

The picture emerging was sick, twisted, and sadly effective.

Daughtry got the girl, the farm with an already legally established youth outreach camp, and Barracutta secured a constant supply of product to sell and use as deemed fit.

Earlier in the night Rip stayed at the farm following the detective's movements on the property. After the coast was clear he went back in removing the signs he'd left in plain sight leaving Daughtry blind to the invasion. He'd replayed news bites on Machias and efforts to find her and identified three members of the special homicide unit. The figure he watched infiltrate the same barn he entered wasn't the oversized Texan or the black man. The female detective, a Jade Carmichael, crossed onto the property using as much stealth as he had. If she'd arrived an hour earlier, they could've come face to masked face inside the barn. He left much evidence for her discovery and planned to follow up the next day. When he'd wrapped his head around the violations littering his desk and decided on the best way to weaponize them.

When Riparian's Ferryman phone rang his glare should've melted it. Instead he considered smashing the shit out of it. Knowing he stood in the center of a war none of his opponents yet knew they were a part of, he inhaled a calm breath, closed his door, and answered.

"This isn't a scheduled call. Is there an issue with the drop?" Rip said, not allowing Barracutta space to control the discussion.

"No. Everything is falling into place as expected. However—"

"So you thought you'd put us both at risk for no apparent reason?" Rip pushed, deliberate in his taunting.

"You work for me, I'll remind you." The voice was irritated and gaining volume.

"I don't, I'll remind you. The gang accepted your contract. I work for them and them alone. Call me out of schedule again and they'll consider the contract broken. If there is a change of plans, tell me now. You have thirty seconds before I hang up." Rip wasn't making friends but the knowledge he held made it all but impossible for him to play nice.

"With the tracker on the vehicle disabled, I have every right to ensure my product is safe and undamaged. I expect—"

"It is. See you on the weekend." Rip hung up knowing there'd be no amicable weekend meeting, pulled the card out of the phone locking it in a Faraday case, and then smashed the shit out of the phone.

TWENTY-SIX

Nickolas appreciated the swimming chamber, its jets simulating river flow, temperature and speed control, array of detoxing minerals, all fully customized for his specific recovery, but its best feature was the mirrored bottom. In it he could study and measure the return of muscle and strength in his legs, know when to push harder, and see the progress from day to day and week to week. It granted him the opportunity to confirm his abilities without his doctors weighing in. Swimming offered him freedom to rebuild and uninterrupted time to plan for the future.

Not the future the doctors anticipated but one decidedly unexpected.

His grandfather stood on his promise to free him of his past crimes by employing a slew of the best and brightest physicians to heal his body and justify a clean break from his previous mental state. Temporary insanity would prove a hard sell when his crimes spanned many years and multiple victims. Despite this, Leigh Senior found not one but three experts to establish a trauma response tied to PTSD and mind-altering drugs he was fed and consumed up until the shooting that placed him in hospital. They were in the background fighting through judicial loopholes never realizing their success or failure mattered little to him.

He existed outside the rule of law his entire life. It never saved him in the past but, in fact, damned him to the worst fate imaginable. He expected it wouldn't prove useful now. The debate was one he wasted no time on, focused on far more crucial matters.

The Candy Storeowner, his past and limited future, now that was worthy of attention.

Long before he made headlines as the Redeemer, Nickolas spent years siphoning through his father's police cases and criminal connections, transferring pertinent details into computer files accessible at any time from anywhere in the world. As his arms and legs fought against the tension of the forced rapids, he recalled the file he read through the previous night while the medical facility and its highly skilled staff slept, unaware.

No small measure, it required all of his adult life to discover why the drug dealer he was abused by as a teen earned the title Candy Storeowner. The file on him spoke of many atrocities expected and some surprising but the link to the trafficking ring, the supply chain of Candy Striper girls acquired on working visas for employment at an elderly care home and vanished by an organization larger than the Candy man's sick residential hub explained everything.

His was simply the first stop. He kept, drugged, and prepared the girls before transport. His housing of them coining the name years back and whether he remained associated today or not the name stuck.

Nickolas certainly wasn't willing to forget it but such clarity was worthless if one couldn't share it.

Accustomed to the dark, he did his best thinking and work at night and last he'd lined up events to ensure his sister could partake in his discovery. Perhaps even make it her own, so to speak. Well, at least after she received his next letter.

Plastering the Candy man, his store, and deeds across headlines would ensure the attention of Jade and her team but public notoriety risked upending Jade's case and all but guaranteed the death of the girl she searched for. He had to employ far more subtle tactics to aid Jade's investigation. As he researched the Candy Store's ties to the larger criminal organization he hit dead ends. The kind that smelled of deliberate corruption and diversion that came with enormous cost.

Calling on several existing connections, all of whom didn't know his true identity and some originating across the globe, he followed breadcrumbs enthused to be unearthing details beneficial to solving the case. By the time a clear picture emerged he'd wished it'd happened in a different jurisdiction. Handing over clues and evidence wouldn't be enough. This time required he be involved on a deeper level.

His arms tired, legs shaking with exhaustion, he hit the kill switch on the rapid feed in the pool and floated onto his back staring up at the stars beyond the glass domed roof high overhead. A flush of cool water encircled his aching limbs, the end cycle running its course. Tracing the constellations overhead, how they all linked, he revisited the merit of his chosen approach.

He'd purchased a large sum of drugs the Candy man relied on heavily and set up a drop point for pickup of a case holding them and an equally sizable sum of untraceable cash. Obtaining pieces from unrelated sources, all blind to the outcome, posed challenges but none he'd fail to maneuver. On delivery of the locked case, the driver would leave for a second drop where his money was waiting, several hours and a state away. Once in place Nick would make a call to a targeted member alerting the gang the Candy man was indebted to for protection of his theft and deception while supplying the code to open the case. The gang would out the operation by eliminating him in the worst way possible, known for using the penalty for betrayal as a violently public deterrent for others in their midst.

The formula was solid but the timing was crucial and so many moving parts were difficult to arrange from a distance but he arranged to watch them play out in real time. Never one to dismiss an offense, he'd purchased the house across the road from the Candy Store when he was twenty-two. It was the second residence he owned, the first being his dead biological father's. Owning properties in several countries, it was one of three he held most dear. Because of this, he installed security measures and many, many cameras, all concealed and several pointing directly at the Candy Man's home turf.

The operation would involve the use of a professional and drones with infrared and zoom capabilities, nothing out of his capacity. Killers were easily bought and he held information threatening an array of them.

Pushing the buzzer signaling his time in the chamber complete and his aide's return to assist him back to his room, he anticipated the final details required to initiate the end of the Candy Man and the start of a bond he waited a lifetime for. Worthy endeavors.

And when his aide retired and he was comfortable in bed, he retrieved his pen and stationery knowing his next letter may be the last requiring more than hand delivery.

TWENTY-SEVEN

Machias woke to the sound of anger, metal and plastic evaporating by means of force. Not afraid, but certain only a disturbance this aggressive was capable of pulling her from exhaustion. Grief had a way of draining the body of its energy so completely it transformed one into a zombie state allowing very little of life to penetrate. She missed Jack, Falcon, and her friends. She didn't miss home for in her view she'd never really been allowed one, a place of comfort, solitude, and nurturing. That existed at Jack and Raven's but she never made it there. Here wasn't as bad as one might think. The bunker, designed to protect from a direct bomb attack, did well to safeguard her from a dangerous world. And, after spending hours reading through the ledgers in Rip's collection her waning faith in humanity and hope for a future she'd want to exist in gained strength.

Machias's abductor was her salvation, of that she was certain.

So when he took to smashing whatever captured his rage inside his room, she decided it deserved his punishment.

Collecting her blankets and pillows from in front of the blackened screen, she noticed his sweater at the end of her makeshift bed, picked it up too, and carried the mass back to her room. Dumping them on her mattress, she rearranged the pillows and blankets, pulled the far too large sweater over her head, and snuggled in beneath the covers.

The destruction down the hall silenced and the bunker resumed its state of protected peace. Cuddled in, Mac considered telling Rip she'd cracked his sequenced passcodes but wasn't sure now was the right time. He was consumed navigating demons from many sides and she refused to be more of a distraction.

She read enough on the contract hits instigated by the gang he worked under to know how high the stakes were. He admitted he hadn't been afforded prior knowledge on the contract involving her. The possibility sent shivers down her spine. Any other and she'd be dead already or living a fate worse than hell. She read the product delivery date fell between Saturday night and Sunday morning of the coming weekend. She wasn't sure how Rip planned to evade handing her over but knew he wouldn't. He wore the regret for Jack's fate in his eyes every time she locked on them. Remembering how it happened, as painful as it was, she didn't see how it could've been avoided.

Her heart ached. Why did Jack run from the van? If he stayed inside maybe things could have gone differently. Perhaps not. Thinking back it was a miracle anyone survived that night. Then, in a horrid flash, a vision of the flesh intertwined in the chain hook inside the back of the vehicle resurfaced. This had to be what fueled Jack's efforts to free them both and what drove him to flee from the van. He couldn't have known then that the Mercedes was the possession of Machias's buyer on loan to Riparian. He collected it with cargo intact unaware of its owner's intentions or the atrocities that took place within it. She considered if Rip saw it for what it was now, a hub of evidence against whoever drugged her and Jack. She pulled the sweater in close and tucked her head into the blanket, sleep weighing heavy.

Rip would have no part in such human depravity. The targets Rip eliminated she measured in lives saved. Most caused torment or death to multiple innocent people, some in the hundreds if you counted the contribution to addiction. And some were pure evil, like her father.

Her mother did what she could to prepare and protect while able. Mac wasn't under the illusion that Lily Lincoln was alive and well living the good life outside Daughtry's control. She remembered the last day with her and the missing person's coverage that followed. Everyone in town assumed she'd left him and her daughter. Mac knew she never would've abandoned her only child to that man willingly.

He had her killed.

On days when he allowed Machias to clean the main house, she'd find reason to sneak into the basement cold storage to stare at the pickling jars lining the shelf. Each one labeled by her mother's hand, dated strangely; Mac never quite understood the perishable timing. They were even given cute names. Seeing her elegant handwriting, the fun she instilled in the process with the names, some Mac created at her mom's prompting, reminded her who she truly had been. The labels were all she had left of Lily. And the only reason they hadn't all been smashed to ruin and suffered the same brutal end the rest of her belongings did was because Daughtry all but forgot about the canning. To him the carefully prepared farm-fresh contents didn't deserve a second thought. The fruits and vegetables were expertly made with flavors Mac could almost taste in memory despite not having enjoyed one since Lily was alive to share it. Her mother, like her, was quite brilliant, though no one was allowed to know it.

Mac could only hope Lily was watching over her and Rip, guiding them to find a way to survive the mess Daughtry cast them in and a path to justice for them both.

Mac hadn't the time to decipher how Riparian became a gang member only that his acquisition occurred following a decorated stretch of time in service overseas. She'd found his medals, not displayed with honor, but stored in their cases behind the shelf of ledgers. A life before, remembered, perhaps cherished, but hidden in the shadow of the deeds of today.

Mac thought back to Riparian's question, "Who is Daughtry to you?"

The method Rip used to categorize and detail each contract assured he would've researched the man who allowed her to be sold into criminal hands. Each contract contained dossiers on every key player involved. Yet he'd specifically asked who Daughtry was to her. She read the disgust and hatred in his eyes when he discovered the abuse she'd endured. Mac found it difficult to imagine Rip returning her to such a damned fate.

Forward or backward, if Rip released her either way it meant the end of who she was and her heart said he would never allow it.

She considered the source of the scar that ran almost the full length of the left side of his face. Mac thought he was handsome even with it but he didn't. Wearing all hers on the inside she still understood how the knowledge of carrying the marks of trauma branded you mentally. You couldn't forget or move on when the evidence peered back at you from the mirror. She wished she could change his mind about it. That was the survival trick her mother weaved into her every day they were together.

Freedom and the truth of who and what you are resides inside your heart and cannot be tainted by what happens on the outside unless you choose to lose sight of it.

Mac promised Lily she would never lose sight of how good she was, that she "came from love but was born into a great challenge of survival." She said Daughtry would do everything to make her forget and never to let him win on the inside even if the battle ended on the outside. It ended for her mother shortly after she vowed to defeat him. Mac was so little, just starting school. Her mother would've made a great teacher, a wonderful chef, or so many other things if she could've escaped him. Now it was left to Mac and Riparian.

One thing Machias was certain of, she wasn't willing to see another good person be sacrificed for her so Rip wouldn't be working alone to solve their situation. Even if she let him think he was.

As warmth enveloped her and her eyes fell closed, she pushed away the echoes of the other girls' screams drifting from memory across from the barn into her bedroom window. Daughtry knew the only torture Mac found harder to bear than her own was that of the girls he moved through the farm. Never there for more than a few days, he drew the time out inflicting damage. With no neighbors for miles, he had no fear of being overheard, so he nailed Mac's window open a sliver and allowed their desperate screams to filter over the land and into her ears as a warning.

If Mac had it her way, she'd burn the barn and the house to the ground with him inside, scorching the earth to rid it of every memory of him and his violations. But first, she thought as sleep set in, she'd really like to watch him pay for them all.

TWENTY-EIGHT

"I don't think we'll hear him revealing secrets tonight, do you?" Jade heard Kane ask the question but her ears remained tuned into the listening device feed from Daughtry's barn and house so completely it didn't register until he placed a hand on her shoulder. "Let's go home. I'll have Callum alert us if anything comes through. He offered to take the night shift so we can refuel."

Sensing frustration building on the back of exhaustion Jade pushed back from the speaker set up in the shop and grabbed her coat. Shaking her head, she glanced up into his stoic eyes. "Pieces. Everywhere. And a clock ticking on the girl's life. I want cohesion. You know? Something that will string it all together because right now I cannot see how the hell it all fits."

"None of us can but that's not to say we won't tomorrow. We're no good to anyone after twenty hours without sleep and…did you eat today?" Kane asked, pulling the chair aside to free her from in front of the monitoring desk.

"Don't remember," she said, too tired to deflect. "I read and reread everything we have and I know there's a crucial link we can't see."

"Honey, can't see much of anything with bloodshot eyes. I hear you but we're closing in." Kane's optimism, usually comforting, had the opposite effect. Signaling he was right, she'd stayed at it past the point of usefulness.

"Okay," she agreed. "I'll pack up my notes so I can review from home in the morning and we'll head out." Folding notebooks closed and gathering the contents of the desk's surface into a case, she was about to throw her jacket on when a familiar face peeked around the edge of the door into Major Crimes. "Axel, did you come to help your dad stay awake? He may need it. As exciting as watching grass grow so far."

"Do you mind?" he asked, entering the room. "Not Dad. I came to see you both, to give you this."

He held out a flash drive. Intrigued, Jade waved him in. "What's on it?" She accepted the drive and walked with Kane and Axe to an empty desk to enter and open the mysterious data.

"I knew Tex was tracing the Merc...the van from where Jack was discovered. I was hanging with a friend who has access to footage of the highways paralleling the shipyards. I asked if he could backtrack it to search for the same vehicle expecting to find nothing but a distraction. Instead he found this." Axel motioned for Jade to shift to allow him to open the clip. She offered him the chair while her and Kane flanked him standing at either side. As the footage played static filled images of highways intersecting the dock he glanced up. "It shows up just before midnight. Watch right here." Axel pointed to the right lower corner of the screen.

Jade's eyes burned focusing in on the grainy image and she wanted to close them, look away, but didn't dare and was glad for it as the corner grill of the van entered the field of view. "You have got to be kidding?" she said without volition.

"Well shit," Kane agreed.

Axel paused the frame and swiveled to meet their stares. "I think they brought the vehicle from abroad, like it came off a ship from an import sea-can. I asked him to run it back to see if it entered the yard before we see it here leaving. He had limited range, two weeks prior to Mac going missing. Nothing showed coming in, just leaving."

"What night are we looking at?" Jade asked, leaning onto the desk for a closer view. She couldn't see a date just the near-midnight time stamp.

"This is from Thursday night. So if Mac was put inside this van before leaving town, she was held somewhere else until it arrived to claim her," Axel said.

"We're assuming she was picked up off the farm's property late that night. Your friend Raven said he suspected that's where Jack was headed to collect her and she hid her go-bag somewhere on the land," Kane said, the timeline flowing together. "She could've been held there for hours. It's our belief they never made it past the fence."

"This is all confidential, you understand," Jade asked, wanting to get it out of the way.

"Yes, I know. Dad trained me well. No one has seen this, only me and my buddy but he didn't know why I was curious about the van."

Jade studied Axel for a beat, sensing no deception. "I found blood in the barn earlier tonight. We won't know whose blood it is until forensics calls but I'm guessing chances are good it's Mac's or Jack's. I'm having it matched against Daughtry to rule Machias out but testing takes time we don't have the luxury of waiting on."

"Well isn't this a happy huddle?" Tex stomped across the shop closing the distance with a Texas grin. "So we've adopted young Axel here? Well welcome aboard buddy. Watch and learn," he quipped before dropping into his large waiting chair and crossing his boots on the desktop with pride. "I have a theory."

Kane turned, inspecting his pleased-as-punch stance. "You can see we were working here, right?"

"My bit is better," Tex challenged.

"How could you possibly know that not having the first clue what we're looking at?" Kane shot back.

"Oh would you two cut it out? What's the theory?" Jade asked, her patience short.

"I analyzed the van in detail, then I had a source review the same to confirm. The vans not from in state, in fact, I believe it's not from our country. Whoever abducted Machias Daughtry and Jack has connections overseas. They imported the van for this job," Tex said it with a tone of overstated accomplishment.

"We were just—" Axel tried to speak but Jade cut him off.

"And how are you so certain of this?" she asked Tex, using her body to block the frozen image on the monitor from him.

"Mercedes made for distribution here in the US differ from those in the UK for instance, and on the one we're after, the lighting package is out, so is the trim level. It's not home grown. This one is built for abroad. So…my news better?" Tex asked, with his expectant Texan draw.

Jade tipped her head, locking eyes with Axel encouraging he take the question as she shifted giving Tex full view of the van on the screen. Despite exhaustion her pirate grin returned.

"I'd say your news is great but not necessarily better," Axel said proudly. "You're looking at a capture of its arrival at the import dock the night of the abduction."

Kane burst out laughing. "Hell, he isn't even a rookie and he just matched point!"

"Well I'll be damned all to hell," Tex said, kicking off the desk to inspect the footage firsthand. At the desk he leaned down, smiled broad, and patted Axel on the shoulder. "If it's up to me kid, you're hired."

"Let's allow him to graduate the academy first," Jade said, energized by the puzzle taking shape. "Okay so Daughtry holds them on the farm, reaches out to whoever his puppet master is, and they use an imported vehicle to collect her," Jade began circling the shop as the men's eyes followed her and the logic. "Jack was an unexpected obstacle so they remove him from the equation before exiting town limits."

"And have no fear dumping him where he'd eventually be found," Tex offered.

"We have to consider that the kid crawled to the edge of the road, scrawled a message for us to follow, and fought to his last painful breath to help us find them and Machias," Kane reminded, then regretted. "Point is, if Jack hadn't put in Herculean effort, he may have gone weeks without being found, maybe longer. Sorry Axel. I know he was an amazing person and your friend."

"We're working it," Axel said, focused on where the map was leading them more than the grief that began it. Jade watched him steel against the emotion, impressed.

"So we need shipping logs," she said, pausing at the evidence board.

"I ran those down and no ships are scheduled to sail from our coast until..." Tex walked over to the board where Jade stood, flipped through a log pinned to the left side and then spun. His words were matched by all of theirs.

"The weekend," they uttered in unison.

"Yes," Tex said. "The date Jack gave us coincides with the export ship's sailing date."

"This is human trafficking." The words left Jade's lips as Grey entered the room behind them. "And we have five days to track the source down, find Machias, and stop the next shipment from leaving port."

"Fantastic," Grey said, walking over to meet them at the board. "I take it we haven't made any headway with the journal entries you absconded from Daughtry's cellar?"

"Not yet," Kane answered, tapping the photos from the secret room nailed to the board. "They're all in code. We're working to crack it but so far..."

"And, to top it all off this came for you but this time via my mailbox." Grey waved an envelope Jade's direction. "I'd say I'd like confirmation on the port connection before I pool resources to throw everything at it but I'd be a little late."

Grey opened the unsealed envelope he held out, smoothing the letter inside across the evidence board, and pinned it down for all to read.

> Dear Sister,
> They arrive from the mist with goods expected but take
> in trade ones rejected. My history being as it is, I could have
> gone for I was his. So start with the link outside the dock,

blood of my blood, can you hear the clock? He sees them not
as flesh but as a toy. The Candy Store though small and coy
is not safe for girl or boy.
    Your Loving Brother, Nickolas

"There's an address typed in the lower right corner," Grey said, checking his phone. "It's in one of the most unsavory neighborhoods but a half hour drive from the shipyard. Makes it viable. I'm thinking you get eyes in the air before—"

"Not a chance," Jade said, jumping in though focused on and meticulously memorizing her half brother's words. "If anyone tips off higher-ups in this criminal chain Mac is dead. Can we cut power to the area?"

"You mean like a rolling blackout?" Axel asked.

"Yes, exactly," Jade said, waiting on Grey.

"I'm not sure but given what's at stake...how significant this operation could turn out to be, I'll fight for it."

"So if we head in and time a blackout to span our sting, we partially cripple their ability to reach out," Jade said, pacing again.

"You could use a jammer," Axel said, following after Jade.

"He's right again," Kane agreed. "If we jam the signal at the same time they'll be blocked from any communication out. Truly in the dark."

Jade stopped up short of dead center of the board with Axel in step, pulled her phone, and snapped a photo of the latest letter. "And we take them all, every person in the place as quickly and quietly as possible. If it were as Nickolas said, a holding site outside the dock, there'd be no reason for interaction until the weekend when product was moved. It might give us enough information to stop it from happening and maybe Machias is there."

"This will take time to organize and coordinate," Grey weighed in, ever the voice of reason.

"Time we don't have, Mac doesn't have," Jade whispered deep in thought. "When did it arrive, the letter?"

"Not certain but it was there when I usually check written correspondence at end of day, so midday?" Grey reasoned.

"We have no choice," Tex spoke for them all. "The earliest we can go in is tomorrow night."

"And we better have every way out sealed," Kane warned. "Any one person escapes and our opportunity to take this down is over."

"Well who's the ray of sunshine now?" Tex said. They checked in with each other knowing the scope of what lay ahead need not be emphasized.

Jade eyed Kane, then turned to Axel. "I need the name of your friend, Axe, and where we can find him."

Kane closed the distance to her and the young man and said, in an almost fatherly tone she seldom heard him use, "It's better we track him down before anyone on their side does."

Jade watched Axel's eyes glaze over with concern.

"He erased all traces of me from his computer. No record of him sending me a thing. And put the footage on the zip so it couldn't be tracked here," Axel said.

Jade exhaled, deciding her next words. "Yes and that was wise but do you know if he erased the link to him viewing it? They may not follow the breach to you directly but if they trace the IP address back to your friend knowing he had no authority to be searching it—"

"It's not you we're worried about, kid," Tex said. "We're with you. He's on his own."

Axel grabbed a pen and notepad and jotted down his contact's name and address handing the information to Jade. "Dylan's place has like ten monitoring cameras at the entrance alone, he's high-tech but a great guy. He's gonna want to kill me for disclosing...for bringing you to his doorstep."

"Nickolas suggested a small outfit," Jade said. "This Candy Store. I'm hoping that's accurate."

"Well you'll excuse me if I don't trust my officers to the word of a lunatic that almost had you all killed." Grey spoke while running a hand over the evidence on the board. "Forty-seven." He all but whispered the number of potential victims spread over the last decade or more. His hand stopped on the name of the cop who committed suicide, missing daughter's name. "I'm having choppers on standby."

"I'll do one better," Jade said, the idea bursting to life. "I'll call Drex at FBI headquarters and see if his buddy who flies covert missions and helped us out during the Occultus case can be ready and waiting."

Grey nodded loving the idea not just of skilled air support but also the FBI backup at the ready. Kane appeared less impressed.

"Okay," Grey said, heading for the door. "I'll talk to the town system operator to arrange for the clandestine blackout. Let me know duration and start time once you have it. As much as you've linked here, it's not enough to think we have a handle on it especially with the Redeemer handing us leads God knows how from God knows where. Tie every loophole you see because if this fails to go according to plan more than those inside that grid will be at risk of feeling their way in the dark."

TWENTY-NINE

Callum used glasses when forced to read gerbil-sized writing on prescription bottles, extra-strength painkillers if he spent more than one night bent over a vehicle engine he decided to tinker with, and regretted numbing the sensation out of his fingertips with too many ski seasons, but there was nothing wrong with his ears. And the sound he registered didn't make sense but was worth replaying for two distinct reasons. One, he was certain he could identify the source of it. And two, it occurred long before Tex dropped Daughtry back off at his property following their interview of him which meant the place should've been empty and silent. Both substantiated distinguishing the area of the recorded feed, amplifying it, and blasting it at four a.m. across the homicide unit's office. Axel, working in a corner, wore sound-canceling headphones. No one else was there to hear it but, if they had, it was likely they would've shared his reaction.

"Who was hammering nails after Carmichael fled the property and before Jackson ever reached it with the suspect?" Callum spoke into the empty space, playing his own devil's advocate. "Someone else was on that land uninvited."

Marking the section of tape and isolating the noise into a separate recording he began cleaning the feed. A talent he embarked on expanding following the death of his wife. One that branded him as a vital contributor to a multitude of cases where listening devices were employed while shielding him from interacting with others on more than a fleeting basis. Having perfected the art and no longer wishing to remain behind the scenes, it opened up new opportunities he honestly enjoyed. Ones like tonight that he hoped stacked the odds in favor of his fellow officers.

Backtracking the time stamp against the order of events he entered, the sound hit occurred approximately ten minutes after Jade confirmed she was back inside her vehicle and exiting the highway access road and twelve minutes before Tex traveled down the one leading onto the property to deliver Daughtry. Whoever held the hammer acted between both suggesting knowledge of Jade leaving and the risk of Daughtry returning.

Their ghost's intentional efforts to avoid contact were telling.

Certain Jade wouldn't be thrilled to learn her actions on the farm were under the surveillance of someone who also didn't have Daughtry's permission to be there, he still wanted her to be the first to hear what he unearthed. He packaged it to send to her phone but held off, wanting to add as much context as possible to the discovery.

Unsure of the evidence Jade encountered, he was blind to how the hammering meshed into the picture. Jade kept in contact entering the barn and the cellar. They coordinated her exit to avoid Daughtry seeing any trace of her. She mentioned little else except for the upper barn windows left ajar when they'd been closed on the prior visit. He made a note of this typing it into the file and then replayed the clean version of the sound bite.

Counting the number of hits and listening attentively as the trajectory of the impacts shifted, first echoing from one side then crossing into the other. Callum never heard the ghost set the hammer or blunt object down at the tail end of the clip, only a subtle shifting of hay, heavy footsteps, perhaps boots receding.

Documenting every detail he could only hope it made more sense to Jade having set eyes on the space where the sound originated. With his intense concentration focused on the task at hand his breaks from the sound analysis were spent studying the case board of evidence. Anything he could add to their understanding had become deeply personal, involving his only child and one he vowed to his dying wife he'd keep safe.

Jack, the young man Axel discovered slain at the roadside, had grown up inside their home along with a variety of characters Axe welcomed in. Jack was special and his presence early after the loss of Axe's mother made a huge difference for them both. He was a wealth of natural humor, not afraid to speak of Sophie and bring memories back to life, and he was a hell of a cook even at twelve. If not for him Callum believed his boy would've wasted away while he struggled free of debilitating grief. Instead he became a star football player. Jack rarely missed a game.

At the crime scene Callum swallowed his remorse showing strength his boy could mirror but when he returned home alone, with Axel fiercely chasing down leads and making rounds to their friends, more than shower water flowed down the drain. Life could be so beautiful and so painfully unfair. He cried a river and blamed lack of sleep for his red eyes.

The more Callum absorbed off the evidence board he'd been entrusted with, the heavier his heart sank. He read the passion in Axel's eyes; the commitment to stay involved, to be a part of justice for Jack. What he couldn't have known was what that meant. This wasn't a simple abduction gone wrong case. Evidence pictures of logbooks and dock sites screamed worst-case scenario.

Nothing targeted teens, opening them to the darkest violations of man, like human trafficking. And that was what Callum was staring at. Not only a random case of it but the organized pattern of criminality evidence said could be held responsible for the destruction of forty-seven lives before it took Jack's and captured Machias Daughtry. Axel, more than a terrific son, an exceptional student, and a fiercely loyal friend, was a beautiful young man. One Callum was terrified of the suspects Major Crimes Division was chasing down getting their hands on.

Knowing every minute brought them potentially closer to Axel his stomach churned refusing to settle regardless of the antacids he popped. So he did what all desperate parents did. He maneuvered to protect his child and asked Axel to stay overnight at the station with him working the case instead of sleeping at home alone. Jade and Kane strictly forbid Axel contact with Dylan, the one who handed over the CCTV van footage warning he could put him at further risk. They'd given him tasks of sifting through logbook entries, knowing his proficiency for mathematics and coding and sympathizing with Callum's plight.

Glancing across the room to the desk in the far corner where Axe sat with headphones on, pouring over the books, Callum breathed in relief and refocused.

Having dissected the hammering section, Callum slid his headphones on and moved backward from the encountered retreating footsteps and hammering. He listened in for mere seconds before jerking backward with force enough to topple his water thermos with a crash as the amplified sound startled him. His reaction had Axel toss his headphones and cross the room in a few strides.

"Dad, what's up?" he said, grabbing a paper towel from a dispenser to block the water from sensitive documents on the desk.

Callum ripped free of his headphones and rescued his paperwork from possible saturation. "I was analyzing subtle trace noise and didn't turn the volume back down. Someone slammed a door, well two doors, and damn hard." Callum said, his ears ringing.

"Doors on what?" Axel asked, tossing the wet rags in the trash. "Where are you at with it?"

"I think it was the doors Detective Carmichael found open in the upper level of the barn. She questioned them; sure they'd been closed when her and Detective Kolton first visited the property. I have to play it again." Callum said, reorganizing his desk and settling the half-empty water thermos at the far end.

"If Jade thought they were closed, they were," Axe said. "Play it out loud, I'll listen in."

Callum disengaged the headphone mode and rewound to the marker he was at before resuming analysis. Setting the volume to a reasonable level, he said, "Close your eyes. It helps isolate your senses."

Axel held a hand up pausing the play and reached for a chair, rolled it closer, assuming a comfortable position with his eyes shut before motioning to start the reel. The sound echoed in the room once at regular speed, then again after Callum slowed it.

"Wooden doors, and heavy," Axe said, his eyes opening. "So we're in the barn. Jade said she crawled through a high first-floor window, fell in after using a log to reach it. You said upper level?"

"Yes. She said the hay loft doors were opened," Callum said, rewinding again.

"How far?" Axe asked, staring over at surveillance photos of the barn in question.

"How far?" Callum echoed, unsure what Axe was getting at.

"Were the doors open all the way, a crack, just one?" Axe's tone was focused not annoyed.

"Wide open I believe she said," Callum confirmed as Axe waved him to play the sound again.

"Yeah, that's it. Someone closed, slammed shut, the upper loft doors. It's the timing of the swing. They would be heavy and have a wide arc and the only doors with those parameters in that barn were the upper ones. I've dropped Mac at the house, even though Daughtry demanded we stay outside of the fence. When she knew he wasn't home I drove her door to door. I've never seen them open," Axel said. "Not once." He reviewed the data in front of them. "When does this sound happen?"

"That's the real interesting part. It takes place after Jade leaves and before Daughtry returns by about fifteen minutes," Callum said, enjoying the enthusiasm and wisdom of his son's approach. "Someone other than the two of them shut those doors."

Axel pushed away from the desk rolling into the room's center and spinning his chair with one foot as he pondered. "What would be the point of opening them? More light? A view outside?"

"More importantly, why close them unless the perpetrator didn't want Daughtry finding them left open, alerting him to a presence inside?" Callum said, sitting back in his chair.

"So our guy, the perpetrator, he opened them initially for Jade to witness them and closed them so Daughtry couldn't." Axe stopped spinning. "Jade said she found blood in the barn. Either our perp was a part of causing it or—"

"Or he set the stage for Jade to find it!" Callum rewound the tape checking his notes and matching a time stamp, then he pushed play. "Tell me what you hear."

After a few seconds, he stopped the tape and replayed the section twice more.

"It's more than stepping through the hay," Axe said. "It's like he's shifting it."

"Exactly like that," Callum said. "Jade discovered a blood pool there. Said it appeared as if pieces of hay were smeared in it. Our guy, as you said, may have cleared Daughtry's cover-up attempt for her. What other reason would he have to recover evidence he knew, from watching her, she'd already discovered?"

"Dad, he made sure she found it," Axe said. "I think he set her up to see everything Daughtry was up to and then cleaned up behind her so Daughtry didn't suspect a thing."

"Detective Carmichael has an insider helping her," Callum said, typing quickly into his computer. "And she needs to know about him at the crack of dawn when we're fast asleep." He smiled at his brilliant son and hit send.

THIRTY

When the castoff of blood splatter coated and blurred the camera feed Nickolas rolled his eyes at the killer's incompetence. He warned him against such things before employing him to do what restraints prevented Nick from carrying out. Family required sacrifice. He understood this at the core of his being in ways few could comprehend. Watching through the limited view from the hitman's bodycam lacked the visceral emotion of being present at the scene, close enough to smell the nitrate-coated air from the bullet blast or the iron-laced aroma of human blood. Nickolas had vast experience in the latter.

Pressing a key, he spoke into the monitor, "There's a second heat signature approaching from your direct west, five seconds to contact."

The silent drone hovering overhead equipped with night vision cameras and zoom lenses went to work tracking the upright bipedal enemy approaching. Before he rounded the corner, Nick said, "Down."

The hit man dropped into a crouch, swiveled to meet the second guard, and fired. Nick watched the man crumple from the drone feed. The silencer the attacker used reduced the weapon's discharge to a momentary pop that mingled and was lost in the fray of neighborhood noise pollution.

Even from a distance, in the dark, and through a limited field of view the degradation of the area over the last two decades was pronounced. And, thankfully for Nick, the Candy Storeowner hadn't been wise enough to sell out. He'd never know who truly ended his life or why but the death, serving a dual purpose for Nick, would be satisfaction enough.

"Okay, drag him into the shed with the other one and circle back to the adjacent house. You stay inside through the hit. The windows have privacy glass and they're bulletproof. I'll notify you when it's safe to resurface and walk out to your vehicle, may not be tonight unless I see a break in the activity. You don't want to get shot in gang crossfire and miss your payday," Nick said, then listened and watched as the hit man followed his instructions. His job had been to take out the exterior guards leaving the target inside without warning when the gang attacked.

By Nick's estimation, they were less than a half hour away and closing fast as expected. "The code for the back door is 04440, it will lock automatically behind you and will not reopen until I activate it. Understood?" Nick asked, watching the head of the assassin nod in agreement. "Good. Go now. And don't worry if anyone comes knocking, the place fits the neighborhood on the outside but she's a fortress."

Nick's eyes followed the man on the feed as he exited out back of the property, skirted a forested dumping ground, and came around the back of his house across the street and down one lot. When he entered and shut the exterior door, Nick watched his security system, open on his laptop, confirm entrance and relocking. Interior cameras tracked the man's every movement. Including his boring if typical raiding of the stocked fridge.

Content with the success and execution of part one of his plan, Nick brought up the camera feed on the side street to monitor for the gang breaching the area. The drone returned to base as instructed and a second, fully charged twin levitated to take its place. He wasn't about to miss a second of the night's activities. The hitman installed two cameras angled into the Candy Store covering the rooms most likely to hold the target. When the drone settled overhead, he watched thermal imaging of those inside. Two outlines were too small to be adult and the pictures filtering back urged him to check the roadway feed.

He exhaled with relief seeing the convoy of bikes cross into the district.

The night of pleasure and violation the Candy man had planned was about to become drastically disappointing, at least for him.

Nick glanced up to a notification in the right corner of his main screen checking the quiet of his rehabilitation center remained. The facility was on such a vast piece of land security drove, not walked, over the grounds in an ATV and anyone uninvited would be seen for miles on approach. Satisfied, he cleared open tabs and focused in on the Store and its owner.

He expected the gang to enter guns ablaze and mow down any and every one in their path, so he'd provided a layout inside the case with the drugs and money coaxing them to enter from the back. By the time they located the kids being held, the threat would be erased and they wouldn't be targeted. Or so he hoped. No guarantees.

The WarMakers chapter was better than he gave them credit for. Even knowing the layout, they surrounded the store before they lit it up. No one was exiting alive unless they granted them mercy. When the shooting started, he witnessed it was in short supply.

Titan had mere seconds to reach Riparian, give him intel on the hit, and secure his place at the front of the building. All he knew for certain was their leader issued a kill order for the drug house owner and any protection. Occupants inside were deemed collateral damage unless an innocent. No hostages, even if possessing action-able inside information on stash, shipments, or incoming cash drops. Apparently, he didn't give a shit. Their one percenters were handed a specific mission. And timing was everything.

Gunners circled the building and the echo of bullets thunking into flesh, furniture, and walls colored the night. Titan and his flank entered the front one after the other, Titan first. Any bullet penetrating the structure's thin walls could hit a brother so they timed the entrance seconds apart, a choreographed brutal play on West Side Story. Titan counted down, broke through the main door, and turned east as planned. With no openings to side rooms until the back of the hall they cleared the distance in four steps. Breaking into the locked room on the right while his shadow took the left, he found a young girl, maybe fifteen, tied to a bed and coherent enough to be terrified. Gagged, she couldn't scream so Titan pulled his blade while whispering in close.

"I'm here to get you out alive," he said, locking eyes so she witnessed the kindness behind his. "Do exactly what I say or we're both dead."

Cutting her left leg free a scattering of bullets rang out in the room sharing the interior wall. Titan sliced the rope, threw her off the bed and onto the floor while sheltering her with his body against possible stray bullets. The firing paused as boots thundered throughout the house. A man was screaming deeper inside the building; Titan knew why and that it would not cease anytime soon.

Plucking the shivering girl over his shoulder, he said, "Hang on and don't look up." Then to his brother across the hall he said, "Innocent, heading back."

"Here too," he replied. "At your six."

In five strides they were all outside the house, three more and the girl and a boy, younger than her by a couple years, wrists raw and bleeding, were set inside a truck that followed the bikes in. He deployed locks for the rear cab and was glad its bulletproof glass protected them.

"Can you take my ride?" Titan barked at their driver.

"Fuck yeah," he said, a new and eager member he sprang from the seat.

"Do nothing but ride it back to Head Q. I'm dumping then I'll meet you there." Titan's low voice and speed of delivery had the guy running for his bike before the punishment began. Screams, shrill and almost inhuman cut the night warning everyone to cover and lockdown, as the Candy man was dragged to the front of the property, naked and damaged but not nearly as much as he was about to be.

Titan jumped in the truck, threw his backup an extra weapon, and nodded his intention to pull out and clear the area before Bull swarmed. If cops were called in, he'd have little to no chance of shielding the kids.

"Go, go, go," his backup yelled, heading full throttle into the chaos.

Titan slammed his door, secured his mask over everything but his eyes, and peeled out smashing over debris in his way. He lifted off two tires bouncing back on the pavement from the back alley where they met the truck, sped double the limit over the side street, and switched over three lanes to an off ramp before checking behind him.

"What are your names?" he yelled over the squealing tires and heated engine. "I'm taking you to safety but I have to call it in so they know you're the ones I'm calling for."

"I'm Melody," the girl said, her breathing ragged but her voice gained strength as she clutched the younger boy. "This is my brother Bobbie."

"Melody, Bobbie." Titan swung a glance over his shoulder to keep the connection. "Can you tell me how you ended up in that house?"

"We were running from a guy at the outreach center in Shadow Hook. He worked there. Attacked us both after pretending to be a good guy."

"He's a fucking monster," the young boy yelled. "His name is Daughtry."

"Okay, you tell them everything you can remember when you get inside," Titan said, eyes on the back road leading to the police station.

"What's your name, mister?" the boy asked. "If you actually turn out to be a good guy I'd like to remember it."

Titan caught a glimpse of the young boy's eyes in the rearview mirror, his pain and fear clear and potent. "Name's Titan," he said. "Tonight I'm a good guy, your good guy."

"Well I'm gonna tell 'em to give you a medal cause no one else is," Bobbie said.

"You can tell them if you want but there won't be a medal, young Bobbie, 'cause I don't exist." The kids huddled close, examining each other and the damage inflicted while he drove.

In no time, with his foot heavy on the accelerator, Titan was within two blocks of the cop shop. He dialed the number from memory and waited. By the grace of God, a familiar voice came on the line but before he could finish his spiel Titan interrupted. "This is Titan. I have two innocents incoming for drop off at the back, Melody and Bobbie, you have one minute." He hung up and turned to the kids. "I'm pulling up to a loading dock attached at the back of the police station, there'll be a man waiting there to help you but I need you to exit this truck like it's on fire. Move as fast as possible, my life depends on it."

The kids nodded in unison, not understanding the why but intent on exacting the how. Evading cameras with a strategic path in, Titan spun the side of the truck up against the dock as the loading door began to rise.

"Now," he said. "Jump and watch the gap!"

The kids did as instructed and before the girl's foot fully cleared, he floored the vehicle away, slamming the door with its momentum, and watching their small figures scurry into the waiting arms of Callum MacLeod.

Safe.

At least two of them were.

THIRTY-ONE

Daughtry would've cut a path in the farmhouse's aged hardwood if it had not been sturdy, his hysterical pacing relentless. The neglected wood planks, sourced off the land originally, were a rare white pine, the floor supported, the walls protected, the workings inside were time-tested and without flaw. The one who tainted the perfection of its design was the only piece within that didn't warrant preservation, restoration, and admiration. His existence cursed it all. Tonight he sensed the historic home and the very land it sat on rejecting him, begging for his undoing. And it wasn't alone.

The call from Barracutta left no room for misinterpretation. Daughtry failed to procure the product assigned to him, after pledging to over deliver with a female and male of pliable age. The business, after all, must continue to produce or be left behind by others more determined. He brought considerable heat to the case by filing the missing person's report on Machias too earlier and awakening an atmosphere of suspicion because of his history and unsavory reputation. Without an upside he became a dangerous loose end and Barracutta made sure he knew it.

He crossed a line.

To make matters not only worse, but possibly unsalvageable, the kid that coldcocked him with a shovel, and fled his entrapment attempt, and his older sister were unaccounted for after a gang raid on the Candy Store. If they made it into police custody Daughtry was as good as dead wading into the realm of liability.

Barracutta's voice echoed in his ears. "If I can't depend on you for delivery and you're leading dogs to my door why not erase ties? You're only as good to me as your last batch of product. If not for the payday this weekend, you'd already be dead to me...and everyone else."

When the line filled with static, he realized he had nothing to barter. No trail to follow and find where Machias was being held, the criminal operation running through the outreach programs lead straight to him, and with eyes on him finding substitutes for the two Barracutta intervened with was out of the question.

A noose was tightening and Daughtry felt it so intensely he ripped off two buttons, loosening the throat of his shirt. They pinged and scattered across the hardwood, disappearing under the kitchen island. In a flash he saw Lily there, challenging him, ready to fight for her daughter and her freedom. Afraid of the venom in her eyes, he backed away. It was the first and last time. She met her fate hours later when he requested Barracutta send help. He eluded Lily intended to threaten the operation and was armed with information to follow through, knowing she'd be killed.

His actions resolved one problem but created far more. In his moment of panic he failed to fabricate a viable explanation for Lily's disappearance and hadn't thought about the community reaction or the consequences of being saddled with a six-year-old the town was ever watchful over.

If he considered *that* a road to hell *this* was eternal damnation.

There was a moment he could've sent Barracutta to prison, stopped the whole enterprise, and may have even come out a hero. Back at the Silver Pines care home, when he'd been approached, threatened with exposure of his drug theft, and enticed with cash and prizes for his recruitment. He could've said no. Reported the criminal leader and associates before they grew to amass a stronghold over the area and ports. Today was the first time he speculated how different life would look if nineteen-year-old him rejected the dirty money and deeds. What did he know? He was a stupid guy facing charges, in trouble, with no options. Too late to do the right thing now.

Barracutta cutting ties meant no way off the property or out of the country, no money or exit strategy, an inescapable target on his back from both directions. The law and the lawless would see him in prison for life or his life ended. And he'd witnessed what retribution entailed on this side of the fence. Served a hundred creative ways, one worse than the next, and none you wouldn't trade for the wrong end of your own weapon. He feared a dreadful fate to match from the other side. Prisoners didn't take kindly to those who violated kids and the labels that would follow him would cast him among the most hated.

Unbearable. Throwing his hands in the air, he brought them down slamming into the wall of brass pots and pans sending many erupting on impact with the counter and floor. Bellowing with the chimed noise the house rattled in its wake. This would not, could not stand. He wouldn't let it.

Having no other choice he ran from the kitchen side door, leaving it flapping open, his feet not slowing until he stood center of the upper barn hayloft. Igniting the overhead light he scurried to the row of antiques piled at the far back and began heaving and pitching furniture until clearing the back wall. There, buried from sight behind a dozen or more pieces, sat a hidden safe. Knowing he was in bed with the evilest partner he'd amassed a string of evidence spanning from his time at the elderly care facility to current day.

Claiming victimization was his only option.

Flipping through files he found the one outlining Lily's departure from his life. Unbeknownst to Barracutta, he'd taken photos for his own security, pictures following Lily walking back after Bible study, the van that swung in to capture her, and the violence that ensued in the interaction. He even managed a few of them departing.

Kneeling on the loft floor, among fallen furniture and a padded file of documentation, he breathed again, the air a mix of hay dust, night mist, and salvation.

"What lengths would a man go to protect his child, bargaining for the return of his beloved wife, against a criminal enterprise such as yours?" he said. "I think people will believe great lengths, very great. Especially once I show them what you're capable of."

He shuffled through photos until locating those most vile and violent. He risked much snapping the shots strictly against policy from the inside of Barracutta's export warehouse and silos. Now he knew it as a risk worth taking.

"And being that you kidnapped my daughter, it'll be no wonder why I lost my mind. Anything I may be linked to will be seen as a justifiable break from sanity," he said, staring at a shot with Barracutta's face clearly identifiable. "You, on the other hand, will be seen for what you are, a soulless violent human trafficker. And if I can end you first, no one will ever know my part in any of this."

The satisfaction he experienced was short-lived as he remembered Machias. He didn't know where she was being held but knew for certain she hadn't been shipped abroad yet and couldn't be until the next boat sailed. Again, this daughter posed the greatest threat to freedom. Foolishly, not wanting to be associated with her abduction, he'd limped back to the farmhouse when Barracutta's men arrived and set a trap to take her. He wasn't informed about Jack until hours later and celebrated still smarting from his attack inside the barn. Served the kid right interfering.

Now he wondered how he could jockey all of it to serve him. Using his knowledge of the inner workings of Barracutta's organization, the evidence he amassed, and the connections, which required severing, he set about mapping an exit strategy that rid him of criminal accountability. Rather be painted a lunatic pushed to the brink than a predator.

Gathering the safe's contents to transport back to the house to work in a more protected and comfortable setting he made his way to the hatch. Turning to back down the ladder he faced the hayloft windows. With the overhead light blasted on when he entered in a rage, the area was lit abnormally bright. And something appeared out of place. The doors were shut and nailed as always but a sliver of wood was missing from the interior frame. Stepping around the hatch he came in close, feeling the raw wood. Setting the files aside he withdrew his phone from his pocket and engaged the flashlight mode. Following the trim around on the inside edge he inspected it. The nail holes remained the same as in memory but they were ragged in places with the nails angled oddly in a few distinct spaces. Standing back he stared at the windows as a whole than extinguished the flashlight, grabbed his files, turned out the light, and left for the house.

"Damn you for making me paranoid," he said, stepping to ground level. "I'll make you pay for all of it as soon as I figure how to get my money out of you first."

THIRTY-TWO

I n Jade's view even the most impoverished and decrepit neighborhoods had their limits and the most wretched the dock district had to offer just met its. He was hanging, disemboweled, from the streetlamp out front of the house known as the Candy Store and it was set ablaze and turned to rubble and ash. The explosions, three before her and the team arrived, confirmed the stash of highly flammable illegal substances literally going up in smoke. And fire and rescue had pulled five dead bodies from the mess. Visible gunshots ruled out inferno as cause of death on three so far. As crime scene tape was being rolled outside a distant perimeter at either end of the properties flanking the east and west side and out of the way of active fire crews. Jade considered encircling the entire district. It wouldn't be inaccurate.

"What a disgusting disaster," Tex said, averting his eyes from the remnants of the drug dealer hanging feet away. "Can we get someone to cut him down?" He yelled at a crew member tasked with that very job only to be told the light standard he was strung up on was live and given the ongoing blaze hadn't been deemed safe for contact.

"Terrific," Jade said, shaking her head at the horror. "Then throw a damn blanket over it. There are children in this fucking place."

The crew nodded and pulled out a fire tarp of some kind readying it to conceal the body from public display. It wasn't them she was irritated at, everyone and everything but the hard working, steal-stomached firefighters. "Thanks, guys," she yelled. "So fucking sorry you're up to your arms in this filth."

"Well if that doesn't send the message not to cross the WarMakers, nothing will," Kane said. His eyes diverted to firemen carrying the charred remains of another person from the site. "How many is that?"

"Seven," Jade said. "If you count the one dangling."

"Great." Kane plucked a motorcycle key off the soiled ground at his feet. "Our approach to this case just—"

"Went up in smoke with about a hundred kilos of fentanyl," Tex said, watching with Jade as a minor explosion erupted at the back of the place. "Maybe more."

"My guess is more," Jade agreed. "Not that we'll ever know now."

"Neighbors won't talk," Kane said. "They know better."

"Haven't answered their doors," Tex confirmed.

"Can you blame them? The view is...sickening. So that leaves us with cam footage to sift through. I'll ask Callum to step in on it and relay anything the gang unit shares. He was one of them and will be a huge asset bridging for us. That team is getting no sleep anytime soon," Jade said. "He sent me messages. Haven't opened them."

"Yeah, to me too but the combustible cul-de-sac took precedence," Kane said, then raised his eyes to events over her shoulder. "Shit, we've got a live one."

Jade spun to see two firefighters cradling a badly burned victim in a sling stretcher. The senior of the two motioned with a nod for the detectives to come running to intercept before he was loaded onto the waiting ambulance. She led the way as all three closed the distance. By the exposed leg outside torn and singed denim pants it was a male, his condition said he wouldn't survive the ride. An EMT sprang from the back and shot him with a syringe of what she presumed was morphine or another potent painkiller.

Jade leaned over the man's face, or what remained of it, in case he could see her. "Sir, you have been badly burned in an explosion and are being transported to a hospital. Do you know who is responsible?" she asked, her voice level and calm.

"Wa…wa…WarMakers," he coughed the word out, and she was certain she witnessed smoke expel from an open wound in his chest. She snapped a couple photos, despite the glares from the EMT. "Got…kids…out."

"Okay," she said. "Hang on." Meeting the confused faces of the medics, she said, "It may help identify him if he doesn't survive." With this, he collapsed and they hoisted him into the back, went to work before the doors closed, and left with lights blaring. The ambulance was still in view when she expanded the picture and searched the frame. "Damn," she said to Kane and Tex who waited for clarity. "He was identifying himself as a gang member. Their insignia is part of his neck tattoo."

She showed them the zoomed-in partial of the crossed ancient Irish arrowheads in the WarMakers branded coat of arms. "Where was he located?" she asked the firefighters preparing to head back into the danger zone.

"Left of the house in the backyard; it sustained considerable damage from the first explosion, may have hit him while he was circling outside the building," one said, before adjusting his mask and disappearing into a gray cloud.

"So this asshole." Jade tipped her head back the direction where the Candy Storeowner's body hung behind them. "Was actively holding kids here."

"Can I say I'm leaning in favor of the eviscerators?" Kane said, his head shaking in disbelief.

"Only if you're real quiet," Tex said. "Maybe whisper."

"No one can hear shit outside the sirens and hoses," he said. "And when they're finished, there'll be zero in the way of evidence."

Jade cast a glance at Kane, then Tex. "Not wrong. We have nothing except a dying gang member's admission that there were kids here. No Machias, yet. None of the dead are her size. If she was here, she's been moved."

"I'm thinking we should disappear." Kane glanced around. No neighbors were out yet with the wreckage being so new, the place swarming with firefighters and cops, and it being the wee hours of the morning. But as dawn broke, they'd line the street and any criminality associated with the Candy Store would be watching faces and seeking names. "The gang unit will keep us updated but we should regroup at the shop."

"Agreed," Jade said. "We better wake up Grey and let him know he can cancel the blackout. It appears this neighborhood will be lit up by the fentanyl fire pit instead."

The trio walked to the truck they'd dispatched in, handing cards to the drug unit lead at the edge of the property. While Kane issued instructions Jade opened the first of a string of messages from Callum. His header advised to read at first light and, as the moonlight shifted to make way for a new day, she shook her head at the irony and hit the recorded attachment. Listening to the clear sounds of someone employing a hammer, she waved the men down.

"Callum got something at the farm. Let's go. He may still be at the shop."

Reading as the truck rolled over debris and Kane maneuvered clear of a stream of first responders, she absorbed what Callum discovered. "He recorded clear evidence of activity in the barn," she said, catching a glance from Kane and direct stares from Tex in the back seat. "It's relevant because it happened after I left, but before you showed up to dump Daughtry off."

"When no one was supposed to be there?" Tex clarified.

"Exactly. And the thing is, I sensed I wasn't alone." Jade spoke with her head bent reading more of Callum's message. When she tipped it back up, she met Kane's concerned gaze. "I was careful, there was no one in close. I thought I spotted a light way off in the distance, deep in the back forested area. Couldn't be certain, it was only a glimpse, but with this and…"

Kane hit a curb and course-corrected. "And what?" he asked.

"The barn. I had to clamber up into the ground-level

window, higher to reach from the outside with the interior floor raised, to enter but the hayloft windows were left wide open. There were nail marks," she began, walking through the logic.

"Like the ones in the staged bedroom of the farmhouse?" Kane asked.

"Yes. And the place I extracted a blood sample from was obvious," she continued.

"Like someone wanted you to find it?" Tex asked, shifting forward to adjust his position crammed in the back of the truck's cab.

Jade leaned his way with her phone so he could read with her. "Yeah, and if this sound, hammering, happened after I left, whoever meant for me to find it also intended to keep that knowledge from Daughtry."

"He cleaned it back up, returned it to the state Daughtry left it in," Kane said.

"We got a gopher," Tex said proudly. "Sneaking in from the forest, messing in the barn, and scurrying away. Interesting. Good thing is he appears to be on our side."

Jade's expression was read before she said a word. Kane glanced at Jackson through the rearview mirror and Tex threw a mouse under the elephant in the room. "So are we thinking this whole mess, the Candy Store explosion and the farm has Nickolas Leigh's signature?"

"He as much as handed the Candy Store to us and had huge motivation for revenge if that sick creep laid hands on him as a kid. I don't know how given the execution was gang orchestrated. But I don't think it was him with me at the farm," she said, anxious to see all the pieces in one room.

"Why, I mean aside from the massive hurdles Nick would encounter coming back to this state with alerts out for him everywhere from train, plane, and automobile rental," Kane asked, turning down the fastest route to the shop. The time of night put them alone on the pavement for most of the drive.

"It didn't feel like him," Jade said, dropping her head again to examine the rest of Callum's messages. "Whoever that was I think Tex is right."

"I'm always right, honey," Tex said, easing tension.

"I wouldn't say always," Kane argued. "Whose idea was the staircase approach?"

"He still blames me for getting shot." Tex shook his head and fell back into the leather seat.

"Always," Jade said, laughing and typing into her phone. "We'll know more laying it all out. We're minutes away. I'm sending Callum a message to meet us. I'll ask if he'll turn around if he's headed home."

"I want his take on the sound grab," Kane said. "He's the expert and we need his ears."

"Jesus, his son might switch career paths after no sleep and a redirect," Tex said.

"He's there." Jade's tone had them both questioning. "Callum's at the shop and not because he was analyzing for us. He had two kids dropped off by a mole inside the WarMakers."

"You're kidding…so kids from the Store are in custody?" Kane said, rounding the last corner leading to the shop's garage.

"Better still," Jade said, readying to unbuckle. "The drop was by a deep cover they thought they lost to the life."

"Seriously?" Tex barked. "What in the Sam Hill is happening tonight or today or…what the hell time is it anyway?"

"After four," Kane said, flashing a smirk at Tex. "In the a.m. buddy."

"So now we have deep cover in on the act? I need coffee for this," Tex said as the truck swung into their parking spot and they bailed.

"Hear that," Jade agreed, sprinting for the elevator. "We'll need all the help we can get. I'm just sorry whoever is upstairs isn't Machias. Callum said all they managed to pry out of the kids is their first names. Brother and sister."

"Ages?" Kane asked, his expression somber.

"Fifteen and ten." As the words left her lips nausea churned her stomach and it wasn't from lack of sleep or missing a meal the night before. There wasn't an age when being sold or perceived as a dispensable object wasn't vile but this was purely gut-wrenching.

Kane placed a hand on her back as they entered the elevator, reading her thoughts and knowing her heart. If there ever existed an ultimate case when the perpetrator deserved to be strung up and gutted this was it. Unable to see all the players involved, she feared the one hanging from a streetlamp was likely not the worst of who they were up against and many more lives depended on them cutting out the heart of the operation, not just severing a limb or two.

THIRTY-THREE

The punching bag Rip slammed his frustration into threatened to dislodge from the ceiling. It wouldn't be a first. His mother taught both her sons to take a hit before giving one in any fight, fearing their size, strength, and flat Irish fists could land them in prison for murder. Again, in their neighborhood, it wouldn't be a first. Envisioning the enemies they stood against, threatening their lives, reining over their freedom, and delving them into a chain of criminal behavior straight out of the belly of hell he stopped short of demolishing it.

Soaked in sweat and panting, he paced the bomb shelter's gym. Once intended as a medic bay, the open space, padded floor, and purified air made for a perfect workout room. Complete with attached restroom and shower. The only thing missing currently was someone to kill and string up from its rafters. Riparian carried a list of favorites. Daughtry and Barracutta were competing for first place.

Titan, with mere seconds to relay his situation, sent him the address of the gang's targeted elimination. Rip drove the second street over from it and watched as explosions and the chemical fed flames like an enraged demon cast the dock district in a red glow.

Too risky to come any nearer, he had to wait not knowing if Titan survived the attack. Forty minutes was a lifetime when you were waiting on news you couldn't come back from.

"Three down, dropped two innocence off. They know I'm alive." In two short sentences Titan changed the tide.

The WarMakers didn't kill children. They also didn't sell them. Falling under the category of *innocence*, Titan had authorization, on locating any during the fight, to dump them somewhere secure. The carnage at the site, costing the gang three of their own, would've been justification enough. For now, Titan remained safe. And so did the kids. Rip knew where he dropped them, the cop shop in Shadow Hook. He also knew their contact while undercover had been told who spared the kids. Titan and Riparian were erased from record once inside the WarMakers' house. Since the battle that marked Rip for life and almost claimed Titan's no one, not a living soul on the lawful side, had heard from either.

Until today.

Rip's brain was performing mental acrobatics, somersaulting over breaking his brother free from the gang's firm grip while he held a kidnap victim down the hall. He recognized the massive void between his brother and him. For all his actions on the inside, Titan hadn't killed anyone. Part of the deal Rip struck. If there was killing to be done it came to him, after all he was the professional. At first the leader didn't trust it, but over time Rip's results sold him. His way out was destined to be a body bag, of that he had no doubt. Freeing Titan before the zipper went up had been his primary goal since being jumped in, but now another life that mattered to him hung in the balance.

Machias Lincoln.

And the only way she stayed safe and claimed the life she deserved was if everyone associated with Daughtry and Barracutta went into the ground before him. He started working on ways to make it happen and the first thought that came to mind surprised him.

The detective. The one he watched sneak on to Daughtry's property, investigating without backup. Jade Carmichael. He researched her using a locked private browser and couldn't help but respect her. She'd come as close to paying for the capture of a serial killer with her life as one could. And more recently dove underground against the Occultus in a territory few entered and everyone feared. Something rare existed in her.

Something familiar.

Endorsing the detective's approach and past determination Rip knew she would never see clear of his involvement with Jack's death. He also researched the young man, though that endeavor proved much harder to stomach. Jack Wells was a powerhouse leader for his generation. He created a social media space that promoted, endorsed, supported, and united fans from every walk of life. His *Getting Wells* podcast boasted a following over thirteen million, gaining more daily, and with the potential to triple in the next year. How the kid created such a safe and inclusive space was birthed out of his recipe of delivering truth with an honest yet frank approach. And he was beautiful inside and out.

The pictures linked to the podcast crushed Rip. In particular one where Jack shared the camera with a compelling young man and Macias against the wall of a deliberately unidentifiable brick building titled *Our New Home.* They were all beaming, rare in their charisma, exuding excitement for their achievement and future. Regret sent him hanging his head over the toilet at four a.m. while Jack's young friend slept in a room strides away.

As relentlessly as he tried, he couldn't stop the images of Jack's body decaying on the forest floor, bugs claiming what once was a vital amazing human being. Degradation that was for most unimaginable, Rip witnessed countless times in his previous calling and during this cursed life he was locked into. The brutality never leaving him.

The unique physical attraction Jack possessed, strangely drew everyone in, woman, man, transgender, nonbinary, non-conforming, anyone with a pulse and he made sure they all knew they were welcome because they shared the one identifying factor Jack celebrated that united them all. He posted and said it often, "to those who are currently living, I am forever with you, among you, and glad you are."

Existence. That was Jack's determination of worth, value, and right to love and respect.

And Rip killed him.

Jack's death wasn't planned. Rip's objective for expelling him on the highway close enough to town to walk in wasn't to end his life but to spare it. If he remained involved past town limits those on the other side of the equation would've seen him as a dangerous liability. Informing them that he'd been tossed out before awakening after Barracutta's men drugged the pair would free him to return to his life. He'd come too aware Machias was gone, in their view, but with no knowledge interfering with delivery of her. When the handover didn't happen, they'd come for Rip, no one else, and he'd be waiting. Rip wanted Jack to live. Now his dream and intention had to live on and the only hope for that was Machias. She loved him and that would inspire her to do right by him. It was blatantly obvious where his heart lay, what mattered most to him.

Rip would not let her die or be harmed. He couldn't.

The memory of pulling that beautiful boy from the back of the van sent him into the gym and now, inside its shower, tears meshed with the water though his body was incapable of reacting more than this. The torment, so innate, blocked the memory in its complete form, delivering snapshots. His strong hand overpowering Jack and throwing him outside to the ground where he took off running, a branch smacking Rip full force in the face during the brief chase, the footfall of ...

Rip's head snapped back out of the shower's rain. He ran a hand over his face to clear the water from his eyes and locked his focus on the memory. He heard the tread of steps behind him. Explainable if Jack circled back aiming to reach the van and speed away with Machias before Rip could close the distance. He wished he hadn't for Jack's sake but for Machias to live free Rip had to take her. He hadn't remembered that piece before. It only added to the ferocity with which Jack fought to save her and the weight of his death.

Carmichael would never trust Rip's help if aware of him, his past gave every reason not to. It left him with only the option of remaining invisible, hinting at leads, dropping signs and clues to spur her in the right direction until Machias could be handed over to her. And being a ghost was only valuable if he could mobilize players constructively and arrange for the poltergeist to rein terror down and punch a sufficient whole in Daughtry and Barracutta's world to permanently yank them to the dark side. And that would take every ounce of strength and concentration he possessed.

Drying off and dressing, he walked back to his office with the determination of not leaving until the perfect plan to accomplish the end of Daughtry, Barracutta, and the WarMakers, in so far as their control over his brother existed, emerged. A black oak table, pushed off to one side, served only to house office supplies. Snatching them up and relocating them to the floor he pulled it center of the room. Staring at its empty surface he envisioned it covered with intel. Collecting surveillance photos of the key figures requiring termination, he placed them side by side with space to amass information below each. He was about to begin the process of organizing by transferring the data from his desk into the operation when something caught his eye, registering as out of place.

One of the benefits to living inside a locked, isolated, concrete building no one accessed was being absolutely certain where everything fit. This didn't and he hadn't moved it. In the row cataloging his detailed evidence journals two were out of order. Though not obvious in a glance, each wore a small flag of color in the bottom right at the end of the binding. The order he devised with the purpose of identifying levels of criminality spanning from an actual simple transport to the kind that move one from this side of life to the other. In a slow gait he neared the mixed-up journals for further inspection, a slew of piled documents to sift through, make sense of, and weaponize against enemies shifted in the draft from his approach. With one large mitt pinning the papers down and the other about to pull the journals free he was startled by the soft slide of feet behind him.

"I think you need my help," Machias said, her voice a calm

whisper. "If you want to take him and everyone associated with him down, I mean so they can't come back, then I'm your greatest weapon."

She shuffled over glancing at the pictures taped to the table to meet him near the journals. Stepping into his personal space she leaned over rectifying the disorder of the books. "I missed the color flags," she said, inches from his scar and smiling a broad mischievous grin. "But I know everything I need to about your life in the WarMakers. So it's only fair…" She shuffled to a chair in the corner of the room closest to the table and pulled it up. "Now you can ask me anything about mine, living with the monster. Have a seat Riparian. Shall we trade horror stories?"

THIRTY-FOUR

T he door to the safe house across the street from the fentanyl inferno opened with a soft slide and heavy thunk as the bolt drew into the housing, offering a return to freedom for the executioner just as the contractor promised. Staying most of the night hadn't been his idea but there were far worse circumstances and he'd experienced several. The fridge was stocked, the place was air-conditioned and clean, and despite the knocks at the door, no one pushed to interfere with his respite. He slept in the back bedroom as the contractor instructed, sheltered from the flashing lights, fire hoses, and sea of first responders.

More importantly, it shielded him from interaction with the WarMakers who became enraged at first light knowing the attack claimed more than one of their own. He watched this from the privacy glass window facing the street. He already witnessed the retribution served on the guy dangling over the front lawn.

Told his payday waited in a storage locker he'd received time-stamped camera footage confirming, he made haste departing. The door slammed locked behind him giving but one choice. Using the back alley to push a street away, he worked down to the crossroad leading to the car he arrived in. Knowing everything left in a vehicle had potential to tie to him he cleaned it after parking. With a full tank and a reliable engine it would make an easy exit from the district. He watched it come into view, veered right bypassing the road, and made for the bus stop. He ensured the previous night the route included a stop near the train station where the locker waited.

He hadn't survived the life by trusting anyone who stood between him and a payday and he wouldn't now. The bus schedule said it'd arrive shortly after five, and he negotiated his release to match it. He rounded the corner while it turned from the opposite direction to meet him.

Seated at the back inside he followed the view of the area as it receded and then vanished altogether replaced by industrial buildings and shoreline. The route ate up twenty minutes of his morning so he used the time to secure a train ticket out of town. He'd buy a plane ticket two states over as an added safety measure. Anything in his apartment would be auctioned off in a couple months when the prepaid rent ran out and the landlord found it abandoned. He didn't care. The payday was a game changer, a life upgrade, and he planned to make the most of it. He also vowed to never return.

Call it a sixth sense, a killer's intuition, or a survival mechanism; either way the contractor that hired him for the hit exuded a confidence and criminal wisdom that unnerved. Too calm.

Before venturing outside to the train station he altered his appearance in the likelihood eyes remained on him. In a baseball hat he lifted off a fellow transit rider and sunglasses he made his way to the side of the station where lockers, color and number coded in line with his key, sat in rows. He stopped short of entering the space. Waiting for a possible target within the early morning travelers, he faked a tremor in his hands, approached a young woman, and dropped his keys bending to pick them up a few feet from her. She watched as he struggled and he caught her eye, removing his glasses with difficulty.

"I'm so sorry. My new meds and my hands don't quite agree," he said, smiling.

"Hey none of my meds ever agree with me." She laughed, reaching for his keys.

"The key is the real challenge," he said. "I may still be here if you come back around tomorrow."

She laughed and eyed him for a second, then said, "Over here?"

"Yeah, I wouldn't ask you for help if—"

"You didn't," she said, walking with him to the bank of lockers in his number range. "Here we are. That wasn't such an imposition, was it?" She pushed in the key, turned it, unlocking the locker, and stepped back not opening the door. "So you're good?"

"Golden. Well no I'm a hell of a mess but I'm working on changing that." He admitted it knowing it was actually the complete truth. "Thank you."

"No worries," she said, vanishing back into the crowd of travelers exiting the building.

Clutching the duffel bag from the back of the locker with steady hands he slowly opened it enough to identify the bundles of cash waiting inside. Seeing no obvious forms of entrapment or tagging he swung it over a shoulder and passed under an arching bridge with no cameras. Locating a trash bin, he tossed the hat and jacket he wore. Heading into a tourist shop he glimpsed a row of dark-blue hoodies, pulled out his wallet, grabbed one and paid cash, ripping the tags free and pulling it over his shirt before exiting.

His train was set to depart in ten minutes when he reached the end of the station where it waited. Ticket checked, he jumped on and made his way to a back seat where an exit existed close by and he could view everyone coming his direction before they saw him. His gut rumbled and he cursed passing by the indoor food truck. It would be a long mildly uncomfortable ride. Small price to pay for freedom from a life that lead to a gruesome death he witnessed the night before in too graphic to stomach detail.

The ride was relatively smooth and the train wasn't packed so tight you didn't have personal space to rest or stretch. Breaching the halfway point into Connecticut his breathing regulated, muscles tense for hours loosened, and his eyes quit patrolling the aisle though no one walked it. He scanned the rows around him, two empty beside and one in front. Then, pulling out the burner he hadn't yet used, he dialed the number from memory. The intention not motivated by revenge or hatred but the hint of good he hadn't completely killed off, that part he aimed to expand from here on.

"Shadow Hook Major Crime Division, how can I direct your call?" a voice said from inside the cop shop miles away.

"Whoever is in charge of the missing girl's case now," he demanded and waited to be redirected.

The one instruction he received that fell out of sync with all the other meticulously clarified orders his contractor issued regarded a girl, specifically a fifteen or sixteen-year-old with the odd name of Machias. If he ran into her his mission directive transferred to retrieving her successfully alive and unharmed and transporting her to the safe house with him to await further instructions. Unlike all the other detailed orders this one stood without elaboration so he dug. In minutes he read the abduction case of Machias Daughtry. He didn't know why or how it was linked to aiding a gang elimination of a drug dealer but he feared the treachery at play and wanted no part of it.

Just the payday.

"Detective Jade Carmichael, do you have information pertaining to a case?" A female voice echoed across the line, interference from a tunnel passage.

"The gang had help and you have a problem. I know because I was the help killing the path in for them. This was about the girl," he said.

"Don't hang up," she said, rushing her words out. "What girl?"

"The one you haven't found." He hung up, pulled the card crushing it under his boot into the metal floorboards, and tossed the phone in the pocket ahead of his seat.

Enemies were everywhere he was one of them, but not today. Today he did the right thing unsure it would make a difference, message delivered, nonetheless. And it gave him a shred of peace, enough to relax into the ride and rest until his stop. Unfolding at the station, he felt the deeds of the last two days, muscles stiffening with extended stillness. Walking off the platform he caught sight of a lunch venue and couldn't ignore his aching stomach any longer. Arranged in old-style diner fashion, he grabbed a booth at the side.

Ordering quickly from a pleasant waitress that smelled of bacon grease, he settled in catching the tail end of a stream of commercials displayed in the large television overhead.

The last one, outlining a later broadcast, captured his undivided attention.

A drug dealer known in the area by police was murdered. His house, unidentified previously despite efforts by authorities and holding a large stash of heroin and fentanyl, burned to the ground in a targeted gang hit. And a car two streets away detonated shortly after five the following morning. The drug unit was investigating the alleged bombing as a related incident but thankfully no one was harmed in the vehicle explosion.

Plucking his fork off the table to dig into his delivered meal the waitress gave him a soft grin noticing tremors in his hand. "Can I get you anything else?" she asked. "Not everyone travels well. Take your time eating, it helps."

She smiled and walked away to tend to other patrons while he stared at the steaming breakfast plate wishing he possessed the appetite to eat it.

THIRTY-FIVE

T he trio entered the shop heading straight for the surveillance desk where they set Callum up the previous day, sharing the weight of no sleep and a download of whirling information and dangerous leads. Jade regretted the demands they'd handed down to Callum and the serious risk Axel faced pulling in as close as he had to the case. But with Axel discovering the body and Callum being former Narcotics Special Enforcement and their on-site expert ears, distancing them was unavoidable. Tex broke free and veered off to the coffee pot to brew fresh while Kane and her met Callum, flanking his desk to listen in as he outlined events from the recorded surveillance and the recovery of two trafficked juveniles.

"First off where are the kids and what condition are they in?" Jade asked, knowing extracting information from youth abused and rescued from such circumstances was delicate and often impossible due to immense trauma.

"They're being examined at the hospital under constant guard and will be kept there at least overnight under false identities until we have more information and can guarantee their safety," Callum said, working the keyboard and bringing information on the surveillance recording from the Daughtry property up on the screen. "They've suffered abuse but not life threatening that we know of yet. We're waiting on blood labs and tox screens. They were more willing to talk when it was only me with them. Said neither had been molested but only due to the timing of the attack on the Candy Store. Melody said five more minutes and...who knows. Their guardian was notified and arrives tomorrow evening."

"Did they reveal anything at all about how they were taken, who grabbed them, or how they ended up here?" Kane asked, accepting a hot coffee from Tex as he rejoined the group.

Jade eyed Callum, noting his hesitation. "There's more," she said, taking her cup from Tex and offering it to Callum. Tex disappeared to fetch another.

"The deep cover that dropped Melody and Bobbie was presumed absorbed into the WarMakers as a full member and likely dead," Callum explained, swiveling his chair, abandoning the keyboard and headphones to command their attention. "Four years ago." He paused letting silence make the point. "I don't know how the hell he survived, where he's been, or how he resurfaced amid a gang war with a drug supplier, but he risked his life bringing them in."

"Where is he now?" Tex asked, coming in mid-explanation. Jade lifted the extra coffee from his hand and smiled her appreciation before gulping.

"He dumped and ran which means he was under a time constraint to return. I caught the kids, literally, but no footage of his truck. I pray he's alive and I hear from him again not only because he was a hell of a cop but, this many years inside, he'll house a wealth of evidence against the gang." It was Callum's turn to gulp, caffeine the only bridge for mental cohesion. Clearing his throat, he focused on Kane. "After I brought them in the building all they would say was that Titan saved their lives. That is my deep cover's real name, not the one I sent him in under."

"And that tells us what exactly?" Jade asked, reading the tension on Callum's furrowed brow.

"Telling them his real name puts him, and anyone related to

him, in grave danger if the gang learns it. That's a trigger for extraction."

"So your guy gave a signal through the kids to bring him home?" Tex asked.

"Not bring him home necessarily but it marks the intention to withdraw, to break cover and come in and soon," Callum explained.

"Christ," Kane said, scratching his head with both hands in disbelief. "So a guy embedded for four years or more wants the hell out the same time we watch the WarMakers obliterate a drug house Narcotics couldn't home in on for years. We've saved two kids pulled into this trafficking bullshit but not the one we're after. And, we have no clue who is behind that part or why they targeted Machias." Kane walked a circle until Tex kicked his size thirteen boot in the way halting him. "Oh…and we still can't tie this Daughtry asshole to it all. Do I have that right?"

Jade raised her eyebrows at him and finished swallowing the last of her coffee knowing the night, soon-to-be day, called for far more. "Yep, that about captures it."

"Well not quite," Callum said, shifting his back to the team to pull up the recorded data. "We may have help in that department. Listen to this. I'm pulling up a section of feed from ten minutes after you exited the barn and were leaving the access road." He turned to motion to Jade and swivel back again. "And about twelve before you"—he glanced up at Tex—"arrived to drop Daughtry off."

Setting down her cup Jade and the men held their positions, locking in to hear every nuance of sound as Callum adjusted the feed to speaker mode. Sensing the room around her as if for the first time, she wondered where young Axel was. The lights were off except for this area of the unit. She assumed he was tucked away sleeping in the break room, it being after four in the morning. The realization made her head heavy.

The first sound was the soft slide of hay. Its subtlety disarming for the next sound had them all jerk back, even Callum and he knew to expect it. Pausing the feed, he said, "This is the start of the event. I clearly identified the closing, abrupt, of two heavy and large wooden doors. I measured the time span of the closure and with that in mind tied it to the upper hayloft."

The team listened in again, this time more guarded, registering what Callum described. Then a distinct hammering occurred triggering Jade's memory. "The nails around the doors," she said. "Someone pulled them out and then replaced them after I left?"

Callum nodded agreement and replayed the piece. When the hammering paused, he stopped the reel. "Now you extracted a blood sample from the loft?" he asked, confirming what he already knew.

"Yes, and it was easy to identify," Jade said. "I discussed it with the guys. It was like the hay was cleared, shifted away from it so I couldn't miss it."

"And this," Callum said, readying to hit play again. "I believe this is him concealing the spot with the hay before he departs leaving Daughtry, literally in the dark on any evidence you found and the devices you planted."

Jade's brow tensed as she pulled back to see the scene in her mind's eye from a macro perspective with a new angle, one that included a watcher who would've arrived after Daughtry was driven away and before she crept in. "Daughtry wasn't exactly diligent in terms of security or diversion," she said, thinking it through aloud. "Hay over a blood pool instead of taking time to scrub it clean, leave no trace. The cameras and drones he left out in the house and lack of family photos. Never using an endearing term to describe Machias. The exterior cellar door left unlocked. They're rookie mistakes and I don't think he realizes what he's up—"

Kane crossed behind the back of Callum's chair and did that thing where he came in close instantly disappearing the room and everyone in it behind him. "Go back. The cellar door?" he asked, his tone a low hush.

Jade's voice dropped a register. "I thought it odd he guarded our access entering the farmhouse but the cellar door—"

"The one leading to the hidden room where you found the logbooks with the potential to bring him down existed?" He stood inside her personal space but instead of irritating it had the opposite effect, strengthening, focusing her.

"Yes. So why wouldn't he..."

"He did," Kane said, turning to open the group back into the conversation. "When we went in, and I was at the bottom of the porch steps I noticed the exterior entry and was planning to take a photo because of the chain and padlock on it. Overkill for a storage area with no direct or easy interior access to the farmhouse. Built a century ago, farm homes from that period all have interior hatch openings that are bolted from the inside of the home. No need to double down over storage, seeds, and canned goods."

"So my watcher from the woods opened that as well," Jade said.

"It's more than likely but the bugs in the cellar may be too far from it to pick up the sound. Now that I know what to listen for, I'll run it through, but why watcher in the woods?" Callum asked.

"I told the guys when I almost reached my truck I glimpsed a light across the forest understory in the distance. It happened so fast I wasn't sure, but now? The timing of the sound clip would match if a person came from that distance in behind me." Jade was about to add more when the officer monitoring the outer desk while they analyzed stuck his head into the room.

"Detective Carmichael hit line three. We've got incoming on the tip line asking for you," he said, before disappearing behind the closing door.

Jade eyed the men, spun on the heels of the fire-resistant Foxhound combats she still wore, and retreated into the dark for her desk. Snatching up the receiver she hit the speaker mode signaling the team for silence.

"Detective Jade Carmichael, do you have information pertaining to a case?" Jade waited as they all listened to echoing static claiming the line. When it cleared a voice broke through.

"The gang had help and you have a problem. I know because I was the help, killing the path in for them. This was about the girl," said a male voice, clear, not distinguishable.

"Don't hang up," she said, rushing out the first and most important question. "What girl?"

"The one you haven't found."

"Are you—" Static resurfaced then a dial tone reverberated from the speaker. "Fuck," she yelled. "And who the hell was that?" The room fell silent again and Jade fought the urge to break it by testing her boots on the nearest trash can. Pushing another button on the phone she spoke into its microphone, "Did we get anything?"

"Too quick," a voice said from the monitoring desk.

"Of course not." Whether exhaustion or converging lanes of thought, her frustration hit a new high until Callum, holding one headphone to his left ear grinned at her.

"I don't know who but I may know the where," he said. "Your caller has a train announcement in the background and the 'next stop' is Connecticut."

"I don't think we have a choice now," Jade said, knowing her next sentence wouldn't be well received by all. "I have to call Drex at the FBI. This is expanding beyond our grasp and we cannot risk allowing any of the key players to slip through our fingers due to a lack of manpower."

Tex eyed Kane, then her before speaking. "You're not wrong. We have evidence and details coming in after the sunrise. I say we hit the sack for a few hours and reconvene here at noon. Call in the cavalry after we have more to go on."

"Honestly, my ears are shot," Callum said. "And my kid has been sleeping twisted in a chair for too long."

"Okay," Kane said, addressing her directly. "We go home, wait to see what else shakes loose and then plan next moves. I think it's obvious it won't get easier from here. Our abduction and murder case seem to be but one fly caught in a web so large we can't see the edges."

Jade stomped from her desk to Kane in three brisk strides. "What did you say?" He read her eyes recognizing a moment when she was sitting in front of the backdrop of her mind and clearly equating clues.

"The case is like a fly caught in a web?" he said, questioning what his metaphor triggered for her.

"Damn, I didn't put it together," she said, darting to the case board and searching through the letters Nickolas sent her. "He told me…" She sifted through the pile tearing the copies off the board.

"I hope those aren't the originals," Tex said, casting a worrisome glance.

"Copies," she said, pulling the one in question free. "Look here." She slapped the folded copy on Callum's desk where they could all read the writing.

…the reach of the threads of this nasty web. They stretch as far back as they could forward and must be severed severely to kill the spider at the center. So I'll ask you this, what is true about the maker of the web?

"Nickolas knew we'd be here facing this exact situation, caught in the center of a web," she said, not facing them but frozen over his letter and wishing she'd paid them all more attention. "If we'd heeded his warning—"

"We'd end up right here," Kane said. "Listening or not, we still don't know what the hell he's saying. If he wanted us to gain insight, he would hand us the fucking lead, but he's not doing that."

"Really?" Jade asked, too weary to fight but not willing to concede. "I'm not so sure he didn't do exactly that. Whoever is at the center of this, it started back with Nickolas's father. He had direct ties with the Candy Store owner. The other letter confirms it. The 'I was his' part. His father. It tracks; someone from that timeline is calling the shots. This all started back then."

"Then why was Machias targeted?" Kane asked, not looking for an answer but connecting the pieces and players out loud. "Whoever did this had to predict it'd bring heat."

"Jack's death brought the heat, and I don't think we can assume they expected his involvement. If she's right, and buddy she usually is, the part we need to fear is that even Nicky wants them beheaded," Tex said, directing his attention on Kane. "He hired an assassin, from god knows where to guarantee the Candy Store hit was a success. And since it was, he may be checking the next name on the list. Having his goals align with ours in allocating blame? Well, folks, that ain't making me sleep better."

THIRTY-SIX

Max followed early morning sunshine lighting the stone pathway leading to the Dutch door at the side of Amy and Errie's renovated home, his heart sinking recognizing the alteration of the steel replacement. Safety measures abound at all of the homes owned by the Major Crime Division members, her included. Jade, Kane, Jackson, and even Grey employed new methods of monitoring, protecting, and defending their private worlds from the dangerous one that spilled over too easily. Hell, Jackson owned so many weapons Max was certain he could launch a full-scale military attack if necessary. Establishing his practice in Shadow Hook and a lifetime of memories and clients, Max never would've imagined it a place where regular locks were simply not sufficient to keep his community safe. Lately it seemed everyone had been transformed by uncomfortable realizations that tested their foundations.

Walking in when Errie opened the door, he hoped not to find any new ones today but expected to be disappointed.

"Dr. Max," Errie said, stepping carefully aside, her leg in a brace after a recent corrective surgery. "Please come in. Amy is out picking up ingredients for me."

"Thank you. How is the leg doing? With Amy on leave I don't hear updates as often." Max relished seeing Errie in good spirits. She earned the admiration of all Amy's fellow officers with her resilience in surviving the not-so-distant attack on her life. She earned their love far earlier in the relationship by being Errie.

She waved him ahead into the family room and followed behind. "No dancing in my future, but I should be able to kick someone's ass about it in a few months."

"Glad to hear some things haven't changed," he joked, referring to her mastery of foul language and knowing she tamed it in his presence. "Can I see where she's been working?"

Errie sighed, studied the hardwood floor for a beat, and then pointed to the sunroom at the end of the hall. "Brace yourself, Doc. It's like Van Gogh and Michelangelo swapped paint for a pen in there. Tormented talent."

Max's smile drew tight imagining the challenges Errie was enduring while Amy, forced off work, delved into her former case around the clock here at home. Her inability to close the case in her own mind was what brought Max to their door. "I figured," he said, turning the corner into a cascade of index cards, brutal evidence photos, and page after page of manic notes.

He figured but missed the mark, the wall covered from floor to ceiling and end-to-end was worse than expected by double. Pointing at the wreckage, he asked, "Do you know—"

"Shit no. Not a damn thing and I don't want to. Have enough PTSD of my own to work through. I don't come past the entrance. Except to hand off food or messages. Their lot is a special breed. I love 'em all to death but understanding the way they think is a whole pot of hellfire jambalaya I couldn't swallow. Good luck. Amy should be back in ten. I have meds to take and a Zoom instruction to prepare so if you're okay?"

"Oh, yes. Don't let me keep you. I'll wait for her here if that's all right," he said, his eyes scanning for an area to sit and finding none.

"Have at 'er. Holler if you need anything or you begin drowning in fucking paper and can't find your way out. I'll send her back when she arrives."

Errie departed quick enough for Max to recognize this wasn't her favorite place in their home, definitely one she avoided. He couldn't blame her. The scene was macabre and overpowering in all the wrong ways. But to understand how to help Amy he was willing to look at the picture she'd painted as grim as it appeared on first glance.

Watching where he stepped, the floor littered and unrecognizable, he neared the wall and found a space cleared. Stepping into Amy's shoes, his eyes traced the evidence making sense of the patterns existing there. It wasn't delusional rantings. Amy dissected the Redeemer's victims, Nickolas Leigh's victims, their backgrounds dating to childhood, for clues to why he'd chosen them and who associated could harbor revenge for their deaths.

On the surface it appeared she was meticulously seeking any hint to lead her to uncover the individual responsible for the attempted murder suffered on Nickolas while he was comatose in hospital fighting to survive the bullet wound from Kane's gun. The fatal shot would've killed him if not for the expert efforts of the EMTs and team of trauma doctors.

On a second, educated, analysis, Max couldn't fathom Amy's true purpose for dissecting the data when she, in fact, admitted to the crime. Watching the massacring he created and having intimate knowledge of his life-sustaining machine, Amy schemed to kill the serial killer while hospital staff ran ragged fighting to save her brothers and sister in arms.

Amy crossed the line and though none who knew were willing to admit it, speak of it, or allow that truth to impact her legally, Max was standing in the destruction it caused her mind.

Reading a document he recognized as a clinical analysis of an injectable substance he wondered if Amy stumbled onto facts previously missed and haunting her. The cocktail deciphered was found in trace amounts in the blood of two of the murder victims. Max knew this because Amy wrote exactly that on the bottom of the page with a further note that read, "speak to Sarah." Max noted this and moved on scanning the wall.

Under a heading labeled *Suicidal Tendencies* substantial evidence filtered down to conclusions, all of which said each woman Nickolas handpicked attempted to end their life on more than one occasion previous to his capture of them. The only one who didn't but fell victim to him was the one who lived, Jade.

It dawned on Max who Sarah was, the victim left in a coma that recently woke from it. Sarah was the only one besides Jade to survive after being marked for death but, as Max saw it, the sole survivor wounded but never questioned.

Not grasping everything before him but absolutely clear how Captain Grey would see it, Max snapped multiple photos, then stored his phone as level footsteps approached. They couldn't be Errie's.

"You care to explain," he said, spinning to face Amy as she walked in, her expression guarded.

"Would love to when I reach an understanding myself, as of now I can't say where the evidence will lead," she said, scouring the area and shaking her head resolute in her objective.

"Okay, let me put this another way. What the hell am I looking at?" Max asked, his patience dissolving in the presence of a case they celebrated closing and feared every moment it remained open.

"Motive," Amy said, setting down a paper coffee cup he hadn't noticed. "He granted me freedom while holding the facts to send me downriver. When you examine his victims, those with a desire to live, you recognize a pattern. They all did. I don't think it was our involvement or fate that caused that." Amy walked the wall, touching photos of evidence from all the murdered victims. "I think he knew and granted them life."

"Amy, why are you delving, and off the deep end to put it mildly, into a closed case that is long over with justice in the courts?" he asked, tracking her movements to the far end of the board where a horrific photo hung of a male victim. "And what the hell is that? That's not from the Redeemer case."

Amy's voice hardened when she spoke. It gained venom with each word. "Because he isn't done and this isn't over! This is from the Candy Store raid yesterday!" She was ranting while she smacked the photo. "And this undesirable motherfucker had connections with

Nickolas Leigh's biological monster. And I believe…" She shuffled through a pile of documents with rage fueling her hands. "I believe Leigh had him eviscerated to exact revenge for some past crime and to hand him over to us…well to Jade."

"What past crime?" Max asked, coming closer to examine the scene in the photo.

"How the hell would I know?" she said, staring up at the wall as if pulling from it a hidden message.

"Why the hell—" Max fought to follow her logic but feared interrupting would throw her off course and she was clearly down a dangerous road.

"I don't know yet, Max, but I'm damned determined to figure it out," she said, still foraging for something in the mess. "Have you read his letters to Jade?" she asked while handing over a copy with every word scrutinized.

"I have," he said, hesitant to say more and risk influencing her opinion. "He thinks he is providing her assistance."

"He doesn't just think it, Max, he is. Like he did bailing me out of a potential attempted murder charge. The only reason for that is Jade. It's what she'd want him to do and that is why he did it. He is winning her over, one move at a time. And what I fear is him returning to do it in person." Amy wasn't facing him, but when she swiveled, he read true terror in her eyes.

"He is paralyzed from the waist down, under medical and judicial supervision, and restrained from exiting any care facility rehabilitating him." Max heard his voice ring back unconvinced.

"You sure?" Amy said, collapsing on a stack of boxes. "'Cause everything I've spent countless hours sifting through and unearthing only confirms he was always way ahead of us. And Max…" She gazed up at him, defeated. "Nothing has changed."

Max stood there absorbing the room and the chaos. "You realize I can't clear you to go back, not with…" He shook his head, his hands palm up holding the disaster in front of him. "This. This is worrisome on so many levels."

Amy's head was down, her eyes studying papers on the floor. "Yeah, I figured you'd say that."

"This time was for you to heal. You're not doing that and no matter what is on the horizon you're better meeting it intact." He crossed the distance between them and stood beside her. "You are a valued member of the team and they, we, would all like you back."

Amy met his gaze, her eyes glazed with a film of pain. "I know Nickolas Leigh isn't done with us," she whispered. "And I don't know how but he's connected to this latest case. I can feel it."

"I know, his grandfather, the judge, and his mother and I were good friends once. Nickolas is in a wheelchair fighting for mobility probably at a cutting-edge, expensive, Swiss rehab center. You need to be concerned with here and now." He walked out the way he came in leaving her to process but the evidence she gathered wasn't without merit and that was what he planned to submit to Grey, along with the photos he'd taken. The possibility Amy was correct and Leigh's goal was to reinsert himself into their lives wasn't a consideration Max chose to entertain. It didn't mean she was wrong.

THIRTY-SEVEN

A hurricane landed, ripping and smashing every solid foundation of the enterprise Barracutta dedicated twenty years to perfect into ruin. And countering with a shitstorm of wreckage to crush those responsible was the only directive capable of righting things. Surveying the factory from the highest perch in admiration of the seamless process one couldn't see past its inevitable end. A timeline existed and couldn't be altered. Days. Not weeks or months. Holding the illusion for days would set the last shipment out to sea and leave Barracutta a break in services to relocate to one of the other three properties on standby. This was not the first brush with the law, rivals, or unforeseen complications like a global fucking pandemic that threatened the business and altered travel methods overnight. If you were good, you adapted. And that was why alternatives existed to pivot at a moment's notice. Losses were an unfortunate consequence but there were ways to regain and Barracutta knew them all. Balancing the books on the other side would wait. Turning the tide on enemies would not.

The gang's execution of the Candy Store owner and the way in which they handled his termination, public and marking the house where his business survived unbeknownst to police for over a decade and a half, annihilated that particular branch of criminality. But not just for the criminal eviscerated and positioned for display.

They'd cut off a key avenue integral to Barracutta's organization without thought or word. A hidden gem on a street where every resident remained conveniently blind and mute to the flow of product in and out of the house, be it drugs, or juveniles awaiting processing. Instead of stashing product there under instruction within a system of order and compliance, new methods would need to be sought out, tested, vetted, and established. And all demanded time and money with no guarantee of success. This equated to one of dozens of complications sure to eat into the profit margin and heighten risk and stress levels in every phase.

The mere thought made Barracutta's jaw clench, ricocheting shards of pain out like an internal Tesla experiment gone awry.

No place to house the girls. No way to tame them with drug addiction, no time for it to take hold. And no conditioning meant no compliance leading to nothing but trouble. Loading a group of placid pawns onto cargo freight was difficult enough but if fight remained in any one it could turn the whole lot rebellious. It never ended well.

And this wasn't the worst sin for the gang. Their haste in retaliation left no opportunity to ensure any trace evidence capable of tying the house to Barracutta's much larger organization was destroyed. Yes, the inferno raging on the back of a combustible chemical composition burned at such a high heat and for a duration that left only ashen land behind it, but what of survivors? At least two made it to the hospital alive. If either one had anything to say it threatened the entire operation.

All they had to do was hold and deliver safely one girl. To say they failed didn't even scratch the surface. The first problem was they still possessed her and no one outside knew where.

According to the informant working out of the WarMakers no one inside did either. The Ferryman who collected her for transport ran a tight ship guarding his cargo and the safe harbor he governed.

The informant could be trusted; he couldn't talk or walk ever again but the information was solid.

All these factors gave reason for swift exacting measures to be taken, but they'd have to wait behind the most immediate threat.

Someone uninvited breached Barracutta's cyber security crawling in and watching through the camera optics of the factory, in his own backyard. Wanting to know how such a thing was possible fell far behind the desire to ensure the backdoor closed hard on their unwelcome visitor. Barracutta decided preferably with his or her body on one side and head on the other. Home turf was not to be shared and invading it at a time when so much had already been violated, well it begged to meet the sum of Barracutta's rage.

Pushing off the catwalk railing outside the office, Barracutta drew a deep breath and turned face back to the nerd on the computer tasked with backtracking their intruder's pathway into the source. Entering to hover too close over the boy's shoulder, allowing hot breath to fall over him, was an intentional intimidation. No time for drawn-out tactics, Barracutta set the rules. "Find what I need and you're free. I'll instruct my men to drive you to the edge of the nearest town and you can find a way back to your life from there. Don't and you're in a shipping container for a very long, devastating ride across the ocean to an end far more unpleasant than you could imagine. Understood?"

"Yes. Of course. Whoever crept in is not good, they're the best I've seen in years," he said, nervous but impressed, nonetheless.

"And you are better, correct?"

"No. I'm not but I'm unconventional. I skirted around the regular searches and looked for the easiest way in." The kid was proud and forgetting where he was.

"Don't waste my time."

"No. I found him. See here?" He pointed to a line of code. Barracutta hated computers, technicians even more. Seeing or not, the kid was prompted to continue. "The easiest way to hack a system is to be the one who built it and build in a backdoor for emergencies. It was a long shot but you don't have a mole. It was just your cybersecurity designer. Probably checking on efficiencies."

"And who is he? An address and you're on your way home," Barracutta said, expecting the question to be met by excuses as to why unearthing an identity wasn't possible.

"His name is Dylan Barclay; the address is in a nice neighborhood. I linked it to the directional search so you have multiple routes in. It should be in the inbox of your phone."

Barracutta checked the house cell phone. A new link waited with name, address, and directions. The kid was more of a complication to keep around and witnessed very little of the true business conducted there. Two of the most trusted men were given instructions. "Get him out of here. Drop him at the bus station a town away with cash and no identification. And wait until he is on one out of town." Breathing too close again the kid was whispered at. "If you remember anything of who I am or what we do I will find you again and there will be no negotiating for freedom."

"Yes. Of course. I know nothing," he said, tremors in the tone sold his conviction.

"Now out!" In seconds, the room cleared while the address and name glowed from the phone screen. Waving in a couple of the handpicked special guards, Barracutta shared the information and thoughts on exactly what was expected to happen.

"In daylight?" one asked. "I'm only clarifying boss not questioning."

"Yes, daylight. And call me when it's done."

The other, senior guard eyed the younger then asked, "Have you any directive for us on your decision on the other issue? We could swing by on our way back if that works for you?"

Barracutta liked this guard and labeled him number one for good reason. He waited patiently, averting his eyes and training the others to follow his seamless subtle actions demanding respect for the boss and the hierarchy of the enterprise. They were all expendable but few, like him, earned their place.

"Mm-hmm. Call me when the first is complete and I'll instruct from there. The problem isn't with the decision, it stands, it's the timing that requires consideration." Barracutta finished speaking, the guard nodded and ushered the other out ahead of him.

Daughtry was a marked man but as Barracutta saw it so were many others. An expert multitasker proficient at bringing order to even the diabolical, Barracutta retreated from the oversight office and made for the back elevator. Regular personnel acting as cover vacated the property under notice of a possible gas leak inspection, leaving outer guards at every entrance to the main building and the property as a whole.

Frustrated to be forced to abandon a space that worked so efficiently, the factory's newest edition beckoned for a visit even if it would never serve the purpose inspiring its development long term. The industrial elevator doors opened to a guard who waited to assess its occupants, twisted back into a monitoring stance, and lowered his weapon. The other one awaiting Barracutta's visit walked over, head bowed in acknowledgment, and said, "It's ready whenever you are, boss. Everything set up as requested."

"Nothing more to be done?" Barracutta asked.

"No, except for you to try it out. Nothing until tomorrow. What time would you like me to send the cleanup crew in?" he asked, his face tense but revealing little in the way of emotion.

"Your name?" Barracutta asked.

"Frank."

"Frank, can you be here tonight at…say, seven? I'd like you to look after things. The fewer involved, the better. You understand?"

"Yes. I'll be at the gate quarter to and here at seven," he said, still with no hint of remorse.

"That works nicely. You can both take second position now at the outer yard." The heads of both men bobbed in agreement and they filed out of sight.

Barracutta stood at the entrance of the concrete steps leading into the new below-floor safety enclosure feeling relief wash over. Everything was going to hell but there was a calm knowing the plan in place assured a list of enemies would arrive first into its depths. Meantime, given a three-hour window before activating part one of the shutdown and relocation, it was only right to make the most of the hard labor that designed and built the soundproof, impenetrable torture chamber.

No one called it by that name but it fit.

Testing the coded lock, Barracutta entered the date of the first sale for exploitation under the new regime, 04, 17,13, and listened as tumblers aligned and suction released a burst of air ahead of the opening door. The room boasted a state-of-the-art air filtration system. Still, notes of cement dust lingered. The temperature dipped inside. Barracutta sensed a waft of warmth following the path in until the door resealed and it mixed with the interior air and dispersed. The silence inside would've been impressive if not for the moaning.

It was endless.

The female chosen, selected the night before after attempting to climb the interior wall of the gravel holding tank, hung from a rack Barracutta designed personally. High enough off the ground to prevent contact and extended for optimal positioning but damn uncomfortable, excruciating over long periods of time. The product, delivered and restrained, had been waiting for seven hours. No direct harm had come to her other than the circumstance surrounding her current pose.

That Barracutta insisted on handling alone.

And the metal table affixed to the far sidewall offered an array of options on its surface. Having the tools of trade out in the open freely without fear of being snatched up by any unruly occupant was liberating. Barracutta smoothed a hand over each item, cataloging that all on the list existed. Clinking the chain of a nunchaku against a set of typical metal handcuffs alerted the dangling wall art to a second presence in the room. Her breathing quickened, the moaning intensified, and her eyes, landing on Barracutta, became wild.

Reaching for a hairbrush sitting inconspicuously at the end closest to the girl, Barracutta dangled it between two fingers and closed the distance. The wall art came to life squirming against her restraints in vain.

"Why waste your energy fighting, my dear?" Barracutta breathed the words in the girl's ear as she struggled to inch away.

"We have uninterrupted hours together. And one truth I will share with you is this…" Raising the brush to her eye level and releasing a wickedly wide grin, the body pushed back as if fighting to be absorbed into the concrete wall. "You will definitely need to conserve your strength if you have any hope of surviving me."

THIRTY-EIGHT

Jade woke unable to catch her breath, jolted into consciousness by a vision of Machias, her beautiful young face imprinted over Jade's mother's on the day of her murder. Lifted out of the house by then Detective Grey back when Jade was eleven; he said to close her eyes tight. She meant to but her body betrayed her in shock and she glimpsed the scene. A fraction of a second and the violent destruction of the most beautiful human she had and would ever know burned into her psyche forever. Asleep, in the throes of a nightmare brought on by a detrimental mix of the case, tension, and exhaustion, the face she glimpsed on the corpse transformed into Machias. Shuttering in gulps of air, she threw her long legs over the edge of the bed and focused on the view of the backyard her and Kane loved so much. Slowly its calming effect returned her breathing to normal but the brutal vision remained clear in her mind.

Like her mother, Machias was a rare human being who never deserved the fate she'd been handed. Jade studied the case enough to know the differences between the two were as numerous as the similarities but she cared about only one.

Machias, because of her value to the men who snatched her from the world, was alive and recoverable.

Jade turned to watch Kane sleeping glad this time her bad dream didn't wake him. She drank in the cadence of his breathing, the rise and fall of his strong chest, the comfort of their home and the view to strengthen her before the war resumed. It struck her; she'd never witnessed the memory of her dying mother with another's face before. Kane told her every woman she ever fought to save wore her face and metaphorically speaking he hadn't been wrong. But this, the actual switching of one for the other, hit hard.

The girl at the center of the case had shifted and locked inside a place in Jade's heart she couldn't break her free from.

Leaning back onto their bed, running a hand across Kane's shoulder, she kissed his neck and slid away to head for the shower. They were expected back at the shop at noon and it was half past ten. Angling to stand, she lost momentum. Kane countered her rise, catching her at the waist with one strong arm wrapped and drawing her backward.

"You don't sneak away that easily," he said, shifting to kiss her. How she wanted to fall back into his arms and stay. She kissed him deeply, maybe too deeply, but pulled back and out of reach.

"No time, my love," she said. "We have a stop to make before the shop. I'll be out of the shower in ten. We need to be gone in twenty."

"I can do a lot in twenty minutes," he said, his smile infectious.

"I love you," she said, before closing the door. "The things I sacrifice," she whispered to no one.

Catching her reflection in the mirror she watched the smile fade. But knowing how the morning started, how the previous night ended, she considered Kane her miracle maker. He brought the light to her darkest corners and she allowed the feeling to sink in to memory to revisit when she needed it.

The problem was knowing she would.

Like the day beyond the windowpane, overcast and growing darker under thick rolling clouds, Jade sensed a blackness seeping in.

It didn't happen in every case or, if it did, was fleeting during the most difficult challenges. Today it claimed territory with a force that said it sought a new permanent home. She didn't know quite how they'd fight off the oppressive criminal undercurrent, only that they must.

Twenty minutes later, she typed an address into the truck's navigation system while being stared down by Kane. "Here." She pointed at the onboard map. "It's on the way."

"Are you planning to explain what was more important than—"

"Quit pouting and drive fast. Axel sent me a request and I plan to deliver. I promise to make up for our lost morning too," she said, pulling on her seat belt.

"I promise to hold you to it," Kane replied, selecting the most direct route and dropping the pedal.

Eighteen minutes later they arrived in an upscale area of newly constructed walk-ups. Dylan Barclay's wouldn't be difficult to identify given the abundance of security cameras around the landing to the front door. The door was set back so Jade couldn't see it from street level, but two cameras monitoring the stairs up and the landing entrance hung in clear view.

"The one on the left," she said, unbuckling. "With all the security."

"Smart kid," Kane said, jumping out. "So…unexpected welfare check?"

"I thought if we arrived without warning we'd get his honest reactions."

"Agreed. The kid designs high-tech cybersecurity systems. You never know he may have captured more than he suspects. How did Callum's boy convince him to search the dock cams for us?" Kane asked as they closed the distance to Barclay's stairs.

"Onyx." Jade swung her head back to raise her eyebrows at him. Scanning him from head to toe, she loved the way he walked. His cool guy saunter.

"Are you serious? The coffee you keep telling me about?"

"Yep," she said, this time not turning but focusing her eyes dead ahead and up the landing. Each riser she cleared brought more of the entrance into view. With three steps to go she glimpsed the contemporary front door slightly ajar. On the second from last she saw its splintered lock. She cleared the last riser in a full-out run. "S.H. Unit officers require assistance, 10-64, dispatch backup to Barclay residence, 1311 Lake Docks Road Unit 17," Jade barked into her radio notifying the shop of a crime in progress, glanced back at Kane while pulling her weapon, and, seeing him armed, pushed through the smashed doorframe.

You never knew what waited on the other side but always hoped for the best. Today, that hope plummeted. The entrance to the home opened up to what planners would label a family room but in Barclay's case had been adapted to a computer hive. And the hive had been raided and decimated. Jade's feet slid on broken screens, shattered parts, and blood. But the scene paled in comparison to the sound of the boy dying. A gurgling, raspy, doomed battle for breath drew her.

Her eyes scanned the scene absorbing the evidence of a brutal attack and tracing its path to a pair of feet visible on the floor at the tail end of the kitchen island. Blood dripped from its top and mixed with coffee grounds. Tins tumbled off a coffee bar shelf, broken in the struggle littered the floor. Raising her head to the shattered window wall, she caught one boot and the gloved hand of a perpetrator fleeing out the back around a cement privacy barrier and motioned to Kane.

"Go, go," she said. "I've got him."

Diving into the mess behind the counter, Kane flew by in pursuit of the attacker. "Kolton in 10-43 out back of building, heading due west on foot. Victim down inside home. Requesting ambulance. He's a kid, guys!" Jade released her radio to assist the young man on the hardwood, but nearing realized that time may have passed.

"Dylan, I'm with you. You are not alone." She spoke not sure if he could hear her, the beating he sustained so violent his face was left distorted, his skull visibly crushed, and thick matter mixed with blood dyed his once golden locks into matted chunks amid crimson clumps of destruction. Leaning close his ragged breathing drifted up weak and slowing.

"Fuck," she cursed the room and reached out finding and

holding his left hand. "I'm Detective Jade Carmichael, Dylan. I'm a friend of Axel's and I really want you to hang on." The words left her lips and his hand clench hers, briefly, with little strength, but he'd heard her.

"There are so many people in this town who love you. Axel loves you and he really needs you to survive this," she said. Dylan clenched again. He knew that too but it held little sway with the state of his body and its chance of survival.

He separated two fingers from the others. "Two? There were two attackers?" His hand bared down on hers, and her head whipped up scanning the space surrounding them. If the other attacker chose to stick around, she was more than happy to fill him with lead. The house was silent, already mourning its owner.

With her free hand, she accessed her radio. "Two attackers, possibly both on foot." Kane was alone in pursuit of a hitman who evidence said had lethal mitts and reinforcements.

THIRTY-NINE

Kane sprang through the shattered floor-to-ceiling window, touched down skimming a foot across the smashed glass coating the grass, and caught the cement separation barrier with one hand propelling him out of Jade's line of sight and after a killer. Dylan was a kid and a good one, and that was motivation enough. Between protocol and training there existed a fire that ignited when a detective faced down an adversary such as this. It exploded inside solidifying every bone, muscle, organ and cell into a conductor with one goal. Catch the criminal.

The residential area was new, and having never seen it before, Kane weaved by one half wall of cement to find a maze of others and the perpetrator two ahead. He didn't tell his legs to pump faster, his feet to channel the best halfback the Eagles ever signed, or his upper body to take on moves like a young Ali in the ring. It did all this without prompting. The guy deked left thinking it'd trip Kane up at the last second to follow. Instead, Kane flew over top of the barrier coming down closer than the guy expected but a hand's length away from grabbing him.

Swiping a decorative yard statue, the guy pitched it without aiming. Kane watched the stone break as he angled left then right to avoid its pieces and the plume of ceramic dust it sent into the air.

Too slow, asshole.

Kane never pursued a criminal without becoming a data storage bank on the fly. Dylan's attacker was five-ten to five-eleven, shy of six feet, black hair, no gray, young, he sported a tattoo incorporating a wing on his left forearm and was still donning the gloves on hands that beat young Dylan.

"Stop!" Kane yelled, closing in and raising his weapon. "Police, I won't warn you again and I'm a fucking great shot!"

The perp gambled, ducking as he dove over a waterfall feature's boulders. Kane, running with his head up and eyes open glimpsed the signs of unfinished construction receding down the embankment behind the feature. Slowing up to brace, he peered behind the side of the feature's rock wall and saw the criminal fighting to navigate a gravel and boulder covered, half-built rock garden against too much speed.

Oh this was brilliant, he thought, aiming his weapon.

The reverberation from the blast jolted the guy midstride, but the ricochet of the bullet off the rock ahead of him caught him in the calf muscle of his right leg plummeting him with full momentum into rocks below. His screams echoed among them as Kane approached.

"Don't move or you'll have more than a limp to deal with," Kane said. The guy was disoriented and covered in injuries from crashing hard against the broken stones. Kane had him cuffed without resistance but had to stand over him to pick him off the ground, dislodging the tangled mess of his body from rock. About to lift him, he sensed eyes on him and stared up. Dead ahead, lower on the back of the hill where the ground leveled out and natural forest left unchanged by the developer resumed, stood a man.

A second attacker waiting on the first.

"Fuck," Kane said, knowing steering through a virtual quarry on a hillside so an armed assassin could take aim and blow your head clean off before you made it halfway down wasn't a wise option. "Detective Kolton, back side of the residence, rock quarry due west. I have eyes on a second attacker at the forest tree line. I need backup from the undeveloped side to block his exit. And eyes in the sky."

The shop called back confirming both had been dispatched on Carmichael's orders and was within range. They hadn't signed off when he heard the rumble of the chopper closing in, its path set to fly directly over head of him and the stooge he had his foot on. As it did, he waved signaling the trajectory of the second man and watched them drop in pursuit.

"Your partner better stand down or they'll shoot him down," Kane said, as the deafening noise of the propeller blades dissipated.

"He won't," the guy said, turning his bloodied face sideways to speak without eating rock dust. "You catch us we're dead either way."

"Well then I'll make sure you live long enough to shift loyalties," Kane spoke, scanning the distance around them for sharpshooters. The guy wasn't marked as a WarMakers gang member and history never had them attack or involve youth in their business. This was something else. An organization much more dangerous and far less scrupulous. "Tell me who hired you and I'll get you in alive and request a protective move."

"Unless it's to Monaco, you can't protect me even if my knowledge is worth the effort," he said, spitting blood out across the rocks. "This job was my way out and look how that went. I never wanted to hurt a kid. There's no escape for me but a hole in the ground now that I've talked to you."

"You haven't even been brought in," Kane said, his eyes ever watchful surveying all sides but knowing their low placement among the large rocks made targeting them difficult and sheltered them from a sharpshooter's line to a clear shot if one was hiding low in the forest. Open, grubbed land on either side of the rocky hill prevented other options. At least the guy drove them to a defendable position.

"Doesn't matter. I'm dead. No way around it now."

Kane switched positions, leaning down to make eye contact

suspecting what hung in the balance. "I am your way out and the only one."

"You stop it and I'll confirm the head of the enterprise," he said, then turned his face back collapsing it on the ground, bloody and defeated. "If you survive."

Kane didn't like the way the comment landed. The man at his feet hadn't been in custody for more than mere seconds and he fully expected to be killed. A response reserved for those in deep criminal organizations with connections and defenders everywhere. Kane's mind began running down possibilities and didn't make it past the obvious when the sound of shots fired down from the chopper rang back from the forest.

"See what I'm saying," the guy said, resting his cuffed hands over the back of his head as if awaiting execution. "We're all dead and that means you too."

FORTY

J ade recognized the echo of heavy cowboy boots approaching from the stairs of the walk-up through its opened door. Jackson was never one to saunter in lightly to any scene but this time relief came with every footfall that brought him closer. "Jade, I'm here," he called out from the foyer. "You're surrounded by us and Kane has one cuffed and the other fled the area under chopper pursuit and won't get far."

"Ambulance?" she asked, timing Dylan's pulse at his wrist.

"Pulling in," Tex said, following a path in to meet her.

"Is this over the camera footage?" she whispered close to Dylan, knowing but requiring his identifying for future prosecution.

His hand gripped and then fell slack too quickly. Jade heard the ambulance's sirens reverberating up from the parking lot. "They're here, Dylan. Please don't stop fighting. I've been where you are, don't leave." Water dropped onto the side of Dylan's bloody, muddied face, and Jade realized it had fallen from her eyes. He was a kid. This was despicable and her heart broke. If they checked on him sooner, arrived ten minutes earlier, put him in protective custody or never involved him at all...

The thought hit her hard as EMTs flooded in beside her, ignoring the wreckage to do their job. She didn't want to release his hand; sensing doing so would cut the only tie linking him to this world. As they braced him for transport, sliding a body board under him, supporting broken bones and stabilizing his head, she spoke through their movements. "Dylan, you helped in this fight. I know you saved lives and I want to thank you for that when you recover, keep fighting for all of us."

The paramedics lifted him and Jade put one hand over and one under his escorting them out, not willing to let go until the doors closed. To carry him they skirted by the coffee bar angling for the front door and the ambulance backed in at the foot of the stairs. With the mess of coffee smearing her as she pushed out of the way, Dylan squeezed her hand. Tighter than before or perhaps she assumed his strength increased having been surprised by it. He released as quickly, his hand so slack it slipped from hers.

She reached to reclaim it but Tex stopped her, gently ushering her aside to take her position and help lift and carry the dying boy quicker into waiting transport. Wiping her eyes, she walked behind them, digesting the scene outside. A gathering of police vehicles, undercover and labeled, and officers assisting Kane with the apprehended trash, cuffed, shot in the leg, and shoved into a back seat for transport. The less trained part of her wanted to pull her gun and riddle him with bullet holes. Instead she turned to watch Dylan be loaded, hooked up to an IV and monitors, and prepped for blood transfusion.

From the corner of her eye she saw Axel fly out of a still-moving truck, door thrown open, abandoning it adrift and coasting to rest against a parking block. Racing to intercept, she bound off the steps for the grass hillside flanking it. Sliding more than running to its bottom, she pummeled into him midstride. Knocking him off his trajectory to reach Dylan and the ambulance. Catching Axel by the jacket, she pleaded, "No. Axel, you don't want to see—"

Axel pulled his arms back in a flash, dipping his shoulders as the jacket came free and Jade was left holding it as he ran for his friend.

"I'm responsible for this," he said, springing into the back of the ambulance before the doors closed. "I'm not leaving him."

"Christ," Jade breathed it as Tex braced her and the two stood watching its doors slam shut, lights swirling as the driver punched its speed onto the main roadway. "That kid doesn't make it and the other one will blame himself for the rest of his life."

Her words landed as Kane met them. Tex's eyes held a wealth of sorrow but it wasn't only for the boy. He knew she was speaking from experience and chances were in the space of a couple hours she wouldn't be alone.

Axel was about to join her.

"You have one. Any news on his partner?" Jade asked Kane who appeared no worse for wear.

"Shot and killed," Kane said, lacking remorse. "Idiot shot at the chopper's gunner."

Without acknowledging the weighty stares of her partners, Jade stomped across the pavement for the cruiser readying to transport one of the men responsible for the attack on young Dylan. The area swarmed with first responders, all of them engaged in aspects of processing and protecting the scene. Clouds remained overhead but a break in them cast a slice of sunlight brightening the lot, reflecting off the roof of the car as she met it. Not knowing but assuming, if she had questions for the criminal she'd earned the right to ask, Kane and Tex granted her space and hadn't followed. They didn't start running until after she threw open the back door, grabbed the guilty assailant by an arm cuffed behind his back, slammed him to the pavement, and started kicking the shit out of him.

"He isn't even twenty, you sick motherfucker!" Jade cursed over him with every kick, aiming her steal-toes for optimal impact. "He had nothing to do with any of this, you piece of shit."

She landed three solid boots into him before the officers in front leaped out, hesitant but knowing their obligation. "He'll pay for this," one said, tentative but moving to intervene. "We got him. He's going in."

"Not without fucking liver damage," she said, landing a final kick before Kane lifted her off the man while Tex plucked him from the ground and tossed him back into the locked back seat of the cruiser.

"Go for Christ's sake," Tex barked at the officers, who ducked into the car and sped away.

"What the hell are you thinking," Kane said at an octave meant for her ears only.

"I'm not thinking," she said, catching her breath as the ignition of rage burned down and the volume of her voice rose. "I'm *feeling* a twenty-year-old kid with huge potential was beaten almost to death and I'm *feeling* pissed about it!"

"We all are," Tex said, locking eyes with her. "So are we heading back inside to find evidence to end this shit or staying out here until we make the news again?"

Jade yanked free of Kane's grasp and stormed up the steps and back inside the house. Stopping abruptly before crossing into the kitchen, she analyzed the scene. The perps entered through the back, smashing their way in. It appeared they grabbed Dylan in the kitchen, possibly right off the chair with its back to the glass. A computer tech, Dylan may have had noise-canceling earbuds in and never suspected a thing until they were inside and on him. A path of debris cut from there to the front room so it was likely they dragged him in, and by the wreckage and blood, questioned and tortured him there.

Kane pointed to a blood smear connecting the room to the area where Jade found Dylan in the kitchen. "He may have crawled his way there. Searching for a phone to call for help?"

Jade nodded agreement while Tex held a cell phone between gloved fingers. "One here so it's possible. Won't know 'til we run numbers."

"Did he speak or—"

Jade cut Kane off answering, "No, not possible by the head trauma but he squeezed my hand. He heard me. That's how I knew there were two attackers and…"

Careful to preserve the scene and remain on the grid they used previously, Jade neared the coffee bar. Above it an untouched photo of Dylan and his two brothers at a Cuban coffee farm sitting proudly on bags labeled dark roast toasted with clay coffee cups. The encased memory survived the assault but the beaming young man in its center might not. Standing before it she drank up every detail, from the crushed and scattered tins, strewn coffee grounds, smashed cups, and shattered china to the broken upper shelf. Her eyes rested there as Tex crossed over to join her. "How tall is Dylan?" she contemplated. "Slightly shorter than you." She spun Tex to stand in line with the edge of the disheveled counter. "If you were beaten and half-blind…"

Tex, sharing her line of thought, hunched and reached out. "He pulled it down reaching for?"

"Where was the phone?" Kane asked. Tex answered by pointing across the room opposite to where they stood.

Jade searched the ground and soon all three were kneeling just outside the evidence. "What are we looking for?" Tex asked.

"Onyx coffee," Kane said it as Jade located the tin. Taking photos, Tex nodded it was safe to extract and with a gloved hand she lifted it out of the chaos. Throwing napkins from the far end of the table down Jade set the tin in the center. They gathered as she flipped the grounds upside down and watched a flash drive dent the hill of coffee.

Dylan *had* gripped her hand tighter; he was telling her what he fought for and how she could beat their enemies. She prayed he kept fighting until she could bring him results and prove his efforts weren't in vain.

Kane's smile beamed at Jade. "When this is over and we roast their asses to celebrate I'm buying you a truckload of Onyx and, I hope, Dylan a lifetime supply."

As Kane repeated the name a slinky Havana brown cat with electric green eyes leaped out of hiding from a trash can spilling paper all over the floor.

"Damn," Tex said, startled but wanting to calm the pet. "It's okay, buddy, we're the good guys."

The shocked feline scurried to Kane's side, the one among them who preferred dogs. "Really?" he said, staring down at it as it brushed into his leg.

"You called the smart fur bag out of hiding by name," Tex said. "So suck it up and grab Dylan's cat. He's going home with you until the kid recovers."

FORTY-ONE

Riparian mastered the art of listening intently without reaction or interruption while in deep cover and the service. Never a big talker, he found it an easy adaptation. As Machias relived the trauma of growing up knowing Daughtry was violating young girls on the property and there was nothing she or her mother, when alive, could do to prevent it, he found keeping his mouth shut difficult. The bastard deserved to suffer a thousand deaths, slow and painful, one would never suffice but it was all he could give her.

Well, perhaps not all.

When Mac was very little, Lily Lincoln, who always stayed with her in a bedroom upstairs, lined the window with pillows. Mac didn't realize, until Daughtry caught her and proclaimed Machias old enough to learn the consequences for badly behaved girls, Lily was shielding her from screams echoing across their property.

His victims never remained there for long, a day or three at most, before they were picked up and driven away. Never to be seen or heard from again. Mac said her mother would wake the morning after another was lost and begin canning fruits, vegetables, stews or sauces depending on the time of year. Relentless, she wouldn't stop until the shelves in the cellar gained a new row. In her teens Mac decided this was where the idea for the cute labels was born. A tribute to those they couldn't save.

"Cute labels?" Rip asked, finding interest in Lily's process. "Like you colored them or drew pictures for each?"

"Gosh no," Machias said, shaking her head while sitting on top of the table in his room next to the mapping of involved criminals, Daughtry's picture inches from her scarred feet. "My mother would never have allowed me to touch them, the labels. She was never mean. I had coloring books and loads of craft supplies she brought from the church. She said labeling them correctly was incredibly important."

Rip thought for a minute, walking around the table as Mac followed him, spinning on her butt with legs crossed like a gymnast readying to tumble. "What was on the labels?" he asked, collapsing into a rolling chair nearby.

"We came up with names, not real ones but like short form or abbreviations. I have trouble remembering," she said, her head dipping low. "I think because of what happened before. I mean, I won't touch anything in a preservative jar and I'm pretty sure that's not because of the contents. I love jam but won't open the jar. Jack said I require a tester."

Rip pondered this then rolled closer. "You said 'relentless.' Lily did this every time a girl left the property. Without fail?"

"Every time I can recall," she said. Her pretty eyes locking on, he watched her wheels turn deciphering the destination of his train of thought. "What?"

"I have trouble remembering whole events, PTSD from war. It helps if I don't think about it directly just things surrounding the event like what color the kitchen was that she prepared the food in or what spices and smells were your favorite."

"Okay, like a memory trigger game. I can try that." She scooched closer and closed her eyes.

"Don't fall off the damn table," he warned. Sliding her away from its edge.

"Not worried," she said without opening her eyes. "You'd catch me first."

He smiled though she couldn't see it. She grinned mischievously as if sensing his reaction. "Think back to the kitchen," he said. "And know you are completely safe viewing whatever comes."

"I know that part," she quipped.

"You're not focusing," he said.

She peeked at him slyly with one eye, then closed it and settled in her position. "She put me on a café chair so I could watch her. I don't like the smell of cinnamon, more vanilla and eggnog. We should have eggnog; I make it from scratch."

She was veering off topic but he knew better than to interrupt. He gave her space to drop into the memory. "Were there lots of ingredients?" he asked, prompting her.

"It depends on the recipe. I loved her caramelized applesauce. We made it a lot because I ate it during the fall and winter. Appley Ann, Saucy Sahara." Her eyes burst open. "I remember those two."

"Where on the label did Lily write the name?" he asked quickly not allowing the memory to fade.

"In the middle of the front, her handwriting was pretty like calligraphy, below the dates," she said, her eyes peering through him back in time.

"The date canned?" he asked.

Her brow furrowed and she shook her head, staring down at the table but seeing a moment in time. "They don't make sense. They were always backdated. I only know that because we canned once the day before Christmas Eve. I knew it was the next night. She brought me to the church celebration every year and he left us alone. I got presents. The date she put on the jar was five days earlier. Maybe she was making sure we didn't save it beyond its spoil date?"

Rip stood as Machias opened her eyes. Facing the table of amassed evidence he stared at the surveillance photo of Daughtry. "You said he only kept them on the property for a matter of a few days."

She nodded but didn't speak sensing him in contemplation.

Stomping over to his desk, he pulled a burner phone out of the drawer and checked the time. Early enough that gang members wouldn't be filtered into the clubhouse yet. He dialed the number. Titan picked up on the first ring.

"You alone?" he asked.

"Yeah, Gunner and Road Cap on their way in but go," Titan said.

"Can you send me the dates of denied transport from ten years ago or more? The ones rejected by the gang?"

"Yeah. It'll take me a bit," he said.

"Say you think the last was an overlap. Tell them I'm suspicious of this contract and we're back vetting it," Rip instructed.

"Okay. They're already pissed and out for blood over the takedown."

"Good. That may work for us."

"Rip?"

"I may have a way out, stay quiet, bro." Riparian hung up to meet cornflower blue eyes ablaze with questions.

"I knew it!" she said. "You're not a member by choice."

"It doesn't matter," Rip replied, riffling through logs of his own, those he'd managed to put together for the sake of evidence against the gang when he believed there was a way out. He brought back to the table one log cataloging contracts from just before Mac turned six and her mother vanished from her life. Slapping it down near her, he flipped back to a rejected run in December of the previous year. His finger traced the information until coming to rest on a date. "Could that jar have said December nineteenth?"

Machias closed her eyes. When they opened shock altered them, like ice on fire. "Oh my god. She was cataloging the kidnappings."

"I think so. I can't be certain without corroborating evidence but when I hear back from my brother, I'll know more."

He watched as the blue in her eyes shimmered with tears, her body trembled, and she grasped her knees pulling them tight into her.

"You're not going back there until he is no longer a threat," Rip promised. "Until I know who is behind this and they are no longer a threat."

"It's not that," Mac said, breathing through pain where others would sob. "It's the shelf, Rip. I can see the shelf. There were so many jars before she left. If we're right, and I know we are, he has done this a hundred times."

Rip placed a hand gently on her arm coaxing her to stare up. "But never again, Machias."

Her focus locked bravely on him. "Okay," she said. "Never. We won't allow it."

"I have a job for you," Riparian said, pulling the oldest of his journals recording gang transports from when he was first jumped in, and events he backtracked with Titan's help planning to use them as leverage someday. Someday had arrived but now they'd be used to protect the gang, Titan, and Machias.

"What do you need me to do?" Mac asked, eager to be a part of the solution.

"Look at every transport rejected." Rip showed her an example of how he categorized them. "Anyone with a black 'X' here." He handed her a new journal from a package in the drawer. Noticing unused ones, she came over, selecting a black one instead of the brown one he held.

"Black is fitting given what we're doing," she said. "And?"

Rip gave her a pirate's grin and nodded his agreement. "Write down every date chronologically with any associated details and leave space for more information to be added when we have it."

"You're going back there," she said, her face awash with worry. "To see the jars."

"I am. I'll photograph the shelves. Don't worry, Daughtry isn't a threat to me. We'll match as many as we can."

"You're helping the cops," she said, flashing her own pirate's grin to mimic his.

"I am. Well, we are." His computer alerted the search he set up met with results halting further discussion. Without pause, Mac bound off the table and followed him to his desk.

"It found the source," she said, crossing the room.

"It sounds like it," he replied, pulling out his desk chair and pointing to another for her to join him. The Mercedes vehicle's GPS receiver was integrated with a cellular modem; Rip used this against the contactor, transmitting the GPS information to his own server to store and sort through. If they'd been stupid enough to use the vehicle for multiple runs, he'd have record of them all. Better still he was about to see where the vehicle considered home. If that turned out to be a rental lot it wouldn't be particularly helpful. He clicked the link to expand the results of his search, copied the home base address, typed it into a refined location search with satellite view, and zoomed in.

"Well that's not a rental company and it's not a residence or clubhouse," he said, viewing the location from every angle.

"No. It looks like the coast? An industrial area? Can you zoom in to..." Machias pointed to an area of interest on the screen. The real-time satellite feed delivered an increasingly grainy view with lower resolution until the picture distorted beyond recognition. "What?"

"Whoever owns this place doesn't want eyes on it," Rip said, pulling the perspective back to identify nearby landmarks. "They're likely using lasers to counter the imaging."

"Is that..."

"Legal? No. If what they do there is already illegal I guess they're willing to take the risk and blame the distortion on a glitch. It doesn't matter. I know exactly where this is," Rip said, switching locations and resetting. In seconds a new search brought a much clearer picture into view.

"How did you do that?" Mac asked, impressed and curious.

"I'm tapped into a newer satellite equipped with AI tech for clearer resolution but targeting from the nearest property, turning it to face this site's direction."

Mac smiled, studying the screen. "That's industrial. Is that a shipyard?"

"Close," Rip said, tweaking the trajectory slightly. On a second link, he searched through municipal road documents of current construction, centering on the area in question. Before long he was sending information to print out and matching details. "It's a section of the docks currently being used as a staging area for highway construction. And it's close enough to the shipyard to offload victims without ever venturing off the property while restricting access from outsiders." Rip studied the view, printing out imaging from all available sides, until he caught a glimpse of Mac's confused expression. "It's a human trafficking transport site," he explained.

"Where he was sending me," she said, her eyes narrowing as she studied the property. Her face was so close to his, the warmth of her breath tickled over his neck soft and gentle despite her rage. He turned to face her. If she had reason to reject his scar she didn't show it. Reading his thoughts, her eyes drifted over the mangled flesh. "I think it's cool," she said. "Far better to wear them on the outside."

His heart cracked open and he knew he didn't want to let her go. Not to confine or restrict her but because he couldn't protect her at a distance and didn't want her to ever be harmed again. "You know what I'm doing...you'll never see Daughtry again. I am ridding the world of him permanently. No jail time, no apprehension. No chance of parole."

"I know," she said, the blue of her eyes so vibrant they appeared out of sync with the dark subject matter. "And the only thing I'll regret is that I can't do it myself and you're adding his death to your list of burdens."

"I won't consider it a burden," he admitted. "More of an honor. Like it will be to destroy this sick enterprise." He tapped the site of the criminal cohort on the screen. "By the looks of it, it's a big one. Now we know where they are and what they are, it's time we paint a clear picture and share the news."

FORTY-TWO

Nickolas Leigh adjusted his position before the aide wheeled him into the boardroom of waiting judicial officials. Not unlike the intensity of a high-stakes merger or acquisition, the room held an electric undercurrent felt the moment he crossed its threshold. The outcome of this deal though affected by wealth had little to do with it. Instead it was a negotiation for his life, freedom, and future. He wasn't nervous. Nerves were reserved for outcomes that mattered to him and this ultimately didn't but it did to his grandfather, the judge. Claiming the power seat, looking all the man of stature he was even with the eye-patch, he motioned for the aide to seat Nickolas next to him, at his right hand and the table's head. Waiters brought water, coffee, and an assortment of tea to each in attendance, starting with the judge and Nick. Not wanting to disappoint a man who put so much into his rehabilitation, Nick studied for this meeting.

Mastering human behavior hadn't posed a challenge in over a decade.

"We appreciate you all accommodating this meeting to expedite next steps in Nickolas's recovery and placement," the judge began. "I'm assuming you were able to review the outcome of the four medical and psychological in-depth assessments performed over the last six months of rehabilitation. I don't believe, having been performed independently and in confidence at your request, they have left any room for questioning the validity of my initial findings. Nickolas cannot and should not be held accountable legally or morally for actions taking place under the direct and intensely powerful mind-altering drugs forced on him during adolescence and disguised to continue to be consumed without his direct knowledge or intention into his adult life up until and during the period marking the crimes of the so-called Redeemer."

He was good. Nick said nothing, sitting stoic and unreadable but proud beneath it all.

"We all know as lawmakers and upholders there are no grounds for holding a person responsible when it is found that their actions took place under circumstances where personal choice and aware-ness could not be reasonably given. His choice was all but eradi-cated and that is no longer my opinion but a solid fact supported by our behavioral science industry leaders times four. Any opposition to these findings, or can we agree and move forward to decide the outcome from this perspective?"

The faces of those around the table either relaxed into the proceedings in obvious agreement of Leigh Senior's position or faltered lacking the backbone to argue against him. Nick read five for him, three against, but a weak three. Shockingly good odds given the seriousness of the crimes attributed to him.

"What I propose is an extension of the private care with allowance for continued rehabilitation but with the monitoring component left in place, your honor." Nick recognized the man representing the state's position. The tricky part was his career required him to operate in front of the judge on not just this case but also many others. "Acknowledging the strong findings contained here, we still have a multiple homicide case with the families of those slain desiring justice."

"And what is your recommendation when Nick is healthy enough to leave care?" the judge asked, staring down the man.

"At the very least in similar cases—"

"There has never been a similar case to this," a woman representing the joint opinion of the medical experts blurted out. "Really, any directive should come from our side of this equation. And we don't oppose incorporating a monitoring component but not at the expense of Mr. Leigh's mental health. To be incarcerated would completely diminish his ability to heal both physically and mentally."

"I anticipated this would create an impasse so I am proposing a solution I hope we can all arrive in agreement with." The judge spoke while waving in two assistants who entered and prepared a screen at the far end of the room and handed him a remote. After a few minutes of setup, they nodded and bowed back out closing the door behind them. "This is Shadow Lark," he said, filling the screen with a drone sky view of a property on the far outskirts of Shadow Hook. "Located an hour west from the center of town it is a private residence, equipped with security fencing enclosing the thirty-acre parcel of land it sits on, a full-scale monitoring system within, and a trained team of guards. If we could agree to allow my grandson to be transferred here, he would have access to continued rehabilitation, complete privacy, 24-hour care and monitoring while remaining separated from society. This way he is not posing a threat to the community or it to him. No one will know he is there. We can revisit terms every twelve months."

As the faces in the room struggled to absorb the images on the screen, some scribbled notes while watching depictions of the land, AI-enhanced monitoring systems, the guards and their extensive backgrounds with his type of criminal, and fence tests that would deter anyone with half a brain from challenging to break in or out of the perimeter.

A woman Nick couldn't put a name to broke the silence. "So you own this property? Bought and devised this large-scale upscale halfway house just for him?" she asked.

"I don't think that is the concern," the prosecutor chimed in. "The issue is does this work?"

"Yes," Granddad said. "And I'd do it ten times over to protect my family and my town. Consider this a pilot project the state isn't being billed for. With Nick's success I may open Shadow Lark to other individuals deserving of these measures."

Nick sensed the perfect moment to strike, he always had. And this, with all of the decision makers devoid of arguments, was it.

"If I may," he said, waiting on Leigh Senior's nod of approval to continue. "I can only imagine the difficulty, the burden you all carry in making a choice such as this given the severity of the crimes I am associated with and the extreme loss resulting from them. I am not blind to the weight in this room today. I am, however, blind to the reason…the motivation for them. I cannot fathom the how or the why any more than you. I feel nothing but extreme shame and remorse though there is much I cannot remember. For that reason alone, I wouldn't feel just in walking free. Perhaps with monitoring, in time, we'll all have clear answers. Until then, at least at Shadow Lark, I could establish a system of normalcy and heal without risk to anyone." He met the eyes of each person, revealing no fear, judgment, or rage, then said, "Thank you for hearing me, and I will accept your decision with gratitude."

He knew what he was doing. And when they signed off in agreement, he knew what it meant. Not a routine behind a guarded and fenced-off private prison. It meant he would be closer to home. Closer to Jade. Close enough to effect change. And as the members in the room put pen to paper, they sparked new possibilities.

The target was set days earlier, but Nick didn't know then he'd have a front-row seat.

"Thank you," he said as members shook his grandfather's hand and took their leave. "You'll never know what this means."

Nick wasn't surprised, not one of them stopped to question why he dropped the "to me" part of the expression.

FORTY-THREE

Killian, the WarMakers leader or Taoiseach, son of its founder and considered royalty in their hierarchy, walked while thinking especially when the lives of his crew hung in the balance. A routine the gunners and road captains were all familiar with and instantly claimed positions to accommodate his protection. Titan sat across from Killian's head chair in the clubhouse, waiting patiently to answer any questions and be given orders once arrived at. Waiting on Killian was never a comfortable situation but it became less troublesome once trust had been established. The price for trust was loyalty and his brother's services until such time as Killian released the two and both knew, outside of extreme circumstances warranting that trade, he never would.

"We're down two members and a prospect killed or wounded beyond recovery in the hit. And Riparian believes there may be a link between the betrayal of the Candy Store dealer and the contract he's holding?" he asked to confirm, already knowing.

"Yes, Rip said when the contractor called outside of the set time he sensed unfounded anxiety during the call. They questioned his disabling of the location tracker on the Mercedes, their vehicle. Logic said something else tied to the contract, so he started digging," Titan said, speaking to the empty chair as Killian continued pacing. "And this is where it gets costly. The contractor handed the cargo to Rip mid-transport. As always, he dismantled its GPS before hitting his holding site but it didn't come from the location we were told."

"So not from two towns over where the cargo's family paid to reclaim her and was traveling to make the exchange?" he asked.

"There is no family to reclaim," Titan said, choosing his words carefully. "Rip back traced the GPS to a location at the docks and confirmed a massive operation running from a construction site. The kind we don't touch."

With this news, Killian spun on the heels of his biker boots and stomped back to his chair. "Are you saying Riparian is certain this last transport is linked to body sales?"

"Yes. The delivery date for the girl matches a shipping vessel's set-sail date off the coast. He also believes the Candy Store was involved and now so are we." Titan had more to say but let the risk gestate.

Killian shot a glance at his acting president who immediately joined him, sitting at his left. "This is not a deception to facilitate transport. This is tying us to the human trafficking organization running off the docks?"

"Rip is confirming details and has a package to send awaiting your request," Titan said, knowing if the danger was taken seriously, it opened the door to an opportunity they'd waited for. "The sensitive nature of the information puts in jeopardy anyone in its possession so he said it's your call."

"There are three problems as I see it, and Gerard, let me know your view. One, we have men dead because of shady business in our territory and disrespect running rampant, another organization is bringing serious heat to our home turf with trade I don't sanction, and whoever runs it fuckin' lied to pull us into their shit!" Killian wasn't happy.

"Agreed," Gerard said. "And it can't stand."

"There's a consideration Rip said I must voice," Titan said, waiting for the nod to proceed. "If we make any move on them, it will further involve us and the gang will be seen by the watchdogs as equally guilty. The whole club could be hunted down in association and if the head of the traffickers is taken alive it benefits to blame us, after all we're holding product."

"Holy fuck!" Killian's face gained a red undertone and his eyes narrowed.

"He has a solution, Chief. He didn't want to land this without one," Titan offered quickly to maintain control. "He takes them out, all of them...and I help. If we're caught, our background establishes credibility for the hit. It'll look like a planned rescue. If we don't make it, we deliver beforehand the saved product to show the gang's opposition to the body thieves. And we feed the law intel from rejected runs over the last decade to exonerate the WarMakers."

"This is to get you both out," Killian said, but his expression wasn't one of hatred or anger. He understood what Rip was truly offering. The fierce protection and defense of organizations such as this meant certain death to anyone interfering with its two hundred and fifty billion dollar business.

"Kill, there's only ever one way out. I guess this is ours." Titan kept his focus firm allowing truth to pass between them.

"Tell Rip to deliver the package. I'll review it and decide." Killian's expression said he rested knowing he had established an assassin capable of protecting his organization even from one worse. "Did he say anything else?"

"Yes. By his estimate they've run well over a hundred out of our turf in the last ten years." Titan waited.

Killian licked his lips then wiped them with the back of his lethal hand. "Reach out to your brother. I will deliver whatever he needs to do this job if the evidence is solid. And, tell him for me, cut them all down. Every last motherfucking one."

Titan nodded, containing his relief at the prospect of following Rip's lead out of their entanglement with the WarMakers and believing trading their lives for freedom came with a survival clause. "I'll reach out and advise when the package arrives," Titan said, standing and walking to the dartboard area of the club. "In the meantime, having a better read on the connections, what would you like to do with him?"

During the conversation, a hostage extracted from the Candy Store had sat chained to a chair, gagged, sporting a blindfold and noise-canceling headphones. The guy sustained initial injuries from capture and delivery but was left relatively unharmed.

"We know what information we need now so go get it. And I want the delivery from his mouth filmed and showing no coercion. You make him understand, if he wants to live, he hands them over with specifics, all of it. And tell him they won't be capable of vengeance when we're finished so he has nothing to fear in this state. He may even consider a new alliance. See where it takes you," Killian said, then motioned for the sergeant-at-arms to oversee the proceedings.

"Set him up in the back," the sergeant said. "In case he's a bad decision maker and this gets messy."

FORTY-FOUR

Jade looked on as Callum cleaned the zip drive with the caution of a restoration expert assigned to newly discovered Sumerian cuneiform containing the secret to eternal life, knowing the information's cost and being the father of Dylan's friend. He did it while the team stood guard waiting. When the information filtered across the screen Callum began translating even the obvious.

"Okay they're video clips, all except these two. The numbers at the end are the time and date stamps and the capture begins last Wednesday to Friday and jumps a couple days to end Tuesday night," he explained.

"Can we open the one from Thursday night first, the night Machias was taken?" Jade suggested. "Activity may give us the time frame, or we may catch her being moved."

Callum nodded and brought up a close-up feed stamped after midnight, its image grainy at first, cleared in increments drawing them all into a visual game of deciphering aspects within until the truck materialized.

"No way did they leave it in plain sight," Tex said what they all thought.

"They are so comfortable in their operation they never imagined anyone would get eyes inside their domain," Kane reasoned.

"Well Dylan did and that is Jack's truck," Jade said, walking over to the shop's evidence board to confirm the plates matched. They did. "They didn't even switch his plates."

"Bold," Tex said. "Can we pull back, zoom out or—"

"No. Dylan tapped into their cameras but any alteration he made would've been instantly detected. It's like seeing through another set of eyes, you can't control where they look," Callum said, replaying the clip. "But I can make a copy and zoom in."

"They did detect he was inside and traced back to him so how would they?" Kane asked.

"They probably locked onto his IP address but I won't know without a real analysis of all the data." Callum pointed to a clip near the end of the row. "This contains a larger quantity of megabytes." He opened it to reveal a circular storage container two stories high and large enough to hold a town's yearly supply of grain. Gravel trucks nearby suggested that was its purpose. A few seconds in two armed guards appeared in the far corner of the clip, moments later a row of females one could only describe as victims filed out, cuffed and chained together.

"Count them," Jade barked, rushing to her desk, snatching her cell phone, and searching its screen to autodial the private number of FBI Agent Drex Lafine. He answered with pleasantries which Jade cut off abruptly. "Drex, I'm looking at video footage of…how many?" Jade called over.

"Twenty-two for sure," Kane said, double counting with the others.

"Twenty-two victims of human trafficking being actively held at a dock site just outside of town. We need your help. How quickly can you get a team ready to infiltrate?"

"Whoa. No hello, just assemble a team for a covert op to recover multiple victims. Is this a thing with you?" Drex asked, referring to the last case they worked together involving multiple victims and requiring delicate infiltration. Spanning across seaboard states and being orchestrated by one perpetrator it shared no other similarities save the need to combine efforts. Jade was glad she reached him and he answered the call.

"Apparently," she said, slowing her delivery. "We're working an abduction and homicide case locally and it spilled over into human trafficking. We have visual confirmation of the victims, cuffed and chained, in footage taken within a week and solid intel on the export date from the first homicide victim. He left a note with a timeline. We have three days maximum."

"Does his timeframe match outgoing export manifests?" Drex asked, following her evidence.

"We don't know yet. We do know there is far more at play here than we can keep eyes on and if the intention is to put them on a ship it's your jurisdiction." Jade glanced over to her team who listened in and shared her foremost concern. "Drex, if we don't have backup equal to their strength the girls are gone. And since the head just sent mercenaries to kill the young man who caught the footage, we're thinking it's a safe bet the organization will dismantle or relocate and we'll miss taking them down if we don't act now. The only card we have on them is we're not their first adversary and they don't know we've identified them yet."

Jade heard Drex issuing orders to junior agents in close proximity. "Hold on, Jade," he said, continuing a list of demands to those on his side. Jade muted the mic and said, "He's on it. They're checking coastal export manifests for our area." She waited watching the team react to something Callum had on the screen.

"Jade, three possibilities match from the nearest port to you. One is unlikely because it's also carrying military weapon parts and will undergo extensive scrutiny with limited vetted personnel. Of the other two, one leaves tomorrow midday. Did it appear they were being moved for transport?" he asked, still networking his team in the background.

"Is there anything showing the victims in transport to the dock area?" she asked Callum.

"No. I watched the same feed from two days ago and it's the opposite. It appeared they were moved into a silo on site and locked in," Callum said. Kane and Tex nodded agreement with him.

"Did you hear that?" she asked Drex.

"Yeah, got it. Okay, so we're flagging the freighter and its cargo. What do you have on the location?" he asked. "And if you're not their first adversary, who is?"

"We can clean this up, gather all our intel and patch you in. Give us a couple hours. We'll include local knowledge on this site. There was a hit taken out on a drug dealer, a place called the Candy Shop, Narcotics had been searching for it for years but never landed it. Our local biker gang, the WarMakers obliterated it and it's connected. We're thinking turf war, but the gang had help. A hired assassin tipped us. He was paid to pave the way in for the gang. We don't know by who or why yet," Jade said. "And Drex, the traffickers left the vehicle owned by the young man murdered in plain view inside the staged construction site. Whoever is running this isn't afraid of us and has been around for more than one dance."

"It's like diving in deep water for the first time," he said. "My instructor said if it's not afraid of you, be afraid of it. Don't move on anything until I've weighed in. Jade the operation will come from me and you will all shift to a backup position."

"On the trafficking ring, yes," she confirmed. "But the abduction and murder we remain lead. I want your word."

"You have it," he agreed. "Why can't you ever call to say hi?"

Drex was joking to lighten the intensity of the situation but truth belied his tone and Jade turned her face away from the team and Kane before speaking. "I will. I'm sorry."

"I know. Me too," he said before disconnecting.

Jade hung up and rejoined her team empowered by the support coming in but nervous about how badly they needed it. The scope of criminality was spreading. The picture emerging confirmed the black cloud she sensed moving in. But she'd been wrong about it. It made landfall long ago and set up shop without any of them taking notice. It was right there, as she walked by the forty-seven names of the missing associated with the outreach programs Daughtry took part in. Staring at the evidence board while her partners viewed more footage a dread awakened.

"Oh shit," she said, turning to the team. "The bus route."

Kane heard her and registered it first. "The one heading out of state," he said. "It picks up at the corner of..." Kane walked over to the case map and ran his finger down a road located in the center of the three main areas where possible abductions occurred at the church, a wayward teens house, and Daughtry land. The bus station, connected by a huge parking lot to a full-service truck stop, was minutes from the farm on a highway heading out of state. "Aw, shit."

Kane picked up a black felt pen and marked an "X" at the station for all to see.

"We need to add any missing person's reports or runaways listed from the bus system from neighboring towns on the route to our potential victims list," Tex said. "These numbers are getting scary."

"Tex, you run the list. I'll put together our case file with Kane, and Callum if you can package the footage highlighting key evidence we can send everything we have over and start working on a takedown operation with Drex tonight."

Jade stared at Kane for a second, gathering calm. "Did you see Machias in that row of victims?" she asked. All three men confirmed her suspicions.

"That's what we were watching while you were on with Drex," Kane said. "All this and our victim isn't among them."

"I can't," she said, diving into the case file to organize copy for the FBI. "I won't accept that she isn't still breathing."

"What about Daughtry?" Kane asked. "Do we have anything more from the listening devices planted at the farm?"

Callum waved them back over to his hub, clicking away on his keyboard. "This isn't as earth shattering as the CCTV footage but I think it will be suggestive in any courtroom."

He hit play and set the speakers on so the team could hear Daughtry's voice clearly echoing through the station.

"What lengths would a man go to protect his child, bargaining for the return of his beloved wife, against a criminal enterprise such as yours? I think people will believe great lengths, very great. Especially once I show them what you're capable of."

The audio was interrupted momentarily by a shuffling of papers before resuming.

"And being that you kidnapped my daughter it'll be no wonder why I lost my mind. Anything I may be linked to will be seen as a justifiable break from sanity." Daughtry paused. Jade wanted to crawl through the recording and strangle off his breathing. The traffickers were allowed, or worse, asked, to take Machias by him. Jade fought the images in her mind.

"You, on the other hand, will be seen for what you are, a soulless violent human trafficker. And if I can end you first, no one will ever know my part in any of this."

"And there it is," Tex said.

"I bet the asshole never thought for a second that talking to himself would nail him as aware and party to the larger organiza-tion," Kane said.

"He all but confirmed it," Jade said. "Callum this is brilliant."

"He's not done." After he moves furniture and I hear him going back down the hayloft ladder I can identify him swearing. *Damn you,* I think. But the rest is too distant for clarity.

"It's enough," Jade said, placing a proud hand on his shoulder. "He isn't weaseling out of culpability this time. The real retribution is having his words verify his guilt and involvement with the traf-ficking ring. I just wish he named its leader."

"That would've been nice," Tex said. "Keep listening. The guy obviously likes the sound of his own voice and doesn't have any friends to talk to."

Callum smiled up at Tex and marked the clip to add it to the sound evidence package for Drex and the FBI.

The team was facing the built-out evidence board, sectioned off into divisions. The gang and its take down of the Candy Store, the trafficking site and captures of the footage, the ever-expanding list of potential victims, rows encompassing evidence on Jack's murder, Machias's abduction, and the brutal attack on Dylan. They put Daughtry on the opposite side away from the young people he took part in ruining. The trafficking ring was left with a hole where a photo of its head should be. All the players were known to them save for the hired killer who tipped them off and the vile beast running an enterprise to profit off the forced labor and sexual exploitation of innocent youth. Connections were drawn between those on the board in so many directions when Jade stepped back, it mimicked a spider's web.

And she remembered Nickolas, what he wrote to her.

"The reach of the threads?" She spoke it out loud intending it for no one lost in thought. "Stretch as far back as forward." Kane stopped studying the board and turned to listen. "Must be severed severely to kill the spider at the center." She stepped forward as the guys parted, allowing her close up to the board. Her focus locked on the empty space where a picture was missing. "What is true about the maker of the web?"

"Jade? What are you thinking?" Kane asked as the others waited in silence.

Eyes grazing over the connections on the board, she said, "We hit any of these and our vibration will alert the spider at the center. We take it out and the web collapses. Pray we find Machias and can extract her safely. We may be backup for the FBI on this but threatening a two hundred and fifty billion dollar industry? Have no illusions." She tapped the empty space. "This is our target, we're going to war."

FORTY-FIVE

Axel forewarned the nurses' station using the authority of his father's position on the case and his role of officer in training to make way for Raven's arrival before he stepped foot on the floor of Dylan's surgery. He heard him; the distinct even stride of his gait, before he appeared from the adjoining hallway. And watched two of the nurses lean out to stare as he passed. With the presence and appearance of a movie star he was never without a following. Axel would let them discover for themselves that he resided outside their dating realm but hoped they sensed and respected his distancing. Raven wasn't in a cordial conversation mood and they were soon to realize.

"I don't want any excuses, Axe. What the fuck happened? Why the hell is Dylan in critical condition? Was this the same bastards that killed Jack?" Raven rifled the questions at him, not really seeing. Axel knew this; he'd caught a glimpse in a mirror in the family waiting room and couldn't miss the transformative impact of his guilt.

"Rave, they gave us a room to wait in. We'll talk in there. It's an active case," Axe said, ushering Raven into the nearby room and closing the door behind them. "Two men, we believe acting on orders issued by the head of a human trafficking ring outside our town, attacked Dylan because he accessed their internal camera footage. It exposed their involvement in Machias's abduction and Jack's death."

Raven was circling the room like a caged lion not willing to find comfort in captivity. "How? Did it show…oh Christ! Does it have Jack's murder on film?"

"No, Rave. Please sit down. It shows Jack's truck arriving and being stored inside their fortified property." Axel fought to maintain a level tone.

"I'm not sitting down. Why the hell did Dylan break into their footage? Is this a cyber security leak or—"

"No. It's a my fault thing." Axel's head dropped despite his best efforts to keep it level and take the reprimand he earned. "The detectives were searching for vehicle footage. I knew Dylan had access to dock cameras and asked if he could scan through the footage for the vehicle Machias and Jack were taken in. He went a step further and used the internal construction site security feed to see if the vehicle in question came off a freighter. The trafficking ring must've detected his intrusion and marked him for execution so he could never share his discovery. And I didn't…I never thought to…"

"So you think because he was trying to help, like you are, this is on you?" Raven stopped pacing and stood directly in front of his position blocking his view until Axe peered up. "This shit, every last ounce of it is on them, whoever the fuck they are! You couldn't have anticipated them coming for Dylan. Did you even know he dug deeper?"

"Not all of it but—" Axe didn't turn away; he owed Raven that.

"But fucking nothing! If Jack expected the worst and thought everything through, he still wouldn't have made it out of this alive. Don't you get it, Axe? The deck was stacked against us from jump. No way could we have imagined Daughtry's twisted abuse of Mac would lead us all here!"

"What twisted abuse?" Falcon, creeping in quietly using a cane and wearing a leg brace hadn't been heard entering. "Rave?"

"Shit," Axe said, overwhelmed by emotions he'd forgotten Falcon said he would drop by. "You better sit down for this, buddy, and anything we tell you can't leave this room, understood?"

Raven ran a hand through the silver waves in his hair, walked away, and stood with his back to them both staring out the window at the park across from the hospital. "Mac wanted to tell you everything," he said. "She talked it through with Jack and I more than once. She thought if you knew how bad her upbringing was you wouldn't want anything to do with her. She felt sold long before she was. He made sure of it. This is about as bad as it can get and it's for her to tell." He paused, contemplating but not turning.

"As bad as…are you saying she was molested?" Falcon asked and Axe watched fire ignite behind his eyes.

Raven spun, leaning with his back against the glass pane. "No. Not yet. Physically abused but strategic so no one could see it, mentally in so many ways, and horrific because she was certain he had her mother killed. Never sexual, small mercy."

Falcon looked like Axel felt, gut-punched and worse.

"I knew in some way I sensed it and there were signs with his control and her fear, but I wasn't sure. If I was wrong, I mean…" Falcon closed his eyes to process the anguish of his missing girlfriend privately.

"I've reached my limit of decency and tolerance," Raven said. "What did Dylan find? I want to know who is at the heart of this shit and where I can find them."

"We don't know who, but they've been operating here for years and they'll kill you at first sight or worse," Axel said. "You can't be involved in any of it."

"Any of what? You tell me all of it, Axe. I want to see the footage of Jack's truck."

"The cops found Jack's truck?" Falcon asked, sensing he came in at the fourth quarter but determined to keep up.

"Dylan did," Axe replied.

"Oh you've got to be...this is what landed him here?" Falcon had both hands holding his head together.

"Yeah, and you'll be next," Axe said, directing the comment at Raven. "No way are you or any of us capable of—"

"Maybe not alone," Raven suggested. "But together we might make a difference, sway the odds in Mac's favor. Our friend in there might die for this intel. I'm not sitting around waiting for Mac to end up in the operatory next to Dylan's."

"Okay," Axe said. "We can go over what I know and see if we can offer any insights to the unit, but no playing fucking John Wick on me."

Raven was about to speak when a nurse opened the door. "Mr. MacLeod? The surgeon would like to speak to you. We've been unable to reach Dylan's next of kin and...he asked me to fetch you."

The cohesion sustaining Axel's life force to his body separated and though he knew he stood up and stepped forward, one foot in front of the other, he felt no ownership of the movements. Present but watching the scene play out without volition, he saw the nurse's lips moving but couldn't hear a word, not the standard chaos in the hallway, or the opening of the door to the back room where Dylan's surgeon stood in full operation garb. She ushered him to the right to seal the door but he didn't feel her hand on his arm, the draft of wind that ruffled papers on a corner desk, or the doctor's grip when he shook Axe's hand. Everything around him wore a layer of vibrating energy like heat rising off pavement it shimmered in a wave of distortion between him and the rest of the world. Until, in a blinding rush, life resumed with the word "alive."

"Did you hear me, Axel?" the surgeon asked. "Your friend came out of surgery well and is alive and resting comfortably."

Not functioning normally, Axe nodded to prompt the doctor to continue his explanation giving him time to regain his senses.

"When he arrived, I think we all feared a terminal diagnosis seeing his condition but he must've put up a hell of a fight. The matter mixed throughout his hair turned out to be blood, syrup, and coffee grinds. In this case, I'm happy to report his head trauma appeared far worse off than it was. I'm hopeful for a full recovery but we're having trouble reaching his parents if—"

"I'll call them," Axel said, finding his voice. "Thank you. I'm so grateful. Do you know when we can see him?"

"He'll be out for some time and when he does wake, he be groggy and in and out of consciousness until his brain has a chance to recover. The guard is staying?" he asked, referring to an armed guard his father posted at the unit's request.

"Yes, for as long as is needed. And no one goes in to see him without first being cleared by Detective Carmichael's team," Axe warned.

"I'd take your friends and go home and get some rest. I'll have the nurse call if there is any change. He'll need days, not hours, but he'll get there."

Walking back to tell Rave and Falcon the good news Axel stumbled in the hall almost collapsing, using the wall to brace his body against a fall. The weight of the case and damage to his group of friends, and the violent turmoil clouding any resolution detected a break in his fortitude and pounced. A nurse witnessed his misstep and came to his side, helping to steady him.

"After your friends leave, if you promise to rest for a few hours in the private family waiting room, I'll bring you some electrolytes so you can finish this fight," she said, a supportive understanding colored her tone. "We all know you're trying to bring Machias home. My younger sister is in her grade."

Recognizing he was good to no one if he couldn't function well enough to walk down a hallway he nodded agreement. She waved another nurse in who handed him a drink in a tall paper cup with a straw. "It'll help with the dizziness." Checking his stability she released his arm.

Righting himself he exhaled the fear of losing Dylan with the confirmation his injured friend was watched over by a caring team who was invested in his recovery.

Once anxious facing the challenges of the academy, current

circumstances proved excessive as an emotional training template. If anything Axe would walk in overqualified.

As the nurse departed, he gathered strength to face the two men waiting in the room ahead for a vengeance he feared wouldn't be delivered without coming at a price none of them, not even the detectives, were prepared to pay.

FORTY-SIX

Riparian delivered a package Killian couldn't deny earned the brothers freedom and distanced the gang from any perceived involvement with the trafficking ring, whether he'd risk the fallout for what Rip requested was debatable. Putting the pieces in place Rip knew the special homicide unit Detective Carmichael operated from was governed by protocol, warrants, and rules of conduct. Riparian had no such restraints and planned to use his current position outside the law to maximum effect in dealing with each enemy.

Daughtry earned first place on the list of targets.

Not only was he the one most deserving of the placement but Rip understood how the police worked and was determined to stay a step or two ahead. Before apprehending Daughtry they'd require warrants and decide timing based on their course of action with the case. Pick him up too soon and they tipped their hand to those associated, too late and they risked him fleeing custody. What worked against them Rip capitalized on.

"Is that all of them?" Machias asked. Her eyes drifted over photos of the missing organized chronologically dating back from the year she was born. The older missing poster captures appeared adolescent in their delivery when compared to the most recent. Times had changed but the brutality and injustice never faltered.

"All the ones we were able to track down and match convincingly to your mother's list," he said, appreciating how the sight of so many victims would impact her especially knowing her fate was to be among them. "You don't have to stay for this part."

"I know. I'm staying," she said, her voice firm and strong.

"She's proud of you." He said it, deliberately avoiding eye contact to grant her privacy in her reaction. "Wherever she is now. I guarantee it."

"So what happens now?" She left the table and returned to her favorite chair beside his, the pillow she added to its seat waited for her unchanged.

"I wait for Killian to accept terms and then he orders the…he sends enforcers to carry out his orders. Their methods will come from him."

"How will they make sure the police know everything?" He expected she'd ask. It mattered to her.

"Before they capture and detain Daughtry they'll remove all your grandparents' belongings from the barn to the one next in line and further from the main house. They have the package and will nail the missing photos, in order, to the wall behind where they have him restrained so when they film inside the detectives will be given the information they require to connect him to the trafficking ring and them to confirmed victims."

"What if the gang's leader rejects the plan?" she asked. Worry clouded her eyes.

"I revise it or carry it out myself." Rip's phone dinged and he pulled it from a pocket while explaining. "It can be accomplished by one man, faster with a crew."

Scanning the screen, he shot her a grin. "Faster," he said.

"He said yes?" Her enthusiasm squashed any concern he carried over how she would take Daughtry's undoing. Staring at her, there was no question she'd be just fine.

"He did," he replied. "So here we go." Rip wasted no time bringing up the feed from the surveillance he set up in the forest at the tree line of the property. Mac scooched her chair closer and leaned onto the table, her image reminding him of kids leering in on their favorite scene in a movie.

But this was real life and if he had to rate it, he'd give it a hard eighteen plus for gory content.

There was nothing left to protect in the main barn, Daughtry transferred all the valuables and sensitive documents into a rolling suitcase, packed and ready to travel. Using jerrycans he ensured the new truck he paid cash for and kept hidden from townspeople was fully fueled with out-of-state plates tracing back to a new identity he established months prior when he struck the deal for Machias. He hadn't had time to sell off the expensive farming equipment but any attempt to do so would be flagged by police following her abduction. Too risky. Instead he amassed a small savings skimming from the church and selling valuables from Machias's inheritance, obvious pieces of art or jewelry her grandparents left to her that were easily liquidated. More personal possessions, recognizable or traceable like wedding rings, family heirlooms, or engraved items he left in the house safe to revisit once Mac was declared. He packed only the basics of clothing, intending to buy new and alter his appearance with an upscale wardrobe. Carrying the last of his essentials to the detached garage, at the back of the third barn left of the main farmhouse, a sense of relief washed over him.

Soon he'd never again breathe the manure tainted farm air, he couldn't wait. Knowing Barracutta wouldn't be in any position to hunt him down after he sent the documents he stored as insurance to authorities sweetened his exit. Thinking back to the start of their business dealings it was fitting. Barracutta blackmailed him into compliance then. He earned the last laugh.

Loading the final items into the truck's back seat, he locked it, turned off the garage interior light allowing the truck's access lights to illuminate his way out, and locked the building's exterior door. When the delayed truck lights extinguished through the windows, one remained, but not in the garage or barn he exited from the main.

Strange that he'd missed one the last time he'd left it. Probably on his way off the property to clean out and cancel his post office box and pick up a few travel items from a town over where he wouldn't be spotted. He was normally pretty disciplined about turning them all off but it had been light out when he left so he hadn't noticed it from outside. Now, hours later it stood out. Occasionally he'd forget a lamp or flashlight. And with the tension of everything he had to prepare to ditch this town and life it was no wonder he wasn't at his best. He considered leaving it, with no one else on the large section of land. But with the police challenging his innocence he didn't want to spur further curiosity if a patrol car ventured near.

Flipping his truck keys from hand to hand, he crossed the expanse between the two barns remembering a discussion he had with Lily over buying a guard dog. Lily thought of it as a protector and pet for Machias and her, he considered it only as a fiercely trained weapon against intruders. In the end he decided against it, not interested in the noise or cleanup. Maybe when he settled into his new life the addition of a canine made sense.

Entering the barn from the main door put the first light switch two steps to the left along its outer wall. Reaching out, he found the switch flicking it up. Nothing. The overhead fixture it activated remained shrouded in blackness. It couldn't be an electrical problem as a light, small but visible from outside, shone in the upper hayloft. Faulty wiring or a burned-out bulb, he decided. Not planning on this excursion he hadn't brought a flashlight. He could, knowing extras were stored in the back workshop cupboard, navigate the main floor by memory in the dark. And he considered it for a few seconds before deciding he didn't care enough to stumble through dangerous rusted tools for one damn light.

What were the chances of the nosy cops sending a cruiser by to monitor his activities at the farm? Could they even see one small light source from the roadway?

Choosing sleep over possible injury he swiveled back toward the door, a bead of moonlight from beyond it guiding him until the bead broke.

A breath caught in his throat but before he swallowed and was able to speak a voice did the talking for him.

"Leaving so soon?" it said, deep and gravelly. "That'd be a shame given there's so much to discuss."

Daughtry's mind spun. This wasn't a cop; the possibility was off the table. "Barracutta?" he said under his breath. "Whatever you're being paid I can double it and believe me when I say being loyal to Barracutta won't serve you for long."

"Barra who?" the voice said, before a light beamed on blinding him in its path. Spun to face the illuminated storage side of the barn, he considered the two armed men before him unrelated to his current plight. The storage was gone. The area picked clean of every stitch of furniture, tools, and equipment once littering the space. *Thieves*, he thought.

"Look, you can keep the items you stole. I don't care enough to bother police over them but I suggest you leave before they make their rounds. My daughter is missing and they're keeping a close watch over the place." Daughtry hoped letting them off the hook would speed up their departure.

"Not that close," the more vocal of the two said. "And we didn't steal a thing. Actually we came to protect the valuables for their owner, sort of a safekeeping measure." The larger quiet man stepped closer than was comfortable as the other spoke, blocking Daughtry's line to the exit.

"I am the owner," Daughtry said, confused and annoyed.

"No. Machias Lincoln is the owner and this is for her." Without warning, arms clenched hold of him while a bag completely blackened the already dark space. One second he was struggling to move the next he was airborne, no contact with the ground below his feet. One of the goons clasped his arms in front of him and slapped metal cuffs on his wrists. He fought to speak but drawing breath drew the bag into his mouth gagging him. Then, in one fluid sequence, his arms pulled over his head, the bag tore free from his face, and he found himself dangling, suspended a couple feet above the now bare barn floor from the chain and hook he used for his toys.

His first thought was to demand an explanation, revisit Barracutta's possible involvement in this attack, or question if any connection to Jack existed but he voiced none. His eyes, adjusting to dark then blinded by light and back again, cleared to the image of a hundred or more faces staring at him, lining the barn wall ahead of where he hung. Focusing on one, he read a word echoed over each photo from black and white to color, out-of-date hair to recent styles.

MISSING.

Daughtry swallowed, fighting to moisten an increasingly parched throat while narrowing in on a recent picture. He recognized the girl. She was about Machias's age when he had her chained in the very place he now occupied. His head swam, struggling to process and the man closest noticed.

"Want me to throw you a line here?" he said, evil casting a solid encasing stone color into his eyes. "You violated every one of these young people in the photos we've decorated with. They're in chronological order by the way. And now you pay for it. Not nearly as much as you should, but it's a start."

Daughtry's panic intensified but was dampened by the display. He couldn't understand, in a state of trauma, how these men collected all the missing, ordered them, and attributed them to him. "Who the hell sent you?" Dry mouth or not he spit the words out. "You better release me. This will mean war with criminals the likes you have never seen."

The more vocal of the two stepped forward. Not close enough to reach out and touch him but within clear view. As he neared, he smiled a slow devious grin, cocking his head to one side, exposing a prominent tattoo etched into his bulging neck muscle.

"Do you know what this is?" he asked, enjoying the interaction far more than Daughtry wished.

Daughtry shook his head, his arms already aching from his suspended body.

He stepped closer. "It's my brotherhood. We're WarMakers, you

piece of shit, and that war you mentioned is right here and now."
He laughed, nodding to the other man who withdrew a hunting
knife from a side strap on his belt with gloved hands. "I'm fairly
certain it's one you won't have the balls to survive."

Screams erupted as the butcher stomped across the dusty floor,
cut through Daughtry's belt and jeans, tore them and his boxers off,
lifted his member, grabbing his balls in one hand, and sliced clean
through. An arc of blood washed across the wood paneling. He was
effectively neutered in one foul sweep. The blinding pain landed
with utter shock and he knew he definitely should've bought
the dog.

The screams were coming from him and they weren't likely to
stop anytime soon.

"Daughtry will be punished for his crimes and while that is
happening the others will dig the fire trench around the barn." Rip
watched Machias carefully as he delivered the plan. She didn't
flinch.

"You said the cops planted listening devices?" she asked.

"The boys have been told where they are and will transfer them
silently to wait until it's over, then they'll put the one back into the
new barn with a message."

"So they are like claiming responsibility?" He sensed by the
uptick in her voice, she feared them being caught.

"Not really," he said, smiling. "They have ways around that."

"Okay, good," she said, pulling her legs up to spin in her chair.
"I don't want anyone but the bad guys paying a price for this."

Rip turned away sorting files so she couldn't read the
inevitability in his eyes. The gang could escape this war, most of
them, Daughtry wouldn't but neither would he.

FORTY-SEVEN

The FBI didn't revel in flying in and taking over a case local police were efficiently handling but Jade knew when it spilled into federal territory it was expected and they were damn good at it. Drex more than most, in her opinion. Watching Captain Grey and him in a huddle deciding particulars she could only hope her team's primary objective to bring Machias home safe wouldn't be compromised by the larger operation. Which had enough moving parts to make your head spin. The Coast Guard was on alert and putting measures in place should the freighter attempt to leave port, the Feds had jurisdictions on either side of their county waiting to lock down exit routes, and the agents that landed sectioned off areas of infiltration. There was debate of when to hit the trafficking site, in daylight or the cover of night. The hold back being the twenty-two plus victims and ensuring their best chance of survival.

Criminal enterprises such as this had no issue insulating with human shields and watching product mowed down in the crossfire.

While Grey and Drex were confirming every possible escape was covered and defended, Jade and the team ordered and analyzed evidence for any detail to illuminate Mac's location or the identity of the one Daughtry was speaking about in the last recorded clip from the farm. Jade scanned the unit seeing every detective's head down and fully focused and feeling it still wasn't enough.

Tex amassed information on the missing from the bus system and appeared swallowed by it, everything but the cowboy hat. Some days he refused to take it off, this was one. Given an empty evidence board on wheels hours earlier, he'd all but covered it and would likely need a second. The loss was repulsive.

She was about to join Kane to review evidence focused on Daughtry when her phone alerted to an incoming call. Answering amid the chaos in the center of the hub, a few strides away, in any direction, from any one of her fellow officers or agents, the sound around her vanished as her ears strained to hear the voice on the line. She hadn't yet identified herself when a man's voice said, "Machias is alive, safe, and protected and will remain so until it's over."

"Say again," she said, her tone catching Kane's attention. He stared across the room at her, reading the situation and waving everyone to shut up.

"I said Machias Lincoln is alive, safe, protected. She'll be brought to you when it's over. Watch the feed, Detective Carmichael. You are not working alone."

"What feed? Can I speak to her? Don't hang...dammit! Machias!" Jade yelled to Kane and Tex who were already glued to her next words. "The caller was male, low voice, said she was alive, safe, protected, and would be delivered to me when it was over! How the hell? Who would know we're in the middle of taking down...Oh the feed." She walked over to Kane's desk, closest proximity, as they all crowded around; Drex heard her and came to stand at her left. Being his credentials outranked all of theirs she glanced and he locked eyes.

"Wait." Pulling out his cell phone and setting it to record Drex scanned the foursome readying them to remain silent. "Can we cast it to a larger device without compromising it?"

"Yeah, airdrop it," Callum suggested, bringing Jade's laptop from her desk and setting it in the center of the group he duplicated the original and dropped the feed, expanding the picture on the larger screen.

The team adjusted for optimal viewing.

Drex glanced to Jade, his eyes preparing her for the worst. "Okay, hit play."

It wasn't what they expected. No victims being tortured or killed as a warning or deterrent. Instead the camera angle of the feed showed a wall covered in *MISSING* posters, then it zoomed in slowly and carefully following the order of them, row after row, side to side. The camera dipped and Kane spoke first.

"That looks like barn floorboards, the wall too," he said. Drex nodded agreement but didn't speak still recording.

When the filmmaker drew the camera up off the floor the image became far less agreeable. Blood followed feet suspended off the ground, legs coated in more blood then a scene no man wants to witness and as it tracked over the chest and neck Jade spoke.

"Daughtry," she said. Drex questioned her with his eyes, and her and Kane nodded the victim, still breathing as the footage was filmed, was Mackenzie Daughtry or what remained of him.

The camera panned away from Daughtry catching a small table in the foreground for a split second and Tex piped up.

"Were those his balls sitting on that table? Well that's one way to make a steer."

Drex shot him a glance and Tex shrugged in response.

The feed returned to the wall of pictures and a voice broke the quiet. "He says to match the jars, Carmichael. And know you have help."

Kane's eyes revealed anything but gratitude and she knew what he was thinking. Before he said a word the camera flipped to the back of a leather biker's jacket. The feed ended with the emblem of the WarMakers.

"The gang is helping?" Drex asked.

"It appears so. I don't know that they aren't using it to settle their own scores but this is a bold move," Kane said, scratching his head. "Dispatch to the farm?" he asked Grey, who nodded.

"Wait," Jade said. "Won't the traffickers have eyes on Daughtry's place? Should we go in lights and sirens?"

"Can't leave him there to bleed out but I hear you," Drex said. He tipped his head up staring overtop of them all, even Tex's hat, to Grey. "Everything ready to go on your end?" he asked.

"Yes. Your guys have Coast Guard and Navy on standby and we have locals for three districts on road closures and reinforcement." Grey pointed to CCTV linked up covering major routes, revealed in a cycle of views from multiple roads with an equal amount of law enforcement. No one was standing down tonight.

"Then I say we use it as a distraction. If our target doesn't know we're onto them they'll fear it with Daughtry's involvement after we go in but while we're busy at the farm they may think it's the perfect time to move the victims," Drex said.

"So we send help to Daughtry loud and visible, the head will have guards gauging activity around there, and go in when they least expect us," Jade said. "And what about the gang?"

"I'm guessing they can handle themselves. It's turf related with the execution of the Candy Store owner. He must've been working for them. Now Daughtry. They're eliminating the trafficker's supply chain one piece at a time," Drex said.

"Yeah, well somehow Machias is caught right in the middle and excuse me if I don't buy the promise of someone who just mutilated her father to keep her safe," Jade said. "If she's not at the site and they've claimed possession she's with the WarMakers."

"The caller said him," Drex pointed out. "One of the WarMakers. Either way we can't take on the gang and the trafficking ring in one night and the primary concern is at the docks."

Jade felt anger swell and Kane, knowing her so well, pushed up against her to calm her. "She is why all of them have a chance at survival and I'm not losing her."

"The gang is local, correct?" Drex asked, and Kane nodded agreement. "Have they ever been associated with harming a young person, kidnapping, rape?"

Jade exhaled seeing his point.

"No one wants this girl left out there but she is actually in safer hands away from all this, including her criminal father, until we take down the threat. The risk I see." Drex walked to the video capture of the victims being lead on the site, chained and cuffed. "Is freeing theses ones without drawing a firefight right at them."

Jade followed Kane to the evidence board where all the missing victims were being matched to organizations Daughtry was connected to. Jade stopped, her head panning from it to the image of the barn wall frozen on the computer screen.

"What?" Kane asked, watching her as she searched through photos from the night she installed the recording devices.

"The jars! Mac's mom's canning jars with the names on them. He said to match them." Jade shuffled through to grab the photograph she took the night she set up the listening device in the cellar. Snapping a copy of it she focused in on the shelf of preserves. Blowing up one, its label life size, she yelled to Kane. "Is there a victim February of 2021 with the name Margret?"

"Holy shit," Tex said, staring over Kane's shoulder. Kane nodded and asked if she saw a Nancy in April of the same year. Jade confirmed it and Drex stared back and forth between them.

"Our missing girl's mother canned preserves on the farm. It appears she was tracking the date and a version of his victim's first name to confirm Daughtry held them there first," Jade said.

"So we have a history, a record of a good number of victims?" Drex said, then he waved in a junior agent who was listening from the sidelines. "Match them and duplicate everything they have for prosecution."

Tex raised his brows and shook his head. "Prosecuting Daughtry might be a long shot. He's missing his balls and currently dying."

Kane shot a glance over at Tex and mouthed the word "ouch" before shaking his head at him.

Their conversation had taken all of a couple minutes but it was time Daughtry didn't have to waste. The decision was made to send a large and loud response team to the farm. Once in place, the unit, FBI team, and support would move in on the dock. On the outskirts of town, the time it took for them to drive in using back roads from various directions would give the farm team time to make themselves known. Whether Daughtry lived or died, Jade was relieved they had the evidence needed to tie him in as an integral component in the trafficking.

Jade made a mental note to check back on Lily Lincoln's history when they knew more.

The team began packing up and preparing for the hard night ahead. Jade helped seal Kane's bulletproof vest over his scarred side. He glanced down and smiled at her. "Can't happen twice," he said.

"Won't let it," she said. She watched the certainty behind her words trigger a deep concern in his eyes but her phone buzzed distracting them both. The words "it's live" appeared followed by a feed, Daughtry's farm from a distance far enough back to view the whole exterior of the barn.

"Live feed," Kane yelled, drawing in Drex, Grey, Tex, and junior agents. They barely crossed the room when Jade, focusing in, spoke up. "Am I seeing a hill or a…is that a trench?" she asked.

"Oh shit," Drex said. The words left his mouth as an explosion on the screen jolted all listening in. Jade had the volume cranked for everyone to hear during the previous feed and hadn't adjusted it lower. The plume of smoke, fire in a range of colors, and extent of instant damage said Daughtry was no more. But more than that, the barn was a complete inferno. A contained inferno but unquestionably set to burn to the ground.

"Your bikers dug a firewall around the building. Am I the only one here who is getting the feeling we are falling behind?"

"Let's go!" Grey hollered. "Locals lead the teams in on the fastest routes to the dock site and everyone keep your damn heads down! I want them on your shoulders when this is over! Any support members, you hang back unless or until called in!" To Drex Grey lowered his voice. "We have the hospital on standby for the victim transport and anti-human trafficking services is sending support staff there."

"Thanks," Drex said, his voice stealing center stage when he spoke again. "You heard the man. You all know the drill now execute it without casualties, folks, and stay on the radio. Keep in mind the photos of our possible criminal targets. One of those we've identified but haven't yet captured could be our prime suspect here. Any identification and we all want to know about it, perpetrator, victim, or weapon. Clear and quiet. Hold no illusions, whatever you're carrying, they have more firepower." Heading out he shot a glance solely intended for Jade. She read the emotion in his eyes and hoped Kane hadn't.

"Tex, you're with team one approaching from due west. Kane and Callum team two going head-on from the south. And Jade, you're with me coming in from the east side where the victims are likely still being held. You know your jobs, go get it done." Drex motioned for a team in jackets identifying them as crime scene officers, to step forward. "When apprehensions are secure, I want you on the scene before they're loaded. This is a major federal takedown with tendrils that could literally span the globe so everything, and I mean everything, is recorded, cataloged, and contained!"

Jade paused and Kane stopped beside her. "What is it?" he asked.

"When I was at the farm, I sensed someone there with me. Whoever is feeding us this information is steps ahead. I don't think this has to do with Nickolas, Kane. It has to be someone with inside information from the gang side. They're working with him."

"And?" he asked, waiting for clarity from her while Tex shot him a hurry-your-ass glare.

"I want to know who this is," she said, walking out with him. "I think when this is over, I might want to shake his hand."

FORTY-EIGHT

Riparian read the bridled fear in Machias's eyes though she voiced none as he handed over the code list for the bomb shelter. "You only use them if I don't come back. Wait until morning, it will take me at least that long. And if you don't hear from me or I don't walk back in by noon you start deciding when you want to go. You call the number of my friend and he'll figure out how to get to you and bring you in safely. Daughtry is gone, the police know the truth and will protect you from here out." As he spoke, she nodded but her breathing was ragged, her body trembled under her sweatshirt, and resin coated her electric eyes.

"I won't be out there alone," he said, the half grin she came to mimic held until she absorbed his words. "I plan to always watch over you. I think you know that one." He used her phrase against her but she didn't smile back.

"If you don't come back, I'm staying here," she said, determined but fracturing.

"No you are not," he said, reaching out to enclose her in his hug. She cried, and he let her, knowing it could be the first and only time he was permitted to comfort her pain in this way. "I will fight to come back for you." He pulled back enough for her tear-stained face to see his. "I might not be as pretty as I am now."

"You're not pretty," she said, staring into his eyes. "You're handsome. I'm pretty."

"Yes. Yes, you are." He let go, threw on his jacket, and walked with her to the man door of the shelter. His weapons and supplies were packed while she slept. Without warning, she ran up and grabbed him in a bear hug. *One last time*, he thought.

Pulling away, she steeled herself against what came next. He'd witnessed it before, a behavior she had no choice but to learn to survive the brutality of her life so far. If there was a way he could make it back, he would, if for no other reason than to prevent adding to her pain.

"When this is over, we should get a dog," she said.

"Good idea." He threw on his skullcap and mounted his bike outside the door. "You think of names instead of worrying. I'll expect a couple fantastic ones to choose from when I see you."

"Rip?" she called out as the engine started to drown their voices. "I see you, but I didn't expect you'd see me. And now you have. I really need you to live."

He couldn't speak. Wouldn't make promises he couldn't keep. Instead of offering platitudes or false hopes, he tapped his chest where his heart was breaking and raised one single gloved finger before barreling into the night to meet Titan and finish what he trusted no one else to do. She was the only one inside his heart that he would carry regret for to his last breath but until he took it, he'd do everything to kill everyone who had a hand in her pain.

As the shelter faded from view in his side mirror, he prayed she found the package he left for her when the morning came quiet and dark and he didn't call. What were the chances of survival? Even Titan didn't know what he'd done to ensure justice was delivered to the head of the trafficking ring.

It took Killian nothing but a day trip for a couple runners to nail down all the details surrounding the fictitious construction site Rip targeted using the transport van's GPS. He had no problem convincing a regular worker at the site to call in sick and map out the entire area. The threat of gang retribution coupled with a hefty bonus went a long way to building singular loyalty. The guy had nothing to lose; Killian said he brought up photos of the Candy Store owner's punishment and said the fate of those controlling the site was far worse. There'd be no job to return to come Monday. His was an early severance.

The WarMakers runners delivered packages at strategic places for Rip and Titan. Their first order of business was extraction of the victims held captive on the site. The runners waited with eyes on throughout the night and into the next while others dealt with Daughtry.

At the farm, Riparian ordered the enforcers to burn everything associated with the man stored in the new truck hidden in the garage, fake identification and all evidentiary documents in his possession were set in a pile inside the house. The vehicle was left completely clean of history for Machias to claim on her return. It was Killian's decision to burn the barn with all its bastardized uses "to the motherfucking ground." Rip liked the idea. Mac deserved a fresh start, new fertile soil, no reminder of Daughtry.

Killian didn't announce Daughtry would be made a part of the ashes until he sent the documented feed through. Despite their vast differences, mutually shared directives existed.

The WarMakers monitoring the trafficking site, with knowledge of its inner workings and a map, narrowed down areas where victims could be stored, the guard cycles, and easiest exits. Using this Rip planned for Titan to help rescue the victims, forcing him to remove them from the area. Transporting them to safety in the five-ton truck the boys hid nearby, he'd be tasked with dropping them off as he did the kids to Callum. This action solidified the WarMakers opposition to the ring and made Titan their protector in ensuring that understanding.

When Titan left, Rip's private war would begin. By the time he returned it'd be over. All but the cryin' as they say.

The WarMakers stood against several rival gang takeover attempts, a list of indictments, and the odd attack by someone they pissed off along the way. They did it successfully by being smart.

Everything came down to timing, information, resources, and accuracy. They were disciplined in all four. So when Rip traded the back roads for the highway with direct access to the dock flanked by five other riders sporting the same emblem, he wasn't surprised. When Titan pulled up matching his speed, he fought the emotions buried down deep and contained for years from erupting to the surface. Hell-bent on meeting his goal he gave him a gloves-up from the bars and drove on for miles in the hum of the bikes and calm of sharing a singular mind. When Titan and he were within five miles of the site the other riders peeled off, disappearing down intersecting roads as smoothly as they first materialized. And for the first time in many years it was him and his brother together in peace on the highway experiencing the freedom of the ride.

It wouldn't last but for a stretch of common pavement Riparian remembered joy.

So, when the site came into view, his anger rose untamed and fiercer than it might have if he'd forgotten it altogether.

Rolling the bikes under the cover of thick foliage in a ditch not far from the closest undetectable lookout, they traded skullcaps for black balaclava to match their night gear and move out for the first position. The transport truck was loosely concealed by the foliage of a grouping of trees and sat waiting nearby with keys under the front wheel well. The gang mapped the easiest way in, out, alternatives, surveillance risks and dead ends laying the groundwork for success. Attaining it was left to the brothers alone.

Titan grabbed Rip's arm before they exited their cover. "We come out of this alive, brother," he said. "Or it's all for nothing."

"That's the plan," Rip replied. "We'll get as close as is safe and wait for the next guard sweep. They leave, we go in. We'll have less than fifteen minutes to free them. The boys couldn't get close enough to know how the complex is fortified. If they don't stay quiet, we all die."

Titan cocked his head as if to say it figured and ducked low heading to the location where the boys left bolt cutters for them. Recovering the tools they each took a side and clipped through creating a hole wide enough to rush victims out of, meeting in the middle. It wasn't electrified or even the strongest gauge of chain link, just typically used on such sites. The problem for the traffickers was fortifying a location that shouldn't require it in excess while maintaining the illusion of being nothing more than the front they were using.

One strike for the good guys.

Rip surveyed the area before stepping through with Titan close behind. Dropping down an embankment to level ground near the largest warehouse where the gang confirmed sightings of victims. They approached from its back, using equipment, storage bins, and vehicles to snake their way up against a front loader and its exterior wall.

Two hefty guards filed out, armed with semi-automatics, and broke left away from them to make a sweep of the area. They stepped clear of the corner and Rip and Titan rushed into the space they'd exited between the warehouse and a storage silo, staying low and watching for active camera surveillance. Noticing one pointed left of its entrance, Rip signaled to Titan and they put coverage between them and it as they moved. Sheltered by a wall in a strange metal hallway they located a secured access door. Titan rolled his eyes and mouthed the words "Fort Knox" as they searched for another way in.

Rip heard his blood pulsing through his body echoing in his ears. You always expect difficulties and worked the problem but it didn't make it comfortable. He motioned for Titan to check ahead for another door while he jumped back outside to do the same. Coming back together seconds later they decided on a smaller access door at the far end. If guards were present, there'd be no way to get to it so it shouldn't require the same level of security as the outer one. Titan pressed his ear to the door and signaled for Rip to do the same. Voices, female voices echoed through its hollow core.

"If we take it out by force the reaction from inside could end us all in this hallway," Rip cautioned.

Titan pulled a kit from one of his many pockets and picked the lock in relative silence. Knowing he had entry, he nodded. Rip pulled out a small flashlight, pointed it up to his face area, put a finger over the hole where his mouth was signaling silence, and gave the okay.

The traffickers had no reason to expect two men to enter their compound alone to mess with their product and live to make it back out. No vehicles approaching from incoming roads meant anyone monitoring wouldn't anticipate visitors. The tip-of-the-spear approach had benefits unless or until they were made. Preventing that was the challenge made worse when dealing with large numbers of terrorized victims.

Titan opened the door, not knowing if more guards were set up inside. While Rip walked in lit like a candle Titan dropped low to shoot out adversaries if necessary. Seeing none, Rip spoke evenly and calmly to the huddled girls.

"Don't make a sound. We're here to rescue you, but have no backup. Any noise could cost lives. Follow us silently, even if you're scared or in pain and do exactly as I say until we are out of danger." Rip carried a badge, it was official, just not his. Pointing the light to it he flashed it from one side to the other, then waved the victims to follow Titan out. "I will follow behind to protect you. Do as he says, stay silent, don't stop or look back."

Titan motioned his intent to execute phase one of their plan but whispered to Rip as the victims aligned behind him. "No time to check other spaces until they're safe."

A woman slightly older than most of the others heard him and whispered back, "They only hold the living here."

Rip felt a wave of nausea twist his insides thinking of Mac and witnessing the condition of the victims. Some had to support others to walk and reminded him of prisoners of war, mere waifs and equally brutalized. As they passed by him following Titan back to the break in the fencing, he repeated, "Stay low, quiet, and keep moving."

Watching them file out following each transition from outside the holding silo, which was more of a barn on the interior, to the hallway, and out into the compound to weave back to the embankment, forest and truck, he wondered how many would make it?

During the planning phase, Rip made Titan promise to

abandon the victims if it meant his life for theirs. Knowing brotherly sentiment wouldn't commit him, he hung the responsibility of returning to protect Machias on him. As the girls snaked away with him in the lead, Rip hoped Titan held to his word. Though they didn't have far to go, minutes from freedom and potential escape, the chances of them all, including those suffering withdrawal and in physical pain, creeping the distance without a sound wasn't good.

Rip watched his brother leading with the strength of a warrior and grace of a savior then he turned his back. It was a good last memory if it had to be.

Checking his watch beneath the rim of his glove, they had all of five minutes to make it up the hill and out of direct line of sight. Rip backed out, defending their exit, selecting a halfway point to operate from until they were clear. Facing the direction of the returning guards, he waited, glancing back as the stream of young girls disappeared further up the hill. Four were left to crest the embankment when he heard footsteps, but they weren't coming from dead ahead as one would predict. And they weren't a singular set.

Death in war was often delivered from that one unexpected ambush, or so Riparian learned losing many team members to them. He survived by anticipating every possible move, putting himself in the shoes of enemies. Even here he thought the best way to cover the compound would be to break off, opposite side searches, and circle back midway to catch any intruder off-guard. Rip wasn't surprised by their approach.

The fact that they doubled in numbers was what threw him.

Poised between a hill of wood pellets as tall as him on the right and a small front-end loader he had some measure of cover from the two flanking, but not when the initial guards returned from dead ahead. Following Titan's path out would only draw fire and attention to him and the victims squashing any hope of their escape. Moving forward would have him meet his end quicker in close range. He glanced inside the loader considering for a fraction of a second, if the keys were in it, driving his way out. By the time it started up he'd be riddled in holes. Deciding slamming to the pavement and rolling under it was the only option, he hit the ground and was mid-roll as boots cleared the corner dead ahead.

From his horizontal position upside down he couldn't discern, in the shadow of night, if either guard spotted him. Then one dropped his head to the sound of Rip sliding over loose gravel. Figuring this would not end well he thought of Machias and how much he truly wanted to be the one who returned, put her on the back of his bike, and drove her out of the hellish life she existed in to a new and better one. It was a flash.

No. It was muzzle flare. And the odd thing was it wasn't aimed at him.

Pinned half under the dozer he watched the guards smash into each other, their bodies flailing from multiple impacts. When their weapons dropped from hands made useless, Rip spun back out, sprang to his feet, and turned his weapon on the guard on the opposite side of the machine. Distracted by the executions, he never saw it coming and Rip's bullet put him down with one hit. The suppressed snap of a Max Nine said the guard advancing from the left would come no further. Rip knew all his weapons by sound especially gang favorites. Spinning back he trained his gun on the scene ahead and then dropped it to his side as WarMakers brothers strode in beside him, watching in a sweep for any other enemies.

"Hey, brother," said the one they coined "Tracks" because rivals made them whenever they saw him coming. "You didn't really think Kill would let you fight alone, let these pricks kill one of ours after the shit they've pulled on our turf, did you? He says well done, by the way."

It was difficult to process the conversation standing in the center of four dead guards on a compound full of hedonistic killers, but Rip got it. He nodded and the guy motioned back to where Titan exited with the victims.

"We're driving them in for delivery so your brother's safe and our part in this is clear. Meantime we have a mess to make of this tidy enterprise. Lucky we reached you. She's sprung a leak." Tracks pointed at the dozer. "You smell like fuel man. You would've lit up like a firecracker. Dump the jacket, it's go-time."

Rip swung a cautioned glance at the embankment and watched WarMakers scattering and lying in wait ready to defend the transport. He exhaled. The air released like he hadn't breathed for several minutes. He signaled the enforcers flanking him and motioned for the main offices on the site with one thought in mind.

Kill the head and the body dies.

FORTY-NINE

Imprisoning product and enemies was the one talent Barracutta excelled at above all others, and ensuring even if escape occurred it only led to a worse fate, especially if betrayal accompanied it. The Candy Store owner failed to protect their arrangement and inspired retaliation from the WarMakers that spilled onto Barracutta's ground and he died screaming. The kid who cyber-snaked into their surveillance cameras had been beaten to within an inch of his life for it but hadn't been pronounced yet. The guards Barracutta sent to the hospital to replace the one killed by police and the other taken into custody from the Barclay hit couldn't reach the one survivor capable of confirming Barracutta's identity. The other was comatose and, as the guard who witnessed him said, "crispy and days from cremation finishing what the fire hadn't." Leaving one tasked with eliminating the surviving witness before any interview could take place, Barracutta tied another loose end even if the final knot wasn't yet cinched.

The WarMakers required swift and final revenge but an all-out war with them would enlist the full arsenal of the law aimed the wrong direction and that wouldn't allow Barracutta a quiet exit to sail for calmer waters and a new staging location. Reaching out to put wheels in motion, by the time Barracutta's feet met new soil it'd require days not weeks to reestablish a reliable production pipeline.

With a worn out welcome Barracutta couldn't wait to push off shore but not without delivering a gift of vengeance to the gang that cost so much in revenue, and the stage had already been set days earlier. Utilizing the threat of a potential gas leak to clear the compound of regular workers tied to the highway construction, Barracutta placed the risk in the minds of many. Now, when the leak ignited into an explosion, strategically positioned and vast enough to eradicate every shred of evidence tying Barracutta to any crime or hint of human trafficking, the validity of such claims would be in question. And Barracutta could watch it play out and dissolve in the news media cycle while living abroad.

Daughtry was troublesome due to their long history and his knowledge of the inner working of the business. Still, with his credibility in question, a missing wife declared dead and now a missing daughter, he didn't have much of a leg to stand on. But when the footage from the gang informant landed Barracutta realized he didn't have legs at all. Apparently, no balls either, that outcome was fitting. The clip's heading said **Next** in bold large lettering. If the gang were willing to bring the war to the compound, it'd take all of them.

And that was exactly what Barracutta banked on.

The holdback was the product. Three and a half million waited to be delivered overseas. The particulars of this victim pool fetched a higher price than most shipments. Three of the girls were ordered as future brides for royalty reaching prices between a quarter of a million to over one million, Daughtry's girl winning the highest price tag. Walking from the obligations on the other side of the world wasn't an option, it'd threaten future business in a region paying top dollar.

And there was still no sign of the Daughtry girl though three of the best were inland following every lead to locate her or her transporter. Barracutta sent the two who handled the handoff in the van because they could identify the Ferryman by more than the scar they described. Hunting him down with more than a few outlandish predictions of where he may be, they were all highly motivated. When the gang was weak, engaged in fighting their way off the compound, Barracutta would send the signal to hit the clubhouse to search for her. She was the one Barracutta wouldn't leave without. The sale of her, and the promise of more, too great to disrupt. If the instructions on her care hadn't been so explicit Barracutta could've avoided so much trouble and stored her like the others on site, but one word from her confirming the existence of any others and the deal was dead and so too was Barracutta.

Alone in the secure office, Barracutta awaited the check-in of the latest guard rounds. And began counting minutes when the radio didn't sound at exactly eleven fifteen. They weren't flawless and, if they encountered an area of concern, had a twenty-minute window of grace to make contact. Flipping through internal camera angles didn't reveal anything amiss so Barracutta switched over to exterior feeds. Nothing until camera five, directed at a subsidiary road that merged with the major highway leading back to the town of Shadow Hook. There, the lens caught the tail end of a vehicle but most of the capture happened prior to Barracutta logging in. Rewinding the feed, in night vision clarity, exiting from the direction of the compound was a five-ton cargo truck.

"Did we have deliveries?" Barracutta questioned aloud. It wasn't a stretch to assume supplies of some measure were dropped off. It occurred regularly during construction and drops required for work scheduled the following day often happened at night or in early morning hours.

Scanning a loading area feed where concrete materials, asphalt, erosion and sediment control products like silt bags were routinely delivered, Barracutta zoomed in on a pile of recently dropped silt fences, bags, and division barriers. Explainable, but as the minutes ticked by the thirst for confirmation grew.

Calling down to an exterior guard walking the perimeter of the compound Barracutta enlisted it. "Hey, you seen any deliveries since you came on shift?"

"No, Boss. I haven't been on the outer track for long though," he said, the radio clear of interference.

"How long exactly?" Barracutta asked, impatient.

"Eleven minutes, give or take," he said.

He needed a smack, give or take. "Leave the perimeter, check on the main and the diesel hold tank and check back in. You have ten minutes."

"Leaving now," he said.

Barracutta dropped the radio criticizing privately. "Well I should fucking hope so."

Perhaps this was the paranoia creeping in? With so much at stake, piles of dumped wood chips soaked in fuel surrounding the site, money at risk, and a clock ticking, fears were taking hold. Analyzing the situation while waiting Barracutta remembered that no one in authority knew enough to identify who held the reins of the operation. Daughtry was dead, the Candy man dead, the witnesses from the hit dead or on their way, the Barclay kid too. Who was left? Those in Barracutta's employ would never. They knew the cost of betrayal.

Exhaling Barracutta pulled up the offshore account padded for moments such as this. As the balance, in excess of two million, danced across the screen memories of the tropical hideaway came to mind delivering the calming effect that always followed. Teal oceans, white sands, a new name and...

"Dead bodies! Boss? They're dead behind the main. Cut to pieces! We have company!" The guard from the perimeter made it inside and, according to his panicked description, wasn't the only one.

"Check the product hold! Go now! I'll send you backup," Barracutta barked into the line seeing blood red but knowing taking the gang down before leaving couldn't happen if they didn't breach the gates. It required them all to cross onto Barracutta's turf. They just arrived slightly ahead of plan. Placing an all-out alert for intruders and securing of the product Barracutta went one step further.

"Move the product now to the sea-can and do it fast! I need

three of you to move them and the rest find our intruders and take them down, understood?"

Each guard checked in confirming orders except the one closest to the main building where the girls were held. Barracutta reached out twice and when there was no response realized the WarMakers were living up to their name.

FIFTY

Sectioned into teams, FBI, detectives from Major Crimes, and various support were suited up and crossing the lot to pile into vehicles when Jade saw Callum, receiving a call and listening intently for a few seconds, wave wildly drawing them in. Drex, Jade, Kane, and Jackson halted and redirected to where Callum stood, an expression of bewilderment on his face. Before addressing the questioning faces of his colleagues he swiveled around searching until locating Captain Grey. Grey locked eyes, reading the urgency, and ran the space between them.

Slightly out of breath, he asked, "What is it?"

"I need you to contact all of the medical support staff and send them in. We have over twenty victims incoming, sir. My deep cover is driving the trafficking abductees to us inside a motorcade of biker protection. And the WarMakers are responsible for the rescue."

All eyes on Callum, stretched by disbelief, left the space around him silent until Drex filled it. "Taylor, I need you on organizing and activating all the medical support staff immediately. Stay with Callum and pull a team for protection during transport to the hospital. French, send agents ahead to prepare the hospital for incoming and shut 'er down! No one in or out without identification checks matched to patients. And watch the handoff for signs of deception. Make it happen, now!"

Agents scattered breaking from their previous assigned groups and reorganizing to help Callum, who was struggling to process. Two heavily armed officers from the tactical team read Drex without words and broke to flank the back deck where the previous drop occurred. Weapons capable of firing rounds fast enough to shred an army in seconds in such narrowed proximity would meet any vehicle or motorbike crew entering.

"Whoever your deep cover is, Callum, can we have him when he's ready?" Kane asked, patting Callum's shoulder. "Definitely worth keeping on active duty."

"Titan," Callum said, his tone registering pride. "That'll be up to him."

"How far out?" Grey asked.

"He said six minutes," Callum said.

"You heard the man," Drex said. "You have five minutes to turn this cop shop into a med-bay." Glancing to Jade, he said, "That means they infiltrated the compound by the docks and we're coming in late to the party. New plan, six of us drop in by air and the rest follow by road."

In minutes Jade's unit, Drex and two agents were seated in the chopper Drex had on standby and he was coordinating from a headset inside as it rose off the ground. Jade watched the lights of Shadow Hook fade and the coastline appear. Seeing the dark water she couldn't help recalling the last time her and Drex shared a helicopter. Glancing up his eyes met hers confirming he was thinking the same thing. Kane was debating approach strategies with Tex and she was glad for his distraction.

Dropping in an empty parking lot on the opposite side of the compound where enemies may have heard the aircraft but wouldn't see it, Drex gave orders for the bird to stay out of direct line of sight until he signaled them in. The night was black outside the reach of city lights and so was the bird.

It lifted off and the team huddled making last-minute adjustments. "We will not be there alone and if the gang is pissed at law enforcement it'd be the perfect time to take us out so head on a swivel," Drex said.

"If the victims are gone what's your target?" Kane asked.

"You take one side we'll take the other and we radio at first sighting. We lay in wait until we're not alone and backup arrives unless unavoidable and we put them down one at a time. Remove their radios with weapons. Don't want them issuing warnings."

Everyone broke out but not before Kane smiled at Jade. One of those 'don't worry about us we're great' smiles. Jade and Drex veered left losing sight of them rounding the north building staying low and dodging cameras along the way. Coming to a gated entrance for workers in the chain link fence, they expected monitoring. The camera overhead was busted and dangled from a frayed wire. The lock was useless, the attached sections dismantled by bolt cutters. Drex pushed it open. "We're not the first ones through here."

"Well he won't be checking our credentials," Jade said, motioning to a body half inside a booth located just beyond the gate. She confiscated his weapon handing it to Drex, lifted a badge from his chest, and removed his radio checking its volume. A quick glance at his head wound and she didn't need to check his pulse. "Double tap," she said.

Drex nodded and they pushed on. They hadn't made it ten steps when Drex flattened Jade against the exterior wall of the building they were passing. Without a word he pointed up. Her eyes followed his finger in time to see a shadow passing by a window on the second level of the adjacent building. Taking cover behind a pile of broken-down boxes the size of refrigerators they watched movement above.

"I don't think it's an employee," Drex said. The figure shadowing them seemed aggressive, not careful. An enforcer on a mission.

Jade nudged Drex in the side and tipped her head. Another broken lock and man door paralleled a bolt cutter left outside. "WarMakers," she said. "If you ran this enterprise and feared a breach this wouldn't be a power position."

"Agreed," he said, holding his radio open on his shoulder. "We have one, possibly two, WarMakers in the north building second floor, one employee down, and radio access. Moving further in."

Acknowledgment came in the form of click backs. So far, the others hadn't encountered resistance.

Jade gave a vertical hand chop in the direction of a building closest to the docks. Drex nodded and they moved silently toward it. There was a stretch of five or six strides in the opening between buildings. Drex would cover her as she crossed, coming in behind. Jade hadn't made it two steps when her phone buzzed, not pausing she sprinted the remaining distance, pinned against a metal wall, and answered.

The voice was male, deep, fast, and out of breath. "Detective Carmichael, your team is not alone, we've cleared all the building except the dockside. Remember we had your backs and don't come for us. Two of our members will stay and take the fall if one is coming. Aside from them...you're on your own and the head isn't dead."

The line went dead before Drex reached her, his eyes questioning. "One of ours?"

"One of theirs," she said, surveying their immediate areas of risk. "Didn't identify directly but WarMakers. They cleared the site for us, all except..." She pointed to the area they intended to search. "They're leaving two enforcers behind. And said whoever runs this hasn't been located by them."

Drex nodded and said, "Our turn." Depressing the radio he spoke into it for all sharing the channel. "Be aware WarMakers on site are pulling out, do not engage. They've left two enforcers with us, watch for emblems and do not fire on. The boss of this bullshit is hiding here somewhere and it's on us to find them and take them down."

Knowing the rest of the team would filter through to their current position, Jade was highly motivated to take out opposition before they arrived. At the building's edge she dropped low and peered around the corner. A small yacht bobbed just off the docks at a lone harbor. Not illuminated but reflecting in the moonlight she couldn't see any movement or signs of activity aboard. Still, it seemed a viable safe zone for anyone intent on avoiding capture.

"The boat?" she said, stepping back for Drex to eye it.

"Yeah, I'd choose it," he agreed. "Can't get to it without a swim and anyone inside this place would spot us between here and the dock."

Jade was about to agree when a window above caught her attention. Ever so quietly someone was opening it. Motioning for silence she pointed above. Drex signaled an approach from the lower access door dockside around the corner. Together they'd flank the entrance, then she'd duck in while he covered and followed. The yacht chimed in its moorings as dark water swelled close to shore.

She couldn't help the sense of dread not knowing what evil hid there.

On three she pulled the door; Drex aimed inside and swept the dark space beyond registering an open sorting area of some kind but no enemies waiting. Jade skirted close, passing under his arm, and was hit by the strong scent reminiscent of kerosene and wood not unlike gardeners chips. Strange pairing. "Wood chips and lighter fluid?" she whispered. "Storing both together?"

"Yeah. Or not," Drex said, following. "Watch where you step and what you brush up against."

The floor inside was concrete, the walls dark gray corrugated metal. Peering high above the distant roof interlaced tracks were too. The day had been hot but the temperature inside was cold, even for night. Like a refrigeration unit regulated it. Beyond the open space a wall separated a bank of rooms on the main, a criss-crossing staircase led to a second floor, a walkway, and recessed windowed offices. They advanced stepping over a body right of the entryway.

Jade slid clear, half Drex's size. He stepped over and was met with a hand grabbing his left ankle. Jade swung back to the sound, searching for weapons and seeing none, grabbed at a radio off the wounded man's belt. Not a WarMakers member but definitely hit by one. Pulling free Drex dropped over him, his knee neutralizing any attempt at movement. "Where?" he said. "Your boss now or you die here."

The man pointed weakly to the floor above and said, in broken syllables, "Catwalk."

Jade rushed into the office across spotting duct tape on its desk. She grabbed it and came back to silence the guy in case he chose call out. When she returned, he'd expired.

Sweeping the main floor sections they ascended the stairs, ever watchful of activity. In the largest of the offices, on the far right end of the warehouse and nearest the docks, a door leading outside to what might be a balcony sat ajar. Whoever used it was in too much of a hurry to shut it.

Jade locked eyes with Drex and mouthed the words "on the run." He reached out pausing her so he could take lead. She knew he feared whatever waited beyond presented the perfect opportunity to be gunned down from an unexpected angle. Outside, the balcony extended into a catwalk over a compound road beneath, cross to a lookout-type structure, and then descend through a set of stair switchbacks to the dock nearest the waiting yacht.

Examining the landscape, Jade said, "I think we're better to go back through the building and out. One of us can cover while the other swims out to it."

Drex, with eyes glued to the distance between the shoreline and the boat, shook his head. "Someone beat us to it." He pointed to the dark water and between the waves the splash of a heavy swimmer broke the surface.

Unable to see clearly, Jade pulled her night vision ocular and zoomed in. "The idiot is going to drown. He's swimming in full leathers."

"WarMakers?" Drex asked.

"Yep."

"Let's give him some backup." Drex assumed the rear while Jade and him ran to ground level, caught sight of a back exit, and threw it open with guns aimed. The swimmer had made strides and was nearing the stern. Moonlight catching glimpses as the waves rose and fell around him. Whoever it was he was a damn good swimmer but the effort had to be taxing. "Scan for movement inside. We see anything headed his way we alert him."

"They're out of range. You're thinking enough to throw them off and give him the upper hand?" Jade asked and Drex confirmed while grabbing his walkie. The fact that they hadn't heard anything for a few minutes wasn't comforting even if expected.

"Boss might be planning to flee using a small yacht at our twenty. Coastguard, pull up and brace for that outcome without making yourself seen and wait on my go ahead. Team check-in." Drex waited as team members clicked back and the Coast Guard confirmed they were pulling into a blocking position if the vehicle left port. Then the walkie lit up.

"Drex, Kane here. We have two employees, both wounded but talking. They were damn anxious to be brought in so we pressed and their boss salted the place with ignition, wood pellet piles soaked in diesel fuel. One shot in the wrong direction and we're in the belly of Hell. The WarMakers retreated and it being rigged to blow may be why."

"Okay, folks, you heard the man. We have an imminent threat to life. Everyone pull back and wait for further instruction. Kane and Jackson call in the explosives unit support and follow protocol. Carmichael and I are in pursuit near the shoreline and will use the Coast Guard for extraction. Drex out."

"I'm not going anywhere until—"

"Yes. I figured. Also figured you'd want to make sure your team, like mine, was in the clear before we take our dip," Drex said, eyebrows raised. "Bring your suit?"

FIFTY-ONE

Rip knew it wasn't just bad luck or code to keep your jacket on when you were gang made; it was a matter of survival. Enemies in a fight were marked by not wearing gang emblems, and tattoos were hard to see when you were covered in blood, sweat, and debris from whatever place you destroyed in the process, but fucking water? And not just water but dark, fuel-polluted, factory-runoff water that you couldn't swallow, burned your eyes, and smelled like the guts of a junkyard dog. If he made it to the boat alive, he was pissed enough by the trip to tear whoever waited there limb to limb. His time with the gang ended when they pulled out of the compound feeling their job done and left him to do what he promised he would. He shrugged the jacket free halfway across and let it drop with more important vows to keep.

Kill the head and take the fall.

Two of the guards Tracks ended broke in the grasp of pain and gave up the yacht and its purpose to provide escape if everything went to hell for the boss. Rip saw problems with the plan. The Coast Guard being what they were in this neck of shoreline, unless the yacht had a custom engine and cloaking capability he gave it no chance at making it to open water. And parked off the only dock it screamed too obvious for anyone as diabolical as this enemy was. Despite these concerns, when Rip spotted the figure hightailing it down the staircase to the dock for the tiny outboard to reach the boat, he had no choice but to follow.

The figure that boarded the boat descended out of sight off the deck and for the galley before Rip hit the water. The engine wasn't humming but the anchor was on its way up when Rip climbed aboard. He swam around the guest docks and slips accessing the fuel dock. The lack of immediate contact told Rip he was up against one perhaps two assailants, no more.

With the anchor being lifted he made his way toward the helm but didn't get far. In the dark of night he couldn't see his enemy laid a poor man's trap, having thrown a net out and shellacked its surface with grease, sunscreen by the coconut aroma. Rip averted doing the splits but couldn't stay upright and crashed into a heap. Struggling to free his gun arm from the netting he heard the cabin door swing open. Rolling off the edge into the water to fight the net from pulling him into the depths seemed a preferred option to remaining an easy target but before he scrambled to the edge a shot rang out overhead, not from the galley but at it.

When the second shot sounded, he caught the muzzle flash from the shoreline. He didn't know who it was but the distraction gave him a chance to grab the rail and claw his way to solid footing. Crushing into a wrapped tarp pinned in the corner he waited until the guy who left the slipstream walked clear, hammered the weapon from his hands, and knocked him on his ass, sending him flying into the heap of tangled netting.

With his weapon aimed and ready to fire he didn't pull its trigger, recognizing the face before him. This wasn't the head of the operation. In a flash Rip recalled where he'd seen him. The night of Jack's death. On the side of the highway. Pieces came forward but not the whole and as if sensing it the guy on the ground tangled in fish net laughed.

"I thought there was something off with you that night," he said. "You hesitated with the kid too. I figured the scar was only the half of the damage when you flaked out." He wasn't shifting and Rip had him at point blank so he asked.

"Where's your boss, asshole? This operation isn't you. You're their fucking decoy and you probably haven't even registered it yet." Rip held the weapon trained on the guy splayed on deck hoping whoever fired from the shore wasn't aiming higher. Either way he wasn't backing down.

"You really think someone who mastered the art of all this would wait around for your biker buddies to take a shot? This is way above your pay grade, asshole." The guy spun, grabbing for a second gun at his back. Rip fired, making a mess of him before he had a solid grip. Stepping back into the shadows he checked the helm and ran the galley. The shooter was alone on board. Before exiting he knocked the anchor back down, pulled his phone and dialed.

"Detective, I'm the one aboard. This guy was a patsy. The head isn't here. And I dumped my jacket in the drink so watch where you're firing." Rip hung up, soaked and sore, and headed for the outboard figuring it not only the fastest way back to shore but one with a view that may help narrow other options for the leader's hideout. With the gang's total incursion on the compound from all sides, no way did the trafficker make it off the property. And now Rip only wanted to end them more.

Pulling away from the yacht he saw a flashlight beam on the shoreline, it waved vertically as if nodding agreement. Detective Carmichael. Deciding to drive across to the spot Titan and him started and where the gang left him supplies, he glanced back to the detective and what must've been her partner, two dark figures in the cast of moonlight. They were gone. As quickly as they vanished a light, singular and moving, reflected high above the second-story office windows out of upper vent spaces in the roofline of the warehouse. The detective couldn't have traversed the expanse between the ground outside to the height in mere seconds.

He called again. "You have company in the rafters inside. Good luck Carmichael and check your mail." He sent a clip of Machias safe and sitting in front of the day's current news feed so if he didn't return, Carmichael would know to keep looking for her until Mac called Callum, revealed her location, and was ready to go home.

Rip didn't care who caught the one responsible for raping the world of innocent young people as long as they were stopped. But the one who came after Mac would not live to do it again. And since the head of this ugly enterprise was one and the same, he made for the stash he requested from Killian. Insurance that the head would never make it off the compound even in handcuffs with a Major Crimes escort.

FIFTY-TWO

A xel delivered as promised and allowed Raven to view the footage Dylan duplicated from inside the trafficking ring's compound and sent to the special homicide unit working Jack's case. But, in Rave's opinion, it identified the 'where' of the criminal responsible for his murder but not the 'who.' All Raven knew was the executioner existed somewhere on the property and he didn't have the restraint to hand his fate over to anyone else. He made that mistake before, stepping back when he should've stood strong. It cost Jack his life. So, as he made preparations for the bastard's undoing, he carried only one thought, which contradicted promising Axe he wouldn't go John Wick on anyone.

Justice for Jack meant a life for a life and Rave didn't give a shit what it took or where it landed him.

Doing his best to conceal the red fire burning behind his eyes when Jack's truck appeared on the feed, he chose his words and reactions carefully. When he and Axe visited Dylan, allowed a brief eyes-on before exiting the hospital, he swallowed the rage. Months from now when Dylan's body had time to heal, Rave prayed he'd make a full recovery. The fact that he shouldn't have been forced to, added ambers to an already stoked fire.

Axel drove him home and they reviewed everything from there. Absorbing the depth and breadth of the exploitation operating in and around their community since he was a child hit Rave so hard he excused himself from the table, walked to his and Jack's bedroom, and into their washroom with doors closed, and vomited. Axe implored him to stay calm and rest knowing the detectives working to bring the trafficking ring and everyone associated down were the very best at what they did.

Rave found it hard to trust, leaving in Jack's old truck from high school, to drive the back roads to Daughtry's farm, only to discover it set ablaze. As the explosion shook the ground and illuminated the sky in red and orange bands, he lost faith in the cops having both hands neatly tied around the throat of the criminal operation. The next stop on his list, while a stream of first responder vehicles rushed passed him on the opposite side of the highway, was to ensure those responsible met the same fate as Daughtry's place.

Rave had never been violent, but he was a quick study.

He fought against the darker impulse listing regrets he'd have, most of them associated with Machias. If she was alive and somehow made it back home, Jack would expect Raven to follow through with their original plans, welcome her into their home, help her rebuild her life, and continue all their directives concerning the podcast.

Taking matters into his hands would not only prevent but completely upend all of it. Jack wouldn't approve but Jack wasn't here. He was dead. And so much upheaval blocked Rave from even considering a proper tribute and service for him. He pushed the thoughts away focusing on the road to the construction site but visions of Jack emerged regardless. Him laughing behind the scenes with podcast bloopers, making flapjacks shaped into houses and taking ownership of the name when they signed final papers for their building, and staring at the night's skyline together.

All of their happy life robbed from them both.

No. Someone had to pay. And he had to know it could not happen again to anyone else, not by the same hands. They had to be put down.

Rave, as Jack said, was a self-proclaimed renaissance man and a diva wrapped in Louis Vuitton. More interested in the latest New York hair trends and international trade issues then how to change a tire or learn the art of boxing. He preferred fencing to fighting and museums to movies but he became an expert at archery when he was twelve, won several competitions locally and internationally, and used the practice ranges as his outdoor outlet for stress. He never used it for hunting until tonight.

Glancing at the high-powered Mongolian recurve compound bow on the seat next to him he questioned how difficult it might be to get within a couple hundred yards of the target. First, he'd be forced to wait for the target to be identified, either by an attempt to flee the sting operation Axel explained the detectives were mobilizing to dismantle the trafficking ring or by coming out of it in cuffs. Whoever the cops were most focused on was about to have a worse outcome than arrest.

He parked a distance away in a makeshift lot littered with several other trucks, most likely used by true construction workers while on shift. The expanse of dirt had no close facilities, no fencing, no cameras. Hiking in a wide arc he approached from the far west side and was glad he didn't veer east after recognizing a stream of black SUVs barreling off the highway below the embankment he climbed for an overview of the site. No way were they not law enforcement. Ten minutes earlier and they would've stopped him right there.

A small voice said he shouldn't be there; this was a really bad idea. He silenced it searching the area for close-range opportunities. If he was in his late twenties or thirties, he'd likely choose the rooftop of one of the buildings but he was young so the landscape spoke a different language to him. Between the main entrance and largest building and a dockside warehouse was a grouping of trees. Most likely planted to offer shade decades ago when the space shared another purpose. Throwing his bow back over his shoulder he climbed the largest of the pack of five, shuffled out on its strongest branch, and found a stable reliable angle.

Waiting for a killer to enter his bow sight so he could deliver the same.

FIFTY-THREE

"T he place is surrounded and the bastard is inside it with us. I couldn't be happier." As Drex said it Jade eyed him like he'd described a peyote high. "What the hell, Drex?" She questioned him racing up the staircase leading to the catwalk at the warehouse's roofline inside the building they left to check out the yacht.

"If he's here—"

She cut him off registering his thought. "It might discourage him from lighting the place up." She didn't slow but listened to his footfall and breathing close behind her.

"Exactly. Unless he's swimming for another continent, and the Coast Guard is patrolling, he comes with us or we all go up in a blaze together."

"Nice," she said, slowing up as the last set of risers came into view. "The light was cast far right." Drex had a point but Jade considered another. "What if there's roof access and a chopper up top? We couldn't do a flyover without alerting. It's possible."

"Now who's being gloomy?" he said. She glanced his way; he was surveying the space above but shrugged and gave her a quick side-eye.

As he peered through his ocular with night vision, she quickly accessed the mail the caller sent her. On silent, she watched Machias perched happily before a large screen with the current day's broadcast. The girl appeared in great health, unrestrained, and even waved at the camera, her expression peaceful. Machias was alive and someone had gone to great lengths to keep her that way. Without time to contemplate the wisdom of her action, she forwarded the footage to Captain Grey, Callum, and Axel. Ensuring she wasn't alone in knowing the girl's status, especially given the uncertainty of the next minutes.

Drex snapped his ocular back in place on his belt and stared at her having caught the end of her typing into the phone. "What is it?"

"Whoever is out on the water sent a clip of our missing teen, she's alive and well," Jade said, unable to conceal the relief in her voice. "I forwarded it so…"

He nodded understanding their position and the odds against. "I see no one above on the areas exposed but if this was his long-term plan who knows what's waiting for us. The catwalk appears solid but don't take chances, use a three-point contact if possible, in case the floor gives way."

"Comforting," she said, scouring the area ahead. "You first."

He huffed a laugh. "I'm twice your weight. This time you're in the lead and I'll cover."

"You better stay close," she said, stepping up on the catwalk but staying low.

"I keep trying to," he replied.

She never turned back, placing a hand on its railing while stepping forward smoothly but feeling for instability as she advanced. If there was ever a place of vulnerability, this was it. One track, no offshoots until the far side, and some thirty or more feet to a cement floor. She didn't gaze over its edge, maintaining her focus straight ahead at the only space the perpetrator could be.

She heard Drex breathing behind her, felt the weight of his steps. Both were a comfort.

On the far side the catwalk branched out to a large loft section almost like a lookout, with horizontal windows on each side meeting at its corner and solid metal barriers instead of continued open rails preventing visual of who could be crouched behind them. Her weapon led the way and the closer they neared the more she fought the instinct to duck.

More than halfway across details were coming into view but there'd been not a shred of movement. The rafters were so quiet she contemplated the chance he'd escaped out the roof and was long gone leaving them to traverse the elevated gangplank foolishly wasting time in fear. Two doors existed at the back of the loft; one labeled Outside Utility Access the other Roof.

Reading them, she swiveled to Drex. "Rooftop access—"

The bullet grazed by her left shoulder, the wind and buzz from it unmistakable. In mid-turn she lost contact with the railing falling fully dependent on the strength of the metal floorboards. She hit it with visions of the ground under her breaking free and reached out for the railing but before she made contact it vanished.

And so did Drex.

He'd had a solid grip on the rail on his left, weapon in his right. The bullet must've compromised an already weak connection in rail sections. It broke free taking Drex's weight with it and he'd succumbed to the momentum. One second he was there, solid like a rock, the next gone.

Scrambling to the edge as a second shot rang out, Jade fired on the area where she glimpsed muzzle flare searching the distance to the ground. Drex was dangling, caught in cables descending to machinery below. "Drex," she called to him afraid he was hit or unconscious.

"Go," he yelled. "Go nail the bastard."

Upside down and injured he never lost directive. Leaping to her feet, anger unleashed, she ran the distance dodging returned fire as she unloaded her clip ahead. A bullet skimmed her free arm. She ran through the force of its impact and kept firing. Time wasted on this bastard meant time in jeopardy for Drex. Jade closed the distance. The target tossed their weapon, bullets spent, but not before firing one into Drex.

Jade heard him cry out and something inside snapped. In three strides she gained momentum and bound over the head of the assailant, crushing them in her fall. Coming down hard, her eyes searched for weapons as she readied to fire. A hand reached out fighting to regain a grasp on a box device. Jade knocked it across the floor, pinned the muzzle of her gun to the back of a head of greasy black hair, and spoke with venom in her voice.

"You so much as breathe too fast and you'll have new places for the air to flow out, motherfucker." She grabbed her cuffs free, slapped them on the reaching wrist and kneed the perp to sit up. Straddling the form on the floor she yanked the other hand close and cuffed it tight and uncomfortable. With no time and Drex at the forefront of concern, she searched around the space, collected the switch box from the ground, located a rope tying off a section of catwalk, untied it and brought it down to restrain the criminal. Securing the rope to an iron brace near the wall they crashed into, she stole a second to identify the adversary responsible for decades of misery in her county.

Lifting the head off the ground where it collapsed facedown Jade gasped, her brow creasing into madness.

"You've got to be fucking kidding! The head of this shitstorm is a woman?" She stood up from the hogtied form, checked the restraints again, yanking hard on each, then tested her newest steel-toed kicks and planted a swift blow into the diaphragm of their capture. "Stay here you piece of shit. I'm not even close to done with you."

Racing with flashlight in hand she radioed the team. "Main suspect apprehended. I repeat main suspect in cuffs at our twenty. Require medical assistance and extraction team. Drex fell from the catwalk and is entangled in…" Peering over the edge where Drex fell, out of breath with adrenaline flooding her veins, she almost catapulted over its edge. Drex wasn't there. Tracing the trajectory of his fall she saw a heap far below. Her eyes adjusted and the heap waved. Drex, a mess but a living, breathing mess, had untangled himself and fallen on top of a pile of wood chips.

"You okay?" she yelled.

"You take him down?" he asked back.

"What do you think?" she said.

"Then I'm good," he replied. "Could use a little help and a couple stitches if you're done playing hero."

"Smart ass."

He tipped his head as the lower warehouse doors flew open and their team, Kane and Tex in the lead, flooded in. Kane searched the area, found Drex, and stared up at Jade.

"You gotta come up," she called down. "You won't believe what we found."

Drex was being helped off the pile, bleeding from his left leg, but still issuing orders. "Anyone who is not absolutely needed pull back into holding position."

As he spoke Jade remembered the device she pocketed. "Drex. The perp was reaching for an activation switch. I have it here can we get explosives up to take it?"

Drex gave orders and Jade watched team members leave and new ones appear climbing to her position. Kane followed close behind them to help escort their hogtied prisoner out. Yelling up, Drex said, "Wait until the area is clear before you move out. I'll signal so we have transport in place and everyone else safe. Once the area is free of us, we'll send in explosive specialists to assess and disable any present risk one building at a time. You and Kane wait on my signal."

"You should be in an ambulance," Jade yelled back.

"Yeah, yeah, a little trapeze attempt and you want me committed." His humor was refreshing, they collectively exhaled, cautious but gaining ease as the compound became more theirs than the enemy's.

Crossing to the staircase Jade handed the device she fought for over to the specialists. They eyed it, then each other and her. "So what is it?" she asked.

"We can't be certain without further analysis but it appears to be part of a wireless mine disposal capability unit." The expert disconnected cables and stored it inside a protective kit. "It's advanced tech with multiple capabilities. We'll get on it."

As the men retreated Kane slid a hand down her injured arm to hold her hers, squeezing it in relief. She read his thoughts but it wasn't the time. Carefully they walked back to the prisoner, who remained face turned away and immobilized. Jade pointed for Kane to walk to the other side and shone her flashlight to illuminate the dark corner of the roofline.

"Holy shit!" Kane said, staring at the form on the floor. "A woman?"

His reaction was met by a bloody grin. Jade kneeled while Kane absorbed the scene. "I'll be happy to kick that smirk off your face," she whispered. The criminal voiced no reaction, trained in the art of evading prosecution, the grin of silence landed more offensive than any vocal response. This wasn't an average criminal you took off the street, Jade thought. This was the one who mastered ruling them.

And the worst part was the eyes staring up from the metal floorboards weren't those of an enemy conquered.

FIFTY-FOUR

A xel kept his phone on his bedside table with its volume on high just in case anyone needed to reach him during the night. He wasn't exactly sleeping peacefully or at all as of late. So, when it lit up the dim room alerting to incoming mail, he grabbed it before the second chime echoed. A video waited there, forwarded by Detective Carmichael. Knowing she was at the docks facing off against the traffickers its importance amplified. Throwing his legs over the edge of his bed, Axel turned on a lamp, cleared his eyes, and hit play.

Machias. Happier than he could remember seeing her and the news feed in the background was current. He knew having watched the same channel hours earlier. His friend was alive and Carmichael wouldn't have sent it if she didn't feel there was a damn good chance of her coming home safely. She wouldn't raise hopes in this situation just to have them crushed.

Raven. Axel threw on sweatpants and a hoodie over his shirt, grabbed his truck keys, and dashed for the door. The news too vital to not deliver in person. Raven needed to see she was coming home and the team was working, doing their job. Raven said little at the hospital and home but his disbelief and anger was palatable. Axe feared if a resolution didn't materialize soon, he'd lose all hope of seeing closure and that was a dangerous place to occupy. Flying down the roads to Raven's place Axe thought of all the ways he could deliver the good news, deciding to take a by the book approach like Jack would've if he'd been there.

Axe still felt him close by.

Arriving in the parking garage, he'd found a spot, killed the engine, and jumped out heading for the elevator before realizing it was well past midnight and Rave was probably asleep. He pulled the house key he'd copied the first night after discovering Jack dead, deciding he'd come in and announce himself as carefully as possible so as not to alarm Raven. He'd been coming and going pretty regularly since Jack's murder and Raven had become comfortable with his unscheduled visits.

He waved as usual to the security camera in the elevator in case the guard was still on duty and monitoring it. At the door he entered as always but crossing its threshold he sensed an eerie chill.

"Rave, it's me, Axe. Are you awake? I have amazing news to share." He called out, his voice met by silence. Walking closer to the master suite he tried again in case Raven had taken a sleep aid as prescribed and was having trouble waking. "Raven it's Axel. I have news. I wanted to..." Axe pushed the door open, eyes scanning the vast room by a singular light left on in the washroom. Not seeing Raven or signs of him having occupied the bed, Axe ran across the bedroom slamming back the washroom door fearing what he'd find there.

Empty. Tidy and left with the light on.

He breathed a sigh of relief, chastising his mind for going so dark so quickly. In the dark he could've walked right by him asleep on the sofa or he could have his earbuds in and not hear a thing while working in the office. It wasn't until Axe spun around in view of the opposite wall, the one behind him when he entered that his heart shot into high gear and didn't stop all the way down to the truck.

Raven's award-winning bow, one he cherished and Jack had mounted high up on their wall was gone. An empty space said

Axel's night just took a dramatic turn for the worse. Locking up in a panic, Axe couldn't think straight until he hit the truck. No question where Raven was going with a high-powered compound bow. The problem was how the hell would he find him before he did something he couldn't take back or get killed by criminals far more equipped at taking lives than Rave ever could be.

Axe's tires screeched cutting the quiet of the night on the way out of the garage. Slamming down hard over a speed bump he took too fast. He stood on the brake jarring to a stop and whipped out his phone remembering the precautions he'd taken without Raven's knowledge worried he may do something stupid in the hours of shock preceding the knowledge of Jack's murder.

Rave had impeccable style and his key chain matched his wardrobe. Along with a Louis Vuitton black star, Rave's keys attached to a mini LV wallet with emergency cash and the company credit card. Never used, Axe thought it the perfect place to conceal an AirTag so if Raven disappeared in those dark hours he could track him. Afterward he forgot to remove it. Fumbling with his phone he pulled the app up and linked in to see if the tag was moving. Not only was it active but it appeared to be inside the perimeter of the construction compound.

Peeling onto the main road Axe fought the urge to call Carmichael, his father, or the shop, but whatever Raven was involved with it wasn't without personal consequence. Instead he sped the distance between town and the site. Pulling into a makeshift lot closest to the tag's signal he spotted Jack's truck from high school. Having taken many a ride inside it, it wasn't difficult to identify. With no weapon for protection and vividly aware the place was crawling with law enforcement for good reason, he wanted to smack Rave for putting him in such a shitty position. As if Jack had a guiding hand in the scene, Axe checked the direction of the tag alert and instead of deciphering which building Rave was in, a small voice reminded him Rave loved heights. It was why him and Jack bought a building and designed their home on its top floor with balconies and high windows.

Axe's eyes locked on the trees ahead as he inched close enough to fear every movement. Without a way to confirm identity from a distance Axe was forced to dodge from cover to cover until he was all but underneath the branches. Peering up he couldn't make out who hung above and knowing he could just as easily be standing under a trafficker ready to shoot him at close range he silently sought to focus on anything able to offer confirmation. A foot shifted positions and for the briefest second Axe caught a LV black sneaker, betting no criminal was throwing down close to two grand for trainers.

"Hey, asshole," Axe whispered from below. "You want to explain what the hell you think you're doing up there or should I just have the team shoot you out of the tree?"

"What the hell are you doing...how did you find me?" Rave whispered back, adjusting his balance to look down. "Why are you here? You need to leave."

"I found you because I'm better at this than you are and we need to leave to make sure you don't piss Jack off screwing everything up right before Mac comes home cause she's on her way there now. Climb down outta that frigging tree before you get us both killed."

"Are you serious?" Rave was backing near the trunk.

"Yes. Now get down fast before we both end up wherever Jack is!" Axe waited until Rave was close enough to reveal him of his bow while he jumped the rest of the way. Then they both hit the ground, flattening as an SUV came careening past them, lights ablaze.

FIFTY-FIVE

Rip made it back to the bikes soaked and cold and knowing dry clothes waited in his saddlebag but not willing to take eyes off the target for long enough to change. The perch above the embankment offered the perfect visual of the interior compound road on the southeastern side of the warehouse Carmichael and her partner were searching when gunshots echoed across the property. He could only hope the heavy fire was coming from them and not their mutual enemy. He fought the possibilities presented if Carmichael ended the bastard for him. If officers on site brought out a body bag it'd make life so much easier and he wouldn't be forced to disappoint Machias and Titan. Not banking on odds for, he located the sack the WarMakers delivered and methodically set up.

The M110 Semi-automatic Sniper System allowed for greater range, accuracy, and semi-automatic rapid-fire follow-up but Rip favored it for its recognizable balance. Sloshing as he dropped to the ground, his Harley boots shedding tainted water; he angled toward the extraction point where the black SUV with armed officers prepared to claim the prisoner. The exit from the warehouse sloped inland so he locked a perfect bead on anyone crossing the distance.

A few, he viewed as support officers, filed out and he tracked three to ensure placement and range to target. Wishing Carmichael wouldn't be placed at considerable risk escorting the piece of shit responsible for ordering Jack's death and selling Machias off to the highest bidder wouldn't change it.

If she took them down, she'd walk them out.

In war there were plenty of occasions where taking out a specific target endangered those around them. And, try as they might, shooters could never trust the moment they pulled the trigger wouldn't coincide with a flinch, head turn, trip, nudge, or unbelievably a fucking sneeze defeating every effort at precision. In a homeland environment like this the risks ran higher but shaky hands couldn't be one of them. Releasing the weapon to its stand, Rip rubbed his hands together boosting circulation, dropped back into position, and leaned into his scope when a sound behind him threw him to grab his handgun. In one fluid motion he released the rifle, rolled onto his back, and had the maker of the sound primed for a bullet.

"Fuck, Rip. It's me," Titan's voice identified him before he came into clear view from behind the trees. "What the hell are you doing? We need to ride man."

"I could've killed you," Rip barked. "Why aren't you with the victims?" Rip's eyes darted from his brother to the view inside his scope. "Get your ride and leave."

Titan dropped horizontal next to Rip and pushed over peering through the lens at his target. "I handed them off to FBI and Callum. A whole team was waiting. I told Callum I had to go back or it'd cost lives. Delivering twenty rescues buys one latitude. I didn't leave him time to debate and his boss is here. Who are you aiming at? All I see is the law."

Rip shouldered Titan out of the way, dug in the sack, and handed him military-grade binoculars. Titan rolled his eyes like he did when they were kids and he was caught playing with his older brother's expensive gear.

"Not them," Rip replied, readjusting back into position. "The one they're about to escort to the waiting SUV so you have to ride."

"Jesus, what is it with you? We finally get a chance at a life, at freedom, and you're gonna fuck it all up the first night by killing a cop by accident or getting arrested for murder?" Titan was pissed and Rip read the fear coming off him, distracting, in waves. Not having the luxury of time or the energy to be delicate, and desperate for his brother to be clear of what was coming for him, he pulled back from the scope and locked eyes.

"You have the chance at a new life, freedom, not me. The deal I made with Killian is to eliminate the head and carry the fall for it. The gang walks, I go down. You survive and stay clean so you can help Machias. I need you to leave…now." Rip didn't want to read the disappointment, the pain in Titan's eyes as he came to understand the true price Rip agreed to pay for his exit from the WarMakers. Instead he tipped his head back down, staring and waiting for the one responsible for every evil piece of destruction and fallout headed his way.

Killing the beast wasn't a hardship. It was the only part of the whole mess Rip looked forward to.

"No fucking way!" Titan's voice could've given their location away if they'd been closer. "We go in and the cops get the truth about all of it and they can deal with Killian, say you were wounded and didn't get the chance to fire. We make some shit up and—"

Frozen behind the scope, Rip didn't move, a statue of elimination, one he mastered years earlier in positions his brother never had to witness.

"You don't leave and you take everything that has kept me alive this whole time away. I love ya, kid, but you have to let me go. There is no way out without this evil motherfucker dying on this hill. They don't drop and we both will. And you know Kill has the power to make it happen. I'm not living with that and either are you. Get on your ride." His voice dropped octaves to a place that left no room for discussion or options and Titan recognized it well.

"Not this time, brother," he said, mimicking Riparian's pose but from behind the binoculars. "They take us down, they take us in, or they take us out but it's gonna be together. I was inside too long to go home without you. I wouldn't last a week and you know it. So, try to hit dead center of the prick so we have a chance at riding out cause you still have a working shelter no one has found and it'd be more fun with company. Besides, you haven't done anything yet that wasn't completely justified by the threat to your own life or mine."

Rip shot his brother a glance; his eyes firm like he'd never seen them. He didn't want to continue hiding from the world, not after time with Machias and reminders of how good it could be. But what about Jack's death?

"Jack," he whispered.

"Hear you, it's too bad they got to him before you could stop it or before the boys did. You can't blame yourself." Titan's words landed like hand grenades between Rip's ears.

"What?" Rip's focus blurred and he blinked through it. "I can't blame myself?"

"Well it isn't like you killed him," Titan said casually.

"It is exactly like that." Rip's breathing was off, confusion was muddying his accuracy, and he didn't know what to say next not wanting to relive the moments in the forest.

"Hey, the boys said after the trafficker's men ran after the kid they coldcocked you with a branch. You went down like a sack of hammers same time the kid was stabbed right in front of you. They stuck around to ensure the guys didn't take advantage and try to finish you off too but had to ride before you woke in case patrol spotted the van with the transport inside. But you didn't kill him. You tried to save him. Let it go, bro."

Riparian, hit with the truth, saw flashes of the branch hitting him, falling to the forest floor, the kid stabbed directly in front of his face. He'd seen it that way, level with the impact to Jack's midsection, because he was on the way down, unconscious until coming too confused and panicked to return to the van. He assumed responsibility because he didn't recognize himself anymore. Machias didn't hate him because she knew it too. He just didn't hear her when she tried to tell him. Maybe his brother was right, together they'd realize another way.

Keeping Titan safe and knowing he wasn't responsible for killing

Jack weighed heavier the task at hand. Because he finally knew who was.

If there ever existed a time to be a perfect shot, this was it. He didn't want to fail, to injury or kill a detective fighting the same fight he was. Breathe. He slowed his heart rate, focused his vision, and said, "When I pull, we ride and never look back."

Titan tipped his head, one subtle nod of acknowledgment setting the stage as the doors of the warehouse flew open, pushed by Carmichael and her partner walking too damn close alongside his target.

FIFTY-SIX

"**H**ow did you think you were ever getting out of here?" Jade asked her prisoner as Kane and her prepared to walk out to the waiting armed and bulletproof SUV transport. "The yacht was too close, obvious choice, and there's no waiting chopper on your roof."

The prisoner, who hadn't spoken a word, decided it worth addressing. "Oh there's a waiting helicopter just not on the roof and my yacht is much larger and anchored further out. She'd be gone now. Your lacking Coast Guard already cleared her."

"You had to know we'd shoot you out of the sky," Jade said, disgusted but slyly gaining information.

"Tell me, Detective, how well armed is your bird? I'm wondering what your budget is for that. Mine is as vast as it is for legal counsel."

Jade fought the urge to trip and tumble the asshole off the same section Drex fell from, aiming outside the cable safety net. "With the intel we've gathered on you it won't matter if your pockets are endless."

"It will," she promised.

Kane shoved her right of the open section as they passed by, a fate far longer, slower, and more painful in mind.

Jade motioned to the crew collecting evidence below them, though Drex sent most out until the place was deemed safe, he allowed a few to ensure the charge against firing on Jade and him stuck. "This alone will put you away for life. You open fired on an FBI agent and detective."

"I don't recall you identifying yourself, Detective, and my property was under siege by a brutally violent biker gang. I was simply defending myself."

Kane couldn't stand it. He paused them all before the staircase down to level ground. "Look you piece of garbage, we have survivors from the Candy Store, witnesses you don't have a clue about, and a boatload of history to put enough nails in your coffin the wood could rot and you still wouldn't escape. Shut the fuck up and walk."

Jade cast him a tempered glance. If the criminal was talking, they were receiving information to be used against her later. He knew it but hearing the arrogant confidence was sickening.

"You sound pretty certain, but your witnesses have to live to be at the trial and trials take time."

Jade realized Kane was holding his rage just fine while hers was about to spill over. Drex limped across the open room to meet them at the base of the stairs and read it in her eyes. One glance and she exhaled the rage. His promised whatever outcome the vile creature anticipated would be sorely over-promised and under-delivered. Then she watched his focus dart from her to the prisoner she guided forward, locking in.

"Barracutta," Drex said, his expression registering pride and disgust in tandem. "It's wonderful to meet you under these circumstances."

"Agent Lafine," Barracutta said, familiar and incensed. "I should've known the locals couldn't have brought me in on their own."

"Oh they could've," Drex countered. "They're generously sharing the blessed occasion." Turning his attention back to Jade,

Drex said, "One of our most wanted and responsible for trafficking in seven countries we know about over the last two decades. Congratulations team. The transport is ready and waiting outside."

Jade checked with Kane, dropped her position next to Barracutta, and waved Drex aside.

"So FBI takes lead on Barracutta and I'm happy to see this one exit our jurisdiction. Will we coordinate on information concerning the murder of Jack Wells and Machias Daughtry's abduction after you've sorted through whatever the hell we've amassed?" she asked.

"How about once we both have our side organized, I fly back and we can all reconvene before setting to prosecute," he replied, his eyes drifting from her to the prisoner and back. "This will take a bit. It's going to be a mess to work through."

"That's what I'm afraid of," she admitted. "Can't make this one pay soon enough."

Drex gave her a half grin and raised eyes to Kane. "We can talk through logistics after we wrap up here."

Kane nodded agreement and waited for Jade to assume her position to handoff outside. Drex limped behind Jade and him as they made for the doorway lit with the first hints of breaking dawn.

Before the trio exited, Jade turned to Barracutta and whispered. "You surpassed expectations for how vile a human can become and I hope you die screaming and head straight to an eternity in Hell. You didn't get Machias and I will make certain you never do. I don't know what your plan for her was but I'm forever standing in the way of it."

Barracutta whispered back, eyes glossy and black with evil. "My intent was to sell her to the highest bidder so she could be used, violated, and spent anyway he wished until he chose to discard her and you can't protect her from the likes of me...I'm everywhere."

"The fact that you're female makes it all the more disgusting," Jade said, louder and no longer caring to conceal her rage. "Women doing this to other, younger, women. I personally hope you never make it to trial. Now move, you bitch!"

The fresh air was welcome after breathing in diesel fuel and Kane and her both drew big breaths with their first steps. Drex hadn't limped his way out the door yet likely delayed by others inside but she glanced back expecting to see him. In that fraction of a second the arm she held, higher up between the elbow and shoulder crossed her vision and impacted the corrugated metal siding, followed by random body pieces.

Without sensing it she'd let go and dropped to the ground, sheltering low as bullets ripped and tore the flesh of Barracutta until only splattered pieces remained. The rolling rapid fire was close, the sound of tin striking, bouncing on collision from spent bullet casing castoff. The sound of destruction in rapid fire, the echo of a war machine.

Screams erupted but Jade couldn't place them. "Cover! Cover! Shooter at large! Down!" Covered in blood and body debris she couldn't tell if she'd been hit. But as the thought registered and the rounds ceased, she rolled onto her side searching for Kane. Agents flew out of the SUV and split rushing for her and him on opposite sides of the mess. Kane was dragged into the back of the vehicle before arms lifted and threw her inside the second row. Drex, sheltered by other agents was half carried and lifted in next to her as a single shot rang out. It wasn't until she perceived the momentum of its tires she caught breath again in her lungs.

Wiping blood from her eyes she felt Drex's hands on her face. "Are you hit?" His eyes sought hers until she focused on him. Nodding that she didn't know, her body started to shake against her will. "Look at me, right here," he said, running his hands over her extremities and checking her head. "I don't think you're hit but you went down hard, we're heading to the hospital. You'll be okay."

"Kane, oh god." She couldn't form words fast enough.

Drex turned away searching the back row and speaking but she lost her hearing and it came in muffled waves. "He's okay, bushed his forearm but he's good. Do you hear me? They're helping him in the back."

He was watching over her, they were safe and alive, she wanted to say thank you but when she went to speak nothing came out. Then, she thought of what Barracutta said. She really was everywhere and in the wake of watching it all Jade saw only black.

"What was it...that took Barracutta out?" Jade asked from her hospital bed as Drex sat at her side, having limped down the hall from triage. "Do we know yet?" She'd suffered a concussion and minor injuries and was under surveillance and not allowed to leave for a couple days as they monitored her recovery but woke wanting every detail feeling the case blew apart with Barracutta.

"A Browning Machine gun, M1917, water cooled beast, belt fed and there were no prints, not a shred of evidence left at the scene to connect its shooter. An emptied war weapon, a dead operator from who knows where, and nothing else. The site is being searched over by CSI with a fine-tooth comb. We've ID'd seven of the twelve bodies on the compound. And one woman was discovered in a holding cellar. She didn't survive transport. We'll work backward until we find the answers but right now you have a visitor. She was very insistent. Reminds me of you."

Machias slid around the corner, grabbed a chair from the side, and pulled it up, invading Drex's personal space. "Hi Detective Carmichael," she said. Jade understood, staring at the teen so close up, why she'd been targeted. The young woman was stunning and completely unaware of it.

"Hello Mac."

Jade smiled at Drex, knowing they both shared an appreciation for the girl's resilience. "It's so good to see you," Jade said. "You didn't have to wait around for me to wake up, we can catch up in a few days after I'm released."

"No. I did. So I could introduce you," she said, her eyes brilliant with excitement. She glanced to the doorway while two large men filed in. Drex smiled at them and waved them forward. "This is my friend Riparian, I call him Rip. He's the one who kept me safe." The girl loved this man and by his expression the feeling was mutual.

"Hello Detective Carmichael," Rip said, and Jade recognized the voice.

"It was you...at the dock," Jade said.

"It was also Riparian who ended the shredding of Barracutta to protect us," Drex explained. "Titan here brought his brother into deep cover with him. Them going after Barracutta to protect Mac and us was their way out. The gang wanted the criminal enterprise shut down on their turf. Good trade if you ask me."

"So where were you this whole time?" Jade asked Machias while a sly smile passed between her and the scarred man.

"I was with Rip, in a safe house from the time Barracutta's men killed Jack until she was killed and he came back to bring me to you," she said. "I witnessed the whole thing and worked with Rip to corroborate Daughtry's part in all of it."

"The jars?" Jade said. "You figured out your mother's code."

"Rip did," Mac said, smiling up at him. He reached out, ruffling her hair.

"As you can see, we have a ton to work through but with Mac's mother's tracking of victims, Riparian and Titan's intel on the gang side with transport evidence, and the documents recovered from the Daughtry farm we'll hunt down every branch associated until the whole operation is dismantled," Drex said. "And the man working for Barracutta that actually took Jack's life was killed on site."

"The man on the yacht," Rip offered. "You helped with that one. If it hadn't been for your shots distracting him, I might not be here."

All Jade could feel was grateful and tired. Despite wanting to oversee every detail to maximize the potential to use against the criminals still out there, her four-alarm headache decided for her it'd be handled in time. There were so many good people working to that end, she had no doubt this criminal enterprise was dead or dying. But the last words Barracutta said still haunted her, she *was* everywhere in one form or another.

As they made plans to stay in touch and filed out of the room Drex passed Kane on the way in, he smiled and said nothing more. Kane heard the fallout while Jade was unconscious and left for them to tell her while he went for a smoothie. Handing it over, she slid slowly upright to drink it. The cup was swirled with colors like strings intertwined.

Jade stared at it not speaking. Kane leaned in, his expression worried. "Are you okay? Should I call the doctor?" he asked.

She looked up, her eyes filling with moisture. "He tried to tell me," she said, tears spilling silently down her face. "I think he tried to warn us."

"He who?" Kane stared at her, not understanding.

"What is true about the maker of the web?" she said. He still didn't remember. "Nickolas. The maker of the web is a woman," she said. "He knew the head was a woman."

"Well he could've fucking said so," Kane said, his eyes flush with anger.

"We wouldn't have believed him." Jade searched her hands, debating her next words, then met Kane's eyes. "I think Drex need to look for overseas ties to the machine gun operator."

"You think Nickolas had her killed?" Kane asked, his voice registering the possibility.

"All I know is Amy was right. He isn't done with us." She said the words as Captain Grey rounded the corner struggling to balance a huge bouquet of flowers and a fruit basket.

"Flowers are to liven up the stark room and mask the sanitation smell and the fruit is for you! And if any of the team starts chomping on it, I'll fire them," Grey said, smiling then read the room. "Everything okay?"

Kane stared at Jade and then Grey and said, "I think we have to talk about locating Nickolas Leigh."

FIFTY-SEVEN

Machias named it the Lincoln Heritage House and used the reconstruction of the property as a way to build a team to run the foundation for youth in crisis moving forward. The foundation, named in Jack's honor, linked to her and Raven's *Getting Wells* podcast and channel so the two could work in tandem and benefit those in need more fluidly. And her supporters were as varied as they were amazing. Staring with the one she considered her brother, Raven.

From the morning Riparian returned to the shelter with his brother to fetch her they became the strangest family. Rip and Titan had select items of her mother's and grandparents' recovered and moved in with her to what was Raven's place but quickly became hers too. Raven cooked with Rip, they ended up with matching tattoos dedicated to Jack, and Rave reveled in Titan's tales about gang life. Raven rode with the brothers, Mac usually behind Rip on his bike where he felt she was safest.

The stories they shared were true, some dark and dangerous, but there was relief and healing in the trust between them. Raven admitted that he'd gone to the construction site with the goal of killing Jack's murderer. In the end, with his face smooshed into topsoil by Axel, he was glad they hadn't been closer when the machine gun ripped the human trafficker to pieces. He also said he didn't regret seeing it as horrific as it was.

"Closure," was all Rip said. No judgment, only complete united understanding.

And they were together when the FedEx delivery came to the door. Rip expected it, no one else. And he appeared hesitant or nervous as it was opened.

"It's from a DNA analysis lab," Mac said, reading the outer packaging.

"Yes," Rip said, waiting.

She caught Raven and the brothers exchanging glances. He'd prepared them some for what was inside but she was shocked when she tore into the document. "He was never my father?" she asked Rip, knowing this was a final confirmation on a certainty he uncovered long before.

"It takes forever for the labs to finish and send results but I wanted you to hold them in front of you before I said anything. Your mother Lily was Daughtry's first capture. The detectives and I believe he may have had a hand in having your great-grandmother killed so he could take advantage of her situation. She was already pregnant with you. Pretty sure Daughtry never knew," Rip said, smiling.

"So she didn't tell him? Left him believing I was his to stop him from…" Mac left the rest unspoken.

"Do you know who is?" Rave asked so she didn't have to.

Rip and Titan shared a glance. "He's a firefighter. Lives two towns away and would really love to get to know his daughter if you're interested," Rip said.

"I checked him out," Titan added. "Good guy and don't say I said it, but he's damn handsome too."

"Well that figures," Rave said.

"I'm not any part of him?" Mac was processing. Rave leaned over closer on their sofa. "You never were or ever could be blood or not," he said. "Maybe we could set up a visit after we check on Dylan?"

"Oh yeah, he has his last check-up today. Cleared for a return to cyber life," Mac said.

"He already sort of started," Titan said. "We checked in with Callum and he went into the station to ID Barracutta's men and everything he witnessed. They said they were there to end him on her orders."

"He's not at the same walk-up though, is he?" she asked, not wanting Dylan to face bad memories any more than she wanted to. She avoided the farm until it became the ranch and all traces of the farmhouse and barn Daughtry used were wiped off its surface. Raven drove the bulldozer and sent photos of the clean earth.

"He moved in downstairs," Raven said. "Well...we moved him in. He hasn't actually seen the place yet. After today and the all clear from the docs his dad said he'd be okay with him going back out on his own."

Rip rolled his eyes, knit his brows, doubting any compliance from Dylan's dad.

"What?" Mac asked.

"Okay he may have made me amp security, hire two full time guards, and put in four more cameras first," Rave admitted.

Mac laughed. "So the picnic is next Saturday and everyone confirmed. Jade, Kane, Tex, and even Captain Grey, Amy, and Errie are coming. Axel is bringing Rocklyn, and Zane, Dylan and Falcon are setting up the music." Falcon hadn't left her side much since she came home and her happiness seemed his priority. She was proud of their relationship and grateful she was free to show it. Even Rip approved. Still, a concern lingered over the celebration. "Rip, are you sure the WarMakers are good with—"

Rip laughed. "They're good. Killian did send a message out this morning though."

Mac still worried about fallout though it'd been weeks and the FBI and Major Crimes Unit had taken down several criminals involved since the night Barracutta was killed. "What did it say?" She set the package confirming her birth right down on the table between them and felt the sunlight from their high windows warm her as it broke through the clouds.

"They reclaimed their brother from hospital and he's making a great recovery working the bar in the club. But he did issue an order." Rip said.

"What?" Mac couldn't give in to anxiety; Rip was flashing his half grin.

"It was for the detectives, so I passed it on to Carmichael. He requested they contact the actual highway construction team to cleanup the dock intersection cause the guys are sick of replacing tires."

The group burst into laughter and Mac listened memorizing the sound. All of them safe, happy, together and healing was not just music, it was a rare symphony.

A LOOK AT:
R.A.Y. A STEP TOO FAR

R.A.Y. A STEP TOO FAR is a heart-pounding medical thriller that explores the fine line between creation and destruction, and the monsters that lurk when science goes too far.

Buy now and dive into this chilling apocalyptic thriller where morality, mortality, and power collide in a fight for the future of mankind.

AVAILABLE NOW

ABOUT THE AUTHOR

As a thriller author, owner of a successful developmental editing company for authors, a ghostwriter, and journalist, J.L. Hughes is grateful to be immersed in her respected field working with other accomplished writers. On the inside cover of dozens of novels, she contributes as editor or ghostwriter to both fiction and nonfiction in every genre from true crime to fantasy, sci-fi to horror—all for the love of story.

J.L. and her family enjoy city life against the adventurous back-drop of the Rocky Mountains.